MW01000544

The FRAMED WOMEN *of* ARDEMORE HOUSE

Also by Brandy Schillace

Mr. Humble and Dr. Butcher

Death's Summer Coat

Clockwork Futures

The FRAMED WOMEN *of* ARDEMORE HOUSE

a novel

BRANDY SCHILLACE

HANOVER
SQUARE
PRESS

Recycling programs for this product may not exist in your area.

ISBN-13: 978-1-335-01403-0
ISBN-13: 978-1-335-92841-2 (International Edition)

The Framed Women of Ardemore House

Hanover Square Press
22 Adelaide St. West, 41st Floor
Toronto, Ontario M5H 4E3, Canada
HanoverSqPress.com
BookClubbish.com

Printed in U.S.A.

To Mark, for celebrating all my various selves
and joining each new special interest with enthusiasm.

1

The house was *enormous*. Jo didn't know enough about local architecture to date it, but the walls stretched up in the damp air, big and dark and lichen flecked. Windows had been boarded up; they wept black mildew creases over sandstone sills. Staring through the car window, Jo dropped her eyes down to the stairs, flanked by columns where Jo imagined regal statues might have stood. Or *ought* to have stood.

"It's...a castle," she whispered.

"It is most certainly *not* a castle," said Rupert Selkirk, solicitor of Selkirk and Associates, in the driver's seat beside her. "Not even the largest house in Abington."

Solicitor. Jo rolled the word around in her mouth. She'd pocket it for later rumination; it was nice to have a word for chewing on. It suggested antique leather chairs and brass lampstands, felt safer than *divorce lawyer*, and didn't trigger the same sort of gut gripe. Rupert looked exactly as a solicitor ought to, with a high forehead, disappearing hairline, and two very bushy eyebrows. He also drove a puddle-green sedan with the steering wheel on the wrong side of Jo's expectations. She wondered if the sense of dislocation would fade with the jet lag. It hadn't exactly improved her first impressions. She forgot to introduce herself, forgot the handshake, stared in absolute stunned silence at the landscape as they drove.

Online pictures had suggested something endlessly green, but the reality was wet and ragged, browned out from the end of winter and laced at the edges with naked tree branches. Jo squinted into the distance, taking in the brackish heath, then trees, then fog. A cluster of trees appeared, lanky pin oaks and a few copper beeches. A crumbling dry-stone wall snaked away from decayed posts; no fence, but the remnants of one. She let her eyes wander its length to a dark smudge of woodland and black bark dotted with lichen. The rest of the hill loomed treeless, stark, and scarred by eruptions of additional stone. *Moors*, she thought. Endless and rolling with dry heather and wet peat.

Jo had pressed herself to the glass, ignoring the steam prints she made. She hadn't brought much with her—certainly not her books. But *Wuthering Heights* might have been a good choice. Relaxation breathing had never been much use to her; whenever she consciously thought about autonomic responses, they went all wrong. So she mentally recited the opening lines of the novel as the car grumbled to a halt in the shadow of Ardemore House. As for Rupert, he was repeating himself.

"—Not a castle. The house is wider than it is deep, mostly to take advantage of the south-facing aspect." Seeing the blank look on Jo's face, he tried again. "In England, south-facing gardens get the most sun. That's where you'll find the Ardemore Gardens. They were the highlight of the property, once. Overgrown now, I'm afraid." Rupert swept his hand across the horizon as if bisecting it. "Everything east of here is rented for grazing livestock. There is also, as you know, the cottage. It helps defray the tax burden."

Tax burden. She might want to hold on to those words, too.

"Emery Lane, my assistant, will be drawing up papers while we walk the property," he said. Jo was starting to run out of processing space, internally. She felt a hiccup of emotion and press-ganged it into a smile.

"Papers?"

"For you to sign. To take over the property as your inheritance."

The smile failed. Better say something like *yes, good. Quite. Exactly the thing.* But Rupert got there first, offering her a hand out of the passenger seat.

"Your mother always spoke very warmly of you, by the way. I was very sorry to hear of her passing."

At these words, Jo quietly abandoned her pursuit of professionalism.

"Y-yeah. I got the card. Thanks."

Rupert was still looking at her. She could tell, but wasn't about to look back. She took in the house, instead, this not-castle that rose straight out of bracken and into a cloud bank.

"I want to go inside," she said. Rupert joined her across the weedy lawn.

"I thought we would see the cottage first. It's at least *habitable*."

He didn't seem to understand; Jo was standing in front of Wuthering Heights, and *no*, she did not want to go poke around a cottage. Not yet.

"Inside," she said. "Please." Rupert sighed.

"All right. But have proper expectations. This property has been vacant for a century, at least since at least 1908."

Now in front of the door, Jo furrowed her brow as Rupert hunted for the right key. That was a surprise, actually. And it didn't make sense.

"But you said my uncle Aiden had the property? In your email—"

"Ah, but he did not live on-site. Had a flat in York, and—" Rupert stopped abruptly and stumbled back. Jo followed his gaze to see a pair of bright eyes peering back at them through the glass.

"Jesus!"

"Tut, now." Rupert waved his hand airily. "That's only Sid Randles, caretaker."

A moment later, and the man himself opened the door. Lean, lanky, all arms, legs, and a shock of red hair. Attractive in the way of highwaymen and pirates, he was either a very well-kept forty-something, or thirty gone to seed. He was also blocking the way.

"Here's a surprise," he said. "This the American, then?"

"Yes. Sid Randles, meet Josephine Black," Rupert offered.

"Jones," Jo corrected. "It's Jo *Jones* now. I mean, *again*." Jo faltered slightly, then dutifully stuck her hand out. Sid tucked an industrial-grade flashlight under his arm and gave her a shake, then squeezed her palm.

"Sounds like an alias," he said.

"Jo Jones was an American Jazz drummer of the Count Basie Orchestra rhythm section from 1934 to 1948," Jo said, then puckered her lips as if that would bring the words back. Sid eyed her a minute, then let out a yelp of laughter, and not very kindly.

"Ms. Jones would like a tour. Sid, will you do the honors, please?" Rupert checked his wristwatch. "I need to take this call and there's no signal inside." He turned away, and Sid grinned at Jo, one crooked canine slipping over his lip like a storybook fox.

"There's no electricity," he said.

"I figured that's why you have the flashlight," Jo said, pointing. Imagining him as *Reynard* from the French fables had done wonders for her confidence. She could almost imagine the swish of his irritated tail.

"Fine, fine. Come on in." He backed into the hall. "Hope you don't mind the smell."

It *would* be hard to miss it. A puff of musty air assaulted Jo's nostrils on entering—a wet, rotten odor. The windows were boarded, and in the slanted peek-a-boo light she could just make out the ghost of a table, a phantom of chairs in the foyer. Sid swept the light across the hall from a dust-webbed staircase to a grand room that opened off their left.

"You'll want to pay respects to the Lord and Lady," he said, then marched her through the pocket doors. The smell was stronger in here, sharper and more tangible. Then, her heart leapt; she'd caught a glimpse of distant book spines.

"It's a library?" she asked.

"Yeah. A rotten one." Sid played the flashlight beam along the mantel of a marble fireplace. "But up there, see 'em? *That* would be Lord William Ardemore. And his wife, Gwen, of course."

The portraits were too large, and the beam of the light too small, but she could make out a frowning man with deep set eyes and a woman with a rosebud mouth, who might have suitably graced a Victorian cookie tin. Family members she had never known.

"Damned odd, those two." Sid flicked the light between them. "Just up and vanished from the place."

Jo sucked a breath. Did *everyone* know more about them than she did?

"What do you mean? Vanished how?"

"I mean just that." He played the light against his own face, campfire style. "Just up sticks and gone. Fired everybody, too, didn't they? Oh, they'd been toast of the town, like." He did an awful falsetto: "*Jobs for the big garden and big bloody house.* Then *poof.* Like they were running from something."

Jo was watching carefully for signs of a joke. There didn't appear to be any, so then she waited for him to carry on. Except he didn't. She studied him for a few silent seconds, until he gave another bark of laughter.

"Nothin' to say about that, eh? Well, the old Lord and Lady are the least of *your* worries, anyhow. There's a hole in the roof upstairs, an honest to God *hole*. Between you and me? Be cheaper to pull the house down than to fix it up."

Jo pursed her lips so hard she felt teeth.

"I just got it! I can't tear it down!"

Sid only shrugged at her outburst.

"Fair, I guess. But what do you plan to *do* with it, then? Look around."

Jo did not, in fact, have an answer to that. Sid apparently meant it rhetorically, anyway, since he was now herding her toward the door.

"To the cottage," he said. "Come on."

Jo found herself taking deeper breaths in the fresh air outside. She also appreciated being able to get a good six feet of distance from the ropy limbs of Sid Randles. Rupert snapped his phone into a pocket as they emerged, and now led the way south. Jo noticed everything; a tangle of brush behind the house, another broken stone wall, a meadow in the distance, a small grove of trees. And just beyond the curve of earth, a chimney.

"*Grove Cottage*, built 1817," Rupert explained as the rest came into view. Whitewashed stone, a thatched roof, bit of ivy clinging to the side: Jo cataloged it against a half dozen examples from literary novels. It beat them all to hell for charm.

"I love it," she said. Sid laughed coarsely.

"You ain't seen it, yet."

Rupert talked over him as though he hadn't spoken.

"It predates the estate house. Not overly large but can be rented as a two bedroom."

"How would you know?" Sid said, lip curling back from canines again. "I'm the one that manages it."

"Properly advertised, it could pull in 300 pounds per week," Rupert continued—to Jo, not to Sid. It was making her brain itch; it felt like two simultaneous but different conversations.

Sid, rather than Rupert, unlocked the door—two shiny dead bolts with brand-new keys.

"Ladies first," he said with a sneer of smile. Jo slipped by him, rabbitlike. The front room had been bisected by a countertop, with fireplace and sitting area in front, kitchen to the rear. She put her back against the counter and had a good look around.

There was an awful lot of junk. Untidy ebbs and flows of secondhand furniture; the cluttered remnants of dishes and crockery on chipped cupboards. Other people's leftover lives.

"There's a bedroom and family bath down this hall," Rupert said. "And then you have the attic space, upstairs—" Jo was already halfway up and peeking into the vaulted room above.

She could hear Sid hollering from below, *"Holiday goers don't wanna sleep up there—no bathroom."*

"That doesn't matter," Jo said out loud. The attic had been finished with painted wood siding, a sort of moss green. Three windows. And no clutter. "It's perfect for me."

"For you?" It sounded like both men at once. Jo ducked back into the living room; Sid had gone fish-mouthed. Rupert, who seemed very good at not being surprised, had nonetheless raised both eyebrows at her.

"Me. I will live here," Jo repeated.

"I see," said Rupert. Sid's eyes roved about the room looking for somewhere to land.

"But maintenance!" he said. "What about the *maintenance*, Rupert?"

"Perhaps Ms. Jones will retain you as handyman for upkeep."

Jo very much did not think so. From the way Sid was leering, she could guess they agreed on that. Rupert just looked at his watch.

"We can discuss this another time," he said. "I'm sure arrangements can be made, but right now, there are papers Jo needs to sign."

Sid nodded, but the tension in the room was palpable. Jo found herself fighting the urge to repeat her favorite words like a talisman. Rupert steered her back to the car as if nothing at all had happened to ruffle him, going on about rental rates and property lines and exactly how much work needed doing.

"And before you lend your signature," he said as they pulled out of the lane, "we are going to have to address the back taxes I mentioned."

Jo's brain threw up a flag.

"Back tax, as in *owed* tax?" she asked. "How much are we talking about, exactly?"

2

Forty-five thousand pounds...about sixty thousand US dollars. Jo sat in a private corner of the Red Lion, nursing a beer and wondering if her stomach would ever stop galloping about. Numbers, though, were always comparable objects. A brand-new Alfa Romeo. A Toyota Prius (two, if you got them used). About a year of rent in Manhattan. And almost exactly, after the exchange rate, what Jo had left to her name after selling her mother's house and liquidating everything else.

Jo pressed palms against her eyes. It wasn't, Rupert had said, an *insurmountable* sum. By which he meant the property hadn't been seized due to nonpayment and transferred to the National Trust. When her uncle died, he'd left whatever remained of his assets to the place; that apparently put the cottage in the clear. But Jo's mother had not touched it—not to take ownership and not to refuse it. She'd spent four years putting Rupert off, making promises, delaying. Then, when the cancer came back, she told him Jo would handle it. Except she never told *Jo*. She could at least have mentioned the cottage, or said how much trouble the place was in. They could have made a plan—

Jo started dialing the number from muscle memory…then hiccupped in surprise. No one was waiting on the other end anymore. And somehow *remembering* her mom's death didn't hurt half as much as *forgetting* it. Jo curled her fingers tight around each thumb. The irony of that hurt, too; she could almost hear her mother's voice, *Jo doesn't 'do' feelings…no empathy.* It wasn't true. Jo did ALL the feelings. She just failed at their articulations. An almost-sob cracked her lips and she drowned it in a gulp of brown ale, choking down a host of unruly emotions.

"Another round, miss?"

Jo looked up to see an attractive, buoyant-looking barkeep.

"No, thank you, I'm just—" She sniffed and dabbed her eyes. "I'm, um. Jo."

"Dinner? We've stew tonight. Popular." His smile was so genuine, it almost hurt. Jo tried to mirror it back.

"Sure. Why not?"

"You're the one bought the old estate, are you?"

Jo started at the question. "I didn't buy it. I inherited it. How did you know?"

"Village news travels fast," he said with a wink. "Plus, there's your accent."

Jo nodded with her mouth shut. Everyone must know about the place, she supposed. It was deeply unfair. She'd only known for three months. Three months almost to the day. *That* day.

She could replay it like a movie clip: it had been raining the way only Chicago could rain. And a lawyer was telling her several things that didn't make sense as she tried to piece together her situation.

"My mom left England more than forty years ago," she heard herself say to the lawyer.

"Yes. The property was in the care of her brother, your uncle Aiden. Then it passed to you, as your mother's next of kin."

Uncle Aiden had always been a shadow figure in Jo's memories. The only other surviving member of the Ardemore family, but she'd never met him. Not even when she lived with her mom in Chicago as a child and came to England on a school trip. Her mother *said* she had written ahead of time, but he never answered.

"An estate," she'd repeated. "And it's mine."

"You have to go there to take full possession, but yes. It's yours."

Except the lawyer hadn't mentioned the back taxes, either. Or why the house had been deserted since 1908—or why Uncle Aiden, whoever he was, had allowed the roof to partially fall in. Unless that happened under her mother's watch. Jo pursed her lips and fought another wave of semipanic. Today, she'd found herself in *another* lawyer's office, and it wasn't mystery mansions with ghosts or locked up heroines or unreliable narrators. Most of the property, like much of the Pennines, wasn't arable. The bit that *could* be farmed had been leased; that kept them out of hock because, as Rupert told her, *steady payment meant no enforcement action.*

Still, signing the papers made it Jo's, and she found herself two Prius' worth in debt from the property taxes, enough to wipe out her finances completely. And it hadn't been twenty-four hours yet.

Jo sighed and fidgeted with the salt shaker, screwing and unscrewing the cap. This *should* be very upsetting. But under her grief, a bubble of senseless joy kept popping up. She'd just country hopped and taken over a massive property, and it felt like free fall and freedom all at once. Her mother had done something similar when even younger than Jo: packed up and left England for Illinois, pregnant and alone. But she never, ever spoke about it, and she certainly didn't celebrate it. Rebecca Jones didn't believe in unpacking "unpleasant" things; you overcame them, or you ignored them. She had a tendency to think of Jo's autism that way, too, and made sure Jo knew it.

But not anymore, she reminded herself. It was her life. The divorce, the loss of the publishing house, and a year spent watching her mother die had only solidified it: This was the life of Jo Jones. Her way. Now she just needed a job, that was all. Surely *somebody* could use the services of a hyperlexic editor with a read rate of 1500 wpm. She'd let her old contacts go fallow for a year, but maybe a call to some writers in need of editors? Long-distance freelance? She had a few weeks to figure it out, at least. Hell. In a pinch, she could—more or less as Rupert suggested—rent the damn cottage, at least until she figured out the next step in her career.

Jo pulled out her phone and opened a browser window for a search, but could find no home page for the cottage, not a Facebook page, not even an AirBnB. (According to Rupert, Sid never finished the application process.) Finally, she turned up a one-sentence description on a travel site's listing of holiday lets. It had a single blurry photo and a number, presumably Sid's. Little wonder he wasn't making a return on investment.

"Hot plate!" the barman said, putting the bowl down. "Lucky you came early—lamb stew makes for a busy night."

A peek over her booth confirmed the place had filled to the point of bursting. It was noisy, too, especially near the door, where patrons stood clinking glasses in raincoats. Jo turned back to her food. The stew was, as promised, phenomenally good. But now that her ears were tuned to the sound of whisky glasses, she could scarcely focus on anything else. Tony, her ex-husband, used to tease that her favorite wine was single malt. He also liked to claim it wasn't a "lady's drink." And that memory more or less sealed her desire. Jo scooched out of her cubby and started across the room to the bar.

"Someone's bought that old estate," said a suit nearby with

his tie tossed over one shoulder. A second fellow sat with him. "Cottage, too."

"American is what I heard."

Jo pursed her lips tight, as though her accent might escape. The suit's companion flagged the barman.

"Ben, you heard about the goings-on up at Ardemore?"

"House is staying in the family, Ricky," Ben said, filling a tumbler. He didn't look at Jo—and she tried to exude mental thanks in his direction. But of course, she still had to use words for whisky, and the suits looked a little too comfortable. Jo cleared her throat and pointed to the rack of whiskies lined up neatly behind the bar.

"Single malt," Jo mouthed, figuring any would be fine.

That earned her a look from Ricky. It wasn't easy to parse, but she certainly didn't *like* it. Ben handed her the glass and she retreated to the corner—except the booth was now half-occupied. Sid Randles was waiting for her.

"Red Lion's on my way home," he explained, lifting a pint of lager. "Can I get you a drink?"

"Have one already." Jo lifted her glass.

"Right." He clinked the rim of his pint to hers. "Cheers, then. I'll get your next round." He sat down across from her, as if invited, and stretched out his legs. Jo sat down, too. Awkwardly. She wanted to walk out of the bar and back to her room, but that was abrupt behavior she'd been taught to keep in check. Most recently, by Tony.

"I'm not having a next round," she explained, adding the obligatory "*sorry.*"

"Aww, come on. You're making it hard for me to apologize," Sid chuckled. "Should I have brought flowers or something? Always worked on the ex-wives."

Jo set her drink down a little too hard. Wives? Plural?

"That's—hard to believe," she said, but he was talking over her.

"Look, I don't think I made the best of impressions, today.

Came as a shock, you moving in on my territory, as it were. I been managing the cottage for years, you know."

"I couldn't even find a booking page," Jo said flatly.

"Well, now, okay." Sid nodded as though they just agreed on something. "You can see why, right? I'm not good with computers. *And* I got on fine renting the cottage without them. I could rent and manage the property for you. See?"

Jo felt an internal tremor of frustration.

"But I am *not* renting it. Remember? I'm going to be living in it."

"Oh, but you can't be serious about *that*." Sid kicked his legs back under the booth table and leaned forward. "I mean, look at you!"

"I beg your pardon?"

"Well, you're just a little thing! Can't be expected to take care of the whole place yourself! Plus women shouldn't be left all alone out there. Miles from town. No neighbors."

Jo was, in fact, five foot three (and three-quarters). She swallowed *fuck you* and replaced it with: "Why do you care?"

Sid huffed into his empty glass. "Look, lady, I'm trying to be your friend, here. That place is a wreck, and you'll need help." He offered her the toothsome smile again. "I'm here for it, see? I'm your man."

His self-aggrandizement was interrupted by Ben, the barman.

"You've a call, Sid. A woman? She's been trying to text you—says you're meeting up in a half hour."

Sid waved him away and dug out his phone. In the moment, Jo found herself considering him afresh. Reynard the Fox was meant to be wily and clever and charming; Sid did *not* live up to these expectations. There was something boyish about him, yes, possibly even disarming. At least two women must have found it charming, and this phone caller might be a third. But it wasn't working on Jo. Her hackles were up, and for once, she was going to trust her guts.

"So?" Sid said, putting the phone away. "What do ya say 'bout me staying on?"

"I say no. Thanks. But *no*."

Jo stood, drained her whisky in one go and set the glass down hard on the tabletop. She wasn't going to wait for a response, either. Partly because she didn't care—and partly because a double in a gulp was going to rob her of uprights pretty quickly. She gave a half-hearted wave at Ben the barman and managed to get upstairs with dignity before the room got spinny. Jo flopped onto the bed, spine greedily soaking up the horizontal. She wanted to hang up clothes. She wanted to take a shower. Instead, she basked in the liquid afterglow of knowing she was single, alone, and in a brand-new country. For the first time, maybe ever, she could do as she damn well pleased.

3

At exactly 9:14 the following morning (as time-stamped on her carefully folded receipt), Jo rented an Alfa Romeo. She liked that name, too. *Alfa Romeo. Solicitor.* The *f* and *m* tickled the lips and the *s*'s whistled in her teeth. The car was manual transmission; she'd stalled it twice already. Driving on the wrong side of the road was wholly terrifying. She and Tony hadn't owned a car in New York; she'd had to learn all over again when she went to Chicago to take care of her mother. *That* had been a five-speed, too, but of the broke-down minivan variety. The Alfa Romeo felt very flash by comparison. And a little out of scale with her destination.

The Ardemore House still had a looming quality, though it seemed less magisterial on second viewing—and more quietly watchful. The stone had been quarried somewhere nearby, she was told. The earth beneath, a riddled network of limestone going hollow. It made her think of a cave she'd once been to as a child. With the flashlights off, black piled on black, assaulting the senses like a velvet hammer. She hadn't liked it. And she'd learned not to trust flashlights.

Now Jo pulled a duffel bag out of the back seat. Plenty of tools, in case she needed them, but more importantly, an industrial light source with wire cage and enormous battery that she'd bought from the hardware store.

Rupert had provided her keys to the house, and she'd also managed to get Sid's extra set of cottage keys before leaving the day before. He'd put a shiny new set of bolts on the cottage shortly before her arrival, and even Rupert didn't have keys yet. Seemed foolish, but then again, there was also nothing in the cottage but garbage. Rupert, for his part, had been surprisingly circumspect.

Jo switched on the industrial light. The front room had only flickered into view before; now it appeared in a single flare, but the bald white light bled the color away. Like standing in an old photograph, almost. And it smelled awful inside. Jo distracted herself by looking at a rough blueprint Rupert supplied the previous day. The little mathematical boxes of rooms made the place feel less overwhelming. She took a mental photograph: A parlor or cloakroom opened just off the main stairs; beyond to the right a dining room wrapped around back to a kitchen and pantry, and a utility closet snugged just beneath the landing. But the treasure lay to the left: Jo adjusted the light so it shone through the pocket doors, and headed into an extensive private library.

The news was good, and bad, and ugly. A gorgeous fireplace of marble with lovely ceramic vases—complete with long curtains and woven carpets—made her feel she'd just walked into a Victorian triple-decker novel. Sadly, two-thirds of the actual books were wet through and rotted. Jo tilted the light toward the ceiling, where cast plaster hung, likewise wet and ragged. Evidence of bigger problems above; she'd have to go upstairs to see the real extent of the damage.

Jo tested the banister. It creaked fiercely, and the steps seemed dry and shrunken. Sid hadn't let her go up the day before, but presumably going up was possible? Jo put one hand on the wall and the other on the rail. Every step squealed in protest. She'd once managed to climb a fire escape from their Brooklyn apartment to a friend's flat two floors up, mainly by holding her breath. It seemed to help, even though holding a breath *in* technically made you heavier instead of lighter. By about 1.225 grams, in fact. Though in theory you *would* be less dense, weight to volume-wise…

These were the sort of things Tony told her not to say out loud.

Fuck Tony.

The house was shaped like a block letter *C*, so the stairs split in half at a balcony. Venturing into the left wing, she discovered a rather grand bathroom with black-and-white floor tiles in octagons. There was a guest room on that side of the hall, too. On the reverse, according to the blueprint, was the master. The door was ajar, though it still had a key in the lock. Jo pushed it open with a satisfying creak and the light revealed deep red curtains around a four-poster bed.

Red room, Jo thought, and her heart gave a little rabbit hop. *"A square chamber, very seldom slept in, I might say never"*—Jane Eyre. Jo smiled and stepped over the threshold, light held aloft. Not quite so stately as its literary companion, and the bed curtains were dust choked, but she felt unavoidably pleased. At least until she saw the plaster littering the floor. The ceiling bore not holes, however; just cracks and some staining. But then, where had all the water come from?

Jo crouched to study the blueprint once more. It showed the master bedroom extending from the bath to the outer wall, but the dimensions were clearly wrong. She had walked the length of the library—it took at least twenty steps, a lot, even on her short legs. The bedroom could only be a third of that.

There must be another room further along.

Jo poked her head into the hall to find she'd been correct: a narrow door appeared at the further end, nearly hidden in shadow. It was also closed tight and a bit swollen against the frame. *Wet*, she thought. So here she'd found the source of the leak, but she couldn't get the door open; unlike the others, it had been locked. She tried Rupert's keys—but none of them worked.

"Dammit." Why didn't she insist on coming up the day before with Sid? She sat back on her haunches and sucked her upper lip (*orangutanging*, her mother called it). Every problem had a solution, though. Some of them were shaped like hammers.

In the end, she decided on a hammer *and* a screwdriver, as chisel. She set the light at an angle and steadied the screwdriver against the lock mechanism. Jo would knock the whole door in together, if she had to. When she struck, the brass rang like a bell, and she winced at the reverberating *ping*. The lock didn't give, but something else did. She heard the *tin-tan-tin* of something small hitting the ground. It had come from the *other* bedroom door that was already ajar. The key had just fallen out of the lock.

"The *key*, Jo," she announced. She should have hit *herself* with the hammer. Jo scooped it up to examine: filed-away edges. It was a "skeleton key," meant to fit any number of locks. Mostly. It went *in*, but still gave the tug of resistance when she tried to turn it. She twisted harder, feeling the rigidity and flex of metal.

"Just a bit more," Jo pleaded. The key trembled in her grip and Jo clenched finger and thumb, white against the shaft. She could almost envision the mechanism as it gave way—and then—*snap*.

"DAMMIT!" Jo shoved her thumb into her mouth; the broken shard had sliced cuticle. The other half of the key remained in the lock, but she'd sprung it after all, and a sliver of light opened in the doorway.

Then Jo forgot her thumb. Unlike almost everywhere else in the boarded up house, the room was bathed in raw daylight. She lolled her head backward. She had thought Sid was being dramatic, but yes—yes there *was* a hole in the roof. She could see clouds as they raced overhead across a cold, blue sky. Where the plaster remained, it had gone soggy; where it lacked, she could see dark, woody splinters. At ANTHONY BLACK PRESS, Ltd, she once published an entire series on architecture. It hadn't made her an expert, but she at least knew beams should meet joists, and that was no longer happening in an area the size of a soccer ball (and roughly rhombohedron). She let her gaze fall back to the warped, wet floorboards. It had been raining indoors, apparently.

"Well. Fuck." Jo sank onto a nearby chest that had remained mostly dry. How long had it been that bad? Surely after her uncle's tenure. She let her eyes wander across the debris-strewn floor. Heavy beams loomed above her, and the stained wallpaper had once been pink floral, High Victorian. The window-wall boasted a small fireplace. It was dry over there, with a single empty nail above the mantel and a small, antique dresser. She ought to assess the damage. And probably call someone about roof repairs. Instead, she started opening all the drawers. They were empty, but something behind the dresser banged against the wall with the effort. A large rectangular something, with one end sticking out.

Jo knelt, careful not to lean against the floor. It appeared to be a picture frame—large, wooden, and gilt covered, like the life-sized portraits in the library. A solid tug slid it sideways. The painted canvas faced the wall, presenting Jo only with the paper backing and its hanging wire.

"Let's have a look at you," she said, grunting to lean it backward and into the light. The varnish had grown cloudy from moisture, but through its haze peered a dark-haired woman with a wide, oval face. The subject was frowning—or rather, not smiling. The mouth pursed into a flat line, and Jo found herself mirroring it, frowning slightly. She looked vaguely familiar, but it wasn't Lady Gwen Ardemore. A similar chin, maybe. But the eyes were dark, moody even, as she stared into the far distance. There was something just a little bit wrong about them, though she couldn't think what. Something *off*. Jo looked for a name, but beneath it all, the brass plate read *Netherleigh*.

"How did you get here?" she asked the strange figure. The style, even the frame, matched the others—it must have been meant as part of the set. Then again, she didn't know who else's portrait would have been painted. She took out her phone, intending to contact Rupert Selkirk, but of course, the house afforded her no signal. Jo leaned the painting back against the wall—and that's when she heard the crash. It sent her racing to her feet, fingers numb-tingling with startle, but by then the cursing had begun.

"Bloody *hell*!" That was Sid Randles. If her guess were correct, he had just tripped over her bag of tools. By the time Jo arrived on the landing, he was standing and rubbing his ankle, backlit by the open door.

"These tools yours?" he asked. "Trying t'kill me?"

Jo followed the banister down before answering. It gave her a minute to try and arrange her brain; his very "being there" was deeply distressing for some reason. She certainly hadn't expected him, but then, perhaps she should have.

"Why are you here?" she asked.

"Why are *you*?" Sid retorted, straightening. "Thought you were moving into the cottage, like."

"I am." Jo checked herself. She did not have to tell him what she was planning to do. She cleared her throat slightly and adjusted her hoodie. "You haven't answered my question."

Sid responded with one of his crooked grins, but he was looking up the stairs.

"I still work here," he said. "You were up there, were ya?"

"I was looking at the roof damage in the little room."

A series of expressions were fast moving over Sid's foxlike features; she registered but couldn't quite read them.

"I told you it was a great ruddy hole, didn't I? Dangerous up there. Might fall through the floor." He moved further into the light and offered her a smile. "Might change your mind about having me around for safety, eh pet?"

Jo rolled the word *pet* around her brain; she wasn't sure what it meant but she did not like it. It ran up a long list of incongruous associations: dog collars, the Monty Python dead parrot skit. She did her best to make forceful eye contact.

"I'm not your pet. And I would like to know what you're doing here because I don't like you. *Here.* I mean." The last part hadn't come out quite as smoothly as she'd meant it.

"What's a matter with you? I'm trying to warn you about this place. God, lady. If that's how you treat people, you'll never make it up here." He turned around and whistled his way through the door, stopping only to add: "Mowing, is what I'm doing. You do that in the States, don't you?"

Jo watched him go in silence. She was still staring after him when the lawn equipment rumbled to life somewhere out of sight. His words had just stung her deeply, for a reason of which he couldn't possibly be aware. *You'll never make it on your own* were some of the last words Tony ever said to her.

Beforetime, mid-May; she had arrived early. Tony booked lunch at his favorite restaurant, La Grande Boucherie. Stained glass, skylights, terribly expensive wine; it wasn't anywhere they'd been together before. She knew, by then, that he'd gone there in other company quite a lot. Jo had worn her battle clothes, which in this case involved all black, right down to the Doc Martens. He would be bringing the divorce papers, and they were supposed to make it amicable. Apparently, he didn't think she'd read them—or do any other digging—or see a lawyer, herself. This, despite the fact she'd been his fact-checker, editor, and person-of-all-work for a decade.

"Hello, Josephine," he said.

"You told me it was a hostile takeover," was Jo's reply. Tony shook his head.

"Salutations, Jo," he corrected. "And we sold the company almost a year ago."

"But we didn't sell it. They went right to the shareholders. That is what you told me." Jo had memorized the details and could list them all, but her voice was shaky with anger. Tony—Tony browsed the wine list and heaved a great weary sigh.

"We've talked about this," he said, running a hand through gray-salted hair. "They were going to absorb us one way or another, remember? So we weren't in bidding position. We took what we could get. You'll have to let these things go."

Jo's fingers had involuntarily closed around the stem of her water glass. She could feel her heart galloping, but the more upset she got, the harder it would be to articulate. *Lucid, lepidoptera, lugubrious*, she repeated to herself.

"Thirty-two thousand," she breathed. "Before tax." Their Brooklyn flat, his car, the business, everything she'd done, all she owned—and it was worth only this? Because a publishing house with a bright future had gone "miraculously" broke with all assets liquidated *just* prior to divorce proceedings?

The waiter had come. Tony poured the wine.

"I'm sorry for how you feel," he said. "I wish it was more, too." Jo steeled herself; she had so many words—but found the act of speaking them harder and harder. When she forced the next ones out, they came through clenched tooth and jaw.

"You did it on purpose."

Tony only looked at her. The same, sad, paternalistic look he had given her for years.

"Jo, no one is out to get you. We've been through this, before. You're not always a good judge of things, and you know it."

She'd wanted to argue. God, didn't she just. But he'd hit her exactly at the fault lines; Jo was wrong, everyone else was right. If she made a social faux pas, it's because she hadn't tried hard enough; if she had a gut feeling about something, she was being "weird"; if she couldn't bear some banality, she was the difficult one. In the meanwhile, Tony kept talking. He handed over some papers to sign, papers that explained how little she would get, how little she had been worth.

"What now?" Jo heard herself say. It sounded weak, and she hated herself for it.

"I don't know," Tony said, looking at her over the lip of his Boudeaux Rouge. "But I do worry about you, Jo. Your future. I worry you'll never make it on your own."

Back in the Ardemore library, Jo dropped a broken slat into a neat pile. Sometimes, she just needed to process with her fingers. And a hammer. And a mini crowbar. She'd managed to free at least one window in the library, letting the light in. Outside, the lawn mower was buzzing closer; she *hated* that sound—the repeated, awful *WHIRRR* got right into her temporal lobes. As it approached the house, Jo pressed both hands to her ears and waited. And waited. It had come to rest somewhere outside the library windows, but just out of sight—and there it remained, coughing and clacking and roaring.

"Oh for fuck's sake—" This was Sid's payback, no doubt. He'd parked it there, just to annoy her. With her hands still pressed against her ears, Jo stalked out of the house and around the far corner. But she'd forgotten the garden wall. Sid hadn't simply left it running next to the house—he'd done so *within* the garden.

She hadn't properly seen the garden yet. Richard Ardemore was best known as a horticulturalist, according to her preliminary research, but the rambling, abandoned house had more or less consumed all her interest. Now she was walking along a wall that stretched far enough into the distance to get lost in the grayish wood-edge. How big *was* it? And why weren't there any *doors*? Jo could hear the mower grinding away beyond the wall, but she'd traveled at least fifty yards from the house with no way in. It wasn't *that* tall, maybe six feet? Jo clenched her fists, then took ten steps running and jumped. Her fingers grasped the edge and she scrambled with her feet against the stone. It wasn't graceful—belly to the capstone, legs straddling, and her jacket bunched up to her bra line—but she was over, having dropped down to a soft landing of heaped dead weeds.

Had Rupert called Sid a *caretaker*? He certainly wasn't a groundskeeper. Jo wished she'd taken a better look from the wall; once on the ground, she could barely see over the winter-blasted tangle of thistle and debris. There were yew trees, a patch of tiny blue-purple flowers, but now was not the time. Following her ears, Jo navigated the bramble and two crooked terraces and found Sid's path of destruction.

It looked like a bad shave: one ugly streak with spit-up heaps of chewed vegetation to either side. At one end, *just* under the library window, growled an orange, rusty push mower, but no Sid. The mower's throttle had been tied in place with a bungee cord. Jo had to uncover her ears to sort it, and when she'd finally shut it off, her whole head was ringing.

"Sid!" she shouted. Jo left the garden (the short, easy way this time) and followed a broken path back to the house's slate steps. He wasn't there; he must've been in the cottage. Had he only been pretending to work?

"Jackass." Jo returned to the library, still gripping at her thumbs. She didn't want Sid hanging around; she wanted ALL his keys—and wanted him gone. Jo turned around and surveyed the library in its partial daylight. Book spines glinted back. The unruined ones, anyway. An ugly black stain sank through the very middle of the shelves in the shape of a parabola. And probably at least three hundred beautiful books destroyed. Had to pitch them. Had to fix the roof, first. Her eyes wandered back to the paintings above the mantel. Those looked all right, at least. Or did they? Jo cocked her head to one side; they weren't centered with the fireplace. Now that she noticed, it was going to drive her to distraction. You wouldn't hang portraits so far to one side unless—*unless* there were more than just *two.* Jo snapped her fingers. The other painting must surely have belonged down here?

Jo rushed upstairs, preparing to fight the door again. But it was already open. She blinked in the daylight; something wasn't right. Like furniture moved from its familiar places, or clocks ticking out of sync. The dresser had moved. Not much. Just enough for her to notice. Jo's heart took a leap, but she knew even before looking:

The painting was gone.

4

Emery Lane, of Rupert Selkirk and Associates, made tea. Jo had met him the day before; pencil thin mustache, pencil thin man; there was something distinctly No. 2 Ticonderoga about him. Watching him bustle about the domestic space of a small back kitchen (with a waist apron) was both incongruous and weirdly placating. She found him easier to talk to, as a result.

"Then, he just left the mower running!"

Emery placed a warmed brown pot on the table in front of Jo.

"Rude of him," he said, agreeably. Jo shook her head.

"Not rude. Planned. He was just distracting me so he could take my painting."

Emery made no remark to this at all, even though it was the second time she'd said it (the first had been in a rush of unpracticed words upon arrival). He did, however, pour tea and offer sugar and little cookies.

"I don't mean to be insensitive, but you didn't really *see* him take it, did you?" Emery snapped a biscuit in two and nibbled one corner. "Were you going to make a police report?" Jo took a deep breath (and a chocolate biscuit).

"I—I don't know. I want him fired, though. How long has Sid worked for Rupert, anyway?"

"Oh, he doesn't work for Mr. Selkirk at all! We are on retainer to the estate, so anything done for the property resides under the jurisdiction of the owners. Sid Randles works for *you*."

Jo set the teacup down a little harder than she meant to.

"I'm *paying* for this?" she demanded. "I thought there wasn't any money in the estate!"

"No, no—not paying! Well. It's complicated." Emery puckered his lips a moment, and Jo worried she'd been rude, even if she couldn't think how. The door buzzer had just gone off, however, and a few seconds later, Rupert entered the kitchenette fully animated.

"Emery, I thought we should—" The words halted and Jo watched him chew back an entire sentence. "Hello, Josephine, I wasn't expecting you."

"We were just talking about Sid," Emery said.

"He stole something from me," Jo cut in. "Sorry—I meant to start at the beginning. He tripped over my tool bag and then left the mower on, and *then* he stole from me."

Rupert had not changed position or expression, except to raise his eyebrows at Emery. Jo suppressed a sigh; *overdirect, inability to mask impatience…salutations, Jo!*

"Sorry. Hello, Rupert—Mr. Selkirk. I, um, have had some trouble with Sid Randles. He took a painting from the estate."

"Of Lord Ardemore?" Rupert asked.

"No—"

"Lady Gwen."

"No, actually. It's the portrait upstairs."

"I don't know of any portrait upstairs," Rupert said, a little flatly.

"It's a woman, dark hair rolled at the neck in a sort of Grecian wave. And she has odd, dark eyes, a blue gown—or blouse, it's just from the bust up." Jo had closed her eyes to repeat this but opened them to share the most salient point: "The nameplate said Netherleigh."

"Which room?" Rupert interrupted.

Jo stood up and made a small circuit of her chair. Why were people always hard? She was better at crowds; that's why introverts could live well in Brooklyn: collective anonymity, the protection of bounded otherness. But if you had to keep explaining yourself, it at least helped if people didn't come at you with prior inquiries.

"The room in the back. With the hole," she said tersely. "Now it's missing because Sid took it. He stole it. I want it back—and I want him *fired*. Like today. Now."

Rupert's unruly eyebrows met in the middle.

"He came to the estate and stole a painting? Why would he do that? Are you sure?"

Jo heard Emery *hem-hem* behind her; he'd asked the same question.

"It was there. He showed up. Now it's not."

"Ye-es. He may have moved it for some reason. Didn't you say it's the room with the most damage?" Rupert asked, as if that explained it.

"Look, he intentionally distracted me, got me out of the house," she said. Except now this sounded weird even to her own ears. What if that was just a prank? What if the two things weren't related after all? In front of her, Rupert folded his hands. He was probably on the verge of asking, like Emery, if they needed to call a constabulary, or whatever. Jo felt her heart grip against her sternum and attempted to beat him to it.

"I might make a report," she said slowly. "But not yet. Right now, I want you to fire him and take his keys. And tell him that, *if* he brings back the painting, I *won't* call the police. How's that?"

Rupert smoothed his lapels, tugged up each pant leg, and sat down in his leather chair.

"You are within your rights to end his employment, of course. It was a contract of convenience, no more." Rupert opened his desk drawer and took out an accounts book bound in green baize. "Sid took no salary; he managed the cottage and grounds and was permitted to keep any funds from renting the cottage. When you move into the cottage, that terminates anyway. You could wait until—"

"I'm moving in tomorrow," Jo said on impulse, but once she did, it seemed a marvelous idea. "I'll be bringing my things from the Red Lion tomorrow morning. Early." The more she spoke, the more real everything sounded. "It's mine, and I'm staying."

Rupert said nothing. Emery said nothing—in fact *he* hadn't spoken since Rupert came in, Jo realized, though his gaze remained fixed on Rupert's serenely professional face. She glanced between them both.

"Please?"

"All right," Rupert said, laying one hand on the nearby telephone receiver. He picked it up, and on that queue, Emery offered to see her out. An alarm was ringing somewhere in Jo's head, but she couldn't grasp what it signaled. It felt awkward enough, but then again, that might be her fault.

"I just want to find out who she is. I mean, it has to be a family portrait, doesn't it?" she asked when they reached the door. Emery was holding her coat, but paused before offering it up.

"It makes a certain sense," he agreed. "The Ardemores were mainly from Yorkshire. Sir Richard and his wife, his son William, all born and bred here. Not William's wife Gwen, though. Welsh. Daughter of industrialists. Davies, I think, was the name."

"Davies. Not *Netherleigh*?" Jo asked. Emery gave a little shrug.

"The only Netherleigh I know is in Belfast. Government building of some kind, I think." He closed the door behind her with a flutter of fingers. Jo could see Rupert Selkirk's back through the window. He was still on the phone.

It was nearly dark when Jo got back to the Red Lion. She'd taken three trips between the town shops and the cottage, stocking in garbage bags and cleaning supplies. It was a mess, too, of course, but Jo itched to get her hands on the bookcase first. Her brain was buzzing with more than anticipation; Rupert had texted to say that Sid would turn in his keys the following day. No mention of the painting—or of Sid's response. It left her with creeping doubts she tried to subdue. *Not everyone is out to get you.*

She'd been right about Tony, though.

Jo pushed open the door to the public house and into a barricade of noise. Standing room only, a blur of faces and colored coats.

"*There* she is!"

A dozen heads swiveled in Jo's direction, glasses plonking the bar top like punctuation marks. She recognized Ricky, his tie flung over one shoulder. *"Hey, Sid,"* he shouted, *"your ex boss just turned up."*

"Oh no," Jo muttered under her breath. She tried to back through the doors and into the hall, but Ben was just coming through carrying a laden tray. Jo spun back around to see Sid leering at her from Ricky's high-top.

"Well, well. Here she is, the tit that fired me," he said. *Pet. Tit.* Jo's mind whirred, but Sid wasn't finished. "I wanna have a word with you, lady."

"I have to go," Jo said. Sid had crossed half the room already, and she winced. *"Don't touch me!"*

"Jesus," Sid sneered. "I *didn't* touch you—what's the matter with you? I just want you to own up. Go on, tell these people what you told Rupert." He spun around to face the room; mostly men, Jo noted. Also a woman with a cane, scowling deeply. She didn't look like safe harbor. All of them were listening expectantly to Sid.

"I been working at that run-down pile for *years*. What do I gotta show fer it? Pitched out for nothin. Not even advance notice."

"Makes her a *real* Ardemore," Ricky sniggered into his beer. Sid clapped his shoulder.

"Don't it, just? But that's not the worst of it, lads. *She* accuses me of *stealing*. And she didn't have the balls to tell me to my face."

People were staring. Some began to laugh. It was noisy. Hot blood crept up Jo's neck and flushed her cheeks. She'd disappeared her thumbs again and a tremor was working its way through her legs. She still managed to get the words out.

"You did steal something. And I want it back."

"I never took no sodding painting!" Sid shouted back. "Why would I?"

Jo couldn't answer. Her throat had seized up, and no words would come out. They fizzled as they left her brain, got stranded somewhere. The light, the noise, and the people—it was too damn much, and she was shutting down. She could sense Sid getting nearer, a looming presence, but she couldn't speak, and she couldn't move.

"You can't say nothing? Not a damn thing?" he asked. "Jest like your uncle, are ya?"

"Oy! Sid! You stop it right there!" a voice shouted. Jo didn't know who it was, but the sound unlocked her legs. She spun around, shoving aside those behind her, and dashed into the hall and up the stairs. When she got to her room, she shut and locked her door behind her, then sank onto the bed, gasping little hiccups. *Why didn't you handle that better for crissakes?* she scolded herself. Jo slumped backward and stared at the ceiling, plucking at brain splinters. Her guts churned with embarrassment; people would be talking. She looked weak to them, but she *wasn't*. She'd just got—a bit—

"'Allo in there?" a woman's voice asked at the door. "Can I come in?"

The accent was thick, round, and warm. Jo couldn't quite place it.

"I've something for you to eat, love," the voice added, so Jo took a breath and got to her feet. It took a moment to undo the latch; standing in the hall was a woman with dark hair, swept back from the temples and streaked on the sides with iron gray. She carried a tray.

"Partridge and rice! Good, too, as I made it. And a little brandy. Drink it up, now, you cannae do better."

It might have been her tone, or maybe Jo just didn't have any arguing left, but she did as she was told.

"Mhm." Jo took a sip and swallowed fire. "You are—?"

"Tula Byrne. Short for Tailelaith. Innkeeper, chef, baker, and the one as chucks out drunken idiots." Tula pushed a fork at her. "I kicked Sid out m'self."

"I'm—sorry." Jo was not sorry. Tula gave her a wide, white smile.

"Sid ain't so good a customer that I'm afraid to lose him. Ben, you might know, he ain't the forceful one."

"I'm not helpless, I swear. I just—it's embarrassing."

Tula leaned against the doorframe and crossed her arms. "Tut, now. S'alright. You're an outsider and I know what that's like."

"How?" Jo asked and was rewarded with a musical laugh. Tula curled a strand of hair around her fingers.

"Ben—the barman? He's mine. I'm an older woman with a young lover, who refused marriage to keep her own name, *and* I'm Irish. It's Satan's trifecta. I been here fifteen years, and *I'm* still an outsider, love."

"Oh," was what Jo managed to say, but that didn't seem to bother Tula.

"Ben told me you inherited that mess on the hill. Yes, I know it's a mess—been that way ages. Fellow who owned it came round some, but not to stay. The young ones used to go up there spoonin' in the hedges. Anyway—I called Selkirk. And you need a roofer." She handed Jo a folded slip of paper with a number written in pencil. "Cheaper than most," she assured her. "Just leave the tray in the hall."

"Tula," Jo said, finally. "Thank you. I mean it."

"No worries, love. We outcasts do for each other."

That night, Jo dreamed of the painting. The eyes were still wrong—more wrong. In her dream they appeared as dark smudges with no eyes at all, and instead of *Netherleigh* the nameplate was blank. She woke up sweating down her ass crack with the radiator hissing; it wasn't a nightmare, but she *was* haunted. *Nettled* was a better word for it, maybe. Rupert and Emery didn't seem to think the painting was even real, much less missing, and *Netherleigh* didn't shed any light at all. Jo tossed the covers aside, took a quick lukewarm shower and dressed, scrolling her phone on her way downstairs to the dining room. Emery proved correct; there was an economics building in Ireland called Netherleigh House. A bed-and-breakfast in Devon had the name, too, but no one explained what it stood for. Over breakfast, she even tried splitting the word in two:

N-E-T-H-E-R. She knew that one; below, behind, bottom.

L-E-I-G-H turned out to be an English surname that also meant "delicate" or "meadow." Bottom meadow? Delicate rear? Field of Butts?

"Here you are," Ben said, delivering a plate of eggs, toast, "bacon," (it was not bacon, Jo decided) and beans, which didn't make any sense. Jo peeped up from her by-now-claimed corner booth; there weren't many people in—and (she hoped) none from the previous night.

"Headed to the cottage?" Ben asked brightly. "Good for a walk if you're feeling brisk. About five miles."

Jo nodded thanks, left half the breakfast, and took a coffee to go. The fog had retreated and clouds pulled like taffy across a blue sky. She wanted, desperately wanted, to start on the house's library. But as she planned to make good on her threat to move in *today*, the cottage needed her attention first. Jo hummed to herself as she unpacked the trunk of her rental: extra-large bin bags, industrial gloves, mold killer. Balancing the load against her hip, she unlocked the door with two reassuring clicks.

The faintest puff of something unpleasant assaulted her nose upon entering. She didn't remember it from the previous day; distinctive, slightly familiar, as yet unplaceable. Jo shrugged and banged the door closed with her hip. A good clean would fix it, she told herself, stepping round the sofa.

Then she saw the whisky bottle and two used glasses. They didn't belong there. But neither did the boots.

They were workman-like and camel colored, with their rubber soles tread-up. More importantly, they had *feet* in them. There was a body on the carpet.

Jo reacted on autopilot, muscle memory dictating her next several moves as she relived eleven months of nursing her mother. Kneel, check for a pulse. *Nothing.* The skin was cold, pasty, the pores closed. Now her brain registered the familiar odor: a metallic tinge of blood and fluids. She couldn't see his face under the mess of red hair, but there was no mistaking Sid Randles.

Jo fumbled with her phone but didn't know any emergency numbers. She tried Rupert, got voice mail. Caught somewhere between numbness and panic she remembered Tula's note. The Red Lion number had been printed on the stationary.

"Tula?" she begged into the receiver.

"Ben, I'm afraid. Who's calling?"

"It's Jo. I—I'm at the cottage—"

"Tula's out in town, but I can give her a message—"

Jo felt like a scream might be bubbling up.

"POLICE," she gasped. "It's Sid!"

"Oh no, what's he done now?" Ben asked. Jo swallowed what was probably bile. That was going to come back (a lot) in a minute.

"He's dead," she said, and just managed to make it to the sink in time.

5

Lights flashed through hazy windows, and Jo found herself focusing on a whorl in the glass. Police with bright yellow vests had turned up first; they put a blanket on her shoulders and left her in the little kitchen where the counter mostly blocked her view. Men in paper suits and gloves came next. She'd seen that before, back in Brooklyn. A man had been shot in her apartment building. It hadn't felt real then, and it didn't feel real now.

"—a shock."

Jo looked up to find a man in a slightly rumpled suit peering down at her. She wasn't sure how long he'd been standing there.

"Sorry?"

"I said I am sure it must have been a shock," he repeated, pulling the other chair forward and sitting down across from her. "DCI MacAdams."

Detective Chief Inspector, Jo thought, her brain translating by rote. Senior investigating officer, UK brand. He had brown hair, shaggy gray at the temples, and a jaw like a mousetrap. Jo noticed that his tie was crooked and that it had dried egg on it.

"I understand you found the body, Ms. Jones?" he asked her.

"I did." She motioned to the yellow and white paper suits. She'd given *them* a very basic explanation, delivered like bullets from a Gatling gun. Plus her name, number, address at the Red Lion.

"I know it's upsetting, but I have a few more questions." The detective pulled out a small notepad. "Let's start with what time you arrived here?"

"11:12 a.m. was when I called Rupert Selkirk."

"Right." MacAdams made a note. "But when did you find the body?"

"I just said."

"You called your solicitor when you found the body?"

"Yes, but he wasn't there. So, then I called Ben," Jo explained. The detective was frowning now.

"I'm sorry, you called Ben—?"

"Well, I called Tula and *got* Ben. At the Red Lion."

"Ma'am, why—?"

"Jo," Jo corrected. Which was also not the right thing to do. She was doing this badly, judging by the look at the detective's face. *Get a hold of yourself*, she thought.

"Okay, *Jo*, why didn't you call the police?" he asked. That was easier, at least.

"I don't know how. It's not 911 like in the US."

MacAdams continued to frown, though the rest of his face remained impassive. Had he practiced that look a lot? Jo found herself searching it for clues.

"How long did you know the deceased?" he asked.

"I didn't. I knew *of* him, but I only met him on Tuesday, and I fired him yesterday."

MacAdams was still looking at her, his pencil poised in midair.

"You fired him," he repeated. "But you didn't *know* him."

"Oh." Jo tapped fingers against her knee to avoid gripping her thumbs into nervous fists.

"Rupert hired him, originally. But he stole a painting from the house, so I had him fired."

"This house?" MacAdams asked, eyes sweeping the cottage front room right to left.

"No—Ardemore House, up the hill," Jo corrected. "Which is my house now. I guess they both are."

For the first time, MacAdams' face betrayed a bit of real expression. Unfortunately, it appeared to be suppressed irritation. He rechecked his notepad.

"You said your name was Josephine Jones, from the US," he read.

"My mother was from York." She pursed her lips. There was a perfectly straightforward way to explain all this, but her mind kept diving sideways into subplots. And frankly, the egg spot on his tie was driving her to distraction. "What I mean is, it's a family property and I inherited it a few months ago."

The detective responded by waving at someone just out of Jo's line of sight.

"I'm going to have more questions," he said. "But in the meantime, Detective Sergeant Green will drive you back to town." A muscular woman with tight box braids joined them. A bit younger than Jo, she had serious eyebrows.

"Yes, sir."

"Hang on—I don't want to go back to town," Jo protested, standing up. She was quite a bit shorter than either of them and instinctively stood on her toes. "I—I live here."

"This is a murder investigation," said MacAdams, straightening the egg tie. "Forensics will take twenty-four to thirty-six hours, maybe longer. We will take you to the Red Lion. Stay there, please."

"I can't stay here?"

MacAdams had almost made it through the door. Now he turned so fast that his coat caught on the handle.

"A man has been *shot*," he said, freeing himself, and Jo shrank into her shoulder blades. She sounded coarse, didn't she? Sid was dead. She fired him, he was dead, and she'd just asked about something useless and banal.

"I'm so sorry—I didn't mean it like that—" she began, but her apology was interrupted by shouting.

"You can't come in, ma'am!"

"Don't you *ma'am* me, Jake, I know your mother!" Tula shoved her way past the do-not-cross tape. "Jo, you okay? Ben told me, and I came straightaway."

She'd nearly made it through the assembled officers, none of whom seemed eager to stop her, when MacAdams put his hands up.

"All right, *everyone* out. You, too, Tula Byrne."

"Boss?" Green asked. "Should I take Ms. Jones, now?"

"No, you won't." Tula put a protective arm around Jo's shoulders and steered her into the sunlight. "I'll get her back all right."

Murder. How were you supposed to get your head around that? You didn't, probably. Jo held a potato in one hand and was making attempts at peeling it; Tula had the forethought of putting her to work in the kitchen.

"Awful business," Tula was saying from the stove. "Wonder if anyone's called next of kin."

"And he was...married?" Jo asked.

"Three times." Tula dropped pasta into boiling water. "And three times divorced. Two of them sisters."

Jo's mouth responded before her brain told it not to: "My God, is there some kind of shortage?"

"Of men?" Tula laughed. "Not to speak of, though I lit the fires of hatred among every woman and not a few men when I took Ben off the market. Granted, we're not officially married. Didn't see the need."

"I was. Once," Jo admitted. "Tony. He was forty, and I'd just graduated college." She pushed the skinned potatoes into a neat pile. "I'm an editor. He had a small publishing house."

Tula had gone about the business of kneading bread dough.

"Ah. Fell in love with the boss, did you?"

Jo blushed fiercely.

"I interned for him, first. We were married soon as I graduated, and *then* I worked for him." Jo nicked her knuckle. *Dammit.* "I worked for *us*," she corrected. "I was the acquisition editor—and a fact-checker. And a lot of other things." Jo had, in fact, been Tony's entire editorial team. She had always been proud of her own instinctive sense for where a text was going, and whether it was derivative, or fresh, or worth bothering over. She thought Tony had been proud of it, too.

"So what did he do, then?" Tula asked.

"Tony? He cheated." Jo tried turning the grimace into a smile but failed. She leaned forward on her elbows, resting her chin on her hands. "Our publishing house got bought out. A hostile takeover, they call it. Buyers go straight to shareholders and then underbid with promises for big returns."

Tula pushed hair out of her face.

"Not sure I follow, quite."

"Doesn't matter. It wasn't true. Well, it *was*. Kind of." Jo sighed, puffing air through her lips like a frustrated horse. "We'd only just *gotten* shareholders. And I didn't know he was sleeping with one of them. Or that she was also attached to the publishing house we sold up to."

"Ah, feck," said Tula. Jo nodded appreciatively.

"Yeah. I thought, you know, it was just bad luck. But as soon as everything was signed and sealed, he asked for a divorce. We split what was left of the assets without bringing it to court."

"So you ended up with half of not much."

"And Tony ended up CEO of the new larger publishing house," Jo added. Tula made a guttural noise and punched down the dough.

"Holy Jesus, Jo! Illegal, ain't it?"

Jo pressed her lips together. Hard to say. Yes? No? She could have fought it. She'd *meant* to fight it. But then she received the telephone call that changed her world.

"My mom got sick. She died. But not right away." Jo spoke slow, worried that if she got started it all might come out like a flood. "After that, my job, Tony, my whole old life—just didn't seem to matter anymore. So, I sold it all and came here. God. I don't know why I am telling you all this."

"Because I asked, love. Pretty sure that's how it works." Tula smiled. Jo wished she could smile like that; a sort of beacon, bright, full of meaning but not wholly decipherable. "I told you, I'm an outsider here, too. I make it my business to also be in charge. No one crosses Tula Byrne, if you take my meaning." She dusted flour onto her apron. "You must be raw, still, over the loss?"

Raw. An interesting word. There was a whole raw chicken on the sideboard, its pink meat pale and flaccid. Raw wind chapped your lips till they cracked, raw onions made your eyes water. Jo thought about the days she cried after, and also about the days she *didn't.* When everything seemed dried up inside.

"My mom and I were close the way you have to be when you're the only ones left," she said, finally. It felt like a bridge too far, like sharing something ugly that she shouldn't have. But hell, she'd come this far and Tula hadn't seemed put off. "She left England unmarried and five months pregnant to live with her aunt, Susan, in Chicago. She never said why. But there are only so many reasons."

Tula was nodding slowly, her hazel-flecked eyes looking at the space over Jo's head.

"And Aiden Jones was your uncle," she said slowly. "Your mother's brother?"

"Yeah. Last branch of the family, sideways from the Ardemores. They didn't get on. Mom never spoke of him and didn't go to his funeral. Did *you* know Aiden? Sid—um," Jo choked a bit over the next part, "He said I was just like him. Last night."

Tula gave her an indulgent smile.

"S'alright, love," she assured her. "I did meet your uncle, once. I remember he once got a little curious about the local history around here. Afraid I don't recall much more than that."

"Oh." Jo cleared her throat. "It's just I never knew him. And I don't know what happened between them. Mom had been hurt somehow. Badly. And now there aren't any of them left. Except me."

Saying that out loud hurt more than she'd expected. But she also felt strangely lighter for it. She watched Tula, who was watching her right back. Might as well lay everything on the table while she was at it—

"Look. I'm on the spectrum, right? Autistic. So if I bother you, will you please, please tell me?"

Tula's look was hard to read. Not patronizing—not maternal, either. It *felt* like a call to arms, somehow.

"I told you, didnae I?" she asked in her soft Irish accent. "We do for each other. I've taken a shine to you, and you're all right with me. I make my friends quick that way. My enemies, too, mostly."

Jo wet her lips, then pursed them together. Otherwise, her heart might get out. Or she might fall weeping at Tula's feet and then curl there in a fetal position at the sheer generosity of it all. Neither of which seemed an appropriate response. In the silence, Tula went on talking.

"Anyway, it's a quiet little place, and mostly good people. Haven't had anything this upsetting happen since that awful car-theft-arson-murder five years ago." Jo stopped peeling potatoes.

"Arson…murder?" she asked.

"Man was burned to death in his car. Ex-military fellow, a local."

"Pardon me, Ms. Jo?" Ben emerged from over the swinging kitchen doors. "Mr. MacAdams is here to see you."

Jo felt her chest constrict; she desperately wanted to know—anything—about what happened. And also dreaded hearing any of it. She stood on her toes to peep over the kitchen door. MacAdams leaned at the bar rail and was looking toward the stairs. He must assume Jo was in her room recovering from shock—or convalescing like a Victorian heroine. And for some reason, she felt an impish rush of playfulness that had absolutely no place in the situation. Keeping the apron on, Jo stepped through to the bar.

"What'll you have, mister?" she asked. MacAdams turned, and it took him at least ten seconds to register who she was. He did *not* register the joke.

"Ms—Jones." He said it as though assuring them both, then took out his notepad. "I'd like to continue the interview."

"Okay. I don't know how to work the taps anyway," Jo admitted, coming round to sit on the stool next to him. His face was wooden and serious, a film noir face. But no one had told him about the egg-tie, and the rumpled too-big overcoat made him look like a deflated elephant. Detective MacAdams looked like Sam Spade tangled with Columbo and got the worst of it.

"I've been to see Mr. Selkirk. He confirms what you say about Sid's contract, and that he was supposed to turn in his keys at eleven this morning. So, if you would, start at breakfast, and trace your movements until finding the body. Details are helpful. Even small ones."

He was in luck. Jo was very good at details.

"I woke up at 6:00 a.m. because I'm still jet-lagged and have no idea what time it is, internally. Left at nine-fifteen for the hardware store because I needed toilet paper and then it took ages to figure out where to buy bedsheets. I left Sainsbury's about a quarter to eleven, I think. It doesn't take long to get up there to the cottage. The door was locked, both bolts. They're brand-new."

MacAdams scribbled all the while, hair falling forward into his face. "You say the cottage locks are new. Did you replace them?"

"Me? No. I've only been here since Monday, remember."

MacAdams stopped scribbling and scratched his eyebrow with the pencil end.

"From the United States, yes. Where?"

"New York." Jo shook her head. "Sorry, no. Chicago."

MacAdams' pencil hovered midair. Jo sighed.

"I lived in New York. My mom got sick with cancer and I went to be with her. I left from Chicago. London, then York, then here."

"And when were you here, last?"

Jo felt twitchy at the flat quality of his voice. Inflection would have been nice. She could've at least worked with that.

"I've never been here before. I inherited the place when my mother died."

"And when was that?" he asked. Jo tried to say, swallowed, and tried again.

"February."

This time when MacAdams looked up, a crease had taken residence in his brow. His face didn't do a lot of expressions, apparently, but this one seemed like actual consideration.

"I'm very sorry," he said.

"Me, too. So. I just arrived, and now there's a dead person in my house."

MacAdams shut the notebook.

"I have noticed the timeline, myself," he said. "It is curious. Do you have any enemies?"

Jo almost choked on her spit.

"*Me?* Shouldn't you be asking if Sid had enemies?"

"Sid has lived in Abington his whole life. The house has been uninhabited all this while, and Sid has been caretaker of the cottage for the last five years. Now, someone has murdered him there. Your arrival represents the only change to habitual pattern."

Jo gaped at him.

"Like what, I'm a harbinger of death? Poe's raven or something?"

MacAdams was giving her a glazed, slightly perplexed look. "Consider, Ms. Jones. Sid may not have been the intended victim."

"That's silly," Jo said. "No one has a reason to kill *me.*" It must have come out wrong, because both of MacAdams' eyebrows had just made a trek up his forehead.

"But there were reasons to kill Sid Randles?" He glanced at his notebook. "Earlier you told me that Sid stole something from you. Were you angry about that?"

Jo felt her face flushing.

"Obviously. I asked him to be fired."

"I see."

"That doesn't mean I think he should be murdered." Jo was getting upset. And that wasn't great for mental processing. First he suggested she might be a target, and now that she might be the villain. MacAdams merely continued, as deadpan as before.

"Was the painting valuable? Might there have been other valuables on the premises?"

"I don't know—how could I?"

"It belonged to you."

Jo blinked. *Yes, of course it belonged to me—otherwise I wouldn't think it was stolen, would I?* She didn't manage to get words out to that effect, though. In fact, she hadn't said anything, and MacAdams apparently wasn't waiting for her to work around to it.

"Maybe something useful will occur to you, later," he said, flipping the notebook closed and handing her his card. "In the meantime, *don't leave town.*"

Jo clutched the card hard enough to bend it. *James A. Mac-*

Adams, the card said. *A* for asshole, maybe. Jo crumpled it and shoved it in one pocket. She'd just found a body on her rug; she was scarcely going to think of anything else for the foreseeable future. Well. Except the painting, which she'd wanted to tell the police about. But if *this* is what passed for detective work in Abington, she might as well set up as a private eye herself.

MacAdams climbed into the passenger seat of a squad car. Beside him, Green wore a hungry, hawkish look. Mostly hungry.

"Could have brought some chips back. Crisps, even," she said. "They have those. In little foil bags."

"Call it a night. We can't do much more until the autopsy is finished and ballistics come back." MacAdams leaned his head against the seat rest. "Murdered in a place he'd worked for *years*. And that woman's only been here three days."

"And?" Green asked.

"And..." MacAdams didn't have anything else. But Green wasn't going to let it go. The engine had been running for several minutes, but she'd taken her hands off the steering wheel to cross them over her muscular chest.

"And what did she *say*. The constables told me she'd been waiting by the dead body—just right there next to it."

MacAdams had been thinking about that. Jo Jones: rather pale, with longish brown hair of the dormouse variety. Took the pulse of a dead body and asked to stay the night at the murder scene.

"Odd emotional reaction," he agreed. "Doesn't square with what you told me about the argument between her and Sid at the Red Lion."

Green had interviewed Ricky Robson along with several regulars. She nodded vigorously.

"I know. By all accounts, she'd seemed terrified that night. Shrinking violet. Ricky said she started it, which I doubt. But most people say she overreacted, shouting at him not to touch her, and then going all mute and wide-eyed."

"What about Ben and Tula?" MacAdams asked.

"Tula takes Jo's side, and she's a hell of a bulldog about people she likes," Green said. This might even be an understatement. "Ben agrees with Tula, as usual."

MacAdams made a dismal note to come back and speak with them personally. It wasn't dislike of the parties involved, but frankly it was the best pub in town and he'd hate getting barred. Tula could be a tough nut.

"Go see Rupert and Emery again tomorrow. I'd like to know if she's got money wrapped up in the estate—or if there's an insurance policy on her."

"Wait, you think *she* was the intended victim?" Green asked.

"I suggested as much to her. She's the only new variable."

Green put the car in gear.

"I don't think I buy that," she grumbled, reversing into the street.

"Consider—she turns up out of the blue. Maybe she's running from someone. Maybe they followed her here from the US and Sid got in the way—was in the wrong place at the wrong time. Or, hell, some Brexiteer might be prejudiced against an American inheriting a Yorkshire baron's estate."

"Prejudiced. Against a *white* lady? Please." Green rolled dark eyes at him. "I got a better one. How about—Jo Jones shot Sid in the back because of the old family portrait she'd been raging about in the inn. Did you ask her about *that*?"

"You think she shot a stranger over a thing she inherited on Monday?"

"Well? You don't know. You said yourself she's the only new thing around here. And she's American, after all. Guns."

She had a point. Green, her fiercely braided hair, cut-stone cheekbones, and machete personality: She was going to run the department someday.

"We'll keep our minds open," he said.

"Good. I'm still hungry, by the way. Rachael's out of town and I ain't cooking. Do you want Thai or something?"

Rachael was the chef of the pair, as he'd quickly learned from occasional invites to their end-of-terrace. And he *did* want Thai. But not tonight. He didn't want to face the autopsy with Tom Yum Goong sloshing about his insides. Whisky and chips, though. That would be proper bracing.

6

Friday

Drinking late night whisky and forgetting that he didn't smoke anymore was not the wisest "bracing" MacAdams had ever done. He stubbed out a cigarette against the brick wall of the station and swigged some mouthwash, but he knew better than to hope it would go unnoticed. Most people were already at their desks of a morning, and Green was scowling from the glassed-in microclimate of his office.

"I thought you quit smoking."

"I did." MacAdams picked up the cleanest dirty mug and assaulted the coffee maker. "What have we got?"

"Coroner wants to see you first thing. Also, Gridley hunted for previous on Sid Randles. I mean, any of the stuff we didn't already know. He got an overnight for drunk and disorderly in York a month back."

"In York, I'm surprised anyone noticed a drunk and disorderly." MacAdams burned his tongue on coffee and winced. "We have the rug he was lying on down at the lab."

"I thought it was a rental cottage—won't it be a mess of DNA?" Green asked. She wasn't wrong. The place was *made* of DNA. But it had revealed an important part of the story.

"They also took two glass tumblers," he explained. "Prints just came back. One set for Sid, the other glass wiped clean."

The announcement perked the ears of everyone in earshot. They had all just jumped to the same conclusion: Sid must have known his killer. They shared a drink together, at least, and whoever it was covered their tracks after. A step forward, though it blew MacAdams' theory of Jo-Jones-as-victim all to hell.

"We need to make a list of all Sid's friends and family," Green said. At her desk, Gridley inverted her fingers, popping knuckles unpleasantly.

"Divorced, wasn't he?"

"Three times," MacAdams confirmed. "He cheated on the first wife with the second, then cheated on *her* with her younger sister."

"They all must be from Newcastle, then. We'd have known them, otherwise," Green said, leading the way out of the room. MacAdams followed, nodding; even he didn't recall the women's names. Sometimes he wondered if that were the point. People knew Sid too well, here in Abington. By the time they had come through high school, there wasn't a woman in town to take him seriously—and not a soul alive who'd lend him money. Still: long, tall Sid, a bit seedy but always quick with a joke. And now, dead. MacAdams pushed through the double doors leading to the station's rear hall, with Green right behind.

"Honestly, Sheila. I just can't think who would do this."

"Well, here's more to chew on," she said. "I had a chat with Emery at Selkirk and Associates. Josephine is the last of her whole family. No parents, no siblings, not even a distant cousin. Divorced a year ago, no current address in the United States, no present employment. Maybe she's a trickier customer than she seems."

MacAdams made a noncommittal sound into his coffee cup.

"Well?" Green needled. "No history… Could be dark money, organized crime."

"*Very* doubtful," MacAdams muttered. Green swatted at him. "Don't you even want to throw in some cheerful speculation?"

They had reached the sterile halls outside the coroner's cold workroom. He could already smell the chemical soup of the place and imagine its grisly gray slabs.

"Sid Randles was shot three times in the back," MacAdams said tersely. "It ruins a morning."

More than this, they were about to view the day-old corpse of someone MacAdams knew personally, with the addition of three holes. He took a breath, then walked through to where Struthers waited. "Let's hear it, doc."

Eric Struthers pulled the sheet aside. Usually, bodies were turned face up with V neck stiches from autopsy. Sid was lying face down, much as they had found him.

"Sorry, it was the simplest way to show you the wounds." Struthers leaned over and pointed to three small holes, purple-red and ragged against skin gone pasty blue. "Small caliber bullet. No exit wound, so most of the bleeding was internal—better for the rug, anyway."

MacAdams had leaned forward as far as he dared to see the neat triangle scatter. Green joined him.

"We are looking for a handgun, then?" she asked.

"Seems so." Eric nodded. "Don't see that much around here, do we?"

It was true—there were plenty of murders, but most were with blunt objects or sharp implements, a few hit-and-runs, strangulation, assault, drownings, an occasional hunting rifle. But not handguns.

"Hell," Green agreed, "there were maybe fifty handgun deaths in all of England last year."

"Quite right." Struthers reached under the sheet and turned

over Sid's right hand. "No sign of a struggle, nothing under the nails, no knuckle bruises. No evidence of a scuffle at the scene, either. He may have been trying to escape, though. Perhaps making a bolt for the door, judging from the angle of entry."

Struthers put up an X-ray slide: one bullet in the left ventricle, one in the lung, one lodged in the spine. He made a bisecting movement, chest to hip, and MacAdams tried to imagine the scene. Sid's glass and the bottle on the side table, Sid on the sofa. Where was his assailant? Standing, perhaps? They spoke. Argued. At some point, things went south. Sid stood and twisted around, making a dash for it.

"Would have taken a minute or so to die," Struthers continued, "but he was beyond getting up again. No powder burns, but this was close range."

MacAdams winced involuntarily.

"Right. We'll want the bullets and casings for testing."

"Sorry, James, I should have said—" Eric gave an apologetic smile. "The superintendent had me send them by courier to York last night."

"Why? They don't have a NABIS ballistics lab."

"No. But they have an ex-military weapons specialist. Can't recall the name." Eric washed his hands. "Semiretired I think?"

MacAdams set his jaw. Outside influence from a retired military expert did not sound like the start of a good week. He waved a hand at Green, a signal for them to depart. They made it halfway to the elevator before he realized she'd been speaking to him.

"Boss—what *is* the matter with you?"

"Sorry. Thinking about Sid."

This, apparently, surprised her.

"Were you that good of friends or something?"

MacAdams sighed. Not, exactly, no, not even as kids. MacAdams was the straight line and Sid the curve. MacAdams never left Abington; Sid always came back. There was a point when he'd prided himself on that—on being the steadfast town boy. They weren't mates, but being the same age, Sid made a fellow look good by comparison. And he was handy. Uncannily so. Sid did odd jobs for everyone. Even MacAdams.

"Fixed a pipe for me last week. Drank a beer in my kitchen on Thursday," MacAdams said. "It's the incongruity that gets me."

"You let Sid in your kitchen?" Green asked, and it wasn't the answer he'd expected. "I wouldn't have. Uniform are at his flat now, on Mill Street. Did you want to follow up with them there?"

"Not yet. Go there ahead of me. I'm off to see Cora."

MacAdams walked the more businesslike hallway beyond the incident room (and it's takeaway boxes). He ought to be mentally preparing his report. Instead, he was thinking about how Sid never seemed like a threat to him—but Green, who stood up to criminals and Yorkshire bigotry, clearly didn't trust him. Jo had also been afraid of him. He might need to adjust expectations. All the same, being shot in the back and left to die didn't seem like someone's reasonable self-defense.

Chief Superintendent Cora Clapham waved at MacAdams through her partly open door.

"Sit," she said and slapped a manila folder in front of him. "Came back this morning."

"What came back, ma'am?"

Cora reached a hand across the desk and flipped the folder open.

"It helps if you *read* the report, MacAdams," she said, settling back in her chair and crossing thick arms over a navy blue sweater. "Ballistics. I sent the bullets and casings last night. They arrived just now."

MacAdams scanned the document in front of him. The National Ballistics Intelligence Service was known for reasonable turnaround; they had the tactical registry and a hub in Manchester...

but less than twenty-four hours was practically miraculous. Cora seemed to read the shock on his face.

"It's not from NABIS. As I'm sure Eric told you, I know a weapons expert in York's firearms unit personally. He was in the RAF when my father was still Squadron Leader."

"Air force ballistics are a bit long-range for this, aren't they?" he asked, already knowing it would nettle her. The look she gave was withering.

"I am aware Sid was not killed with an air-to-ground missile, James. *Detective Inspector* Fleet expanded on his work in military ballistics and firearms as an expert for the Metropolitan Police. He knew my father."

Oh joy, MacAdams thought. Cora's late father had been a proud airman in the RAF, enamored of authority...and a deeply committed social climber. He liked shaking hands with the right people, knew how to smile in photos. MacAdams never trusted the man; Cora, however, *idealized* him.

"Fleet is semiretired now and working in York," she went on. "Without him, you'd be waiting on National to track an unregistered firearm. He's arriving here on Friday to help with the case."

And what? MacAdams had just been asked to process two divergent and unwelcome points—retired Scotland Yard and arriving on Friday—and could not quite work up a *yes, ma'am*. It was enough to keep his already dour expression from getting downright surly. Meanwhile, Cora leaned back in her chair.

"Jarvis was a great assistance after my father passed. They had been close. He came here to help sort through paperwork and military memorabilia. So James? Don't be a prick. Now—look at the file."

MacAdams was not a prick by default. But there was more going on here, and he hated all of it. Still mute, he turned his attention to a photo of the weapon matched to Sid's death: positioned against a ruler for scale was a derringer style handgun so small it could fit in the palm of one hand. Small caliber, by necessity, body of black steel, and a brass tack on the handle. German made, so said the description, and small enough to hide up a coat sleeve.

"Very James Bond," he muttered.

"In the sense of being highly specialized, yes. Very few were ever made. We're checking serial numbers. At least one of these was in a collector's set in the USA."

MacAdams tapped the photo.

"Is that where this one came from?"

"No. It's your lucky day. That one is right there in the North York Police Station. It was seized eleven months ago in a raid of unregistered handguns."

MacAdams absorbed this a moment. Like as not, the thing had been sitting on a dusty shelf awaiting a trial, or processing, or both. It wouldn't exactly take a ballistics expert to identify the specially made ammunition… Fleet's services were essentially moot at this point, and cat and mouse games were not MacAdams' thing.

"Are you going to tell me why he's really coming, or not?"

Cora sat straighter and rolled her formidable shoulders.

"You know I don't owe you an explanation, MacAdams. So take it as a very serious compliment that I'm giving you one. He's coming because Sid was murdered with a handgun Fleet is familiar with, and neither you nor Struthers have the expertise to examine the body. And he's coming because he *offered* to come, and because *I want him here.* Is that perfectly clear?"

MacAdams sucked air, then cleared his throat for the long-awaited delivery:

"Yes, ma'am."

He had let the coffee get cold again and chewed on his general irritation until the microwave did its work. Of course, he'd worked with outside law enforcement before. He'd even worked with Scotland Yard on occasion. But somehow, this had to do with Cora's father, he was sure of it. Fleet was military. Like her father. Like her brothers. Like herself. Every dog wagged for its own specialty. But ex-military *and* ex-Yard? He'd be impossibly smug, probably a know-it-all, and Cora would give him a free hand. MacAdams grit his teeth and shoved his door open, intending to throw himself into the worn-out desk chair. Except someone was already sitting in it.

"Oh! Sorry. This is yours, I guess?"

"Ms.—Ms. Jones?"

"I would have sat in one of the other chairs, but they are full of—stuff." Josephine waved a hand at two filing boxes. MacAdams found himself clearing one, on impulse.

"There is a waiting room," he said.

Josephine scooted around the desk and sat in a plastic chair. "Well. No one told me."

"Ms. Jones, why are you here?" MacAdams asked, still standing, because sitting seemed like an invitation he wasn't giving. His coolness must have been reasonably evident, but Josephine didn't even have the good manners to look uncomfortable.

"I was upset last night," she said, rather bluntly.

"About the murder."

"No. At you." She wasn't looking at him directly. Her eyes strayed to the corner of the room, and when she spoke next it had a slightly rehearsed quality.

"I arrived on Tuesday. That's when I met Sid Randles—twice. He tried to talk me out of taking the cottage, then he got a phone call from some lady."

"What lady?" MacAdams asked—but Jo just held up one hand and went on with the narrative.

"Wednesday he put a lawn mower outside the window, so I went to turn it off. When I came back, the painting I'd just found was missing. Rupert said he wasn't even really on payroll, just managing the cottage. So I had him fired. And then he was a dickhead to me at the Red Lion. The next morning, I went to move my things in. And I found him, like I said. Oh. And I don't know *what lady*. He was meeting a girl."

MacAdams was about to ask for clarification, but she didn't allow him to. She was talking faster now, the East Coast American accent flattening the *a*'s and making her harder to understand.

"Sid was living in the cottage. I'm almost sure of it. He wasn't renting it, but everything had been well used, even the bath taps. So, he was mad I came to take over, and then he stole something to get back at me. He was *supposed* to turn his keys in. He didn't, though. But the painting is gone, and now he's dead. What if someone killed him over it?"

Against his better judgment, MacAdams found he was sitting down, after all.

"Rupert Selkirk said he doesn't know of any painting. And you told the sergeant it was hidden behind a dresser. The only person who even *knows* about it is you."

"And Sid. Who took it."

"You saw him remove it?" MacAdams asked, and she huffed impatiently.

"Oh *this* again. No. But it didn't walk off on its own, did it?"

MacAdams tapped the table with an imaginary cigarette. What was he supposed to do with *that*? Did she mean to be like this? Someone let her waltz right into his office, so apparently she was good at disarming—or dissembling. Then again, the mere fact of her being there was so suspicious that it had the opposite effect. Apparently "cat and mouse" was the order of the day and he missed the memo.

"Ms. Jones, you said all this yesterday."

"Yes, but not in the right order." She took a breath and pulled both hands into her lap. "I wanted to give you everything as it happened, and I didn't do a good job yesterday. You were suggesting I might be angry enough about all this to kill Sid."

She was sitting there as before, upright and bright-eyed, and apparently unaware that what she'd just said was questionable as hell.

"And—you *weren't* angry *enough*," he repeated.

"No. I was angrier at you last night, and I didn't kill you, either." She looked off in the corner again, so she missed one of MacAdams' rare double eyebrow lifts. "And then there was the fight—or whatever. He wanted me to tell everyone he *didn't* steal the painting."

He was about to ask her what Sid had said, exactly, but he didn't have to. She had just repeated the scene, verbatim (according to her), ending with what Tula shouted at Sid before Jo left the room. He found himself writing furiously to keep up.

"Tula kicked him out, then?"

"She said so. And that she'd never liked him much anyway. I was embarrassed, to be honest. More embarrassed than angry, by then. Oh. And I'm not the target, either. You asked if I had enemies, and I don't. I'm honestly not sure anyone even knows I'm in the UK right now."

MacAdams had got that far all by himself. But Green was right; better to find out more, including what she was doing between midnight and four in the morning on Thursday.

"Okay. Talk to me."

Jo pursed her lips and cocked her head slightly to one side. "I lived in Brooklyn until my divorce eighteen months ago. Then my mom got sick, and I moved to Chicago to—to take care of her."

MacAdams noticed a stricken expression flit by as she talked about her mother.

"Employment?" he asked.

"You might say I lost my job in the divorce," she said, deadpan. It carried a stinger, though. One MacAdams recognized pretty well. "I'd been an editor at a publishing house."

"And your ex-husband?"

"Got a job at his girlfriend's publishing house."

That wasn't what MacAdams meant, but it certainly painted a picture. Jo leaned on her palm.

"He didn't leave me with much, so there's nothing I have that he wants."

"What about the estate?" he asked. Jo gave a chirrup of surprise, followed by long, incongruous laughter that almost ended in tears. It was a little distressing to watch.

"Sorry, sorry." She wiped her eyes. "The estate is in debt and has a giant hole in the roof and a totally ruined library nobody wants. You'll just have to take me off your crime scene board or whatever you use over here."

It occurred to MacAdams that Jo Jones perhaps watched too much BBC mystery.

"Thank you, Ms. Jones. Now, if you could tell me where you were between midnight and 4:00 a.m. on Thursday?"

A spark of recognition lit up Josephine's eyes.

"For real?"

"We ask everyone that." MacAdams lied. "It's for your statement, which you still need to sign."

"I didn't leave my room again after I went up. Tula brought dinner, and I slept till 6:00 a.m."

"Anyone verify that?"

She blinked at him, silent. She'd done that the night before, and he still didn't know how to read it.

"I'll check with Tula and Ben again." MacAdams sighed, steering her out of his office and toward Andrews. He would have to pick up the magisterial Fleet at the train station soon. "The sergeant here will take down your full statement."

"Should I say more about the painting, too?"

She fixated on the painting. And MacAdams didn't want it—or *her*—to become a fixation for his case.

"I'm sure there will be no stopping you," he said.

7

Jarvis Fleet arrived punctually at the train station, and MacAdams had no trouble picking him out. Gray suit, fresh pressed; close-clipped hair, brush mustache, impeccable posture. He'd been a Royal Air Force officer under Cora's father Alexander Clapham (Air Commodore, by the time he passed some years ago). He was carrying an overnight bag.

"Do you have a forensic team on-site?" he asked after a firm handshake and greeting.

"Of course. They have been going over both the murder scene and Sid's flat since yesterday morning." Sid's flat was a boxy little place by the station, barely an efficiency. It was disquietingly empty, and it didn't take long to get through it.

"Good." Fleet checked his watch, then retugged his cuffs in place. "I would like to see the cottage first. We can drop my case at the local inn when convenient."

"When—convenient," MacAdams repeated. He'd sent Green back to Selkirk and now regretted it; somehow he'd just become Fleet's chauffeur.

"It can wait until this evening, of course." Fleet gave a stiff bow of his head. "There is quite a lot of ground to cover first, I know. You can give me the details as you drive."

So now MacAdams was also some sort of debriefing secretary? *The details* were rather sparse, and MacAdams in no mood for flourish. Fleet took them in with brief nods, as though checking off some internal list. Everything he asked was perfectly, coldly rational in a book-by-the-letter sense. The Scotland Yard turn, essentially.

"You *were* in Met Police," MacAdams ventured when they pulled into the estate's hill-bound drive. "How did you end up in York of all places?"

"I took early retirement from the Yard," Fleet said placidly. MacAdams dodged a sideways glance at him; grizzled, yes. But he didn't look out of his fifties. "I decided to transfer my skills to a place in my home county."

"London to York is a bit of a step down, isn't it?"

"It's a beautiful town." Fleet smiled slightly beneath the mustache. "Cora tells me you lived there, yourself, once."

Fleet had the story wrong—or Cora did—or the Fates were simply against MacAdams in inconceivable ways. He'd never lived there. His ex-in-laws lived there. In fact, his ex-*wife* now lived there. *And* he found it a pricey, self-important tourist trap of a place, but decided on silent assent as he parked the car.

Inside the cottage, things looked much as before—which weren't lovely to start. MacAdams pointed to the floor next to the yellow, lint-pilled sofa.

"The bleeding was internal, not even a spill on the rug—which they took for testing, anyway. Possible shoe fibers," MacAdams added hastily. A uniformed assistant nodded in his direction.

"We're just about through, sir."

"Find anything?" MacAdams asked. She gave him a thin-lipped smile.

"Found everything, sir. Lots of different prints."

It was going to be a mess of paperwork. They had found hairs on the sheets that weren't Sid's—prints that weren't Sid's—leftover toiletry items that on analysis also weren't his. He turned to Fleet, who was turning slowly in place.

"Rental," he said. "Any number of people may have been through here."

"Have you checked for a register?" Fleet asked. MacAdams stared.

"A guest book? Of course we have, and no, nothing." MacAdams watched Fleet with growing impatience. "You'll want to see the body, surely."

"In time," was the enigmatic response. Fleet had begun to walk the room. When he reached the sofa, he tugged up both trousers and squatted low, his face nearly touching the floor's uneven surface.

"There are marks from a rubber sole," he said. "Didn't you tell me there was a rug here?"

MacAdams found himself dropping to one knee and looking askance in the light. There *did* appear to be a smudge. And not from their paper booties. He hadn't seen it there before. But then, he hadn't been on his knees looking for it.

"Maybe someone forgot to suit up," he said, trying to think back to their initial discovery. Fleet got to his feet.

"Curious," he said. "And no other papers to be found here?"

"Papers? What *are* you looking for?" MacAdams asked. It was past noon already; they still had to see Struthers so Fleet could have a look at the actual entry wounds.

"If you haven't found a guest register, perhaps there's a reason."

MacAdams felt his masseter muscles locking tight.

"Oh, I'm sure there's a reason," he agreed. "The reason is that it doesn't exist. Sid Randles wasn't exactly a tidy bookkeeper."

"And yet, you tell me there are multiple sets of prints and DNA. Someone was staying here, however itinerant." Fleet performed a full quarter turn on his heel, as if for military drill. "This does not have the appearance of a holiday let. But that doesn't mean he hadn't used it for other purposes."

"Meaning what?" MacAdams asked. He had assumed that Sid merely treated it as his personal home away most of the time, probably for an occasional bender with Ricky Robson and company. Fleet straightened back to his ruler-stiff posture. The look on his face had remained cordial.

"Has it not occurred to you that Sid might be involved in drug trafficking?"

MacAdams sucked air: *Oh-my-fucking-God*, as if that isn't the first assumption of any modern detective.

"Yes. It has *occurred*," he insisted quietly. "We've not found so much as a bag of weed here or his flat—and he's never had prior for it. And yes, before you ask, we brought the proper equipment to look for traces. There isn't any reason for you to do a more *thorough* search for the same things."

The infuriating half smile remained.

"All the same," Fleet said, "I'm here to help."

It took less than twenty minutes to get back to the station—an almost entirely silent trip. They had come, finally, to view the body, which wasn't getting any fresher. MacAdams did not want to repeat the examination, but couldn't very well stand outside the door and let Fleet take command. The man had been nothing but infuriatingly courteous, but MacAdams felt like a list was being drawn up of all the ways *he* had violated exactitudes. Fleet wanted to see the estate house; MacAdams hadn't yet procured the keys from Rupert Selkirk. He wanted to go to Sid's flat and be "thorough" there, too, and suggested everything should have been left in situ rather than boxed and brought to the station. *Yes*, possibly things were more lax in Abington CID than Scotland Yard. Maybe MacAdams himself was a bit *lax*. But it was hardly London, was it? Or York, for that matter. MacAdams could still recognize most people by sight, and a good number by name. He'd grown up with half of them.

"James," Struthers was saying, "did you know that a little derringer like that can't fire without a recock?"

"I wasn't aware," MacAdams admitted dryly. He also hadn't been listening all that intently. He brought himself closer to the slab, its occupant, and Fleet, who was leaning very close to the wounds.

"It means the first shot felled him," Fleet said in his measured cadence, "and the other two were fired while the killer stood above him."

"But there weren't any powder marks—" MacAdams began. Fleet raised his hand.

"If I may?" he asked. "That model is very small. It wouldn't leave powder burn unless the barrel nearly touched the cloth. The shooter would have aimed from directly above him while he lay on the floor."

"And he would have had to recock for each shot?" MacAdams asked. Fleet turned to look him in the eye.

"Correct."

MacAdams held his hand up, finger and thumb, as though aiming at a body below him.

"Shot him twice more in the back, even as he lay bleeding out. That's not self-defense, that's hatred in action." He paused. "And yet, they shared a drink first."

"About that," Struthers interrupted. "His blood alcohol level suggests drinks, plural. In addition to the few he'd had before getting kicked out of Red Lion by Tula Byrne."

"Who is that?" Fleet asked. It was MacAdams turn to wave *him* away.

"How affected would Sid have been? Had enough to impair judgment, or perhaps not recognize the danger he was in?" he asked Struthers.

"I doubt it. Sid's liver suggests he was a regular drinker,"

Struthers frowned. "We have no way of knowing how full the whisky bottle was at the start, and both parties were drinking, but I'd guess Sid would have been more or less alert and in his right mind."

Complete consciousness was a mixed blessing, under the circumstances, MacAdams supposed. But assuming the killer had been drinking, too, perhaps liquid courage raised the stakes on an argument.

"It could have been a flash of anger in the moment," he said aloud. "But whoever it was brought a *gun*. Premeditation."

"Yes," Fleet said simply. He rolled off the silicon gloves, inverting them along the way. "I asked earlier. Who is Tula Byrne? You say she threw him out of a pub the night he was murdered?"

MacAdams didn't quite stifle the exasperated sigh.

"Tula is the innkeeper. It's her job to throw people out if they get disorderly—thank you, Struthers."

"Certainly. It was a pleasure to meet you, Detective Fleet."

"Call me Jarvis, please." Fleet shook his hand. MacAdams was already partway through the door. The last thing he needed was the forensic team turning into the man's fan club.

"MacAdams," Fleet said, coming abreast of him with his sharp, measured stride. "I do understand your position. No one likes another DCI on their beat. You don't want me here, and I don't blame you for that."

They'd arrived at the car, and MacAdams felt his fingers clutch hard around the keys.

"But—?"

"Very perceptive." Fleet's smile didn't fade. "*But* you have bias in this case."

"I beg your pardon?"

"And I beg yours, detective. You have already failed to consider those you know well as suspects. Tula Byrne, for one. And what do you know about the American woman who found him? You are too close to the actors in this little drama." Fleet said these words almost without inflection, but MacAdams could feel the heat rising up the back of his neck.

"You think so, do you?"

"Cora Clapham thinks so," said Fleet—and MacAdams threw himself into the front seat of the sedan and slammed the door shut. Which was a wholly useless gesture, since he needed to give Fleet a ride back to the inn. Fleet climbed into the passenger seat, proper as ever.

"You're angry," he said. And for some reason the sheer obviousness of the statement took the wind out of him. MacAdams sighed.

"You want to interview Tula and Jo Jones? You're going to be staying at the Red Lion with them. Do your worst."

It was Friday night and MacAdams was home alone. Mann City would be on the telly; he browsed to the channel and picked up *Motorcycle Mechanics*, which still came regularly (despite the fact he hadn't worked on the BMW in his garage for at least three years). He proceeded to unthaw a microwavable entrée and open a brown ale. *This*, he told himself, *was free living.* The joke had long gone out of it; more of a mantra to mediocrity, now. His dinner had just *dinged* when the doorbell rang. He opened it with beer in hand.

"Sheila?"

"In the flesh," Green said when he invited her in. "Hope you don't mind the house call. I wondered how it went with your Yard detective."

"He would like us to be more thorough."

"Ah fuck's sake." Green shrugged out of her coat, which had been peppered with light raindrops. MacAdams hung it on the back of a chair.

"He's probably interviewing Jo and Tula and half the other occupants of the Red Lion right now," he added. Green barked a laugh.

"You know Sid's exes are gonna be there, too. Arriving tomorrow, I think. Ever meet them?"

"No. Heard plenty from Sid. Mostly not to his credit."

Green nodded, then leaned forward on her knees, hands dangling. It was her get-real pose.

"OK, now give me the dirt. What's the detective really like? He's from Scotland Yard and Cora seems pretty smitten."

MacAdams sat on the arm of his sofa. He was not, himself, *smitten*. But he could see why the Chief might be. Jarvis Fleet in his pressed suit, straight tie, military turning radius, internal rule book. Fleet who also discovered a footprint that shouldn't have been there, and who had shed real light on the murderer through his assessment of shots fired.

"Infuriatingly perfect," he said.

"Uh-oh."

"Yeah." He rubbed at his neck; he'd been clamped down tight all day. "I don't want him on the case—but..."

"But we might need him?" Green finished. MacAdams gave that real consideration.

"*Need* is too strong a word. We can use him, though. What did you get from Selkirk?" he asked.

"About Sid? He confirmed a sort of basic contract for maintenance and gardening. Apparently, he let the cottage in lieu of payment."

"Why in lieu of?"

"Sid got to keep any money he made off rentals," Green explained. "Selkirk figured he'd work harder to keep it up that way. And, if you want my opinion, he probably figured Sid was gonna do shit under the table anyhow, might as well make him responsible for the whole mess."

MacAdams knew from his own occasional employ of Sid that this made excellent sense. But it also meant Selkirk knew about Sid's less-than-wholly-legal methods. Green went on.

"Anyway, there wasn't much money to be paying *anyone*.

The American woman wasn't lying—the estate's in debt. Unless she's made of cash, I don't think she'll be setting up as lady of the manor anytime soon." She stood up, stretched, and retrieved her coat. "Look, boss, you gotta stop with the microwavey meals, right?"

"Rachel worrying about me again?" MacAdams asked with a laugh.

"She's a nutritionist. It's her job." Green slung the coat over her shoulder. "If you don't watch out, she'll start making me bring you packed lunches."

MacAdams could very well believe this; Rachel wasn't maternal or anything of that order. But she *hated* the way police people ate. Bad food at bad hours, too much caffeine.

"Tell her I was making a pot roast when you came, and I won't mention your regular order of curried chips."

"Blackmail," Green said, wagging a finger. MacAdams got the door.

"Whatever works," he said. She chuckled on the way down his drive, a dark silhouette against the streetlamp. MacAdams leaned a moment in his own doorway. The night had turned milder than the day, part of spring's uncertain welcome. He did not want to be in the incident room on a Saturday. He wanted to go for a walk with the dog he didn't have (but kept meaning to get) and have a pint somewhere with real food and the general hum of humans. Murders were damned inconvenient. MacAdams shut the door; he didn't have to *like* Fleet, he reminded himself. He just had to figure out how to use him to catch a killer.

8

Saturday

Despite coming down early for breakfast, Jo had lost dibs on her corner booth: it was now occupied by a newspaper and the top of a grizzled crew cut. Occasionally, a long-fingered hand would reach out for the teacup and disappear once more behind the print.

"You can breakfast in the kitchen, if you want to," Ben suggested. Jo plunked herself down on a barstool.

"Thanks, but here is fine." She planned to live in this town; she couldn't keep hiding from the locals. Even if she found herself measuring every patron against her memory of Sid's little audience the night of—

Well. The night he was murdered. This was the second time she had discovered a body; first it was her mother's. That hadn't been a surprise. But expecting it hadn't made it less surreal. She sat there, waiting for EMS, fighting the association of texture and color that kept threatening. *Dead flesh looks like old plastic*, she'd thought, the pebbled yellowing of ancient word processors in high school labs. And the reverse meant old plastic now made her think, horribly, of dead flesh. And with that, came breakfast.

"You said no beans, I remembered," Ben said, setting down the hot plate. Jo attacked the eggs with gusto, eating one-handed and scrolling her phone with the other.

"What do *you* know about the Ardemores?" she asked Ben. "I can only find stuff about Richard Ardemore up here, mostly about his botanicals. Not much about his son William. Except that he married into industry." She'd had no trouble finding results for the name *Gwen Davies*; more the reverse. There were tons of them. She wondered if she'd stumbled on the most common name in all of Wales.

"Don't really know much. Just that no one was ever around, so it made for a good place to sneak off as teenagers. A fair few parties we had up there," he said with a blush. "Music and drinking, you know."

Jo did *not* know. She wasn't the sort to be invited to parties—or to go, if she had been. But she smiled to show there were no hard feelings. Uncle Aiden and her mother certainly didn't seem to have cared what happened at the place.

"So no local color?" she asked. "No gossip? They left in 1908 and no one's lived there since."

"A bit of a row when they left, sure," Ben said. "People felt hard done by, the ones who worked there."

"Why?" Jo asked. Ben scratched at his chin.

"Hard to explain, I guess. See, around here, there's an expectation: you own the land, you take care of it and the people who work it. Responsibility, like. But that's two generations back, now."

"Ah, but that's the living! Maybe she's asking if there's a disturbed ghost!" Tula said. She'd come round the corner with her apron on, joined Jo at the bar, and troubled Ben for coffee.

"Honestly? I'm just wondering who's in the painting." Jo sighed. (Though having a ghost would have its literary charms.)

"I only had one look at it, but I'm 90 percent certain she must be related to Gwen's side."

"Oh, you and your mystery woman, eh?" Tula laughed. "Going to tell us about her?"

Jo squirmed slightly with anticipation. She couldn't pretend she hadn't been hoping for this sort of opening.

"*Well*, I have been trying a name search without much luck. So I started looking up portrait painters instead—you know, who might be hiring out in the Pennines circa 1908." She pointed to her phone. "Turns out there were all *sorts* of artists up here in the early twentieth century. I mean, there's Peter Brook, he's famous but too late—wrong style. Then you have the Barbizon school of landscape painters and John Constable, he's the one who said painting is a feeling. But in terms of color and composition, I think it looks like an Augustus John. It probably isn't. But it has those brushstrokes, sort of daubs, plus his paintings were so psychological and—"

"Slow down, there, love!" Tula said with a laugh. "I thought you were an editor, not an art historian?"

Jo felt the blush starting and pursed her lips. *You're oversharing again*, said the internal Tony. *Fuck off*, Jo managed to reply.

"I've just been researching," she said shyly. Tula peeked over her shoulder.

"You learned all that from a smartphone?"

"My laptop is upstairs," she said. She'd read close to 40,000 words on art, the Pennines, Richard Ardemore and the many, many Davies since four that morning. "If I'm ever allowed back up to the property, I'll see if the paintings downstairs have the same sort of style. I mean, I'm still looking for connections between the women in the picture and Gwen Davies' family in Wales, too. But this is sort of reverse engineering."

Tula drank her coffee, then leaned her broad chin on one hand.

"You're a wee stuck on this painting, aren't you?" she asked.

That was one way of categorizing the fiery creep of obsession, Jo supposed. There had been so many. Four years chasing every word written by or about Ngaio Marsh, a sixteen-month gestation of Jeremy Brett's portrayal of Sherlock Holmes, her lingering love affair with literary novels, and an embarrassing secret passion for *Voltron*.

"Maybe. A bit," she said. "Come on, though! It's a mystery, right? A woman with strange eyes. Who *is* she? And why wasn't she hanging up downstairs with the other two when there's space? And why was she stolen? It—it doesn't make sense. And that bothers me to death."

"Well, the *who* can't be all that hard," Ben said, getting up to collect dishes. "You just need to find someone whose family's been around forever."

"Oh, aye. Roberta Wilkinson is who you want, though that takes doing." Tula gave another of her bright, laughing smiles. "She runs the museum. Be happy enough to tell you her kin been here thirteen generations."

Jo had just done a little hop on her barstool.

"My God, you have a museum?"

"O' course! Mind, I wouldn't get your expectations overhigh," Tula cautioned. "And she's nary open on the weekend."

Which just figured. Jo turned about to scan the room. The man in the corner booth was standing now; he locked eyes with Jo. She half wondered if he'd been waiting on her to notice, the way wolfish barflies did before pouncing. He was, at any rate, approaching.

Jo responded by scooping the last bit of toast into her mouth, and reciting *don't talk to me, don't talk to me* under her breath. Apparently, it worked.

"Tula Byrne?" he asked, a slight smile under his brush mustache. "I wonder if I could have a word?"

Tula answered in her easy way, whisking the gentleman off to the check-in desk. Jo felt simultaneously relieved and embarrassed. She wasn't socially inept; she thought she'd grown rather good at peopling. It's just that she had enough on her plate already, including a dreaded phone call to Fiennes & Sons about the roof.

By 10:00 a.m., Andrews, Gridley, and Green perched at their desks with coffee mugs and morning buns. Fleet had been late. Upon arrival, he took a seat in the rear of the room, coat carefully folded over his knee and a teacup—with saucer—at his elbow. He must have been granted it by Cora, because the last of the downstairs china met its end in MacAdams' constable days. They were all chipped mugs and paper cups, now.

MacAdams pinned photographs to the board with magnets. Mostly, they were images of the crime scene, the body where it lay, and forensic photos of the doors and windowsills. It *wasn't* like the BBC versions, though, despite Jo Jones' allusions. Or, well. Not quite. He flapped one more photo against his palm: a picture of the German derringer.

"We still haven't located the murder weapon. Uniform searched the estate grounds, but we're operating on the assumption that the killer still has it," MacAdams said. Then he motioned for Fleet to step forward. Fleet gave the usual curt nod and faced the room with hands folded behind him.

"German derringer. Affectionately known as the *pug*. Note the peculiar four-chambered housing. The bore is too small for .22 caliber, so bullets are specially made in limited edition. A colleague of mine who works with antique munitions suggests few were made. It's rare and old enough to be unregistered." He waited for MacAdams to pin the photo before going on. "This particular model is from York search and seizure."

"So the killer has access to an antique weapon that we can't effectively trace—is that right?" Green asked.

"Affirmative," Fleet agreed. Gridley untucked the pencil behind her ear and tapped the desk with it.

"It could have been inherited or collected," she mused. "Whoever has *this* one might have other weapons that *are* registered."

"Already on it," Andrews said. "I've a list of people in the county with permits. We're working through it as we speak."

MacAdams nodded appreciatively.

"Good. But note—only three of four rounds were fired. Even if it *does* take special bullets, we must assume the suspect is armed and dangerous."

"Once we have a suspect, anyway," Green finished. Fleet performed another of his military turns to face her.

"There are always plenty of suspects. Just no present leads."

While true, it was maddening the way he delivered his little corrections. *Pompous git.* MacAdams expected to hear an earful from Green. He decided to steer the conversation elsewhere.

"It's reasonable that Sid knew the killer and invited him—or her—in. Even so, the doorknobs, whisky bottle, and second glass were wiped. Whoever it was had a cool head and presence of mind," he said. "Otherwise, we have all sorts of various prints and DNA on scene."

MacAdams spared a glance at Fleet before continuing.

"And DCI Fleet noticed a rubber-soled shoe tread where the rug had been. It suggests someone left a track after we removed the body. I need to know who has been in there without proper protection on their feet. Forensics says it wasn't one of theirs."

This announcement was greeted with blank faces and no admissions.

"Could someone *else* have a key?" Green asked. "I mean besides the ones Sid had." MacAdams made *another* mental note to get that set from Rupert; he'd been so damn busy carting Fleet around…

"We know Jo Jones has a set of keys," Andrews offered.

"Correct. And she does not have an alibi for the night of the murder," said Fleet. "Neither, I should add, does Tula Byrne. I interviewed her this morning."

"But Tula was with Ben," Green said. "I established that they were at the Red Lion together."

Fleet merely gave a slight shake of his head.

"Tula shut the bar down that night, and Ben was already sleeping soundly when she went upstairs. Tula claims that was just after midnight, which means she can only vouch for Jo Jones until then. And as you say, she has a key."

The room shifted around this piece of information. MacAdams found the idea of Tula *or* Jo stalking Sid frankly preposterous, but saying so would likely get him accused of bias. Again.

"All right, noted," he said flatly. "It doesn't make them suspects, necessarily. But we do need *everyone's* movements. Including Sid's closer connections. His mum went into a care home with early-stage dementia and died last year." He didn't think it necessary to mention that Sid's father committed suicide when he was nine. "No siblings. But there are the exes."

Green put two photos on the board. "His second and third wives, Lotte and Olivia. They are sisters, they are *loud*, and they turned up in here an hour ago demanding release of Sid's body."

MacAdams studied the photos. One was a redhead—bottle red—and the other sported brown hair and heavy fringe. Obviously related, not unattractive.

"Does that mean they are claiming rights as next of kin?" Gridley asked.

"Don't know, but you can ask them as I'm sure they will be back." Green sighed. "They want a funeral at St. George's. Like, tomorrow."

"What about the first ex?" MacAdams asked. That had been years ago; his only recollection was Sid's insistence that she was an "animal" in bed.

"Name of Elsie Randles. We haven't been able to locate her yet." Gridley stopped short; her phone was buzzing and she snatched it from a trouser pocket. "Hang on. It's about Sid's finances. Let me get my email."

"Good," MacAdams said. "We could use something tangible." While they waited, Fleet made a signal as though intending to speak in confidence. He dropped his voice low.

"Tell me, MacAdams, what's this about a stolen painting? Ms. Byrne says that's what started the argument with Sid in the pub room."

"Not quite," MacAdams contradicted. "He'd been fired, and I wouldn't call it an argument—"

"Boss!" Gridley interrupted. "Shit—sorry—but look at these bank statements." She pushed papers aside and turned the monitor for better viewing. She'd highlighted a series of lines, each appearing monthly at around the same time: five thousand pounds.

"Every month? When do these things start?"

"Five years ago, May," Gridley said, scrolling down.

"That's almost exactly when he took over the cottage," Green said—and Andrews gave a slightly indecent chuckle.

"Damn. Either the rental market is better than I thought, or someone was paying him off."

A payoff. MacAdams looked at Green. *Curried chips*, he thought.

"It gets stranger," Gridley said. "Money goes in and then money comes out in smaller, less conspicuous amounts—but it tallies. Cash both ways. Though, I mean, *all* his deposits are cash."

"They would be," MacAdams said, scanning the sheets. Everything under the table, as usual. The amounts varied—and were surprising even apart from the shocking enormity of five grand. He was certainly making money *somewhere*.

"Three questions: Who was paying Sid? For what? And then, who was *Sid* paying?" he asked.

"It's not honest cash, that's for sure," Green said, puffing air. "It *looks* like drugs, I know it does. But we went over his flat and cottage with sniffer dogs and everything. Clean and clean. There'd have to be *some* sign, wouldn't there?"

MacAdams tapped his chin. There were other ways of making money in Abington. Gambling, for one. And some years back, he remembered a car theft ring had been busted out of York and Newcastle, plenty of money changing hands there. Five thousand was, however, a very round and very specific number.

"Let's go back to the idea of a payoff. Gridley, you see if the amount Sid pays out *always* tallies. It could be he's getting a lump and gambling with it, or something. And I want to know about these other payments, too. It could be from the cottage rental—which might tell us something."

"It's gonna be hard to know, boss. It's not exactly traceable." She scanned the file again. "Dammit, though, he makes a good buck. Or would have if he weren't spending it all."

MacAdams looked over her shoulder. Credit card hits went to gambling sites. He knew that about Sid already. But Gridley was right; assuming the rest was truly from holiday letting, it was more than enough to live on. No wonder he was sore about losing it.

"For now, see what you can dig up on Lane and Selkirk's finances, *quietly*, please. They claim there's no money in the property, but the handyman was turning over a few grand a month *and* receiving mystery cash infusions."

"What about the wives? Should I fetch them in for questioning?" Green asked. MacAdams tapped his chin. They wanted a funeral, and that might be a good idea. Better than keeping Sid on a slab and would offer a chance to pay special attention to the mourners.

"No. Not yet. Get Sid's body released for burial, instead."

"Will do," said Andrews. "Oh—the cottage? That Ms. Jones was asking." MacAdams watched his officers head off to their separate tasks, aware that Jarvis Fleet was quietly waiting to be directed. There were times when an officiously civil straight man could come in useful.

"You can release the cottage back to Jo Jones. Fleet and I are going to interview Selkirk and Associates," he said.

9

Emery Lane met them at the door, prim in a pressed brown suit, and told them they were lucky to find them at work on a Saturday morning.

"Mr. Selkirk is on the phone with an important client and has an appointment this afternoon," he said.

"We'll wait," MacAdams assured him. "This is DCI Fleet, Emery. And actually, we came to speak to both of you."

In fact, MacAdams knew all about the day's schedule, thanks to Green, and had hoped to get Emery alone. He seemed the easier nut to crack. Emery's pencil mustache gave a slight twitch as he led the detectives to the front office and offered each a chair.

"Tea?"

"Please," Fleet said stiffly; MacAdams declined and shrugged off his rumpled mackintosh.

"Emery, you told us that Sid Randles became a retainer to the estate three years ago. What was the exact date?"

"I never assent to any details without looking at the files.

The habit of a good legal assistant, I assure you. I'll just pull it up, shall I?"

MacAdams smiled. Not because it set people at ease. On the contrary, Green assured him that a smiling MacAdams was highly unnerving, which alone had encouraged the practice.

"Thank you. While you do that, I'd like to verify a few things. Before the contract, Sid had only been doing the occasional odd job, paid hourly. Is that right?"

"I could look for receipts—"

"I think MacAdams would be happy with a general assent," Fleet suggested. It was well timed and had the benefit of both surprising and unnerving Emery. His face hadn't changed, but now his gaze drifted between the two detectives.

"Then, yes," Emery said, "But Mr. Selkirk can confirm."

"And after the contract?" MacAdams asked.

"Sid Randles managed the cottage on his own."

"You have no documentation for how much he made from these arrangements?" MacAdams asked.

"I don't believe so."

"Isn't that a bit odd? What if the rental were incredibly successful? Wouldn't that matter to the estate?"

Emery wet his lips.

"I will have to inquire from Mr. Selkirk," he said. In the next room, the leather chair creaked and MacAdams heard Rupert putting the receiver down rather louder than necessary. The man himself appeared a moment later, bearing a look of mild but genial surprise.

"Detective Chief Inspector MacAdams," he said smoothly. "How can I help?"

There was no way he hadn't heard the conversation.

"Rupert Selkirk, this is DCI Fleet, formerly of New Scotland Yard," MacAdams said, and much as he hated to admit it, the mention of the Metropolitan Police had just gained them useful footing.

"Goodness," Rupert said, nodded appreciatively to Fleet.

"We're following up on Sergeant Green's report. You see, I would like to know how much Sid made from his cottage rentals. I would also like to see receipts of how much you paid Randles as a retainer prior to that arrangement."

"Of course," Rupert agreed. "Could you step into my office?"

Rupert's office was larger than Emery's, and rather nice: polished wood, rich furnishings. But it felt oddly blank, somehow. Rupert motioned them to a brace of leather armchairs as he unlocked a cabinet.

"Aiden Jones rented the cottage in the eighties and nineties—that would be Ms. Jones' maternal uncle. His health became poor, however, and he was unable to keep it up. He died four years ago. Rather than taking on the estate herself, his sister, the elder Ms. Jones, made the law firm a retainer."

"Is that unusual?" MacAdams asked.

"It is, indeed. But we negotiated to hold the property for her daughter."

"And you were paid for this service?"

"As I say, we were on retainer by the elder Ms. Jones. So, yes. But the estate had been going fallow. The extensive grounds left to go wild, the house in some disrepair." Rupert held up a folder in one hand. "These are the rental records from Aiden Jones."

MacAdams extended his hand and didn't lower it until Rupert surrendered the file. He scanned until he found the entries. There weren't many, less than a dozen or so a year.

"Not exactly lucrative, then, I see."

"No, it wasn't." Rupert settled into his chair. "After his passing, I didn't attempt to rent it myself. It seemed hardly worth the trouble."

"It didn't seem worth your time," Fleet repeated, "as the estate solicitor."

"In point of fact, Detective, I'm afraid I don't have that kind of time. The Jones siblings had an unusual relationship to the property. Aiden had seemed highly interested in its history, but not its *management*. His sister in America had no investment at all. I could not see the point of managing a property on behalf of those who cared so little about it."

"I'm sorry, the estate's history? Explain?" MacAdams asked. Rupert lowered his head slightly, giving MacAdams a somewhat conspiratorial glance.

"No, family history. The estate has plenty of documentation through the nineteenth century—the gardens, at least, were famous in their time. And of course, it's been abandoned a long while. Aiden had some interest in how the Jones side of the family connected to the Ardemores."

"And how does it?" MacAdams asked. Rupert compressed his lips.

"Only just. No progeny meant no baronetcy, but the land parcel passed to more distant family members—of which Jo Jones is the last."

MacAdams weighed these admissions. It raised more questions than it answered, particularly about Jo's family, but also—

"All right. No one cared about the estate. Then why bother with an estate manager? Why not let it go to ruin?"

Rupert made a deprecating noise and shook his head. "Sid was *not* an estate manager. If he called himself that, it was a very grand gesture. We needed the grounds looked after in the most basic way. Keep the lawns short, clear the drains. Occasional upkeep. I just wanted to keep the cottage reasonable until—until such time that the family took possession."

"And you wanted Sid Randles cheap," MacAdams summarized. Rupert smiled and laced his fingers.

"Sid Randles *offered* himself *cheaply*. He agreed to take over renting the cottage in place of a salary. As you can see from Aiden's records, it didn't promise much, certainly not anything of real worth to the estate"—*which means*, thought MacAdams, he *definitely* overheard his line of questioning with Emery—"so the arrangement suited us both. I explained this to your sergeant yesterday."

"My detective sergeant," MacAdams corrected. Beside him, Fleet uncrossed his legs and leaned slightly forward—the bending of a ruler.

"Am I to understand that upon Ms. Jones' arrival, this arrangement with Sid was rendered void? Once she took over the property, it would become her decision, yes?" he asked.

"Yes, but I didn't know her intentions before her arrival," Rupert said—and maybe there was the slightest shift in tone? "As a matter of fact, she only phoned last week to say she was coming, and I notified Sid the day of her visit. It was a surprise to us all."

MacAdams frowned. "The *point*, Mr. Selkirk, is that Sid did not have an arrangement with Jo Jones. Only with you."

"Not with me—with the estate."

MacAdams held up a copy of the agreement with Sid, which Green had taken the day before.

"The thing is, *estates* don't sign documents. And I don't see Jo's name on this. It's *your* name. And—well. And Emery's name, too. As a witness."

Emery Lane looked deeply uncomfortable. MacAdams pressed on.

"As of this week, Sid was losing the cottage—and that meant no more retainer, no more renting the cottage, no more money. Am I following?"

"That is correct," Rupert agreed.

"And then you fired Sid on Jo's behalf."

"She suggested he may have stolen something, and made it clear his services were not wanted. So yes, then I fired him for her."

MacAdams heard the whisper of Fleet's trousers as he placed both feet on the floor. Hopefully that meant he'd followed MacAdams' line of reasoning. He closed his notebook to make the point:

"Ah. But there was no need to fire Sid at all. You just told me Ms. Jones' plans for the cottage rendered Sid's contract void. Or am I missing a legal loophole somewhere?"

That got an animated response from Emery, whose eyes averted nervously to Rupert. The solicitor was still completely at ease.

"I had assumed that a new contract would be drawn up, Detective. The grounds still need basic maintenance and Sid Randles was the obvious choice. Perhaps it's best to say I preemptively relieved Sid of his duties *before* a new contract could go into effect."

"Was Mr. Randles upset?" Fleet asked. Flatly so. Usefully disengaged.

"Naturally."

"Because of all the income he was making," MacAdams said. Rupert took the bait.

"As I have already explained, the income would be minimal," he said. MacAdams nodded appreciatively. He had been saving his best card. Now seemed the time to play it.

"Minimal. So you consider five thousand dollars a month *minimal*?"

For the first time, Rupert started.

"I'm sorry?"

"Technically, Sid was depositing upwards of seven thousand, all cash." MacAdams watched carefully; Rupert's eyebrows migrated to center, the muscle under his brow ridge folded and flaccid by turns.

"Impossible."

"I assure you it's plain in black-and-white. The five thousand, as a single amount, appeared in his account monthly. Every year. Beginning in March of his *agreement* with you over the cottage. Curious, isn't it?"

"But—I didn't know this!" Rupert gasped and looked toward Emery, who hovered at the door. "I don't know what Sid

Randles was up to, but it had nothing to do with our agreement over the holiday let. It *can't* have."

"Oh, I am inclined to agree," MacAdams said, and now that Rupert was good and ruffled, he opted for the natural first question—"Mr. Selkirk, where were you on Wednesday night between 11:00 p.m. and 1:00 a.m.?"

"Here." The answer was immediate and a bit unexpected.

"In your office?" he asked, and Rupert nodded.

"Yes. One of my clients decided to rewrite her will, and she wanted it Thursday morning to show her remaining family members in Uxton. We were both here, Emery and I, until nearly two in the morning."

He'd just given himself and Emery an alibi. And of course, that would be very convenient. MacAdams waved the folder Rupert had given him.

"We will follow up. And I'll just be keeping these if you don't mind. I would also like you to send your financial information over to the station. It will save us the trouble of demanding them from your bank. Fleet?"

"Nothing further," the man said, bowing with absurd civility as MacAdams tugged on his hat.

"Ruffled, I think," he said when they reached the car. "Though, they seemed honestly surprised by the money Sid was pulling in."

"You believe them?" Fleet asked, though it sounded less like a question and more like a subtle accusation. "Solicitors make their living by being difficult to read."

"The same is true of detectives. But I agree that he's suspicious. Too slick in his replies."

"He had an answer for everything."

"Rehearsed, you might say," MacAdams agreed. "Five thousand pounds a month is a great deal of cash, but Rupert probably has it to give. If we're talking blackmail, that is. A lot, but not enough to break him."

Fleet's features had gone rather tight…or tight*er.*

"This has continued for three years. You don't think a breaking point might be in sight? Could *you* part with so much?"

Fleet's point, annoying as it was, had some weight. For the average person, even a Scotland Yard detective, that sort of expenditure would bleed out before long. MacAdams didn't feel like admitting it, though. He started the engine.

"There are holes in the blackmail theory, anyway. If Sid was milking Rupert for that five grand, why didn't at least one of them attempt to hide it? Sid didn't bother to falsify receipts or even a guest book. One look at his bank account and it's obvious he was up to something illegal. Anyway, Rupert just seems too *smart* to be caught up by someone like Sid."

Fleet's impassive face nevertheless carried the essence of a frown. "Are you suggesting Sid could only blackmail someone of substandard intelligence?"

"I'm not trying to insult the victim. But yes. Sid was a small-town type. For all his schemes, he wasn't an outright felon." Fleet's eyes narrowed.

"Jo Jones begs to differ," he reminded him. And of course, he had a point—but Sid had method to his hucksterism. He only took what he thought the world owed him. Granted, Sid assumed the world owed him *a lot…*

"All right. He *might* blackmail someone, but the man was hardly a criminal mastermind," MacAdams explained. "This kind of thing is way over his ken." Beside him, Fleet stared resolutely out the rain-streaked window.

"A man can be smart enough to blackmail and too foolish to hide it well," he said. "You might consider this—Rupert *hoped* Sid would get caught."

"Maybe," MacAdams muttered. "But according to Gridley, the money still *went* somewhere else in smaller amounts. Maybe he owed money somewhere—gambling syndicate? Something. The murderer could be at either end of the transaction."

"Killed by the mastermind and not the blackmailer, you mean?" Fleet asked archly. MacAdams shrugged.

"It makes more sense than being killed over a missing painting, at least."

Fleet cleared his throat.

"I have been meaning to ask about that."

"Oh God, don't tell me Jo Jones has convinced you—" MacAdams began, but Fleet shook his head.

"I've yet to interview her. But you released the cottage back to her care surprisingly quickly."

Oh, MacAdams thought. "Look, Fleet. I can appreciate your skills. But it's not your case—and I won't have you questioning everything my team does. The cottage had nothing in it of value, not drugs, not answers, not the bloody, blessed painting."

Beside him, Fleet turned like a slow-winding spring.

"Let me ask you a question, Detective. If you can answer it, I'll take my leave. I'll get on the very next train back to York. Is that fair?"

MacAdams had steeled himself for a fight; he hadn't expected *that.*

"All right," he agreed.

"Where are Sid's keys?" Fleet asked.

Dammit, MacAdams thought. He was just at the solicitors' and forgot to ask for them. He fumbled out his phone and rang Rupert's office line from his mobile; meanwhile, Fleet kept talking.

"Sid Randles was caretaker to the cottage and estate. He was supposed to turn in his keys to Rupert, but I've not seen them. Have you? You searched his person, went through his clothes, and Green had uniforms all over his flat—"

MacAdams did his best to ignore the running commentary.

"Emery? Yes, it's DCI MacAdams—"

Beside him, Fleet droned on. "In the evidence bag at your office, there are car keys and a flat key. But nothing for the cottage or the estate. And yet, the door had been relocked after the murder. It seems to me the first order of business would have been to secure the keys. And that waiting until you were reminded—again—after failing to procure them—"

Emery's voice came back, tinny on the line.

"—is the pinnacle of sloppy policework, representing either extraordinary overconfidence or a stunning ignorance of protocol."

MacAdams put down his phone. The emotion traveling his synapses at that moment felt a lot like self-disgust, tempered with the horror of having to admit it to Fleet.

"Rupert Selkirk does not have the keys," he said thickly.

Fleet merely adjusted his coat and brushed lint from his trousers with sure and steady fingers.

"And thus, you have perhaps prematurely released the cottage," he said.

MacAdams didn't trust himself to answer.

The world had become a much better place, in Jo's estimation, since the advent of texting. Quicker than email, more immediate results, and most importantly—no need to make a phone call. She preferred, generally, to be the call-er not the call-ee; the sound of a telephone put her right through the roof, for one thing. A vibration was certainly an improvement, but it still resulted in the persistent zzz-zzz-zzz-zzz as opposed to the polite *ping* of text.

The worst part of phoning, however, was knowing when to speak and when to pause. No visual cues, just the sound of your voice bumping into someone else's and having to apologize a lot. In consequence, she'd delayed the roofer call, and the longer she waited the more impossible the task felt. And so, when the cottage was finally released to her, she attacked it with delight, relief, and all the energy of hyperfocused procrastination.

That was six hours ago. Six hours, plus twenty trash bags, three trips to town, two jugs of bleach, and a ruined pair of jeans. Jo sat on the kitchen floor with her legs spread out in front of her. She'd pitched almost everything, especially the horrible sofa, which took some deconstruction before she could get it out the front door. Then, of course, there was *re*-construction. Bringing in linens and cutlery, rugs and lamps, and dishes, too. Other people's dishes had an ick factor she couldn't quite get over. Besides, the old ones had murder on them.

She'd allowed herself a break. Or rather, her body went on strike. She was a gross mess and not inclined to get up. So of course, that's when company arrived.

"Hello, Ms. Jones?" floated in through the open front door. She recognized MacAdams' voice. She could only see his hat over the midkitchen counter. A fedora or something like it, and from the way it turned side to side, he evidently hadn't noticed her.

"Floor, over here," Jo said, holding up one hand to wave.

MacAdams leaned over the island.

"Are you all right?"

"I've been very busy."

MacAdams' head disappeared again as he appraised the state of the cottage.

"You did all this since this morning..."

"Most of it." Jo grunted and climbed to her feet. "Some of it before."

"*Before?* Wait—Jo, were you in this cottage after the murder?"

"You said I couldn't move in, not that I couldn't come *back*." This was technically true.

"You contaminated the crime scene!"

"No I didn't! Your constable wouldn't let me in." This was technically *false*.

MacAdams removed his hat to run fingers through shaggy hair.

"Thank God for small favors," he muttered. "I came with a

question about the case. Did you happen to take Sid's estate keys from him? I—we—want to make sure they are accounted for."

"Why? So the killer doesn't come back and sneak in?" Jo asked, and MacAdams half choked.

"No!" He frowned. "Yes."

"Well, that's covered." Jo pointed to the door. "New dead bolt and three internal lock and chains. I installed them this morning. Seemed a smart thing to do. I'm a big-city girl."

"I see," he said, though he very clearly did not. "Back to the point, please, I need to know if you have Sid's keys?"

"Nope. Couldn't get it rekeyed so I changed the whole mechanism. Shame, though. They were brand-new locks." Jo swigged water from a coffee mug.

"New locks. I remember." MacAdams leaned on his forearms. For some reason, the man always looked tired. Or maybe like he'd just lost a fight. When he next spoke, it was mainly to himself. "What would be the point of that, Sid—what were you *doing*?"

"Do you want to know what *I* think?" she asked, watching him carefully.

"I…am half afraid to ask," he said, rubbing his face with both hands. Jo didn't care. She had a theory.

"When I think about Sid, I think of three things," she said. "His snaggled tooth, the way foxes hide their food, and *Jane Eyre.*"

MacAdams' left eyebrow was on the move toward his hairline. "I'm sorry, *what*?"

"Sid makes me think of Reynard the Fox, being too clever for his own good. Lots of stories about him—his uncle, the wolf, tried to catch him but he often gets away to do more mischief. Then, *in Jane Eyre*, Bertha Mason is a secret wife locked in the attic." Jo knew she was giving points A and D; the trick was explaining the B and C in the middle. "I think Sid liked hiding things, maybe secret things. I'm not sure why the painting was locked up at the house, or why a key to that bedroom wasn't included in the set Rupert gave me, but maybe the whole estate was Sid's private fox cache."

An expression was making its way across MacAdams' stiff features, one facial muscle at a time. Even his eyebrows were operating at different registers.

"You didn't have a key to the locked room?"

"No. And Rupert didn't have a key to the cottage. I got the extra set from Sid the first day." She waited to see if he was catching on, and it was clear the same thought ran through their minds: *people put new locks on things when they are hiding something.*

"Well? What do you think?" Jo asked. It was a hope misplaced. The spark of interest had vanished and the more surly look returned.

"I think we released the cottage prematurely," MacAdams said, though part of him was still processing this information from Jo. "Until we find out who—"

"Oh no you don't! You can't kick me out of here again!" Jo insisted.

"Look, I can get CID to comp your room at the Red Lion." After a moment's silent hesitation, he added, "We can consider it a polite request."

"Meaning I can refuse?" Jo asked. He sighed heavily.

"If you do, it will no longer be a polite request, and that will require paperwork."

Jo considered him a moment. Was he giving her the opportunity to at least be around during the day? Was this a concession? Making up for being a jerk before?

"For how long?" she asked.

"Give me till after Sid's funeral," he said.

10

Jo parked her car behind the pub and pulled her suitcase from the back seat. Her back was sore, and it would be nice, she thought, to finally unpack *for real*. She could scarcely count her mother's house in Chicago; that had felt like camping rather than coming home. Jo hadn't grown up there, anyway; her formative years had been spent between her great-aunt's condo downtown and a series of apartments from Gary, Indiana to Evanston, Illinois. Jo's mother only bought that house after Aunt Sue died, and by then, Jo was on scholarship at NYU. She'd moved into Tony's flat just before graduating—her first "home," even if second-hand, since it had been decorated by his first wife. Jo tugged the stuck suitcase wheel over the curb and hummed to herself. Maybe place-less-ness suited her?

Tula waved from the bar and then joined her at the check-in desk.

"I cannae give you the first floor room back, love. I've put you in the attic suite, though. That okay? You donnae have to pay for it, mind. And I've put in the best towels."

Jo had the fluttery, numb-eared feeling she got when people took extra trouble. She fumbled a thank-you—how was she supposed to repay all this?

"You guys have been way too kind about—well, everything," she said, blushing. "I could help out, maybe? If you need a hand."

Tula laughed. "Careful what you wish for."

It was Jo's first Saturday evening in town. The Red Lion wasn't the only pub, but it probably got marks as the most popular. The dining room had filled to capacity. As a latecomer, she'd have to take a place at the bar.

"Welcome back!" Ben said cheerfully. "Whisky, neat?" He'd already placed it on the bar top in front of the taps. Jo climbed onto a stool.

"Thank you," she said—loudly. The noise had not yet reached panic level but appeared to be rising. Ben filled two more glasses with gin and bitters and handed them down the bar to a red-headed woman with slightly smudged lipstick.

"On the house," he said to her.

"You're a dear man, you know it? After what we been through." The woman spoke slowly, the way you do when you're attempting not to slur things.

"Maybe you'll want something to eat? Do you good," Ben said, but she shook her head.

"Na' for me. You can ask Lotte when she gets back from the loo."

Lotte appeared a few seconds later with heavy makeup and watery mascara, as though she'd been crying and tried to tidy up. You wouldn't ever confuse them, but seated next each other, they made a pair—the faintest hint of family resemblance. *Oh God,* Jo realized with a jolt, these must be Sid's sister-wives. Lotte peered out from blue-black bangs, with a pinch of nose and pouting lips—*Pulp Fiction*, Jo thought. Uma Thurman channeling Winona Ryder. Her red-haired sister had more flesh, broad shoulders, square jaw, a face you'd call pretty—but she didn't look *well*. Sallow. *Fallow*. Jo once thought of Sid as gone to seed, but this was a better representation.

"Chips," Lotte said in a chirpy sort of voice. Ben nodded.

"What about you, Jo?" he asked. Jo wished he hadn't; Lotte's head snapped round at the name. Jo tried to mumble as she ordered the special without bothering to check what it was and scanned the room again, looking for a free table. Too late; her accent always did her in.

"*You're* the American?" Lotte asked, and her sister emerged from the gin and tonic.

"God. You found Sid," she said, her voice slow and a bit slurred.

"I—yes." Jo squirmed internally. What were the right condolences for something like this? They weren't married anymore. Jo wasn't sure how she would respond to Tony's death... Tears? Joy? Nothing? She breathed her comfort words: *Fulcrum, forfeit, feat, fiesta, ffu ffu ffu*. "I'm very sorry."

"*Nobody* is ssorry," the woman slurred, though her voice sounded like tires on gravel. "Nobody even cares. But *us*."

At this, Lotte wrapped one arm around her—which she immediately shrugged off before turning her attention back to Jo.

"It happened in *your* place," she said bluntly. "And everybody says you didn't like him."

Jo opened her mouth, then closed it again. *Everyone*. Did everyone really think that? Granted. She really *didn't* like him. Her heart was beating too hard; how was she supposed to defend herself and not sound horribly callous?

"Were you close?" she asked, finally. Lotte didn't answer. She started to cry, and on cue, so did her sister. Jo felt like she was watching a slow-motion car wreck—and then, Ben rescued her by arriving with Lotte's "chips," thick, fat fries swimming in curry sauce.

"Funeral is tomorrow," he said quietly to Jo.

"Like you lot care," Lotte whimpered. She then stuck a chip

in her mouth like a potato pacifier and mumbled the rest around it. "And after all Sid done for your family!"

Jo had decided to fade quietly from the conversation—but this arrested her. *Don't take the bait*, she thought. Much too late to stop herself.

"What do you mean *my family*?" she asked. Lotte drew herself up.

"*Your* lot promised him work. But they just wanted someone to order around, didn't they? Never even paid him in the end. Bastard."

"What bastard— *Who?*" Jo asked, puzzled. This time the redhead answered. Or tried to. She reached a thick arm in front of her sister to tap the bar in front of Jo.

"Aiden Jones, that's who," she hissed—followed by a hiccup. "Gonna make things right, was he? Na' he weren't. Wanted the history and secrets about the-the damned property, is all. SO high and mi-mighty. *Bloody arse-bandit.*"

Jo felt her insides churn. She picked up her drink and slid from the barstool, intent on putting distance between them—but there weren't a lot of inconspicuous places to stand in a full house. The pub room had a few large barrels-turned-standing-tables near the front window. When Ben delivered her fish and chip basket (the apparent special), she transported it to the first of these and assaulted the fries. Salt. Starch. Breathe. Ketchup wasn't ubiquitous, but she'd developed a real affection for brown sauce; three fries down and a gulp of whisky had her feeling a little more herself.

Had Uncle Aiden hired Sid for something? Maybe. Could it explain his immediate dislike of her? Or was Jo seeing plot where there were only words: just two grieving women picking a fight. It would have to go on her growing mental list of things she needed to find out. Jo leaned on her elbow and let her eyes wander the bar, scanning the crowds—only to make accidental eye contact with one patron in particular—the man she'd seen at breakfast.

Sitting perfectly straight, and neither eating nor drinking, he looked odd and out of place. She'd originally thought of him as a bit wolfish, but now he reminded her of a proctor at an exam. Jo thought of the headmaster in *Hard Times*, Mr. Gradgrind, "ready to weigh and measure any parcel of human nature, and tell you what it comes to." But of course, that made her think of the headmaster in *Our Mutual Friend*, Bradley Headstone, teacher-turned-murderer and a case of terrifying contents under pressure. *Stop that*, she cautioned herself; her brain was about to go on a deep dive through all the headmasters of literature.

"Good evening," said the character of note, "Mind if I join you?" This, Jo knew, was always a trick question. Why hadn't she brought down the laptop? She could then at least pretend to be working. At any rate, the man had already made himself at home—and his first question was something of a surprise.

"Do you know who those women are?"

"Sid Randles' ex-wives." Jo swallowed a mouthful of heavily battered fish. "Well. Two of them. The second and third, I think."

"Have you ever met them before?" he asked, now leaning one hand on the tabletop. It did not make him seem more relaxed. Actually, the opposite, as if he'd just gone against his nature.

"No? I just got here a few days ago." *Introduce yourself*, she thought. But he hadn't, and he started this. "They are here for Sid's funeral."

"I know." He raised one hand, signaling Ben, who set down a cup of tea in front of him. "Police released the body this morning."

Jo paused mid-chip.

"Are you their lawyer? Solicitor, I mean."

He sipped his tea. "You must be from America."

"Oh. Yes. Jo Jones. I inherited the Ardemore House."

"And you discovered the body." His response was as measured and polite (and mechanical) as before, but Jo felt suddenly accused. She stopped eating.

"I did. I don't know why everyone is still talking about it."

"Don't you?" The man tapped lightly at his mustache. "We do not see many shooting deaths here. Not even in London, not by comparison with the United States. Perhaps you have grown inured to such tragedies?"

Inured to tragedy. Jo felt a rising quiver of annoyance and bounced her right leg to hide it. *Just doesn't have any real feelings, does she? No empathy. Jo doesn't do emotions.*

"No. I am not. It's an awful thing to happen. I didn't like him, but no one deserves to die like that," she said stiffly. He, in his turn, took a long sip of tea. When he'd replaced the cup firmly on the saucer, he smiled.

"Why didn't you like him?" he asked. And that was a bridge too far.

"I'm sorry?" Jo stood a little straighter, trying to buy herself some height and maybe a shred of authority. "I don't actually have to tell you that."

"Of course, you are right." He gave a little bow of his head. "My apologies. But there are many reasons for not liking a man. Even Tula Byrne did not enjoy his company, or so she told me."

Jo let out a long breath. She'd forgotten he spoke to Tula that morning. Maybe they knew each other, or were friends? She shouldn't be rude.

"I think he took liberties," she said carefully. "That's all."

"I see. And do you think he took *other* things? Do you believe he stole something?"

Jo picked up the basket and its remaining bits and pieces. Clearly he knew about the argument in the pub room...but enough was enough.

"I have to go," she said. She had a room after all and could return the silverware and glass later—because much more of *that* and she wouldn't have an appetite *at all.*

In her room, Jo sat cross-legged on the bed, fries in one hand and computer mouse in the other. The attic suite sat alone at the housetop, on the third floor (but curiously referred to as the *second* by everyone in Britain). She brushed crumbs from her pink pajama shorts and scrolled rapidly through an online tutorial. Now, to upload her photo of the remaining portrait, the one of Gwen Davies, Lady Ardemore…

"Halloo," cried Tula through the door. "May I come in?"

"Gimme a sec." Jo hopped up and unlatched the door. Tula swept in with her usual exuberance, filling the otherwise empty room.

"Great God almighty and all the saints, those two are getting *mortal* on gin. Olivia, at least—utterly binned." She plucked at her blouse sleeves and then settled on the pullout sofa. "No way to plan a funeral, by half. Ben said they chased you right on upstairs."

"Not *them*," Jo corrected, resuming her cross-legged position and scooping her hair into a scrunchie. "They chased me to the barrel table. It was that weird guy from the bar."

"Which? You don't mean Ricky—"

"No, the mustache man. He was down at breakfast. You know him, I guess?" Jo puckered her brow. "Sorry if he's a friend, but he pissed me off." She'd been worried that Tula might get angry. Instead, she laughed.

"Oh goodness, *we* aren't friends!" She rocked forward on the sofa. "That's a detective! Forget his full name. Something *Fleet*. Working with MacAdams, I gather."

It took a moment for this to fully matriculate through Jo's brain.

"Then *why* wouldn't he say something?" she demanded. "All detectives are supposed to—they say this is detective *blah blah blah* and show credentials!" She did not add that all her sources were slightly out-of-date mystery novels, backed by occasional BBC shows. All the same.

"He must have done? Or maybe he was just making conversation." Tula got to her feet and began collecting Jo's dinner items. "He's from Scotland Yard. The exes were right impressed, they were."

Jo must have looked like an idiot, assuming he was their estate lawyer. It wasn't fair. She guiltily handed Tula her empty whisky glass.

"I was going to bring these—you didn't have to come up, I promise."

"Ah. You've caught me putting it on the long finger. I really came up to ask a favor. You know about the funeral tomorrow?"

"I've been told. Twice."

"Third time is a charmer, love." Tula's smile lines listed leeward. "Seems we're unexpectedly catering the whole affair, *and* we're setting up the graveside service with folding chairs. You asked about helping out..."

Jo felt a bubble of panic but swallowed it down.

"I did."

"Tomorrow, then? Bright and early?"

Jo managed to nod, though not to speak. Tula gave her a gentle smack to the shoulder.

"Brilliant! And anyway, you're less likely to be haunted by a man if you go to his funeral."

Tula let her be, then, waving good-night and backing out the door with dirty dishes. Jo flumped backward on the duvet. Somehow, she'd just agreed to go to Sid's funeral as the odd, interloping "American" who found Sid's body on her carpet and—according to his wives—"owed" him. What exactly did you wear for that?

Sunday

MacAdams supposed he should be thankful that it wasn't raining. He stood with Green near the back of the mourners—what he considered "respectful distance"—as they wound their way from the church to the cemetery plot. *Longside*, they called it, probably because it ran along the park.

"The turnout is…big," Green said.

"Don't be surprised," MacAdams told her. "Sid was a local boy, remember? Grew up here. Went to school here. Had friends here." He could tell by the look at her face that she found it hard to swallow, but this wasn't Newcastle. For all his unfortunate quirks, Sid was one of theirs. MacAdams stopped short of admitting—even privately—that he'd miss him. But he would.

"There's Rupert," he said, noting the sheen of the man's balding head near the front. "And Emery, too." Tula and Ben and a few others from the Red Lion were busily arranging chairs into a semicircle under damp saplings. The after-event had partly been MacAdams' idea, or rather, he planted the seed to Olivia and Lotte when he gave over Sid's body. A mingling of people in the pub room after service would be useful, indeed.

"Are we watching anyone in particular?" Green asked.

"Yes. Everyone. Though I am interested in the Newcastle wives." Olivia and Lotte looked forlorn in black gowns and were weeping openly. They'd made a scene when Sid was carried away by the undertaker; they made a scene at the bar, too. It wasn't that he doubted their sorrow in losing an ex-spouse—hell, MacAdams would be beside himself if Annie died, three years notwithstanding. It's just that their grief had a performance to it, and he wasn't yet sure *why*. Certainly no one here in Abington needed impressing. Perhaps they were impressing one another?

Either way, MacAdams planned to hit them both with questions. Insensitive, possibly, but their guard might be down after the funeral.

"Detective MacAdams," Fleet said, by way of greeting. *He* looked perfect at a funeral. "They are getting underway."

The murmuring rows of people had now gone silent. Graveside service among Anglicans followed the usual route; MacAdams tuned it out. Instead, he let his gaze wander from face to face.

Rupert remained his usual benign and unreadable self; Emery meanwhile nodded sympathetically (nervously?) to whatever the priest was saying. Nervous and sympathetic seemed his primary qualities. Then there was the grocer and hardware clerks, and a half dozen other locals whose faces shone with polite interest, and probably a hope for gossip. Ricky and some of the pub lads, all of them pallbearers, showed a bit of real emotion—if only a bit. And he could see Tula and Ben, heads bowed and wearing their work clothes.

And beside *them*, in a black sheath dress and knee-high boots, was Jo Jones.

MacAdams felt himself straighten involuntarily. What was she doing there? He hadn't expected her to turn up, though he hadn't any specific reason why not—apart from the obvious part she played in finding his body. Perhaps some sort of closure was in order?

Like the very Catholic Tula, Jo kept her head bowed. Unlike Tula, she kept glancing up surreptitiously, and so caught MacAdams' watching eye. The resulting blush crept right up her neck to an untidy bun just as everyone around them muttered a half-hearted *amen*.

And perhaps because he'd been distracted from the general scene, MacAdams *also* heard the quiet sound of car tires on asphalt somewhere just behind them. He turned to see a black sedan ease its way onto the gravel apron. Once halted, it allowed the egress of one extremely high-heeled shoe in brilliant red.

"Oh. My. God."

Lotte's voice, MacAdams thought. The sister-wives had pushed to the front for a better view; now they stood gaping at the woman walking the crescent toward them. Midforties, with swept up blond hair, an extraordinary amount of makeup, long legs, and power-walker thighs. Her stilettos spiked the tarpaulin as she passed Lotte and Olivia, and then, in front of them, dropped an entire bouquet of white lilies onto Sid's coffin.

"Elsie," Olivia spat, and MacAdams swore he could hear the grave dirt crunching in her tightly grasped fingers. Elsie herself said nothing—not with words, anyway. She delivered a look of hauteur to each sister, which, judging by response, must have been eviscerating. Perhaps it was the shock of funeral crashing, or perhaps the *I dare you* expression in her hat-shaded eyes, but Elsie proceeded back down the aisle in unmolested silence. The storm broke as she reached the road, but MacAdams ignored the sisters' shouts of outrage and followed Elsie the distance to her car, away from the crowds near the coffin. It was still running, and now he understood why its approach had been so quiet.

"BMW i3?" he asked, just managing to touch the hood as Elsie opened the driver's side door. "Electric. Nice."

"I rented it, didn't I?" Elsie snapped. She'd managed to get a cigarette to her mouth and lit on the way. After a drag, she blew smoke in MacAdams' direction. "You bastards not going to tell me about the funeral, yeah? Let me find out on my own he's been murdered? Fuck you."

This was not the reception MacAdams expected.

"We did try to contact you."

"Not hard enough."

"I'm DCI MacAdams—"

"Then fuck you *extra*."

"—and I am in charge of investigating Sid's murder." That, at least, stopped her rapid-fire response. She smoothed the sides of her faux leather minidress as if ironing out her next reply.

"Fine. What do you want?"

"I'd like to ask you a few questions. Will you be going to the Red Lion, now?" he asked. Elsie laughed. It wasn't pleasant—a sort of surprised bark through vampire lips.

"With those assholes?" Her eyes wandered over MacAdams' shoulder, where the crowd was dispersing. And then, as if making the decision on the spot, she climbed into the car and slammed the door. A second later, she was backing away, and MacAdams had to jog in order to tap upon the window.

"What?" she demanded through the crack.

"An address, Ms. Randles—"

"Ms. SMYTHE," she hissed around the filter end of her cigarette. "Newcastle."

"Yes, but I don't know where in Newcastle," MacAdams protested. Elsie merely shifted into first gear.

"You're a detective, aren't you?"

MacAdams wisely removed himself from her forward course, and a moment later Elsie *Smythe* was little more than distant taillights.

11

Despite Elsie's physical absence, her name at least had managed to make it all around the Red Lion. She *had* cut quite a figure—and few stage actresses could have enjoyed a more startling entrance. The stilettos, miniskirt, and broad brimmed hat were already legend. The spotlight now lost, Olivia and Lotte took refuge in a bottle of red and were getting through it pretty damn quickly. If they didn't act now, MacAdams feared they might lose the moment.

"DCI MacAdams and DS Green," he said as they joined them.

"Cops again," Lotte sighed. MacAdams judged her to be in her early thirties, with pixie cut, heavy bangs, and an air of unquiet disillusionment.

"We just have a few questions," Green assured her.

"At a *funeral*?"

"We are in a pub, Ms. Randles." Green's delivery never failed to make an impression. Usually by direct impact. But before Lotte could make a comeback, Olivia shoved the empty wine bottle forward, almost into MacAdams' fingers.

"Wanna talk? Buy drinks. Gin this time." Olivia's makeup didn't quite hide the gray complexion and papery skin, evidence of excessive drinking habits. MacAdams noted it and nodded toward the bar.

"Fair enough. Green, would you?" he asked, settling down across from the sisters. "I understand today was upsetting for you both."

"You think?" Olivia weeble-wobbled her glass. "That sleazy little shit."

Given Sid's general reputation, the epithet might have also been aimed at the deceased…but MacAdams knew better after the graveside scene.

"You weren't expecting to see Elsie, I take it."

"She has no right to be here."

MacAdams considered this while Green slid two G&Ts across the table.

"Why is that?" he asked.

"She is an evil bitch, that's why." It had been said, with slight variation, in unison. MacAdams cleared his throat.

"In my experience, it's the first wives who resent the latter ones, not the reverse."

"*I'm* the *latter one*," Lotte assured him. MacAdams watched a parade of emotion march across Olivia's face; she'd been wife number 2, and while she might have no love for Elsie, she'd just dealt Lotte a glare of ill-concealed annoyance.

"Do you know Sid married me on his and Elsie's anniversary?" Olivia asked. "Seems like a statement, yeah? But she never really *left*."

"What's that supposed to mean?" Green asked. Lotte laughed a bubble into her drink.

"Olivia means he cheated," she said.

"Cheated. *With* his first wife?" MacAdams clarified, pencil poised over his notebook. Lotte laughed more openly, now.

"With me! And Elsie, too. God knows who else. All of Newcastle, maybe."

"He cheated on *you*, too, you great hussy," Olivia muttered. Lotte shrugged. MacAdams wondered how on earth Sid managed to inspire so much ardor. He found himself thinking of Jo's assessment, that he was a fox, lean and hungry and a bit wild. Maybe that's what drew them in?

"So he cheated on both of you with Elsie," Green repeated blandly. "And you are sure about this?"

"Didn't you just *meet* her?" Olivia demanded, gulping her drink and then waving it at Green. "Go on—and less bloody tonic this time."

"About Elsie," MacAdams repeated.

"She's an honest-to-god whore. Call girl. Whatever. Sleeps with everybody. You lot should have arrested her."

"Prostitution is technically not illegal," MacAdams corrected. Olivia made a *pffft* sound, though slightly wetter given the creep of intoxication.

"Fine. Then ask her how she pays her bloody rent, and what's she driving that car for? Cheap slut."

The situation was devolving. MacAdams tapped his notebook.

"When was the last time either of you saw Sid Randles?" he asked. This earned him two glassy stares. "Alive," he added.

"Three years ago, after Lotte and him divorced," Olivia said, answering for both. "Came around wanting some more fucking money, no doubt."

"No, he didn't." Lotte wagged a finger in Olivia's face. "You *always* say that. And he didn't. He—he wanted a—a place. I mean, just a place to—" She scrunched up her nose. "I don't know."

"A place to stay?" Green asked, delivering gin the second.

"Money, I'm telling you," Olivia insisted. This time, Lotte's remonstrance came with a shove to her shoulder.

"Just because he took *your* money doesn't mean he wanted

mine," she hissed. "He said he wanted a quiet place to be sometimes. Not like always. Not to live. Just to be."

MacAdams pressed the pencil into the pad till it threatened to break the lead.

"A quiet place in the country?" he asked. "Somewhere no one else would be?"

Lotte brushed hair out of her face with the back of her hand, smearing a bit of lipstick on the way.

"Yeah. Quiet." Tears had begun welling again. "He said we could meet there, too, sometimes."

"And did you meet him there?" MacAdams pressed. Lotte stopped crying.

"No," she said. "I was tempted at first but—I changed my mind."

"'Cause you knew he wasn't coming back to you," Olivia snapped. There was malice in it. "He wanted a shag. That's it."

"So? You *wish* he wanted to shag you!" Lotte hissed, then turned to look MacAdams in the eye. "Didn't want her, did he? Just her money. She gave him ten thousand pounds! After all her hard work, and had to sell her car and—"

"Shut up, you stupid bitch," Olivia groaned.

"—and now she ain't got no savings, no retirement—"

"Neither do *you*."

"—And she's mad at me and Elsie cause at least we get laid once in a while."

Green and MacAdams both saw it coming, but neither could react fast enough. Olivia threw the rest of her drink directly into Lotte's face. And in response, Lotte grabbed a fistful of bright red hair.

"Stop it, stop it, stop!" Green, who was still standing at the table's edge, managed to haul Lotte backward, but Olivia came, too, and the full force of both women toppled her to the floor. MacAdams scrambled out of his booth and hooked one arm around Olivia's waist, but by now Lotte had her fingers into Green's box braids.

"*That* is assault of a police officer," MacAdams boomed. It had the desired effect. For one thing, Lotte went limp as a noodle. For another, Tula had just turned up and wedged herself between the two women as if daring them to feel lucky. The room had crashed into silence, but there had been quite enough activity for the gossip boxes, so MacAdams just quietly ushered the sisters out of the public rooms.

"Go back to your rooms," he commanded. "And stay there. I don't want you leaving town."

"We just said—we're broke," Lotte snapped, wiping mascara from her cheek. MacAdams pinched the bridge of his nose.

"The rate will be taken care of tonight and tomorrow night. Stay here. Stay put." The promise had a surprising effect on them both. No doubt they would be ordering booze on the room tab. He'd have to speak with Tula about that.

Green he found at the bar, seething.

"You okay?" he asked.

"I'm PISSED OFF." She opened and closed her fists, the tendons standing out fiercely. She could do damage, and *thank God* she knew it well enough not to take a swing.

"I know. I'm sorry. But you did good." Green had ordered a whisky and was already drinking it, so this was clearly the end of her shift. MacAdams patted her shoulder.

"Are you thinking what I'm thinking about the cottage?" she asked. "The quiet, out-of-the-way place?"

"I am."

"And you think Lotte lied about not seeing him there."

"I do."

Green nodded at him.

"Bring them in tomorrow?" she asked. MacAdams was about to agree, and to suggest they took them in turns, when his phone buzzed. It was Gridley. He listened patiently, holding one finger up at Green, and then waving across the room to where Fleet had taken up a surveyor's post.

"Actually, no," he said, returning the phone to his suit pocket. "Gridley's turned up an address under Smythe in Newcastle."

"That was quick."

"The proper name helps," MacAdams said as Fleet joined them.

"Rupert and Emery have gone," he reported. "They've been cautioned not to leave town, of course."

"Yes, same for the sisters," MacAdams said. Green, whose fury hadn't really dampened much, scowled.

"And how do we know they won't bolt?" she asked testily.

"Free room and booze. And Fleet can keep tabs on them. Informally," he added when Green seemed about to protest. "Don't worry. You'll be in on the formal interview. I want to speak with Elsie while the funeral is fresh."

Fleet did not comment on his new assignment or on the developments. Instead, he inclined his head in the direction of the corner booth.

"I assume you noticed that Ms. Jones is in attendance?" he asked. "She was with the innkeepers graveside."

"Yes. I believe she's offering them a hand."

"Unusual."

"I don't know about that," MacAdams said. "The funeral being last minute, I'm assuming Tula could use the help." Fleet turned in that precise way of his.

"*Jo Jones* is unusual," he explained. "Abrupt. Loquacious and silent by turns. Doesn't make eye contact. I might almost say *rude*."

Green put her glass down.

"I'd assumed that's just being American," she said. MacAdams shot her a look: *don't go in for stereotypes.* Of course, he'd been thinking much the same thing.

"Was she rude to *you*, Fleet?" he asked. "Specifically."

"Suggestive might be the best word for it. I was asking about Sid Randles; she got up and left in midconversation." Fleet began putting on his coat. "By the way, have you once more made the cottage off-limits? I would like to put in practice my little survey of the place."

MacAdams rubbed the back of his neck. Partly, he felt he owed it—especially as Fleet hadn't rubbed in the key incident.

"No, not exactly," he admitted.

"It seems protocol would demand it," Fleet said primly.

"We've surely learned all we can there," MacAdams sighed. "And anyway, we have four suspects to interview—Lotte, Olivia, Rupert, Emery—plus Sid's first ex-wife. It's plenty to be getting on with, don't you think?"

Fleet smoothed the lapels.

"More than plenty," he said. "It's the narrowing down that matters."

Tula released Jo from service with a beer and a plateful of sandwiches. The going had been smoother than expected; she'd been too busy to feel awkward and as part of the help, no one tried to make conversation. But now, at liberty, Jo found the room a different sort of place. Ricky was seated a few tables away; he'd laughed at Lotte and Olivia's little scene, but now he spent his time casting unfriendly glances at Jo. It felt like high school; an immature means of singling someone out, of making them feel vulnerable. She ignored him. There were plenty of other ways to feel isolated; Tula and Ben were taking their own lunch behind the bar, deep in conversation with some local friends. She could join them, but she'd have to get over the sense it was a huge imposition—and she didn't have the peanuts for it today. So she stayed where she was, eating bread and cheese and thumb-scrolling images on Google.

"On your phone at a time like this? No better than my granddaughter."

Jo looked up to find a frowning woman in Highland tweeds. She looked at Jo through thick, yellow-tinged lenses.

"I excuse my niece playing games," the woman said dismissively. "Because she's a child."

"I'm not playing a game—" Jo said, forgetting that she did not have to answer. "It's a reverse search for a composite image."

"It looks like Google." The woman sniffed.

"It *is*. It's image recognition software. It works by finding distinctive points and comparing them to *billions* of other images. When enough points align, it's a match." Jo paused. The woman's face had not changed, except to deepen the frown. She looked positively marionette.

"Did I ask for a lecture?"

"Um. No?"

"Manners, girl! Don't scowl at your elders." The woman thumped the tip of her cane against the floor. "You made *some* amends by helping out at Sid's funeral. So don't ruin it by being obtuse."

Obtuse?

"More than 90 degrees, less than 180," Jo spat out. It was nerves, and it was the wrong definition, but she felt simultaneously angry, wronged, embarrassed, and guilty. The woman's eyes got wider behind the yellow lenses and she puffed her cheeks.

"I see how it is. You've no breeding at all." With that, she spun about and walked away—nearly elbowing MacAdams as she went.

"Jo, meet Roberta Wilkinson," he said, straightening his jacket. Jo groaned.

"*That* was the museum lady? Great." She put her face in her hands. "I need her to like me!"

"I'm not sure Ms. Wilkinson likes anyone," MacAdams said. Jo peeped at him between her fingers. He appeared to be looking at her shoes. "Good boots, those."

"Oh. They are my security boots for awkward situations."

MacAdams settled on the opposing bench.

"My ex-wife had a pair."

"My ex *hates* them." Jo lowered her hands and picked up her phone again. "There were a lot of exes here today. Not mine, of course. That would be even more awful than *that* was."

"Understood. The late arrival was Sid's first ex-wife, by the way."

"Who could miss it? High heels and leather, Bond girl fancy." Jo gave him a quick glance. "Are you here to ask why I came to the funeral?"

MacAdams looked startled. "Why would I ask you that?"

"When a detective turns up at a funeral, he's working. But me? Here is the American again, trying to insert herself as the help. Inspector Alleyn would be very suspicious of me. So would Hercule Poirot. Or DCI Barnaby of *Midsomer Murders*."

"I see. And so would Sherlock Holmes?"

"Hard to say. He came at everything sideways after going through his mind attic." Jo cleared her throat and managed to smile. "Sorry. Social anxiety stuff. I just got accused of having no manners—besides, you *were* staring at me during the funeral."

MacAdams' forehead creased in the middle.

"I didn't mean to embarrass you. I promise."

"I wasn't embarrassed," Jo insisted.

"You blushed."

"Oh." And now she was probably going to do it again. Well, that made it all much less weird and awkward, didn't it? "I figured you were out of ideas and planning to arrest me."

MacAdams actually laughed. More of a hoarse low-grade chuckle.

"Not yet, Ms. Jones."

"Good." Jo looked across the bar. Ricky—still staring—and probably hoping MacAdams would lead her out in chains. "Do you have a suspect, though?" She figured he'd say *I can't speak of police matters with plebeians.* Instead, he waved at Ben and ordered a dark ale.

"If I had *one* suspect, I'd be in excellent shape," he said, taking his pint from the tray. "But I'm off duty now, so small talk only. I'll tell you about Roberta Wilkinson's famous scowl, and you can tell me why she thinks you have no manners."

Jo sighed. How much did she say? *Actually, a lot of people say I'm rude but I'm just autistic and sometimes don't realize I've missed an obscure social cue and also you keep changing the rules.* Instead, she showed him her phone.

"This. I downloaded police composite sketch software and created an image of the missing painting using my memory and a photo of Lady Ardemore's portrait."

He took the phone and held it at "probably needs reading glasses" distance. The faux portrait wasn't perfect by any means; Jo had trouble getting the eyes quite right. Mainly because they weren't right in the painting itself; she'd just used Gwen's.

"You did this? How did you get police software?"

"If you are willing to pay for it, you can get almost anything." Jo chewed her lip. "It also required getting through a lot of tutorials and reading the forty-page manual."

He handed it back.

"And now?"

"Now I'm loading it into search engines and scrolling through the matches. A lot of junk to sift through." MacAdams swigged his beer.

"I meant what happens if and when you find a match," he asked—but Jo had just stopped paying attention. A flitting image just rang alarm bells in her brain. She laid the phone flat and walked back the search bar. An old photo—a face—

"My God, it's *her*," Jo murmured. Not a painting, but a photograph: the lighting, dress, and posture were different, but the same wide, flat features, dark eyes, unsmiling expression. She looked to be in her early twenties. Enlarging the thumbnail only made it grainy, but the link led her to an eBay page. *Small original photograph, circa 1901*, it read. *SOLD.* Jo clicked on the seller and a contact form popped up with location: Swansea, Wales.

MacAdams was still looking on, as if he expected her to elaborate. Jo couldn't, though, because she was mentally calculating how long it might take to *get* to Wales. Like driving across Pennsylvania, right?

"Sorry," she said. "I've got to go."

12

Monday

The early-morning smell of Costa coffee always reminded MacAdams of stakeouts. As a detective constable in service of a DCI fond of (often pointless) surveillance, he'd managed to get through thermoses of the stuff. By four in the morning, it was always cold, and the burned-in flavor stuck to the back of his throat.

"More milk," he told Green, who was busy selecting two bacon croissants.

"You put three in there already."

"I did." MacAdams pulled out a chair. It had taken less than an hour to get to Newcastle, and it was still only ten in the morning. A little early to start knocking on doors, yet. Green joined him and resumed their conversation from the car.

"Olivia and Lotte are skint, right?" she said, chewing thoughtfully. "And Sid is partly to blame. At least in Olivia's case. I did a bit of looking."

"True about taking her 10K?" MacAdams asked. Green tipped her head to one shoulder, then the other.

"Depends on what you mean by *take*. Olivia apparently busted her ass in her twenties, had aspirations of getting to London. Just a high school diploma, but she held two and three jobs at a time, I gather, and was a good saver. Married Sid at thirty and, according to local gossip, went downhill pretty quick after."

"Still working, now?"

"Yeah. Bartending," Green said. "Anyhow, whether he took the cash or they blew it together, it's definitely gone. Ten thousand is a lot of money to most folks, especially if hard-won. It's a motive."

"It could be," MacAdams agreed. The wind was picking up outside, and he watched a plastic bag gallop its way through traffic. "I'm assuming money is the motive where Rupert Selkirk is concerned as well."

"Right, but the sisters have another beef, too. Sid cheated on them both. *With* the first wife, Elsie."

"We don't know that," MacAdams cautioned. "We know they *think* so. But I agree, that could be a motive, too."

"Two motives. Two sisters. We know they wind each other up." She pointed to the slightly fuzzy section of braiding and what might be a fingernail scratch or two. "Maybe they convinced each other to do a crime neither would try on their own. Then, they come to Abington and play the grieving widows to deflect suspicion."

It wasn't a bad theory. MacAdams had played around with that scenario, himself; could Lotte have been at the cottage? Did she lure him? There was just one problem.

"That doesn't explain Sid's mystery income," he said. "Because Lotte and Olivia aren't pulling in 5K a month consistently, of that I am reasonably certain. I'm not ruling out the idea, mind. But I have a harder time believing they would *shoot* him."

"It's effective," Green suggested. MacAdams finally unwrapped his own croissant. It didn't have the usual appeal; possibly due to the Costa coffee smell that lingered over everything.

"Maybe, but why use a gun at all? And why *that* gun, an antique? And why shoot him in the cottage where he's sure to be found?"

"You're telling me there are easier ways to get rid of your ex."

MacAdams grimaced slightly. That was basically the truth. Sid had used both women and would probably be induced to try again; they could have lured him almost anywhere with promises of money or sex or both. But even poison would be simpler than a gun. Hell, they could have run him over with a car, for that matter.

"There are really two questions, here," MacAdams explained. "First is *who* had the gun. But second—*why* a gun. What's it for? What does a gun give you that pills and poison don't?"

Green appeared to ruminate.

"Power. But I see where you're going with this. It's a risk, so why take it?" She crumbled the sandwich wrapper and tossed it between her hands. "Threat level, maybe? Sid might not respect a lot else."

"Good, yes. So—it's a negotiating tool?" MacAdams rubbed his chin. "That would suggest *not* premeditated murder. But then, why make it look like one?"

Green shook her head.

"You lost me," she said. MacAdams tapped the table.

"If you were going to plan a murder, you'd make it look like *an accident*," he said. "Three bullets in Sid's back in a cottage someone was about to move into, and they didn't even bother removing the second whisky glass; they only wiped away their prints. That's about as far from accident as you could get."

"Hold up," Green put her hands in the air as if trying to keep a thought from escaping. "Are you saying the murderer made it look *more* murder-y?"

"In a way, yes. Think about it—no one was likely to be up there—even Sid wasn't supposed to be. The killer had plenty of time after shooting him to wash and put away the glasses, or even to smash a few things and leave the door open as though it were a break-in. And, since Sid bled internally, they could even have disposed of the body somewhere else with no one being the wiser. There's a bog just by the road. Hell, he was on a convenient rug for dragging." MacAdams waited for Green to digest this; she didn't look wholly convinced.

"All right, but that's a damn cool head—and dragging Sid off would be a heavy job. Could be this *wasn't* planned, and the killer just panicked and left things as-is."

"And still wiped the fingerprints off the glass and doorknob, while locking the door behind him?" MacAdams asked. Green squinted at him.

"Or her," she added. "Okay, have it your way. It's a negotiation gone wrong. But if the killer meant the scene to look like a very intentional murder afterwards, where does that leave us? What would be the point of that?"

MacAdams had been preparing for just this question, and Green would be the first trial of his theory. He sipped milky coffee.

"Maybe the killer was trying to frame someone else."

"Like Jo Jones? But no one even knew she was coming, you said so yourself."

"Okay, fair. Then what if it's a *message*? I maintain Sid couldn't have pulled off hiding the funds successfully entirely on his own."

"Technically, he didn't hide them successfully, anyway," Green offered. MacAdams wagged a finger.

"You say that—but remember, the money went in and then out again. It ended up somewhere else, and we haven't been able to track down the destination yet. There are brains in here somewhere. The killer might have thought so, too."

"An accomplice to Sid who helps him make 5K a month doing—or selling—something," Green said. She shook her head. "I don't know. We've got much less complicated motives closer to home. What if the money and the murder aren't connected at all, and this is just plain revenge?"

She wasn't going to let the sisters off so easily, it seemed. MacAdams stood up and reached for his coat.

"Well, that would be very inconvenient," he said. "For now, let's set about trying to eliminate a few suspects." It was time to find out about Elsie's movements.

Newcastle had its share of postindustrial blight. Smokestacks still rose along the river, though few in use. *Elizabeth Smythe* had a registered address in Elswick that Gridley had found. Green directed him via her smartphone, and they wound their way down a narrow street of squat redbrick buildings. Flats, mostly, from the look of things.

"Smythe is her maiden name," Green said as they parked. "But guess what? She has a brother, last name of *Turner.* Jack Turner."

MacAdams blinked. The name registered—along with a separate murder investigation outside of York—the one tied to the car theft scheme and the arson a few years ago.

"*The* Jack Turner?"

"Yup. Doing time at HM Prison in Full Sutton. Apparently, they were in foster care and only Elsie got adopted. Jack went in service. Hard to know if they're still in contact, but Andrews is following up just in case." Green opened the door and leaned out. "It's that one, number 27."

The door paint had peeled, leaving a stain of weather-beaten bare wood. No bell. MacAdams knocked hard on its surface and waited.

"Any other entrance?" he asked when the silence stretched.

"Not that I can see. I can look round the back." MacAdams nodded and watched Green's navy windbreaker disappear around the end of row houses. Then he peered into the window, hands clamped tight against the glare. It didn't look particularly lived-in. He decided to dial the station and got Andrews.

"Tommy, I need you to get the landlord. We're having no joy here," MacAdams said, nodding at Green, who'd returned mouthing the words *no back door.*

"I've good news, then," he said. "Gridley spoke to the owner this morning as a precaution—said she'd be happy to meet you. Want us to ring?"

MacAdams agreed that yes, this would be expedient, and then headed to the next door over.

"Landlord is on her way," he explained, knocking at the neighbors. Because neighbors tended to know things.

"Aye, what yee want?" came a voice behind the door. A woman, elderly.

"DCI MacAdams and DS Green from Abington CID."

"Howay. I've nowt for ye." The door stayed closed, but MacAdams hadn't expected it to be easy.

"You're not in any trouble, ma'am. We want to ask about your neighbor. Elsie Smythe is her name."

Much to his surprise, this announcement was followed by a bolt being slid. A few seconds later a woman's face appeared in the space between door and lock chain.

"A reet workyticket, she wor."

MacAdams just looked at Green.

"Troublemaker," she translated. Not a Geordie herself, she was at least well versed from her time as a cadet in town. Through her ministrations, they discovered that Elsie's kind of trouble wasn't the specific sort. The neighbor didn't like her look, even if she were *a geet lush* (attractive), and Elsie smoked too much and gave herself airs. MacAdams scratched the back of his neck; maybe she and Sid were a perfect wily pair together. It might explain why Sid kept going back to her—if indeed he did. He had finally met his match.

"Did you happen to see a man about with her, ma'am? Ginger, my height."

She shook her head. And a moment later, the door slammed

shut in MacAdams' face. He took an involuntary step back, almost into Green, who steadied him at the shoulder.

"The landlady is here, boss," she whispered, pointing to a smartly dressed woman on the sidewalk. "No renter wants to be seen jawing with the cops."

It was Green's way of suggesting he avoid reading too much into the woman's response. But overreading was a relatively useful trait among detectives. Nevertheless, he turned a reasonably friendly expression upon the approaching suited woman. Her hand darted out, perpendicular and ready with a single-pump handshake that a City-boy might be proud of.

"Deidre Sloan. Your constable rang," she said promptly.

"DCI MacAdams. Could you let us in the flat, here?" The ask was a formality; she already had the keys out.

"I hope there's no trouble," she said, turning the key in the lock. "I have two buildings in this estate, and I don't want bad press."

MacAdams peered into the snug front room. No mess. But no personal effects, either. Just a careworn sofa, two hard-backed chairs, and the dangling wall wire for a onetime television set. The kitchen told the same story; a few stacked dishes and a coffee maker, but the icebox was empty and the freezer ice half-evaporated.

"Nothing back here, either," Green said, emerging from a mostly empty bedroom. "No clothes, no shoes."

MacAdams turned his attention to Deidre, who was clasping and unclasping her hands.

"I thought you said it was still occupied."

"Yes. But I don't perform surprise inspections. How was I to know she'd gone?"

"I imagine nonpayment would be a clue," Green said. Deidre bounced on the balls of her feet.

"No, no, you don't understand. Ms. Smythe pays for the *year.* She won't be overdue till sometime in July."

MacAdams' shock must have been showing. Green's certainly was.

"Is that usual? Having renters who give you the entire year in a check?" MacAdams asked. "How much would that be?"

"I don't feel I should have to answer that," Deidre said snappishly. But very quickly thought better of it. "The rent is 700 pounds per month. For Elsie. I—I gave her a break for being so timely and up-front. It's not a crime."

Of course it wasn't. MacAdams inhaled slowly and wished he had a cigarette. Mental calculation put the figure for the year under nine grand. Not an insurmountable sum; not proof she'd come into heavy funds. If anything, it showed a canny grasp on the precarity of her chosen profession (assuming the sister wives were right about that).

"When was the last time you spoke to her?" he asked.

"Months. I'm not even sure."

"And how long has she been living here?"

"Three years. Four, maybe."

"We could ask the neighbor," Green said. "For specifics."

"Oh Lord. That's Edith. She isn't straight in the head, so I wouldn't put much faith in her." Deidre was clasping her hands again. "I'm sorry. I really must go see a client. Are we through?"

"We're through. But I want you to call if you hear from Elsie. Understood?" MacAdams gave her his card and waited until she nodded before adding, "We'll give one to the neighbor, too. I'm sure she'll keep sharp eyes out."

"What was that last little dig for?" Green asked when they made it back to the car. He turned onto the roundabout and back to the highway.

"Paying rent a year in advance is a good way to ensure the landlord stays out of your business," MacAdams said. "I suspect that Deidre Sloan will say and do nothing to jeopardize a big check every July. So she may as well know that Edith has our number as well."

Green processed this a moment. Then turned sideways against the seat belt.

"So now Elsie Smythe is a person of interest, too. That's Selkirk and Associates, the sister-wives, and Elsie Smythe. And Jo Jones, of course."

"Because?"

"Boss. Come on. She owns the cottage, she argued with him, she found him."

"By that logic, Tula Byrne is a suspect, too," MacAdams said, not proud to be advancing one of Fleet's theories. "She punted him out of her pub, suggested he never be allowed back, and called him a fair few names. And unlike Jo Jones, Tula at least *knew* Sid. Three bullets in the back says history, to me." MacAdams downshifted. "It might be a debt gone wrong, revenge, blackmail, or jealous rage. Regardless, they are clearly quick to act on instinct, maybe impulsive, but smart, too."

MacAdams shut his mouth then, but it was too late. Green didn't even bother to hide the smug grin.

"A bit like an American who up and moves to an abandoned estate in another country on a whim and knows how to download and use police software?"

The cosmic ironies were against MacAdams, it appeared. He'd only just returned to his desk after their fruitless search for Elsie when the phone rang—and Jo Jones proved his DS very much in the right.

"You're going *where*?" he asked of the phone tucked precariously at his ear.

"To Swansea. It's in Wales."

"I *know* where it is." MacAdams was trying to take his coat off one-armed. They'd only just got back minutes before. "You can't leave town, there's a murder investigation on!"

"You're a little late, I've been on the train two hours already."

MacAdams flattened his palm against his forehead. People

did not "up and go to Swansea." His eyes darted to the wall clock: half past four.

"Why are you going to Wales at all?" MacAdams could hear the scuff of fabric as she switched hands, making herself comfortable.

"I'm on my way to meet the seller of that eBay photograph. He might have more information on the woman in the painting."

"*Might?* Have you even spoken with this person?"

There was a slight crackle in the line, followed by a pause in transmission. When Jo came back, she was midsentence.

"—So I thought you could keep an eye on the cottage for me."

MacAdams had followed all the words, but still not cottoned on to the meaning.

"Are you asking me to house-sit?"

"I'm not asking you to water the plants and feed the cat or anything. I just thought"—more static on the line—"so I left the key in an envelope on your desk."

MacAdams scanned the desktop, itself covered in crime photos, notes, and points of interest in the case. Jo's voice piped back in.

"I stuck it between the lamp and your computer. Your desk is a mess, by the way."

A crisp blue envelope poked to the left of MacAdams' monitor. He'd also just noticed the notepads had been arranged in a stack; she'd been in his office again. How did that keep happening?

"Jo, I really need you to stay put until the investigation is over."

"I didn't catch that? I think there is a tunnel coming up."

After that, the line went dead. MacAdams ran fingers through his hair.

"You're bloody welcome," he groaned to no one. Or rather, to someone he didn't realize was there.

"I'm sorry?" Jarvis Fleet stood in the door, his coat neatly folded over one arm.

"Ms. Jones," he explained, "has decided to go to Wales. And yes, before you say anything, I *know* persons of interest are not supposed to leave during an investigation."

He expected Fleet to cite some rulebook from memory. Instead, he invited himself in and sat in the chair opposite.

"Please explain," he said. MacAdams wished he had the slightest idea how. He half thought of hunting for the bottle of Talisker stashed in his desk.

"She's still on about that bloody painting," he said. "I spoke to her yesterday. She had been doing an image search, looking for information about the woman in it—a relative, I gather."

"The painting she claims was stolen?" Something about the way Fleet said it felt oddly accusatory. It put MacAdams off.

"I don't doubt it's missing. But she said it had been stolen by *Sid*, and we can't prove that. If it even exists at all, Rupert suggested he may have moved it, since the room has a hole in the roof. But we've no evidence of it anyplace, and frankly, what would Sid want with an old family portrait? It's not even worth anything, can't possibly be relevant."

Fleet stroked his mustache absently.

"Odd, isn't it? That she should be in town so briefly, but be the victim of a theft and also a person of interest in a murder."

Something squirmed on MacAdams' insides. Gut feeling, maybe.

"What are you suggesting?" he asked. He half expected Fleet to say she'd made up the theft, maybe made up the painting itself, to get sympathy or throw off suspicion. But Fleet had made a few quarter turns somewhere.

"The painting matters to Jo Jones, so much so that she'd violated orders on behalf of it. If she thinks Sid took it from her, that is a motive."

"Christ, Fleet! You think she killed a man because of a painting?" MacAdams had raised his voice, and now Fleet was looking at him with a kind of measured judgment. It did not bode well at all, so he settled himself back down. "Look, Jarvis. As far as I can tell, Jo isn't even interested in the painting itself. This thing in Wales has to do with a family member. It's ancestry hunting, that's it."

Fleet's thin mouth turned up at the corners.

"You like this woman," he said. And he may as well have added *your judgment is compromised.* MacAdams had to force the next bit through his teeth.

"You find murderers by discovering motives, Fleet. Blackmail is a motive. Revenge is a motive. It's just a matter of narrowing the list."

Fleet nodded faintly and stood up.

"I am in agreement," he said. "But I still think there may be more to Jo Jones than you suspect. Even as there was more to Sid Randles."

"Good night, Fleet," MacAdams said firmly. Fleet waved his hat and disappeared through the door. After a few moments, MacAdams opened the bottom drawer of his desk. The bottle lay neatly against two tumblers. Tempting. *More to Sid Randles.* Sure there was. A family on hard times, a dad who offed himself, an unstable mum. Things hadn't been good for the Randles clan for a few generations. Not that this made crime more palatable—just more understandable. MacAdams bid adieu to the whisky and shut the drawer; the moment had passed, and he still needed to eat something—

And go check on Jo's cottage.

MacAdams pulled into the lane off the main road, very much regretting his conversation with Fleet. He kept the car in the drive and walked along the brick path, revisiting the man's theories. They still didn't make sense. Surely not. MacAdams wasn't playing favorites; he was just following the most salient evidence. Or so he told himself while unlocking the door.

He might almost be standing in a different cottage altogether than the one they hauled Sid's body out of. A standing lamp gave a warm glow to the sitting room. Gone were the leftover furnishings and all the previous knickknacks. Spotlessly clean, but not so much to make you feel uncomfortable; the mismatch of black-and-white photographs, odd modern art, animal print pillows, and quilted throws invited you to make yourself at home. MacAdams knew it was box-fresh—everything brand-new, and he even knew where from. Like a magazine shoot, almost, less a lived-in space than a movie set for living in. "Put yourself here." Did people do that?

MacAdams poked his head upstairs, which was largely unfinished, and then down the hall to the bedroom and bath. On the bedside table was a single photograph: an elderly woman who, given the resemblance, must be Jo's late mother. A few other odds and ends, a book with a cracked spine, a necklace in a clamshell dish. He retraced his steps to the living room and settled into a chair next to the fireplace.

To his practiced eye, what most readily stood out? The books. There were a lot of them, considering she traveled with a small case, and they had been placed *everywhere*. He might almost call them *strewn*, where all else was arranged at right angles. To his left, a stack of used mystery novels she may have picked up at Arthur's Bookshop in town. From where he sat, he could see literary tomes (on closer inspection, Jane Austen and the Brontes, principally). But also *Modern Physics*, a reference on garden herbs, a *Visual Guide to Architecture*, four chemistry textbooks and a *Compendium of Weird Facts*. Cozy, curious, and random met analytical, practical, desperately organized. Jo was an editor, but also apparently an epicure of odds and ends.

Assessment: he'd had it the wrong way round. Far from being impersonal and magazine-like, the retooled cottage spoke Jo into being, even the carved wooden fox that appeared to be laughing at him from the curio table. Without clutter or even many actual past-life items, the cottage felt a bit like Jo in a way that Sid's flat, mostly empty and much too tidy, did *not* feel like Sid Randles.

And that, by circuitous reasoning, brought MacAdams back to his interview with Rupert Selkirk. That office had seemed wrong somehow, and now he knew why. Rupert Selkirk had lived in Abington his whole life, and practiced law in the same office almost as long, and there hadn't been a single personal item anywhere. Despite being a widower with three kids and a grandson, not a single photo graced his office, no memorial to his wife, no kids playing at beaches, no handmade coffee mugs or ashtrays. It made MacAdams wonder just what he was hiding behind the scrubbed and tidy facade.

He permitted himself a sigh. MacAdams hadn't come to check on the cottage so much as to check on Jo Jones. She was a woman alone in the world, trying to make a new start. He more than understood it; he respected it. Annie had done that after their divorce (even if *MacAdams* hadn't). Jo Jones chased new beginnings—but Sid's murder emerged from his past. One suspect down; he'd crossed Jo firmly off the list. MacAdams put his hands on the chair arms and prepared to be on his way.

Then, he heard a *clang*. The unmistakable sound of metal on metal.

His response was instinctual—muscle memory, almost. MacAdams ducked low, keeping his profile out of view in case the floor lamp gave him away. More sounds: grating? Rasping? Prying? He waited, scarcely breathing. The noise hadn't come from the front, but the rear of the house—he would guess the kitchen window casement.

MacAdams crept across the floor in a crouch, using the breakfast bar as a screen. The sink and counters disappeared into shadow, but he could see the window. It was old, the sort that gave just enough room to allow the passage of a metal file, a housebreaker's favorite.

The clock over the stove ticked loudly. His heart pounded. Then he heard it again, the rasp of steel, the jingle of the window latch. MacAdams' palms were slick with sweat. *Rush him*, he thought; *catch him halfway through the window.* He was forty-five and not exactly in fighting trim but chose to ignore these critical details for the moment. Instead, he bounced on his heels, breathing shallow, and watched as a gloved hand pushed through the open casement—

And then his phone rang.

"Fuck—" MacAdams dug into his coat for it, but too late. The file clattered into the sink, and the perpetrator disappeared through the window frame and into the night.

Dammittohell. MacAdams struggled to his feet and dashed for the front door. It took barely ten steps to get around the side of the cottage, but the housebreaker was long gone. A grove of trees backed the cottage, and beyond it the lane. In the moment it took MacAdams to get his bearings, a grim thought occurred to him.

The housebreaker could be the murderer.

And *if* it was the murderer, then he was probably carrying a gun. MacAdams took a breath and dug out his phone.

"Green?" he shouted when she picked up, "Someone's just tried to break into Grove Cottage."

13

Tuesday

It took a *long* time to get to Wales, including two changes, multiple waits on platforms, and sleeping overnight in the carriage for a total of nine travel hours. Yet it wasn't even a whole four hundred miles.

Jo ordered a coffee from the trolley and then went back for a sandwich. It was a deeply sad sandwich, but she didn't want to go hunting for *Gwilym Morgan Estates, Antiques and Books* on an empty stomach. Especially as the eBay seller never did reply to her message. Which meant Jo had just traveled overnight in a coach seat with little more than an address. Now here she was, unshowered on an early Tuesday morning, hoping to God the place was open when she arrived.

"Swansea, Victoria Station," the voice announced. Jo stood as the cars lurched to a halt, skipping through the doors with her bag over one shoulder. The sun shone bright, glinting off university signs that suggested Swansea was a college town, and possibly a rather large one. Except for a change in the lilt of chatter and what might be the smell of the ocean, it wasn't so different from York (though she guessed no one from either city would agree with her on that). Sunglasses on, she made her way across a puddled street, feeling strangely free and easy despite the lack of sleep. That tended to be the way; decisive action, even when it didn't make much sense, was its own reward.

Halfway down the first street, Jo's phone buzzed.

"I'm just arriving," she said—but the answering *good morning, Jo,* was from MacAdams, not the eBay seller. She really needed to add some contacts to her phone.

"Sorry, I thought you were someone else. Everything okay?"

"More or less," MacAdams announced, though he sounded far from convincing. "I'm afraid I have some upsetting news for you. Someone attempted to break into the cottage last night."

Jo tripped over the curb on a loose shoelace. She just managed to prevent herself from skinning both knees.

"Did they take anything?"

"I interrupted them."

"They tried to break in *while* you were there?" Jo tucked the phone under her chin and tried to tie her shoe midair. "Did you get them?"

"They entered by window. Ms. Jones, I think you ought to stay at Red Lion when you return. We have forensics looking at the footprints, but in case there is an affiliation to the Sid Randles case—"

Jo dropped both feet to the ground again.

"Are you telling me the *killer* was at my house?"

"We don't know who the perpetrator was." And that meant, Jo reasoned, that he *didn't* get them.

"But if no one is staying at my cottage, won't they try to come back?"

"I'll post an officer there."

"Okay." Jo let out a long, slow breath. "But if there's an officer there, then I don't need to stay at the Red Lion. Right?"

"Ms. Jones—at least think about it?"

MacAdams made a few closing remarks she hardly listened to; a sort of happy bubble was rising in her stomach. By rights, she *should* be upset. But she doubted the break-in had anything to do with Sid; nothing of his remained...she'd trashed everything but the bedframe. The airy sensation had to do with something else, though. She was doing *as she liked.*

Despite a murder and a detective trying to tell her what to do about it, Jo hadn't budged. The rational response, she guessed, would be an enthusiastic promise to stay far away from the cottage. Or, better, a plane ticket back to Chicago or New York. Chicago, where she'd grown up repressing everything about herself for the sake of "quiet living"; New York, where she'd given up her only-just-realized self-sovereignty to someone who "knew better." Fuck it. She was going to make a stand, this time. Her life. Her rules. Even murder needed to know where to *get off.*

The sun played rainbows in street puddles, the antique shop wasn't far, and besides, she felt like a walk. To be honest, she felt a little bit like flying. A pleasant cluster of buildings huddled near the park. The ground floor placard announced a handful of shops and one To Let sign, but she could see an Antiques sign hanging above a second-floor entry. She climbed the stairs, but it wasn't exactly a public-facing business, so far. Officially *Gwilym Morgan Estates, Antiques and Books* only client seemed to be a stubby-tailed orange cat.

"Hello, there." Jo dangled fingers down its back, which earned her a rusty meow and purr. No Open sign, so she rang the bell and waited. In a minute or two, the cat's ears pricked up. Footsteps, mumbling, and the creak of the door followed, making way for a bewildered young hipster wearing a three-day-old beard.

"Um—Mr. Morgan?" Jo asked. The man blinked in daylight like a ground dweller.

"Yes? Can I help?"

"I'm Jo," Jo said. "Jo Jones? I emailed about the photo?"

He looked at her quizzically and scratched a stubbly chin. Jo was afraid he might shut the door.

"Um. You had a photo for sale, black-and-white, about this big." She made a square with her fingers and thumbs. "On eBay?"

"Oh! You should have *said*." He yawned and rolled his shoulders. "I haven't used that account in years. If I saw the listing, maybe I could remember—oh, em, won't you come in? Mind Puddles, she's a great nuisance to guests."

Puddles darted inside, and Jo followed her retreating steps into a dim enclosure. There were old grandfather clocks, umbrella stands, and chairs with faded fabric; crockery here and there, a shelf with knickknacks and old glass. Untidy, if not exactly a mess, it carried the unmistakable perfume of other people's lives. She felt a palpable itch to straighten the place.

"Apologies for the dust," the man said, padding on bare feet and waving for her to follow. "Most of my material goes to auctions—or through the online shop. Call me Gwilym, by the way."

They had entered a brighter room with dusted glass cases and items with conspicuous price tags. Jo paused over a stone elephant that seemed like a good companion for her wooden fox.

"My photograph studio for online sales," Gwilym explained, sitting on the edge of his desk. Considering he had most certainly just rolled out of bed, his attempt at a more businesslike air came off pretty well. He even put on a pair of glasses and held out one hand. "Which photo were you on about?"

Jo produced her phone and handed it to him. He heaved a sigh.

"Oh dear. I'm always surprised how things persist on the interwebs. This page should have been taken down; the photo came with a box of daguerreotypes, and I sold the lot to a collector of memento mori ages ago."

Jo paged through her mental notes.

"*Memento mori*, photographs of dead children?" she said, "It's a Victorian thing."

He grinned broadly. "Yes! Sometimes the only photo taken of a loved one occurred after death."

"I know! They pose them to look alive." She beat down the urge to froth about the details. "I'm—I used to be an editor. We did a photo collection."

"An editor! Of books! Mam fach!" He handed back the phone with a disarming smile. "I always thought I'd like that. Sorry about the picture. Who is she?"

Jo hiccupped.

"Well, that's the question I had planned to ask you." She tried smiling to hide her desperation. "I inherited this house recently, and there was a portrait in it. I think she must have been a relative of mine, and of Gwen Davies, who married William Ardemore in 1906. Over in Abington, Durham. Can you look up who bought it?"

"I closed my account, not sure I could even get back in. But they aren't likely to know, anyhow. They wanted it for a brace of dead children. What was the name on the painting?"

"Netherleigh."

Gwilym mussed his already fairly mussed hair.

"Coffee," he said. "I'll have a think, but I need coffee. Kitchen in the next room—won't be a minute. Instant okay?"

Jo didn't have the heart to say that she loathed instant coffee. How the British could be so excellent at tea and so bad at coffee always astounded her.

"Yes, thanks," she said instead. *Be polite*, she thought. She'd woken him, and he looked as though he'd thrown on whatever clothes were nearest, rumpled and loose. Unless he was just a bit of a modern bohemian. Probably he could rock a man-bun if he tried. She looked about her again, trying to work out how a young modern hipster ended up an antiques dealer.

"How do you spell Netherleigh?" Gwilym asked, returning with a tray, mismatched cups, and packets of sugar substitute.

Jo gave him the letters, slowly, while Puddles ran figure eights around her legs.

"Could it be a place name, maybe?"

"I googled it, but no luck," Jo admitted.

Gwilym lowered his mug. "Maybe search a local archive?"

Jo grimaced.

"Well, I would. I want to. I—sort of pissed off the museum-cum-library lady." She hadn't really meant to be that honest. But Gwilym hardly missed a beat.

"Oh yeah, I've done that."

"Really?"

"Oh my GOD, yeah. See, I'm into archives myself." He grinned, maybe a touch mischievously, and left the room. When he returned, he carried two enormous atlases under each arm. The first he spread out on one of the glass showcases.

"All the archives. Maps. Geography. Ancestry. Provenance. And I get so tired of people telling me that internet searches are the same thing as research. I mean, algorithms just give you hits *other people* think are useful. Now this—just look at it! So detailed, these old atlases—give you all sorts of place names you might not expect."

Jo followed his fingers as they raced along, so caught up in his excitement that she accidentally drank the coffee.

"I'm not seeing Netherleigh, I'm afraid," Gwilym said at last, running through the index. "Not in Wales, anyway. This other has County Durham."

The second volume was older and tattier. The two of them huddled over the must, fingers sliding together down the tiny print.

"Aha!" He turned a wide grin in her direction, beaming from scruff to eye sockets. "Not quite a jackpot, but *Nethr-lei* used to be a county name in Derbyshire."

"That's more or less where I just came from," Jo admitted. It was slightly deflating, not least because she was very sure of the spelling, and this wasn't it. "Maybe we can search the Davies family, instead? I have to head back this afternoon, and I'd hate to go empty-handed."

Gwilym stared at her like he was trying to guess her height and weight.

"You came all the way to Swansea to see me about that photo?" he asked. "Wow. That's clean off!"

"It's not *that* far to travel," Jo protested, but Gwilym was nodding enthusiastic approval.

"No, no, I get it! It's a compliment! Well, it is from me. Obsession is like that—we're knee-deep in mine, aren't we? I mean, look around." He gestured, then turned pink in the cheeks. "It's also how I annoy folks. Occasionally." He hummed to himself, picked up the horrible coffee, and settled in at his desk. "Davies is a pretty common name. I have access to the archive at Swansea University. What else 'ave you got?"

"They had money. Industrial types."

"Hold on—you don't mean *Davies Colliers*?" Gwilym slid round the desk, wiggling the mouse to wake up his computer. "Charles Davies. Smart man— he started in coal mines and then opened mills and a tool and die plant. The tool and die is still around, just outside Cardiff."

Jo scooted the cat for a better look. Two clicks opened a black-and-white photo. Charles Davies wore a top hat and suspenders; behind him were factory boilers and plumes of smoke.

"Family photo over here." Gwilym fished down the page entry to a grainy sepia print. A heavy-bosomed wife flanked Davies, all in ruffles. On the other side was a boy in short pants and two girls. One was certainly Gwen—and the other?

"Why can't I see her face?" Jo asked looking at the blur.

"Exposure," Gwilym said. "She must have moved when they were taking it."

Figures, Jo thought. Retiring. Shy. Turn your head, don't make it easy for them. There was something just a trifle rebellious in it, maybe.

"Names, though?" she asked. Gwilym rubbed his whiskered chin.

"Not on this page. I know ways to find out, though. If you give me your number?"

Jo took a scrap of paper from her purse and scribbled it down. Gwilym took it thoughtfully.

"You hungry?" he asked. Jo was, but didn't want to stay.

"I've a train to catch. Someone was murdered in my cottage last week, and I'm not supposed to be outside the county, apparently." She knew very well she was bragging a little. It *did* sound very far out, though, put like that. Gwilym almost panted excitement.

"You are a wonder!" he said. "Where do you hail from, mysterious American person? How did you end up in a murder mystery?"

Jo shrugged. Excellent question, wasn't it?

"Just lucky, I guess." As Jo made her way back to the station, the temperature had risen, so she dispensed with her coat, then caught her reflection in a nearby shop window: two-day-old clothes, jacket knotted round the waist of blue jeans and her hair in a knot never to be described as "fashionably" messy. She hadn't even needed the Doc Martens of Security for this trip and found herself rather pleased.

Once settled into her train car, Jo gathered evidence. Gwen had a sister—check. The sister had a portrait painted—check. The painting had *not* been hung in the main hall with the others, and unlike the others, it didn't give a proper first and last name.

What had Rupert told her? The Ardemores lived alone in that house with a battery of servants. No children. No sister. At least, not one anybody mentioned. Perhaps the sister hadn't had a "coming out" yet, so wasn't being flaunted on the marriage market. Or maybe no one bothered with younger sisters in 1908? Or maybe it was something…worse. She picked up the phone, half intending to call Tula, when it buzzed in her hand.

Jo it's Gwilym, read the text. Her name was Evelyn.

14

"MacAdams, in my office, now."

Cora was wearing a pale blue cardigan over her blouse, and it had the peculiar effect of making her look harder rather than softer, like a flower crown on a stone wall. She leaned both elbows on the desk and laced her fingers, which was always a bad sign.

"A break-in. At the murder scene. Which you recently cleared for occupation."

"Yes, ma'am."

"And your evidence to date consists in the victim's bank statement and a metal file with no prints you found outside a cottage window that may or may *not* have anything to do with anything."

Cora licked her thumb, flipped through a report, then tossed it at MacAdams.

"In addition, your sergeant was in an altercation. You didn't report it."

"It wasn't an altercation—"

"Olivia Randles put hands on one of your officers and I had to hear it from local tattle? Meanwhile you and Green and half of forensics were up last night at the cottage. What were you doing there in the first place, James? Start talking, and impress me, because it's not been a happy Friday."

It occurred to MacAdams that answering the questions might involve admitting he was doing a favor for Jo Jones, a person of interest in the case. So he ignored them and got on with progress.

"We have four leads. We've discovered that Rupert Selkirk had signed over the business of renting the cottage to Sid Randles. We know Randles received regular payments of large sums that we can't account for. Fleet and I put pressure on Rupert before the funeral."

"And the other two?"

"Olivia, Sid's second ex-wife, had given him a lot of money to help him out. Sid also cheated on both Olivia and Lotte. There may be a connection to the cottage."

Cora unlaced her fingers, but the expression on her face had not improved.

"You know all this, and you haven't brought anyone in for questioning?"

MacAdams resisted the urge to shift in his seat. He'd meant to start this yesterday, but the break-in had shifted their focus. Cora did not appreciate his silence.

"Rupert Selkirk, then. You said you had put on some pressure—well, Detective, that's what interview rooms *are for*."

"Apologies for the interruption, ma'am." Fleet stood in the doorway. "It's ten fifteen."

"Jarvis, sorry to keep you waiting," Cora said, with a dose of gentleness that MacAdams had not once heard, ever. It was enough to knock you sideways.

"Not at all, ma'am. Also, MacAdams? Jo Jones has phoned to tell you she's back in town."

MacAdams groaned internally. He should never have told

Fleet she'd gone—that was a fool's mistake. He could feel Cora's eyes boring into him.

"Is that so? Listen up, MacAdams. You bring Selkirk in for questioning, *today*." She shooed him out of the office and joined Fleet, darting MacAdams with one last stinger: "Don't make me take this case from you."

Fleet only tipped his hat. It wasn't *his* fault, not really—but MacAdams was willing to make it his. Dammit, fellow DCIs ought to know when to back each other and when to keep mouths shut. He watched the two of them marching in lockstep down the corridor and decided he didn't want to know where they were going. He secretly hoped Fleet wasn't the reason Cora wore the fuzzy cardigan. And he really, really hoped Fleet wasn't going to be a permanent fixture about the place. But it wasn't looking good.

God, he wanted a cigarette.

Green was waiting for him outside his office. She looked tired, though not altogether worse for wear.

"Did I come up in the meeting with Cora?" she asked.

"Only once."

"And?"

"We're moving too slow." MacAdams sighed. "She wants us to bring in Rupert and Emery today."

"Shit, we'll lose the sisters, then. They are checking out at noon—and you know Gridley can't find anything—and I mean *anything*—wrong with Rupert's finances. We can't charge him."

"Nope. But we can question. Make it look like we're doing something." MacAdams ran his fingers through his hair, aware that he hadn't combed it.

"We *are* doing something," Green insisted and gave a very not-secret sign to Andrews, who stepped into the office with her. "Tell him what you found."

"It's what I *didn't* find," Andrews corrected. "You told me to look up Elsie Smythe, right? She's got an account in Newcastle.

It's reasonably sized, bit of income, bit of outflow. She pays utilities direct deposit. But she *isn't* paying her rent that way."

"No check to Ms. Sloan once a year?" MacAdams asked, lifting slightly in his seat.

"No, sir." Andrews smiled hopefully. But MacAdams shook his head. It wasn't a smoking gun; possibly she paid in cash, under the table to avoid tax.

"It's worth asking the landlord, but it's still pretty thin good news," he said. Andrews only grinned.

"Not to worry. We were saving the best for last," he said. "It's from our team in legal. And it's going to make you very happy."

Rupert and Emery came quietly and were presently installed in separate interrogation rooms. Meanwhile, Green and Gridley took turns bringing MacAdams up to speed on the general legal discourse necessary to see how, precisely, Rupert Selkirk had been cooking the books.

"It's not the strongest case, I'll grant you," Gridley explained, tucking a pen behind her ear. "Not money laundering or anything that egregious. But a family solicitor simply *cannot* sign over property under only his own signature."

"Because?"

"Because it's the same as saying you owned it," Green explained. "Like, imagine I have a car, and I loan it to Gridley—and then she rents it to you without my knowledge. Get it? Now, Rupert is smart. He tried to get around it in the contract by signing over *only* the cottage, and not the ground it sat on. A loophole of sorts, like laying a squatter's claim to the floorboards and plaster."

"And that's not legal?" MacAdams asked, because he'd better be sure. Green shook her head.

"Not without input from the family, it's not. He's not the signatory or the executor."

"That's the best part," Gridley said as they arrived at the interrogation room. "Selkirk signed it *as though* he were the owner of the estate and not Jo Jones. Emery signed as witness."

MacAdams peered through one-way glass to see Emery, sitting straight and stiff. Little wonder he'd been jumpy when they started asking questions; his boss had involved him in something *definitely* illegal—on behalf of Sid, now dead. What could possibly be that important?

"Give me five," he said, then he opened the door. Green would join in a few moments. The disruption to tension always aided the process, MacAdams found. And he liked to be the first to begin.

"DCI MacAdams to interview Emery Lane," he said into the recorder. "Mr. Lane, do you understand why you are here?"

"I'm assuming you have more questions about Sid Randles," Emery said quietly. MacAdams tapped an imaginary cigarette against the steel tabletop.

"I'm actually here to ask you how you feel about your boss."

"About Mr. Selkirk? He is an excellent employer."

"Upright and aboveboard, then?" MacAdams asked. Emery seemed to have just reduced his surface area by internal contraction.

"I believe so, yes."

"I see." MacAdams pushed forward a piece of paper. "I have given the subject a document," he said for the tapes, then turned back to Emery. "Can you tell me what this is?"

"A contract between Sid Randles and Rupert Selkirk."

"Good. And can you tell me what is wrong with it?"

Emery's face was a blank. "Wrong? I don't understand?"

At that moment, the door opened and Green announced herself. She had donned a sleek charcoal blazer and, with her hair replaited into ferociously tight rows, a look of almost frightening professionalism. She then launched into a short, sharp explanation of exactly why and how Rupert's contract represented illegal action, witnessed by Emery. MacAdams could not help but be gratified; there was something in the way she led with her chin—her whole face a chisel edge.

"In summary," she concluded, "This document could be used to charge Rupert Selkirk with perjury, false attribution, and usurpation of property."

Emery cleared his throat and reached for the plastic cup of water.

"I am not trained in property law," he said in a hoarse voice.

"Are you suggesting you did not know this contract was illegally drawn?" MacAdams asked. "Or that in signing it, Rupert pretended to have rights to the property?" He gave that a moment to sink in, then leaned forward onto the table, Cora-style. "It's very odd, don't you think, that the moment a real heir comes to take possession—unexpectedly rendering the contract void—Sid Randles ends up dead. What do you think of that?"

Emery drank more water.

"I'm waiting for my solicitor," he said.

"Your solicitor is in the next interrogation room over," MacAdams reminded him. "I'm asking you a simple question. Did you know Rupert was engaged in illegal activity?"

"He wasn't." It was almost too softly said to be audible. MacAdams nodded to Green, who took the fore again.

"Mr. Lane, I'm sure you'll agree that Rupert Selkirk's clients would find a false contract over property a fairly illegal action"—Emery had blanched at the mention of Rupert's reputation, so Green pressed the advantage. "Clients need to trust their solicitor. And as you can see, we can find other solicitors happy to act as expert witnesses to the clauses in this contract."

"Witnesses?" Emery asked.

"At trial, yes," MacAdams said, mentally calculating. No one had brought charges yet, but it could be done in a hurry now that they had some evidence of wrongdoing. "It's enough, at the very least, to have him disbarred."

Emery's throat constricted so hard that MacAdams almost

heard the click of tonsils. He was shrinking further into his carefully preened suit.

"It will be a murder trial, Mr. Lane."

"Not murder!" Emery half choked.

Now it was time to play the bait. MacAdams pushed back in his chair.

"You are free to go, Mr. Lane, as you've assured us you have nothing to do with it."

Green knocked his knee under the table. She didn't know where he was going with this. He knocked back, in an attempt to communicate *wait and see* with a side of *no interrupting.*

"Mr. Selkirk has done a foolish and risky thing, and I wouldn't want it to smudge your own character," MacAdams pursued. "People often do foolish and risky things when they are being blackmailed. Don't they?"

Emery was now parchment white. His eyes didn't rise even to meet MacAdams' tie. MacAdams arranged his face into a look of concern, not wholly invented, either.

"Mr. Lane? What might Mr. Selkirk be blackmailed for? Such an upright person, long established, professional, lots of friends and associates. He wouldn't risk all that for nothing, would he?"

Green seemed to be catching on.

"Could be protecting someone else, maybe," she offered.

"You said he was an admirable employer, Mr. Lane," MacAdams went on. "Is he also—your friend? A man you would lie for?"

Emery made a groaning sound and put his face in his hands. MacAdams allowed himself the breath he'd been holding and a quick look at Green, who nodded. They had hit upon it at last.

"You don't have any family here in the North, do you?" MacAdams asked quietly. "And though Rupert Selkirk does, there isn't a single memento from his life of almost forty years in this town as a family man."

Across the table, Emery's eyes peeped between his fingers.

"*You* are his family, aren't you, Emery?" MacAdams asked, and Green decided to go for gusto:

"You are Rupert Selkirk's lover."

Emery took a shuddering breath, then slowly raised his eyes to meet theirs. It wasn't an admission for the tapes, no. But it was an admission all the same.

"Sid Randles found out, didn't he?" MacAdams asked. "And he threatened to publicize it."

"We did nothing wrong," Emery whispered. He was shaking. Across the table, Green's stone-cold demeaner had softened.

"Not for loving each other, you didn't," she agreed. "Not for *that*. But a client needs to trust the solicitor, to know he's on the side of law."

MacAdams felt suddenly self-conscious. After all, Green and Rachel had recently become engaged, and extended family hadn't exactly turned up with Pride flags. Abington had two pubs, a village hall, cinema, and a players theater, a dozen decent restaurants; it wasn't *provincial*. And yet. There were the homophobic jokes he'd heard in pubs, and the way new constables looked at Green like she was an exotic plant. All Selkirk's relationships had been built on his role as a local family man; all those cookouts in drizzly weather with his kids playing with all the other kids, and his wife making punch before her passing. Idyllic. Stifling. A two-sided trap.

"Sid was going to tell people that Rupert had lived a lie. Is that it?" he asked. "Or—perhaps he planned to tell Rupert's own children? Threaten his reputation and his family all at once?"

Emery Lane had sobered and recaptured some of his wary reserve. He was too clever not to see where this was going.

"Say what you will. We had nothing to do with what happened to Sid," he said. "And I've said all I'm going to say."

"Interview terminated." MacAdams switched off the device and turned to Green. "Fetch him a cup of tea, would you mind? He probably needs it."

★★★

MacAdams expected to find Rupert Selkirk cold and unflappable. He was only half-right. Rupert sat quietly, hands folded on the table. But you couldn't call him *cold*, almost the reverse. The man looked oddly beatific.

"Good morning, James," he said. MacAdams wanted to reply in kind, but that wouldn't do, not today.

"Detective Chief Inspector MacAdams interviews Rupert Selkirk," he said to the tapes, and Rupert ducked his head in agreement.

"*Detective*, yes," he corrected. "I know why I'm here. I won't mislead you further."

"So, you admit you lied to me," MacAdams asked as he took his seat and resettled his rumpled coat.

"I was not honest about my contract with Sid Randles. You know that now, I assume."

"We know you illegally overstepped your role as solicitor and that you misappropriated your client's property."

"Yes."

"And you did this to keep Sid Randles from publicizing your relationship with Emery Lane."

"To keep him from further damaging me, yes." Rupert took a breath. "Surely you get lonely, Detective? Since your divorce? It's human. I'm human."

MacAdams kept his voice firm and even.

"Explain yourself, Mr. Selkirk."

"I'm trying." Rupert took a breath, calculating how much he needed to reveal, no doubt. "I used to go to Newcastle. To meet other men. And before you ask, yes, this started before Bethany died."

MacAdams kept his face impassive as ever. He did not approve of infidelity. But neither was he above comprehending it.

"After her death, I stopped being *careful* about where I went or with whom. And by then, I had been keeping company with Emery on a more—exclusive basis."

"I see. Sid found you out." MacAdams waited for the denouement, but Rupert offered him a sad smile.

"Ah. Yes." Rupert shook his head sadly. "I told you truth about hiring Sid to mow lawns at Ardemore. He'd done it before, or so he said, for Aiden—but he wanted the role of caretaker. Frankly, I said no. But he offered to prove himself by doing some work gratis. If I found him competent, would I reconsider? He came to replace a window in the drawing room of my home and decided to explore where he was not invited."

MacAdams considered his bathroom tile job afresh. Had Sid gone snooping in his house, too? Perhaps he was afraid to press his luck with a detective.

"Emery fancies himself an amateur photographer. There were—photographs—in the bedroom side table. Intimate, you might say."

"Sid blackmailed you."

"Yes—and no. Not in the way you seem to think. I've already surrendered my finances. You'll know I did *not* cut checks for five thousand pounds a month. I was as shocked as you about Sid's sudden riches," Rupert assured him.

"Mr. Selkirk," MacAdams said, his voice reclaiming its professional—and more biting—tone. "Were you blackmailed, or were you not?"

Rupert arranged himself as though it were he, and not MacAdams, conducting the interview.

"To be caretaker was all he asked for, and the cottage, to do with as he pleased. And while I understand the implications of that legal document you have just shown me, I was within my rights to act *on behalf of* the family for the maintenance of any building on the property."

MacAdams didn't believe him. Increasingly, because believing him was going to be very inconvenient for the case.

"Look, you will have the sympathies of any jury. To be blackmailed in larger and larger amounts, to know your family would be damaged by his knowledge—"

"James, listen to me. I am a gay man. And if you want to malign my character, you could say I'm a *coward*. I didn't want my private life aired in public, and it was such a small sacrifice—give up a cottage no one wanted and my relationship could stay secret."

"Ah. But then Jo Jones arrives to take it over. And you knew then something had to be done."

Rupert smiled. Indulgently.

"I made a realization, yes. But only that playing along with Sid had been foolish. I still thought some arrangement might be made between them, but on the very first day, I had already taken the precaution of—of having Ms. Jones sign an agreement about the property that retroactively gave me permission to do exactly as I had done with the cottage."

"You—What?" MacAdams sounded exasperated and knew it. "Why would she sign something like that?"

"Because I told her to, as her solicitor. Because she had just arrived and needed someone to handle things, and I *was* handling them. Frankly, because she didn't know any better. I'm not asking you to approve of my methods, Detective. I'm not proud of them. But they were not *illegal*." MacAdams felt a wave of frustration snake round his insides.

"You took advantage of your client's trust!" he barked. Rupert smiled thinly.

"Sadly, that is also not illegal. If it helps, it worked to her advantage in the end. She had just given me power to hire Sid, which meant it was my duty to fire him. And I did."

"And *then* you murdered him." MacAdams pressed (a little desperately). Rupert shook his head.

"Murder requires a motive, Detective. I simply don't have one."

"I beg your pardon?"

"Sid wasn't the only one who found out about my double life." Rupert's face crumpled slightly, and it made him seem older, less polished. "Not quite a year ago, Emery and I went to our usual hotel in Newcastle. I didn't know my son was staying there, too. He told my daughters. They felt...*betrayed*."

MacAdams noted that he named none of his family members, even though MacAdams had met Ruby and at least one of the daughters. It was as if names, like photos, were too painful. It explained the hollow office.

"They cut off contact?"

"Something to that effect." Rupert gave a resigned sigh, but his previous demeanor crept back again, along with the long-suffering smile. "My youngest lives in town, however, and has made it his mission to disabuse my clients. I lost about half of them. I kept more than I expected. A quiet gay man in proper tweeds and good shoes is given more leeway than you'd expect. Especially if he keeps his relationships—discreet."

MacAdams gave thanks for his own unexpressive face. Rupert, sly old lawyer, had set MacAdams up for this moment and played his hand beautifully.

"I no longer have a secret to protect," Rupert confirmed.

MacAdams turned off the tapes and watched his case slipping away.

15

Cigarettes. MacAdams kept an emergency pack in the car. He snatched it on the way out of the station, then walked as far as Robbie Park in a drizzling rain. When he reached the bridge over the duck pond, he lit one and inhaled deeply. Air, quiet, and space to think: that's what he wanted. What he was about to get, however, was company. And not the sort he enjoyed. Because Jarvis Fleet, blazing blue umbrella and all, was approaching from the bandstand.

"Good afternoon, lovely day for a stroll."

There wasn't even a hint of irony in the statement, even though MacAdams—hatless—was wet through and smoking ferociously.

"I thought you were out with Cora."

Fleet responded by pointing beyond them, into the hazy distance.

"Yes. At Longside. We were visiting the grave of her father. It's the anniversary, today."

Oh. MacAdams felt the creep of self-reproach and stubbed out the cigarette.

"You knew him well, I hear."

Fleet joined him, offering his edge of umbrella.

"Very well. From my earliest days in service. I owed him a great deal."

"Cora tells us all about his perfections," MacAdams said. It sounded sour, but was the absolute truth; she worshipped the man. Fleet didn't reproach him, however.

"It isn't slander to admit a man is only human, and to mourn them despite their faults."

MacAdams agreed with these words so heartily that it gave him a turn coming from Jarvis Fleet. He summarily cast his mind back; old Alex Clapham always seemed a sort of board game version of himself, *blow hard and rattle the pebble monkeys*[1] or some nonsense. The sort of man who referred to all police personnel as "snowdrops." His daughter excepted, no doubt.

"You weren't friends?" he asked.

"You mistake me. I was very fond." Fleet adjusted his mustache. "I came to the funeral."

"Cora mentioned it. Said she found you invaluable at paper sorting."

An anemic sort of smile creased Fleet's stiff features, and his mustache gave a fractious twitch.

"Odd that you have a reputation for being taciturn. Yes, I came to help during the period of grief when personal effects were too much for Cora to consider." He paused. "You did not like the commodore?"

MacAdams was being chastened, and he deserved it. He was nettled, but it had a lot more to do with Cora's lack of faith in *him* than her preference for *Fleet*. Annie would have said this was unbecoming of him, and he would have to agree.

---

1 Junior RAF officer, the nubile version of Rock Ape (RAF regiment member)

"Honestly? I didn't. Why did you?" he asked. Fleet stepped closer, the umbrella over them both for a moment.

"We held things in common," he said. "We served in Afghanistan together. You might say we bonded over a mutual admiration for military mechanism."

"I assume you've seen his War Room, then." *War Room*, everyone in a hundred mile radius had been invited to see the air commodore's museum of medals while the man lived.

"I am led to believe that everyone has," Fleet said, and for a moment, MacAdams almost caught a hint of companionable humor.

"We may as well walk and talk," he said, making an *after you* gesture in the direction of town. "The Selkirk interview did not go well. We can't actually pin him with anything appreciably illegal."

"Ah. I understand your frustration. Lawyers are particular."

"It's not just a lack of evidence," MacAdams admitted. "I'm struggling to find a motive. I thought Rupert was being blackmailed for being gay, but Sid lost that power over him a year ago."

"Can you be certain?"

"Easy enough to check. We can ask his son or past clients to verify. Apparently he lost a few. Emery and Rupert are still each other's only alibi, but that checks out, too, and has come with an admission that they shared a hotel room in Uxton."

"Ah," Fleet said. MacAdams sighed.

"Meanwhile, Green suspects Lotte and Olivia have motive, and then there's the first wife, Elsie, who has been conveniently difficult to find. But none of *them* broke into the cottage last night."

"You're sure?"

"I usually can tell a man from a woman," MacAdams said testily. "The window prowler was tall, thin, squarely built, with the arm strength to bend a metal casement."

"That's rather a lot of information from the glimpse of a hand," Fleet said. "And Green may correct you about the necessary strength."

Dammit. She would, too. MacAdams attempted to smooth his bristling ego.

"It wasn't Olivia or Lotte. They might be taller than Jo Jones, but they'd be reaching up through the window, not downward. Elsie might be tall enough, but doubtful she's the sort to do her own dirty work."

Fleet maintained silence for a few moments, long enough for them to reach the station's car park. When he spoke again, he'd taken an entirely different tack.

"Perhaps we'll start from the other direction, then, objects and not subjects. The painting, let's say."

MacAdams shook himself, divesting water in several directions.

"You can't be serious."

"Why not?"

"Yesterday you suspected Jo of murder." MacAdams pulled the door open and ushered them both inside. Fleet gave a faint, though oddly precise, shrug.

"Everyone is a suspect. But she did not break into her own cottage."

Fleet had just given the enormous compliment of taking MacAdams' word for it.

"Go on," he said. Fleet acquiesced.

"The murderer wants something. Perhaps that something is still here—or perhaps one of the suspects you mention has it in possession."

MacAdams felt the heavy pressure of coincidence descending. Because, of course, the theft of the painting immediately preceded Sid's death. But if Sid *did* steal it, they didn't know *why* or even if the two events were related.

"So how do we find a missing painting?" he asked.

★★★

"What do you mean, *flirting*?" Jo asked. The ground beneath her feet squelched uncomfortably, and she was grateful for the bright blue wellies that Tula insisted she borrow.

"Jo, darling-heart, don't be dim." Tula lent her a hand. "Mind the stile as you come over, this one's a bit rickety."

"I'm not being dim," Jo insisted, trying not to slip in the mud. The path began near Ardemore garden wall and led the back way into Abington, a good three miles one way. *Right to Roam*, they called it. "I just don't see it. At all."

"Gwilym asked for your number."

"Yes, so he could call me with any answers—"

"And he texted before you even left the train station. Which means he surely knew already or had means to find it while you were still there. He just wanted your number. I'm surprised he didn't ask you to lunch."

"Oh. He did."

Tula fairly cackled at this. Jo puckered her brow.

"At least I came back with her name!"

"You almost came back with a Welshman," Tula chuckled. "Charming, the way you described him. Unkempt, mayhap, but charming. And he deals in antiques?"

"I think he *means* to," Jo said. "He's like a collector-gone-awry. Has subscriptions to all the ancestry sites and probably a few for treasure hunting or cryptozoology. He said he'd like to be an editor."

"Instead?"

"In addition, I think. I'm not sure he collects antiques, really." Jo ducked under a low-hanging furze. "I think he collects hobbies."

"Oh, la—you snap him up, quick, then! He must surely have money, because if antiques were his stock and trade, he'd starve."

Jo considered this. She'd meant to make a list of her old contacts by now, send a few emails. Get the ball rolling on her (not quite formed) freelance ideas. The murder had thrown off her plans a bit. Much the way her mother's death had done. But if she planned to stay in Abington, she'd better start job hunting soon herself. The taxes were looming. Maybe marrying for money wasn't all bad.

"Tula? How did you meet Ben?" she asked. Tula stopped walking and leaned against the wooden fence lining the path.

"Met him my first night in town. Was passing through for a walking tour, met at an open-air concert. Had him all night, by morning, he'd damn near proposed." She coiled a strand of hair round her finger. "I might have agreed, but I was against marriage on principle. Then."

"Not anymore?"

"I've softened in my years. Was bang against it, young. Left Limerick when I was seventeen, been everywhere—Australia, South Africa."

"The States?"

"Nah, you all've quite enough Irish already." She smiled, a little less sunny than her usual. "Started off following a man. Then followed a band. Ended up in the Peace Corps a few years. By the time I knew't ten years had gone."

"Did you go home, then?" Jo asked.

"I am home, love. But nay, I never went *back*. Not to Limerick." She started walking again, and Jo followed. The old brain bell was ringing, and dots connecting, and she felt a sudden unutterable sadness.

"You see yourself in me, don't you."

"A bit," Tula admitted. "Fellow outsider, and such." Jo put her hands in her pockets.

"I guess I see *myself* in *books*," she said. "Always. I love words. The way they look and feel and smell. It's hard to explain. Words have just always been my people. And I don't forget them after I've read them."

"Ever? Like a photographic memory?" Tula asked. Jo scrunched up her nose. She'd never liked the term.

"It doesn't work quite like that. I can recite from most of the books I've read—but it has to be triggered. I don't have a search engine in here. But—" she looked out over the heath, the rolling hills dark with wet winter weeds. "This makes me think of 'The Darkling Thrush.'

'... frail, gaunt, and small,
In blast-beruffled plume,
Had chosen thus to fling his soul
Upon the growing gloom.'

"And the estate, that's been mostly *Wuthering Heights* and *Jane Eyre.* The words just come, and I make connections."

"And you really never forget?" Tula's features had lit up, suddenly, in a quick burst of sunshine. "That's incredible."

Jo shivered a little all the same.

"Maybe. Mostly it's just very crowded up here. And sometimes lonely."

Tula had come a little closer; protectively, perhaps.

"Lonely how?"

"It's not a perfect system." Jo shrugged. "Sometimes the connections I see aren't really there—I've just made an association. But *sometimes* it means I see connections other people can't see—or a lot faster than they do. Plus, even though I never forget things, other people *do.* Often, I'm left living in a memory that has vanished for other people." Jo tucked her fingers into her armpits. The cold was starting to seep in, despite the filtered sunlight. It was unpleasant to think about. She wanted to change the topic.

"On the day of Sid's murder, you said something else bad had recently happened in Abington. Arson, or something?" *Nice topic change, Jo,* she thought. But Tula didn't look put out.

"Oh, aye! Awful business. The victim was local, name of Douglas. His Da owned a garage in town, and handed it down. Now, when I met him, I'd have said he was an able-dealer, a real schemer if you know't? But you know how it is—grew up here, so part of the fabric. You'll never hear a word against him. And no speaking ill o' the dead."

Jo started. "I thought something was just set on fire?"

"Aye. Douglas himself. Or his car, rather, with him in it."

"Shit." Jo tried hard not to focus on the forming mental image. "Who did it?"

"That's where it gets messy, like," Tula said. "They arrested a Newcastle fellow, can't remember the name. Jack, maybe. Turns out they'd been stealing cars, and using Douglas' garage to chop 'em. Somehow or other, this partner sets him ablaze. Get's done for murder—manslaughter, I mean."

Jo processed this: a *manslaughter offence constitutes homicide*. Involuntary meant you hadn't meant it to happen—negligence. But this sounded a lot voluntary.

"That's awful."

"Too right, it is. Violent and vengeful. Sort of thing just doesn't happen around here, especially not to people you know."

Jo understood the sentiment, but it seemed everyone knew everyone, here. In Chicago, in Brooklyn, it didn't work like that. Yes, Jo knew her immediate neighbors. But she'd left the country with none of them the wiser. She thought she preferred it that way. And by circuitous reasoning, that made her think once more of Evelyn.

"Someone must have known Evelyn. I mean, someone must have been *friends* with them, right?"

They had come to a slight rise in the path, which gave a decent vantage. Green and black hills, rumpled like bed skirts, with great gray billows overhead. Bracken and heath and stretching shadows, and here and there a bright spot of vanishing sun.

Tula gave her an open-mouthed smile.

"That's right out of clear blue, love."

"No it's not! You know about a murderer victim's dad's *job*. Somebody must know about Evelyn."

"Aye. Roberta Wilkinson," Tula said, and Jo flinched. She hadn't made a great first impression.

"Right. Yes. It's just working up the nerve to talk to her. Hell, I haven't even called the roofers, yet."

"You're joking! Jo, you *must*! We've storms all spring long!"

"I know, I know." They'd arrived at the stone steps leading up from the path to the streets of Abington. Jo already agreed to dinner at the Red Lion, but she still planned to go back to the cottage. "Can we stop on the way? I need cheese and wine from Sainsbury's."

After three soggy miles, shopping, and a lot of brisk wind, Jo was in pursuit of the pub's enormous fireplace—and a glass of something cheering. Tula had paused to hand over the groceries to Ben, and Ben had done some rather theatrical pointing in the direction of the far booths. Jo followed his mime to the back of a head, and an unmistakable flop of hair inexpertly trussed into a man-bun.

And because fate was a beast (and because Tula had just said Jo's name, loudly), Gwilym turned about to wave.

"Oh. Dear." Said Jo, but Gwilym had already bounded in her direction with the enthusiasm of a golden retriever.

"I should have called—I know it—but you said yourself, it's not *that* far to travel."

Jo wet her lips. Those had been her words, all right.

"Tula," she said, because Tula was hovering rather gleefully at her elbow, "meet Gwilym."

"Aye, and welcome!" Tula practically embraced the man. "Jo's told us *so much* about you!"

"So you see, I have an account with each one of those ancestry sites," Gwilym was saying. He went on to explain how he'd cross-referenced the Davies family with his archive, been through two library databases, and called a meeting with colleagues before deciding to come in person to Abington. But the fact he'd done it all in the last thirty hours for an almost perfect stranger meant it didn't *exactly* look like a research trip. And it didn't help that Tula could hardly keep from giggling out loud.

"That's—a lot," Jo said. Because frankly, she was impressed.

"Oh, it gets better!" Gwilym pulled out his laptop and turned it toward them. "You told me that William and Gwen Ardemore didn't have children, right? Well, the Davies family line were *fantastic* breeders. Family tree like a willow hedge."

Jo did not know what a willow hedge looked like. But from the diagram, it apparently meant lots and lots of kids.

"Every single member of the Davies family had more than five children a piece, right up to Gwen, Evelyn, and their brother, Robert." Gwilym used his butter knife as a pointer. "Then Robert had eleven children, enumerated here. Gwen had none. That suggests someone was sterile, and I sort of assumed it was William. Syphilis, you know? All men had that back then."

"Can't be true, can it?" Ben asked.

"Oh, it really is," Jo agreed. "One in three Victorians, by some estimates. And then there was all the congenital stuff, what they called saddle-face, or the stumpy little vampire teeth kids developed." Jo chewed her lip at Ben's horrified exclamation. "Erm. Sorry—I edited a series in the history of medicine. Anyway, that helps explain how my family had come into the property. I mean, we're a distant branch. But what does it say about *Evelyn*?"

Gwilym's face fell slightly.

"Not much. That's why I thought I'd come down. The best history is always local history."

So he had said. Tula rapped the tabletop with her knuckle.

"Perfect! Jo can introduce you to Abington's local historian and museum keeper. She'll *love* you." Jo gave her a panicked look, but Tula *tsked* at her—then waved her toward the kitchen.

"Look at him, lass!" she said, pointing through the swinging doors. "He'd charm Satan himself. You bring him round to see Roberta. If he can't melt her, no one can. And—there's someone on the phone for you."

"Which phone?" Tula handed her the landline, its cord stretched long from the bar.

"This one. I've got Fiennes & Sons on the line. Now order in some proper roofing before you've naught left of the mystery room at all!"

16

Wednesday

Morning arrived with MacAdams' head hammering like a woodcock on spring detail. A spotty memory of how many whiskies he'd put back before bed told him it was plainly too many, *and* he was out of Nurofen. Coffee, black. Necessary. He assaulted his machine and settled into a kitchen chair next to a semifull ashtray. Apparently, he was smoking again.

"Perfect," MacAdams muttered and got down to being especially displeased with himself.

The problem wasn't losing his case against Selkirk. He hadn't been entirely convinced of it, anyway; the man wasn't a murderer.

MacAdams' problem *also* wasn't Jarvis Fleet. In the cold light of day, what bothered him the most was how often Fleet was right about MacAdams...especially where he came up short. And *that* reminded him of Annie.

MacAdams had been considering the kitchen drapes as he thought this. They were the ugliest toile he'd ever laid eyes on. Why did he still have those? Because, as with most things, he just hadn't got round to changing them. The house he lived in wasn't a grand place. It needed paint on the outside and new plumbing within, and the radiators could stand a flushing. He didn't mind all that. He didn't mind his horrible striped housecoat complete with ash burns, either. But they were all a very present reminder that nothing about the house had *changed* since the day Annie walked out of it. Himself included.

He stood up and tugged at the fabric, blue and white with little farm scenes. The curtains had been part of an upgrade that never fully materialized—Annie's hope of turning the cottage into a country house. But this was Abington, not York. He liked it here. He liked *himself* here. And Annie—well. Annie had wanted more. Not buckets more, not millions and tennis courts and cocktail galas. Just a bit more comfort, and money, a tap that didn't leak all the time, and maybe a partner who could get behind change now and then. Some men complained of a nag; his ex-wife wasn't one of them. She urged and she appealed, and she encouraged and exhorted. And then, one day, she just got tired.

The most awful thing about MacAdams' divorce wasn't that Annie fell out of love with him. It's that she fell in love with the man he might have been, but never got round to being. That she waited seven years before giving up the ghost didn't make her selfish. It made her a fucking saint, and he missed her every damn day.

He'd also missed a crucial detail in his own present case, which should have been glaringly obvious. When it came to motive, especially in a case with undisclosed cash, he'd always followed the money. He still believed it had to be relevant, but Fleet had made a brutal point. The day of the murder: What was different? What had changed? Two things, not just one. Yes, the painting had been stolen. But that was hardly all. Jo Jones' arrival meant Sid *could no longer use the cottage.*

Selkirk had been surprised by this, too, and set Emery to

drawing up a retroactive document while he showed her about the property. Sid was already there when they arrived, and he heard from Jo herself that his keys would be demanded of him after the painting incident. He even tried to forestall the event by entreating Jo back at the pub to keep him on as property manager—and then, when that failed, trying to shame her in public, all to no avail.

Sid had one night left. That was the night he died.

"So you're saying Sid basically invited his own death?" Green asked. She and the others had gathered around the whiteboard with anticipation. And pastry. MacAdams nodded slowly, still blinking away his headache under the office fluorescents.

"In a manner of speaking, yes. It was important, this meeting. Because it was going to be the last one at the cottage," MacAdams said. "What I want to know is what made the cottage, the estate itself, so important?"

Green pushed her chair back and draped one arm over the side.

"It's out of the way. Far enough from town—or any neighbors—that no one heard the gunshots. Could make for a safe trading zone, away from prying eyes. But if it's drugs, then it's *damn* well hidden."

"Yeah, couldn't have been cooking anything up there, or storing it, either. All tests came back clean," Gridley agreed. MacAdams nodded.

"All right. So what else do you need a quiet, out-of-the-way place for?" he asked. Andrews waived a Chelsea bun at him.

"What-ab-d…" He swallowed pastry. "What about other kinds of trafficking? I mean, like…people?"

"Shit, really?" Gridley asked. "Sid?" MacAdams felt a hitch somewhere south of his liver at this idea, but Green held up one hand.

"I wouldn't put anything past Sid," she said, "and we certainly had enough DNA samples to suggest a lot of folks were around.

But—and I *only* say this because I've seen trafficked houses in Newcastle—it didn't have the right signs. None of the windows were locked on the inside, and no signs of prints on floors. People would be sleeping on every flat surface, dishes would be dirty, you'd see a lot more footprints around property, probably a lot more cars in and out. SO—not impossible. But unlikely."

"So you're in favor of the blackmail theory?" Andrews asked.

"Nope." Green swigged her coffee. "I think revenge."

"Walk us through it," MacAdams encouraged. Green walked to the board and tapped the photos of Lotte and Olivia.

"We have a cheating ex-husband and two very jealous sisters. Jealous of each other, but also violently jealous of Elsie Smythe. Her turn-up at the funeral suggests she and Sid might *still* have been an item. Or at least that he wasn't *nothing* to her. *And* there's the money he took from Olivia."

"Can we prove that?" Andrews asked. Behind him, Gridley nodded over her foam cup.

"I think we can. Green had me do a deep dive into finances. I had to go back a way, but Olivia always had the same bank. When she was still married to Sid, she took out two sizable chunks from her savings. About cleaned it out."

"Right," Green agreed. "And no deposits except what she makes from her job. It's not much. Lotte's accounts are all over the place. She works temp jobs."

Andrews frowned. "But still, there was money leaving Sid's account and going *somewhere*."

"Did you see them at the funeral?" Green asked with a side-bob of her head. "If either thought the other was getting rich off Sid, they'd have killed each other first."

"So you think they *knew* about the money, is that it?" MacAdams asked. "He's on easy street, they've been jilted?" Green nodded at him.

"You're the one who said three bullets in the back means

hatred. I think it's a revenge job, and the sisters certainly had a right to it."

It was a fair point, and she'd made it already several times. MacAdams decided to give her the lead.

"All right, Green. You take on the sisters. They're back in Newcastle, now. Andrews has the address. Press them on the cottage. Now, about the painting—"

"Are we talking about that again?" Gridley asked, wiping raspberry Danish off her shirt.

"Yes, we are," he admitted grudgingly. "We have to take it into account—it went missing the day he died. And maybe, just maybe *the painting* might have been important on its own."

"Because?" Gridley asked. MacAdams grimaced a smile upon realizing he was repeating what Fleet had said the day before. To soften it, he repeated what he'd heard from Tula Byrne.

"Ms. Jones thinks the painting might be a well-known Welsh artist, Augustus John. They sell at auctions, and some of them fetch upwards of 400,000." MacAdams rushed this part. He had looked it up on Google about ten minutes before the meeting. "But a few hours later, Sid gets shot in the back by someone he let into the cottage and had a drink with. The murderer leaves with keys, we know. But he can't get back in because Jo changed the locks. What happened next?"

Green palmed her forehead.

"The cottage gets broke into. Shit, I see where you're going with this. He can't get back in, so had to try through the window." At that point, as if on cue, Fleet came through the far door, carrying his teacup and saucer in a military march. Green carried on: "Just one problem—we know the painting wasn't in Sid's cottage."

"We know that," MacAdams agreed. "But did *he*?"

"Or *she*," Fleet said, sipping Earl Grey.

"Fine, or she." MacAdams managed to get the rest of the éclair down in one go. "Maybe the painting is the point."

Green's eyes flashed. She sat taller in her seat, too.

"Jo said the painting was like the ones at the estate house, right? Great big things in wooden frames? Surely a quick look around would have told the murderer *it wasn't there.*"

"Only—" MacAdams interrupted, "Only if you knew what it looked like. Paintings can be any size. Suppose for a minute the killer only knows he's getting an Augustus John?"

Green looked deeply suspicious.

"Thin, boss. And anyway, if Sid wanted to secrete something, it would have made a lot more sense to keep it *in* the estate house. It's big and creepy and probably full of hiding places."

Fleet turned slowly to face her—then a full quarter turn to MacAdams. "Has anyone searched the property?" he asked. "A *thorough* search?"

The answer, of course, was *no*. Because the murder hadn't happened there. Because it was a falling down heap of a building—but mainly, because MacAdams just hadn't thought it important to do so. He shook off the creeping sense of incapacity—once again.

"I will arrange for that," MacAdams agreed.

Jo wiped her brow. She'd brought gloves and a ventilated mask and a LOT of garbage bags. There was a "keep" pile, too, but it was already apparent that *most* of the estate's library was going for the trash. Jo dumped them by the armload, humming "You Never Can Tell" by Chuck Berry. It had been stuck in her head since meeting Lotte. It was her ringtone, too: picked that morning because Tula was afraid she wouldn't hear the vibration buzz while working. That *didn't* mean she wouldn't let it go to voice mail.

They had failed at the day's first mission—Roberta Wilkinson wasn't open on Wednesdays. Gwilym had offered to come help with the library cleanup, but Jo needed a people break. She also wanted some alone time in the house.

That wouldn't make sense to most people, she guessed. Above her, stretched tall ceilings that should have been magnificent. Instead, dark corners sent tendrils of creeping mold through sagging veils of cobweb. Beyond her well-lit space, the dark maw of further rooms, boarded windows, and the looming hulks of unused furniture.

Jane Eyre. Red Room. Red, red, Reichenbach. Jo tied up the latest bag and puffed hair out of her face. This was her Gothic novel; these were her pages. A nice thought, punctured slightly by fourteen shiny black trash bags—and three small (neat) piles of salvaged work. *Alfa Romeo, alphabet,* she whispered. It wasn't the wreck that bothered her, it was the waste.

Jo slid into a cross-legged position on the (recently swept) rug. If she faced away from the bookless shelves and black bags, it looked nearly presentable. Dustcovers had been removed from faded gilt-and-velvet chairs; she'd wiped down the coffee table and shined the antique lamps. Electricity had made a difference, too; bless Ben for making the appropriate phone calls (he also left her a whole box of fuses and candles for the inevitable failures). The library remained dim, drafty, and still—but all her own. And as a reward, she could finally peek at her salvaged booty.

Jo ran her fingers along the embossed leather cover. *Crime and Punishment* by Fyodor Dostoevsky; her heart gave a little leap. That was going right down to the cottage, by God. She'd also located *Madame Bovary* and Gaskell's *North and South*. Jo felt her lungs compress in a tight *squee*; it finally escaped as a delighted (if slightly manic) chirp. She'd hoped against hope she might find a Dickens, or something by Darwin. No luck. But she'd rescued a slightly stained copy of *On Liberty*, and two books by Kierkegaard. Over and over she turned the pages; they still smelled damp, but they were intact, and her eyes scurried rapidly over every word. *Savor it, savor it,* she commanded, forcing herself to skim and move to the next.

As she opened *Three Years in Pacific*, a section fell out onto the floor. She picked it up gingerly, but it wasn't part of the book itself. It had been folded like a map.

"Gardens," she said, opening the first third at the crease. In color, enormously detailed. She recognized the outline of the house's rear walls and traced her finger along the property's spreading enclosure. There—the place where she had climbed over. There—the spot Sid left the lawn equipment. But on *this* map, there were beds and borders, exotics and water features, terraces, trees, and sculpted lawns. She closed her eyes but could only see the tall weeds impeding her view, the bank of violets, and the bald scrape of Sid's careless mowing. It definitely called for closer inspection.

Jo carried the map to the table and switched on the smaller lamp. As if on cue, the house electrics flickered.

"Not again!" she begged. The flutter stabilized, and Jo let out the breath she'd been holding. She turned back to the drawings, only to find herself suddenly in darkness.

"Dammit." Jo fiddled with her flashlight and headed to the closet under the stairs. It looked a bit Frankenstein in there—not a modern fuse box at all, but knobs and tubes and an enormous power switch. Which had shut itself off. Jo considered it carefully; had that happened before? She stuck the tiny light between her teeth, gripped the switch with both hands, and heaved up. A sizzle sounded in the copper, and behind her, light once more flooded the library.

Jo peered out of the cupboard. It shone on, steady. But Jo had only just made it back to the book wall when the sizzle repeated, and she was once again without power.

"Oh, for God's sake," she hissed, and slumped onto the settee. Call an electrician? Call Ben? Call it a day? In the relative dimness, sound amplified, and she could hear the flap of the tarp presently covering the hole in the roof.

Jo let her eyes travel up to the ceiling, and perhaps because all her attention was now focused on it, she thought she heard something else. A faint tap. No. More a *skif-thup, skif-thup.*

Footsteps.

Jo froze, the sweat on her neck turning suddenly chill. She let out a shaky breath. *You are making this up*, she told herself… Jane Eyre, hearing her "peal of strange, eerie laughter echoing through the house."

But then again, Jane wasn't wrong.

She waited, listening. And the sound came again, a faint slow tapping, heel to toe. Jo sucked air, trying to think of all the things it might be—and still ending up with *a murderer in your house.*

Jo picked up the broom. It was coming from the little room where the painting had been; she was sure of this. But could someone have gotten past her, without her hearing? *Yes, you dummy, you were looking at books.*

Skif-thup. Skif-thup.

The steps continued. The roofers had been in; maybe they left something behind? *Not a metronome, Jo,* she told herself. Then again, the repeated sound might be loose plastic. Or dripping water. Did she dare turn the lights back on?

Yes. Yes, she did. Jo crept to the closet, sensitive ears straining to hear soft tap-tap in focus. Someone had broken into the cottage. Someone might be in the house with her. Just like Sid had been…

Thud, thud, thud went her heart, and she reached for the main switch, once again in it's downward position. Her fingers wrapped around it, clammy and cold—

"YOU NEVER CAN TELL!"

MacAdams hailed the uniformed officer outside Jo's cottage. "Bryce, isn't it? This your first detail?"

"No sir, I did surveillance last year. I'm used to this sort of thing." He seemed pleased about this, though MacAdams assumed his last assignment didn't involve a murder case.

"All quiet?"

"Yes, sir. Ms. Jones left the cottage this morning to clean up the big house."

Of course she did. Somehow she was always in the next place MacAdams wanted to look. But that might explain why she hadn't answered his calls. He put his hands in both pockets and headed up the hill toward the estate house—only to see Jo running full tilt *down* it.

"Ms. Jones?"

She skidded to a halt, blinking and gasping. MacAdams noted she was streaked with dust or soot, and that her shirt clung to rusty sweat patches.

"Are you—all right?"

Jo worked her mouth a moment, then straightened herself.

"Just. Fine." She did not look fine.

"Are you sure?"

"NO. I'm…?" She made some wild gestures with her arms, then hugged herself tightly. "I, uh, scared myself."

"Okay," MacAdams said gently—she looked feral and frightened. "How did you do that?"

"I hate phones. I never have my ringer on. But I did. Chuck Berry. The lights went out, and I thought I heard something. Then my phone shouted at me, and I fell down the front steps getting out the door." Jo rubbed her nose. "I thought I heard someone upstairs at the house."

MacAdams insisted on going, and Jo refused to be left behind. She's mostly got hold of herself again, and led the way back up the hill explaining as she went.

"It was probably a tarp or something—there's a hole up there," she said. "You don't have to search—"

"I was coming here specifically to get your permission to search," MacAdams interrupted. "A police search."

Jo didn't even complain. That apparently surprised MacAdams into extreme politeness.

"I'm sorry for so much disturbance," he offered. They'd arrived at her front door, which Jo hadn't relocked. She had meant to, but was too busy running away like an idiot.

"I was sort of panicking," she said by way of explanation. MacAdams just pushed the door open. The lights were on again.

"Wow. Incredible place," he murmured. Jo supposed it was, too. She was struggling more than usual to make eye contact, but she followed his gaze—up it went, to the carved wooden staircase, across the scalloped ceiling and back to the stained glass in the window above the door.

"I was in the library. Sorry about all the garbage bags."

She stepped around two of them, full to brim with rotten books.

"I was standing here. When I heard. What I think I heard." MacAdams crouched on the floor near the spot, his eyes trained upward.

"Describe it for me," he asked.

Jo hadn't had a lot of time to process, in between the phone ringing and running out of the place. She took a moment to collect herself, straightening the book piles and refolding the garden plan she'd dropped before.

"A sound like footsteps, but they didn't go anywhere. Just tap-tap above my head in the same place." *Just say it, Jo.* "I think I overreacted."

MacAdams stood and cleared his throat.

"A man was murdered on your property. Then someone tried to break into the cottage. And this place is big and empty—"

"And dark. At the time," Jo added. He nodded.

"Yes. You aren't overreacting. I shouldn't have cleared the property until we were sure the killer had no further interest in it. That's my fault. I want to bring a full team out here and search the premises."

Jo quirked up an eyebrow. This put a very different light on things; it also made her intensely curious—and simultaneously unlocked her tongue.

"You think the killer *will* come back. Why? It must be—because he is looking for—something." She turned rapidly in place, almost a pirouette. "You know it's not in the cottage because that's been totally emptied… Plus, I looked everywhere for secret hiding places. And I'm surprisingly thorough."

"Somehow I don't doubt this."

"Right!" Jo wriggled with anticipation, all former fear dissolving in light of new data. "So, what would Sid have that the killer wanted? *Oh.* He had something that didn't belong to him, is that it?"

"Ms. Jones—" MacAdams' interruption hadn't slowed her brain down in the slightest. *Sid gets shot in the back; backstabber; backstory.* If you wanted to kill someone over something they didn't even have, what was it? Information? *Forensic Files Case Study*; they published that years ago; Murder happens for four major reasons: money, love, revenge, and—

"Blackmail! Is that it?" she asked.

MacAdams cleared his throat again. "You have a disconcerting amount of energy. Do we have permission to search?"

Jo considered this. "Can you at least tell me what you hope to find?"

"Clues," he said. But he was looking at the paintings above the mantel. Unconsciously, Jo realized.

"After blowing me off, you're finally looking for my stolen painting, is that it?" she asked. MacAdams turned to face her a little too quickly. He didn't have a lot in the way of facial expressions, but Jo had spent her life studying hard for clues to read people. Even if she didn't always get it right, he was up against an expert.

"Ms. Jones, I did not say that."

"You didn't *not* say it. Also, I hate the sound *Ms.* makes. It's just Jo." Jo chewed the side of her thumb. "I'm all for the search. But you can't stop me from being here."

"We just want to stop the murderer from being here. Have you considered that you may be in danger?" He probably meant it kindly. She did not take it that way.

"I'm a grown woman, you know. I'm not helpless. Want proof?" Jo fished about in her pockets and held up a small canister of pepper spray. MacAdams squeezed his eyes shut and spun around to face the wall.

"I'm not gonna spray *you*—" she began, but MacAdams only grimaced.

"Ms. Jones, that had better be breath freshener. In fact, don't *tell* me what it is! Pepper spray is banned under the Firearms Act!"

"Since when?" Jo demanded.

"Since 1968—just *get rid of it*."

There were two blue-glazed vases on the mantel, and she chucked it in one.

"Okay, safe. But it's not an assault rifle, why is it illegal?"

MacAdams had managed a complete facial expression this time, and it was grumpy as hell.

"Why are assault rifles *legal* in the United States?" he asked. "You can get up to a year for possession of mace."

It had just dawned on Jo that MacAdams was giving her an easy out. *Breath freshener indeed.*

"Thanks. I really didn't know," she admitted.

"I figured you didn't. I'm more worried that customs ever let you in with it." He uncrossed his arms. "Now. About this light switch. If I'm sending a team up here tomorrow anyway, we could maybe have someone look at it."

It broke a tension Jo had only just registered.

"Sure. It's in this little closet thing." She opened the door to reveal the fuse box and enormous hand switch. MacAdams began counting down the porcelain fuses.

"It wasn't those," Jo interrupted. "I think there's a short somewhere. I'm guessing the surge must have thrown the switch into its *off* position."

"A surge would blow the fuses, not throw the main."

Jo had never read about electricity. An unpardonable lacuna.

"Oh. The switch must be loose? Maybe it fell down?" She closed her eyes a moment, remembering her fingers as they wrapped around it. "It had definitely been in the down position."

MacAdams let out a long slow breath, as if he were blowing cigarette smoke.

"Jo? Did you turn the lights back on before your phone rang?"

Jo felt her spine ice over.

"I—no. Maybe?" But she hadn't. She knew that. And yet, the lights were on *now*—and even if a switch fell *down*, it wouldn't fall *up*. "Oh shit."

17

"Two whiskys," Tula said, winking. MacAdams tried to push his away.

"Ah-ah—it's on the house, James. You can't *still* be on duty—be gracious, there's a lad." She patted his shoulder then hurried off, leaving them in Jo's preferred corner bench seat.

"Cheers," Jo said, clinking his glass. "I feel like a fool, to be frank. I should have known the switch couldn't throw itself. But I was on the ground floor the whole time, and the door was locked."

"Yes," MacAdams said, a little darkly.

"Oh." Jo sunk her head into her hands. "The murderer has the keys."

"We don't know that for certain," MacAdams said. Though, really. It was the only thing that made sense. Somehow, they had given up on the cottage and decided to sweep the estate house, just a day before MacAdams planned to search it. It felt like the murderer was always one step ahead of him. How?

"I just don't get it," Jo said, swallowing two mouthfuls of stew.

For a small person, she ate with absolute gusto. And there was something oddly satisfying about this. "If this is really about the missing painting, and the killer still doesn't have it, wouldn't it make sense to keep Sid alive till they did?"

This had occurred to MacAdams, and was infuriating.

"Yes. Yes it would," he admitted.

"Unless you thought someone else had it, and Sid got in the way," Jo added. "But I can't see how you blackmail somebody with a painting."

"It may not be blackmail. There are a lot of possibilities," MacAdams felt compelled to say.

"Like maybe the killer was just really, really mad?" Jo blinked at him. "Are you going to eat and drink or just watch me, because it's a bit weird."

There were times when better judgment won out.

This wasn't one of them.

"I'll have what she's having," he told Ben. With the estate roped off till morning, what was the harm?

Jo Jones liked whisky almost as much as MacAdams. By the time he got his dinner, they were both on their second round—and deep into the weeds about composite image software.

"You mean you can take the features from other paintings and not just the existing ones in the database?" he asked.

"I was trying to match the texture. Reverse image searches pay a lot of attention to detail. The algorithms don't see a face. They see bits of data. I mean, when you *read* that's true, too—you might have a whole scene in your head, but you're also processing text, a letter at a time." Jo paused for air. "Most people do, anyway. Unless I'm editing for errors, I usually take in whole words at once."

"Speed-reading?" MacAdams asked, putting his cutlery across the emptied bowl.

"Sort of. *That's* acquired through techniques like chunking, minimizing, and subvocalization"—words MacAdams had never even heard in the context before—"Basically, learning to absorb phrases or sentences or paragraphs all at once, instead of reading individual words."

"But that isn't what *you* do?" he asked. Jo had a way of scrunching up her nose, as though corkscrewing herself into being understood.

"It *is* what I do. But I wasn't taught to, so I learned it sideways. Obviously, I can't do that while I'm working. Then you have to care about the individual words quite a lot." She finished her second whisky and took a deep breath. "I think I might almost be coming down, now."

MacAdams swirled the remainder of his Talisker (neat) and considered her afresh. He'd almost forgotten how utterly unnerving all of this must surely be for her. It was easy to do: she seemed oddly unsinkable. Fleet found that suspicious, but if MacAdams were quite honest, *he* found it compelling.

"Why did you come all the way to Abington?" he asked.

"I'm pretty sure I said."

"You told me you inherited. But you don't have plans to go back. And I wondered why."

Jo leaned her elbows on the table and settled her face into both palms.

"Honestly, there isn't anything there."

"An ex, you said."

"Oh yes. Jackass. Are you divorced?" she asked. MacAdams started a bit; a bold question baldly put.

"I am, in fact. Her name is Annie. She remarried a little over two years ago. Has a kid and one on the way." MacAdams drained his glass. He shouldn't be talking to Jo about Annie. But fair questions should get fair answers.

"You don't sound bitter." Ben came to collect plates and Jo ordered another whisky. She probably shouldn't *have* more. But MacAdams had made that sort of suggestion once to Green and nearly got his head kicked in.

"I'm not. I guess."

Jo had been making fairly regular eye contact. Now her gaze shifted up to the corner above his head.

"I guess I'm not, either, about the divorce part. It's awful living with someone who doesn't actually want you to be—you. I'm bitter about the *marriage*. Maybe that's Lotte and Olivia, too." Jo chewed her thumb. "They don't seem to like each other very much."

"And yet they still live together," MacAdams said.

"You're joking? Why? To double the almondy? Alomny. Shit."

MacAdams assumed she meant *alimony*—what he would call *maintenance*.

"No. Sid wasn't the type. And he had no money." In fact, as they were learning, that wasn't true. At least, not in the last three years—he was positively flush. But Sid made money and lost it as fast; he'd not have given them a cent. Across the table, Jo made a valiant effort to sit straighter.

"No money. Steals a painting. Rupert said it's not worth anything." She sipped the renewed whisky.

MacAdams frowned.

"You told Tula it was an Augustus John."

"Oh." She rubbed her chin. "I thought. Maybe. But only saw it once. Dammit." Her lean against the table had become precipitous. "I thought—maybe—he brought it back? S'why I went to look at the cottage the night after."

"The night—after," MacAdams repeated. Jo gestured vaguely with one hand.

"Ooopsies. Hadn't meant t'tell you that."

"Jo! You went to the cottage on Thursday night?" MacAdams rubbed his forehead. That explained the shoe track. "You contaminated a crime scene!"

"Dinddnt. Did *not*. I just looked in and went right back out again!" She blinked glassy eyes. "Barely two minutes. Minutia. Mmm."

"You know I could book you for that," MacAdams said. But

he didn't get an answer from Jo because she'd just slid sideways in the booth and passed out. He sighed and raised his hand and waved for Tula.

"She was planning to stay the night, anyway," he said, hunting about for his wallet. "What's the fee here?"

"James Arthur, I will take that as an insult," Tula warned him. "She's friends, and good people, too. Let me get Ben."

"I can help." The offer had come from a weedy-looking chap with a dirty-blond bun and scrubby-looking beard.

"*You* will absolutely not help," Tula cautioned the man. "I've got the policeman—he'll do." She got one arm under Jo and lifted her out of the nook with strong arms. Then she handed her to MacAdams. "You don't mind, do you?"

He had an armful of unconscious Jo Jones. It didn't really matter if he minded or not. She wasn't particularly heavy, but not as light as he'd expected, given her size. Fitting, somehow. As Fleet might say, there was always more to Jo.

When he reached the second floor, Tula opened a dormer room.

"I should just make this Jo's room—be a dear, put her on the foldout."

"Not the bed?"

Tula gave him an indulgent look.

"I've got to get her clothes off, don't I?" she asked. MacAdams did as he was told and beat a hasty retreat. He had unfinished whisky. And his ears were burning.

Downstairs, the weedy young man was still waiting somewhat eagerly by the bar.

"You're a police officer?"

"Detective Chief Inspector."

"Wow." He sipped his beer. "That's due to the murder, then?"

MacAdams gave him a closer inspection. Very clearly not local. Welsh. And not allowed to help a drunken Jo Jones up to her room.

"You're the one she went to see in Swansea. William, or…?"

"Gwilym, actually! Same name, only the Welsh version. I deal in books and antiques. She asked me to help find a family member."

"And did you?"

"Sort of. Her name is Evelyn Davies—she's the woman in the painting. I heard you talking about it." MacAdams was forming *opinions*. In part because they discussed the painting hours ago, and Gwilym had likely been listening the whole while. MacAdams abandoned his seat, joined him at the bar, and opened his notebook.

"Your full name, please. And how long have you known Jo Jones?"

"Omigosh, am I a suspect?" Gwilym said with something a little too like glee. "I knew I wouldn't regret coming down here. Nothing ever happens in Swansea."

MacAdams put the notebook away. This was not a dangerous man.

"She's really something, isn't she?" Gwilym asked after a few minutes' silence. "I mean, you just don't always meet people like that. I bet she's neurodivergent. I have ADD, and we can sort of recognize each other. Good thing, since you lot almost never do."

MacAdams wanted to ask what he meant, despite being sorry he'd started the conversation. *Neurodivergent*—something, something spectrum disorder—

"Autism?" he asked.

"Awesome," said Gwilym. "I'm helping her with research tomorrow."

MacAdams had his own research to do. He also had to tell Green about the property incident—and didn't relish it.

MacAdams had driven Jo's rental to the Red Lion, leaving his own at the property. A lucky thing, in the end, as he had to walk off the whisky—and getting home would take him just past the row of flats Green shared with Rachel. Theirs was a ground floor end-of-terrace, with independent entrance. He paused at the bell and checked his watch…half past ten. He had just determined to call her mobile instead when he heard the latch.

"A bit late for a social call, isn't it?" Rachel asked. She wore a scrubs top with flannel pajama bottoms and blocked the doorframe like a petite linebacker—or possibly a bulldog. She waved a mug at him that read, simply, *FUCK*. "I don't like it, James."

"I'm sorry, Rachel. I won't be a minute."

Green had just appeared behind her, bending low enough to rest her cheek against Rachel's.

"Stand down, boss," she said, giving her a squeeze. Then she laughed. "*Other* boss, come on in."

"That's okay, I promised to be brief," MacAdams said. Rachel gave him the two-finger "I'm watching you" as she walked away. Slighter than Green, who most men wouldn't cross, and yet on balance Rachel was far scarier. Fireplug tough.

"We have a bit of a situation at the Ardemore House," he said to Green.

"*Now* what?"

"Nothing much. Someone appears to have been up there, though. Prowling. I stationed a guard till we can search it tomorrow morning."

"Uh-uh. Gotta be afternoon. I've got the sisters in for questioning tomorrow, bright and early at eight."

"They agreed?"

"Didn't give them a choice. I'm just trying to get them in before happy hour starts." Green wet her lips. "I'm not sure what's up with those two, but they were a long way from sober when I interviewed them today at noon."

"Smart. Night, Green—my best to Rachel."

"Always," she said with a grin. He heard the murmur of comfortable talk and laughter as she shut the door. A warm, bright space, he thought, and wished it didn't make him ache so much.

18

Thursday

Daylight. Already.

Jo woke to a ceiling that looked all wrong. She *had been* dreaming—the painting again, except it was in the cottage, and for some reason Sid's sister-ex-wives were there. Now that she was awake, she heard the clink of plates and a baby crying and street noise. Jo raised her head just slightly; yesterday's clothes were in a heap on the nearby futon. She wiggled her toes and felt sheets on skin. She was mostly naked under there, apparently. Wincing slightly, she reached her hand left across the mattress. No warm depression, so she was alone (thank God). This must be the Red Lion; yes—she remembered that part. Though most of the previous evening was a blur.

There would be no skirting the hangover. And despite shower and toothbrush and even a bit of makeup from her purse, she still bore the hangdog look that often accompanied a morning's walk of shame. Sadly, last night's clothes always looked like last night's clothes. Jo grimaced at scattershot sunshine in the stairwell and made her way into the kitchen.

"Morning!" Tula sang as she pulled a rasher of bacon out of the oven. Jo smiled squeamishly. *None of that*, her stomach cautioned. Ben's face appeared above the swinging doors.

"How are you feeling?" he asked. Tula leaned forward to kindly remove a dot of shave cream still lingering behind Ben's ear.

"She'll need a bit of toast and tea, I think." She tugged at Jo's arm. "Your Gwilym has been waiting, but I warned him to let you have the first half hour to recover."

Jo lowered herself carefully to the wicker-bottom chair; the room still felt a bit spinny and she'd only processed about half of what Tula said. Something, something, Gwilym, tea. Ben poured her a hefty clay mugful.

"You'll like this," he whispered. "It's Tula's Cure."

Jo didn't know what that meant, but given the leather hammer beating at the back of her brain, she was willing to try anything. Jo took a sip of tea and almost coughed it onto the checkered tablecloth. The second sip went better. And by the third, the hammer dulled out enough to think straight.

"What is that stuff?"

"Ireland's best." Ben winked. "Moonshine and tea. Now try some toast."

Jo blinked, a little bleary-eyed.

"Better," she agreed. "Coffee."

"How about espresso?" Ben smiled at his half-dome chrome machine *from Italy*! he'd told her. "Two shots?"

Caffeine came with a side of Welshman. Gwilym looked quite different this morning, however. For one thing, he'd shaved. His fresh face perched over a collared shirt, an actual tie, and a herringbone tweed sport coat. He wore the same glasses, but now they made a kind of intellectual statement.

"Feel okay this morning?" he asked, setting down the demitasse next to her.

"I think so, except now I might be hallucinating a professor."

Gwilym colored from neckline to ears.

"Oh, this? Well. I mean. I *was* a lecturer for a while. And a university archivist after that. Specialized on the seventeenth century."

"You were an academic for real?" Jo massaged her temples between sips of coffee. "That's why you had friends at the university."

"Correct. But, well. You might be surprised, but there isn't a big market for archivists."

Jo was not surprised.

"So you started with antiques?"

"No. That is, I ended up with them." His color had faded, but now it returned. "My aunt left me a tidy sum and a lot of household goods."

Jo nodded. Because of course she did.

"That doesn't wholly explain your new look, though," she admitted.

"I'm incognito!" Gwilym flapped his arms, birdlike. "It's archivist uniform. I'm headed to see Roberta Wilkinson."

"You know her?"

"Of her. Dynamo with agriculture texts. You should see her work in the Newcastle botanical archives. Plus, Ben warned me to be charming."

Jo didn't feel well enough to be excited by this information, but the fact that Gwilym had access to real honest-to-God research sources was definitely increasing his market share with *her.*

"Excellent," she said. "You're a much better version of me."

"Oh, you'll be there, too," Gwilym assured her. Jo dropped her toast.

"Oh."

"It's your obsession, remember?" He'd already popped out of his seat and donned an overcoat. "It's not far. We can walk."

That sounded like a terrible idea. For one thing, the sun had come out, and everything, everywhere was much too bright. Jo looked a mess, it was 10:00 a.m., and she had a raging hangover. She wondered if this were Gwilym's way of getting back at her for forcing him out of bed on a Saturday, unshaven and barefoot. Jo worked up a grimacing smile—and walk, they did.

"You and the detective are friends, I take it?" Gwilym asked as they ambled up the high street. Jo fished about her bag for sunglasses.

"Eh? Sure."

"Nice, is he?"

"Efficient and trustworthy," Jo confessed. "Not much of a talker."

"He talked a lot last night."

"You were listening?" Jo asked. She had unfortunately fuzzy memories. "Did I miss anything at the end?"

"I think you confessed to crossing do-not-cross lines," Gwilym said. Jo would have smacked herself in the forehead if it wasn't already hammering so hard.

"Crap. I didn't mean to." She paused. "I didn't mean to pass out, either."

"Tula got MacAdams to carry you upstairs," Gwilym offered. And this was even worse.

"Oh my God." Jo rubbed her temples. "That's embarrassing."

"*He* didn't seem embarrassed. I would have done it, but Tula wouldn't let me." Gwilym's tone had gone just a touch rigid. Jo gave him a hard look.

"Tula says you are flirting with me."

Gwilym rubbed at the now-absent beard.

"I *am* flirting with you."

It was hard to know what to do with this admission. Jo felt a slight flutter of—panic, possibly. It had been a long while since she'd been on the dating scene, or anything like it.

"It's probably best if you warn me in advance," she said, finally. They had just crossed the last lane. Beyond was the main road, the trailhead back to Jo's cottage, and, at the edge of town and perched on the stream: a wheat-mill-turned-museum-library. It looked charming as hell in the sunlight, even if Jo had to shade her eyes from the sparkling water below.

"Oh. You know what this means." Gwilym rubbed his hands together. "There will be *really* good stuff."

"Because it's old?"

"Nah, because its tiny. Unimportant. It's the best way to hide treasure."

Jo agreed. The trouble was pleasing the treasure-keeper.

The interview rooms at Abington CID didn't look remarkably different from your average utility supply room. Because, MacAdams mused, at least one of them did double duty that way. He'd had Andrews clear away floor cleaner and extra toilet tissue before the interviews with Rupert and Emery, however, and so the rooms were ready to receive Lottie and Olivia. They would be interviewed separately. For obvious reasons.

MacAdams poured coffee for himself and Green; he'd already ensured the sisters were caffeinated and supplied with some biscuits. He was in no position to judge, considering his last two evenings, but Olivia appeared to have one hell of a hangover.

"I'm surprised you didn't use the morning to search the cottage," MacAdams said to Fleet, who had parked himself (with tea) behind the two-way mirror.

"I'm intrigued by your theory of Sid working with an accomplice," he said. MacAdams burned his lip on his coffee.

"When did I say that?" It was actually something Jo had hinted at the night before. Fleet waved a teacup at him.

"You suggested Sid wasn't bright enough to carry out this

business all on his own. I am inclined to agree. I thought an extra set of eyes might be useful."

MacAdams could agree to that, but as he peered at Olivia through the glass, he couldn't help but feel this was *not* a criminal mastermind.

"Good morning," MacAdams said, entering the room and settling down across from Olivia. She nodded a perfunctory hello and threaded her fingers around her cup.

"I'm here. Ask your questions."

"Thank you. I don't think this will take much time, Ms. Randles."

"God." She lowered her face into her hands. "Just Olivia, for fuck's sake. You don't happen to have something for headache on you?"

MacAdams waved through the two-way glass and waited as water and aspirin were delivered—and a coffee refill requested. It pleased him to see he'd been right about the hangover. Not because he needed the confidence boost—though it did give him a gratifying one—but because it provided context for the red-rimmed eyes and slight tremor. Coupled with Green's report of day-drinking, it could mean one of two things: alcoholism, or extreme stress and strain. Both were worth exploring.

"You have many mornings like this?" he asked, knowing it would be offensive. Olivia, however, only shrugged.

"It's what, Tuesday?"

"Thursday."

"I haven't been sober since the funeral."

MacAdams pushed the packet of biscuits at her, and she took the hint. One dry swallow down and she took a long breath.

"I know what you think. And I know what we looked like at the—thing. Lotte going for your officer. You know she didn't mean it."

For all the venom he'd seen the previous week, it was something of a surprise to see Olivia come to her sister's defense.

"Tell me about Lotte."

"Why? We've got alibis, remember?" Olivia snapped the biscuit in half. Technically yes, they had alibis. But as with Rupert and Emery, they vouched for *each other.*

"I'm curious, that's all. Sid left you for her, and yet you defend her actions."

"Pfft. I didn't defend them. I said she didn't *mean* them." Olivia rubbed her palm over her eyes. "She's just a bloody berk, got an empty head. And Sid didn't leave me for her."

"He cheated on you with her, and then he married her."

"Doesn't mean anything. Sid cheated on everybody all the time, and we all knew it and learned to put up with it."

MacAdams had been married and divorced only once, and it wasn't a picnic. He decided to ask the obvious question:

"Why bother getting married at all, then?" Olivia's eyes were still watering, but she focused them on MacAdams.

"People don't cough up cash and presents for shacking up, do they? Look. I don't feel like playing around. What do you want for real, because I want to go home."

MacAdams leaned on the table, cradling his elbows.

"Okay, I'll be fair. Anyway, I've been where you are."

"Hungover?" Olivia laughed harshly. MacAdams waited until she'd quieted, then let the silence stretch a moment.

"No," he corrected. "*Grieving.* You more than the others, I think. You loved him, didn't you? Even though he took advantage of you."

Olivia's face went stony for a moment, then a quiver trembled at her mouth and jaw until a retching sob escaped. She swallowed it down with more coffee. MacAdams decided to press on.

"Is that why you wanted to arrange the funeral, Olivia? To show you were the one who cared? I thought you were putting on a show. But who for? Who did you want to impress if not your sister, Lotte?"

"She didn't love him," Olivia said, her throat catching. "She wanted him. That's all."

"She wanted him because you had him?" MacAdams asked, wondering suddenly if this was about the problems of shared ownership. Olivia shook her head, a stuttering action. She sniffed and tried to master herself.

"You don't understand the situation." Olivia blinked tears. "See, Lotte and I met him in Newcastle when Elsie was still his wife. He hung out in Bigg Market where the stag dos were, and he chatted us up."

"Both of you?"

"That's what I'm telling you. We—we *shared*." Olivia didn't strike MacAdams as easy to embarrass. But she did avert her eyes slightly before going on. "It's just a thing we did with guys, okay? Sid was fun. He was just so carefree, wild the way kids are. Like some goof of a boy. He made us laugh, you know?"

"And you fell in love with him for that?" MacAdams was partly trying to keep her talking. But he honestly *did* wonder. Olivia let out a defeated-sounding sigh.

"I don't know. God." She took another biscuit. "Nothing was ever serious with Sid. Made you feel like—like you were all right and the world was wrong."

MacAdams imagined Sid drawing Olivia into that world; the one where it's other people's fault. He could see its seductiveness.

"Go on. What went wrong?" he asked. And for the first time, it seemed Olivia was glad to talk.

"Me and Sid, we were good together. I didn't even care so much about him seeing other people, see. Elsie was jealous, wanted him all to herself. We was in bed one night, and Sid said *I should just marry you, instead.* I said *go on, then.* Why not? Left her the next day, moved in my place." A sad little smile flickered over Olivia's ashen face. "Elsie was fucking pissed. Evil about it. She sent me dead roses on my wedding. Then one day she met me at the pub and laughed in my face, saying *I'd see.* Sid wouldn't love me half so well now there was a leash." Olivia's fingers clenched into a fist against the table. "But that wasn't it at all. It was when the debts got bad."

"Gambling," MacAdams said, because it wasn't a secret to anyone. Olivia nodded.

"Little stuff at first. Lost on a horse race or whatever. He was working at the chicken farm, then, Glencroft Poultry. Part-time. I had the cleaning job and the bartending. I took a shift at the grocer. It was fine." She grimaced. "Until it wasn't."

There had been a bit of trouble. MacAdams already knew that. Partly because Sid came back to Abington for a few months to lie low.

"Some creditors aren't very nice," he said.

"They were threatening him. So—so I started paying them off. He went away awhile, laying low. And he needed money for that, too." She pushed her head into her hands, squeezing at the temples. "Us against the world, and nothing mattered, did it? I gave him whatever I had. And that was that."

"He left you," MacAdams said, trying to get the train to station. But Olivia jumped tracks.

"No. He married Lotte, sure. But he didn't *leave*. We all lived in my house." Olivia's hands were trembling. "He didn't take Lotte's money. And he didn't take Elsie's, either. He didn't depend on them like he did on me."

MacAdams should have asked, and didn't—now he had very strong reasons to know:

"Olivia, did you *pay* for the funeral arrangements?"

Olivia gave him a watery smile.

"I put it on credit," she whispered. "See? He's still mine. Bought and paid for."

MacAdams traced his steps back to the break room. There was a lot to unpack. Sid was a complete shit. And Olivia loved him—and believed he loved her, too, despite the cheating and stealing and divorce. Hell, MacAdams wanted to believe that, himself, for her sake. On top of it all, it seemed Olivia and Lotte—and maybe Elsie?—shared Sid in some as-yet-to-be-determined manner. It was messy. And it might yet have bearing on the case.

He'd left his coffee mug in the interview room and so opted for a paper cup and the grit left in the bottom of the carafe. He'd have Gridley go get some proper breakfast for the sisters, since they still had a wait, and then settled himself in front of the whiteboard.

"Does it improve?" Fleet asked, taking a seat nearby.

"Not especially." MacAdams sighed. He turned to Green, who was just coming in. "How did yours go?"

"Lotte is a very energetic person," she sat down next to him. "I am 100 percent sure she was off her trolley yesterday and continued to drink after I left. But you wouldn't know it. Bright eyed, makeup. Fresh. Very, very talkative."

"Youth, how I miss you." MacAdams sighed. "Give me the highlights."

"She and her sister might have been co-shagging Sid," she said. And while there were many, many ways of saying it, somehow this was probably the worst. MacAdams grimaced at the mental image threatening to precipitate.

"Yes, so I heard."

"I wonder if you heard in as much detail as I have. I'm all for getting your freak on, but that was *a lot* this early in the morning." Green cracked her knuckles.

"Quite," said Fleet, who had been observing both by turns.

"*But* the most interesting bit of information doesn't have to do with Sid. She knew that Elsie's brother was Jack Turner."

Fleet put his teacup down.

"As in, Jack Turner in prison at Full Sutton?"

"Yeah, we did the same double take," Green said. "They were separated as kids, grew up in different cities."

"We aren't yet sure if they kept in touch," MacAdams added

for Fleet's benefit, then back to Green—"How did Lotte figure all this out?"

"Apparently she stalked Elsie awhile, some sort of revenge for getting dead birds in the post." MacAdams made a mental note: *dead roses, dead birds.* Elsie was quite something. "But," continued Green, "Jack isn't Elsie's *only* kin. Lotte said they also have an aunt named Hannah Walker, and Gridley turned up an address in York. It's our first real lead."

MacAdams brightened considerably.

"Address?" he asked, opening his notepad.

"Bootham. It's fancy. Looks like she bought a new house a few years ago down there. It's in your phone already."

"Green, I could hug you."

"Owe me a beer." Green checked her watch. "We gonna let them go or not? Forensics is packing up to go over the Ardemore estate house in an hour."

MacAdams got to his feet and gave the whiteboard an appraising glance. Murder victim, sister-wives, five grand a month in mystery cash, a missing painting, Elsie, her criminal brother, and now an aunt in the rich suburbs...and still not a lot of connecting threads. He turned his attention back to where Fleet waited.

"You were the extra eyes," he said. "I don't see either of these two being capable of murder."

"One has a problem with alcohol, with previous for impaired driving. The other seems psychologically unbalanced, possibly manic," Fleet said matter-of-factly. "That does not rule out either accomplices to Sid's crimes. More likely than ever, perhaps. But no, we do not have evidence suggesting they are killers."

It was close enough to agreement for MacAdams, who pounced on it.

"Good. Let them go home. Tomorrow we'll hunt down Hannah Walker in Bootham. Maybe we'll pay a visit to Elsie's brother, too. *One* of them might know where she is."

★ ★ ★

"Brochures?" asked the girl behind the museum counter, hastily putting away what appeared to be nail polish.

"We were hoping to see the archive," Jo began—only to watch the girl's eyebrows climb right under her bangs.

"Oooh," she gasped. "You're the *American*. The one with the murder."

"VICKY!"

Everyone winced, even Gwilym, but Jo felt her head reverberate. She took off her sunglasses and did her best to smile at the sour little woman in tweeds.

"Roberta Wilkinson, please meet Gwilym Morgan," she said. Gwilym fairly pounced on her aged hands, taking them in both of his and pumping enthusiastically.

"I've read your compendium on Durham sluice gates," he said. "I used to be at Swansea—it's *so* good to meet you in person!"

It got better from there. Gwilym's reception could only be described as *glowing*; he showered Roberta with compliments, but not empty ones. In fact, the more he talked, the more impressed Jo became with both of them.

He'd clearly made an impression on Vicky, too, because even Jo had caught her un-subtle hints about being single and having the evening off. The only downside to this acclaim was that Roberta gave them a *two-hour tour.* Jo's headache had dulled by their arrival, but not enough to fully take in a monologue on sixteenth century farming techniques.

They had ended, however, in the botanical section—and she was surprised to find a portrait of Richard Ardemore in state above the last display, labelled with his name below it, *and* a framed garden plan like the one she'd found in the library.

"I have one of those," she said.

"Bequeathed at the time of his death, along with his entire collection on herbology," Roberta announced. Jo nodded and tried to look as appreciative as she felt.

"I'm glad. The rest of the books are more or less destroyed."

Roberta looked at her over her glasses. "As I feared. I wish I could say I'm surprised. Richard Ardemore dedicated his last years to those gardens." She sniffed. "He spoke the language of flowers."

Jo *almost* interrupted with the dictionary definition—a sort of cryptography through flower arrangement for message sending. She press-ganged the impulse into a question instead.

"Did he design the garden that way?"

"He designed the garden in sympathetic relationship with the house. Each individual plant should be studied for culture, habit, foliage, and color to achieve a practical, beautiful, and appropriate effect," Roberta said—or rather recited. Jo was sure she'd read that somewhere before. It also didn't answer the question. Gwilym took the next stab.

"But he knew William wouldn't. Knew it even *then*. No sense of tradition. You said everything was left to the library, here? By who? To whom?" he asked. Roberta swelled like a pleased pigeon.

"By Sir Richard, himself, in his will. My grandfather was curator then. The Baron knew his son would be useless, you see. William never was *true* Yorkshire. No surprise when he left town."

Gwilym and Jo exchanged a quick glance; obviously the abandonment had surprised just about everyone *else*.

"I thought," Gwilym said, taking the cue, "no one knew why they went away?"

"Pish posh." Roberta gazed down at Jo through lamp lenses. "There's no mystery at all. *William* was a spoiled and irresponsible boy who married a city girl. *She* didn't like it here, so off they went, leaving all those families without work."

"They fired the servants," Jo said to Gwilym, but Roberta interrupted her.

"AND the *gardeners*. Didn't I just tell you? No gardeners, no garden. Let it go wild, trees falling down and the walls crumbling. There was an army of gardeners under Sir Richard. Want to know more? Go ask those what suffered most—the same as tended and loved what he loved."

That was the first good idea Jo had heard since breakfast. She pulled out her phone. "Who are they? Can I meet them?" Roberta's lips formed an ironic smile, but no warmth, no joy.

"*They* are *dead*," she said, then turned back to the framed garden plans. "Just *look* at them. See there, terraces, heated water pipes to the orangery, fountains, a sunken garden, rare plants? He might have made his name on his plans, though he never drew up another. Then bang, they were closed up for good."

"When?" Gwilym asked.

"Before I was born," she huffed. "One lifetime to build a garden, one lifetime to lose it."

Jo pursed her lips and closed her eyes. *Roberta had never seen the actual garden.* Technically, Jo hadn't really, either. Not in a way that mattered, or one that made sense of the admittedly beautiful plans. Maybe there was a trade in the offing. It felt like jumping off a high dive, but she got the words out:

"You should come to the house," she said. "When I'm allowed back. I can show you the gardens."

Roberta did not suddenly warm to her, but a noticeable softening had occurred. *Stay with it,* Jo told herself.

"I haven't really seen it all myself. The police keep taking it back from me. Today they're searching it. Looking for my stolen painting, I hope."

"What painting?" she asked.

"It's a portrait of Sir William's wife's sister," Gwilym said, managing to make it sound not-weird. "Evelyn Davies. We don't know much about her, but thought maybe you might? Everyone says your family have been here for generations."

Points had just been scored by them both. Jo felt herself daring to breathe as Roberta smoothed hands against her woolen jacket.

"Thirteen generations," she said. "Farmers, all of them. Worked hard. Some of them even dug the foundations of the garden."

Oh, Jo thought. *They're all dead* hit differently, knowing that.

"I'm sorry. I didn't realize your family were the ones," she said. Roberta gave a little shrug—a shake of her wiry frame.

"Not the only ones. Randles, too. Sid Randles—he was last of *them*."

"Sid!" Jo had almost shouted it. A shock and a sucker punch to the gut all in one, it had effectively disengaged her social graces. Roberta shrugged.

"Obviously. Like his father's father." She waved her free hand toward the rear. "There's an archive—don't think I didn't keep every scrap of news, just because I didn't like the way the family turned out. You want to find something? That's where it's like to be. I'll take you down."

She led them past a small kitchenette to what appeared to be a cellar door. Roberta flipped a switch and led them down basement steps, each sinking in a slightly different direction. The windows overlooked a drop to the water below.

"Old mill," Roberta explained. "Wheel is gone now. Over there's the catalog. Other one is microfilm. You want the younger Ardemores, I expect you'll find them in the *society papers*. They liked the spotlight."

Roberta opened up a cabinet at the rear of the room and pulled out a sort of hanging shelf. On it were rows of small boxes.

"The 1900s start here," she said before ambling up the stairs again. Jo gulped air as the tension receded.

"Amazing! This is so old-school!" Gwilym ran his fingers along the row of boxes. "Where should we start?"

"William and Gwen Davies got married in 1906," Jo suggested. "That would be a big occasion." She plucked the box with the right label and handed it over. Gwilym scooped it up lovingly.

"God, I LOVE this stuff. Mostly everything has been digitized these days, but nothing beats microfilm. Check this out."

He settled himself at a computer attached to a microfiche. Jo had seen but never used one; it looked like a small copy machine.

"First we toggle a few settings," he said, then slid the glass plate out to load the film.

"Are they searchable?"

"No, we'll just have to read through them," he said, "It's going to take ages." Jo felt herself grinning. She tapped Gwilym's shoulder, then shooed him out of the way.

"I only have one superpower," she said, "but this is it. I don't suppose you could charm Roberta out of a cup of tea?"

Gwilym headed upstairs, and Jo concentrated on the little screen. It would have been *much easier* without the still-there headache, but soon she had a rhythm and was flying through the images. In the end, it didn't even take that long—and you would have to be blind to miss it. June 13, 1906, a full page spread and a wedding gown that went on for days. *Baron Wm. Ardemore weds Cardiff Beauty.*

"Vicky said she—" Gwilym began, but Jo cut him off.

"Look! Look here!" She snapped her fingers and pointed. Spreading across the bottom of the June 13 edition were the combined families of Davies and Ardemore. "That's Mr. and Mrs. Davies—I remember him from the photograph you showed me."

"I don't see Sir Richard?"

"He died beforehand—and his wife before that." Jo wasn't looking at that side of the family anyway. She tapped the screen. Gwen in her gown stood at William's side, all heavy-lidded gaze and heart-shaped mouth. Just behind her and carrying a small bouquet were the faraway eyes of Evelyn.

"That's not just her, it's the *same*," Gwilym said. "Do you still have the picture of my eBay photo?" Jo pulled out her phone and held up the thumbnail to the larger photo: a perfect match.

"That's strange," she said. "It means someone cut her out from the rest."

"That would have been a pricey photo to be cutting up," Gwilym said. Jo nodded.

"Yeah. I mean, Kodak introduced the Brownie in 1900—it's one of the first cameras that individual people could own and reload. But I'd say this was film plate, so not cheap. And you didn't get doubles back then." She added the citation on impulse: "*History of Medical Photography*, 2014."

Gwilym leaned on his elbow.

"You're like a dream editor, aren't you?" he asked. "I should have done that. In college I did a little bit of everything, instead. It's a great way to spend six years not getting a degree."

Jo chewed her lip. A cut-out photo. But it was the *rest* of the family photo they ruined and, possibly, threw away. Was she being erased or preserved?

"You said that lot of photos sold years ago, and you didn't remember who bought it. What about who sold it to *you*?" she asked. Gwilym rearranged his man-bun.

"Hnuh. Maybe? I might still have receipts, but I wouldn't want you getting your hopes up. The big estate auctions are usually put together at random. Unless provenance comes with the item, the seller isn't usually real helpful."

Jo only heard *I might still have receipts.*

"Good. Let's see if there's a lead here someplace. Someone clearly thought she was important, right? Or why frame her separately?" Gwilym didn't have a chance to answer—tea had arrived.

"Knock-knock!" Vicky rapped on the stairwell wall with one knuckle. She carried a tray down with cups and small sandwiches but handed them to Gwilym.

"It's almost three o'clock. We close shop in half the hour," she said. "And I'm free after that. By the way."

"Me, too," Gwilym offered enthusiastically. "I'm going to spend the afternoon tracing this photographer's insignia. You can just see it, here?"

Jo had taken a sip of Earl Grey and now nearly spat it out again. *That* was the line he'd used on her. Did he not see it coming from other quarters? She felt bad suddenly for Vicky, who looked crestfallen.

"You could probably get dinner first, Gwilym," she said, trying to be helpful.

"Aww, thanks!" Gwilym said—to Jo, not Vicky—"But I paid ahead at the Red Lion for board."

And Jo decided there was a sort of comfort in that.

The Ardemore estate's circular drive now hosted three blue-and-yellow police cars, Eric Struthers' minivan (with forensic equipment), and MacAdams' sedan.

"You really think Struthers needs to be here?" Green asked. "You aren't planning to find more bodies, are you?"

"It doesn't hurt to have him look at the scene. Jo's roofers will be here tomorrow, and there won't be any point looking after that."

Teams of uniform officers spread out belowstairs. MacAdams and Fleet ascended to where Struthers had already set up shop.

"A lot of debris." He pointed to the hole in the ceiling. "Jo said the painting was in here, behind the dresser. Taking a hell of a chance storing something in here—but you can definitely see where it was." He pointed to a long stripe on the floor behind.

MacAdams pulled out his notebook and consulted it.

"You're assuming someone put it there on purpose?" he asked. "Couldn't it have fallen off the wall?" Fleet answered before Struthers.

"It was originally over here, instead. Above the fireplace."

He pointed over the mantel. "The paper is brighter there, and look close. A nailhead."

MacAdams slapped the notebook against his thigh.

"So it had been in this room, hanging on the wall—then was shoved behind a dresser? That doesn't make any sense. Unless you *meant* to hide it." He rubbed a circle into his temples. "Struthers, *how* long had it been back there?"

"It's hard to say without—"

"I don't need the address, just give me the neighborhood. Days? Months? Years?"

"Not years," Struthers said. "Probably not months."

"You seem to think it's important," Fleet said, rounding on MacAdams. "Enlighten us?"

MacAdams very much wanted to but felt the idea might flit off if he didn't approach it just right. And dammit, if that didn't sound like a Jo Jones thing to say…

"Let's review movements on the day of Ms. Jones' arrival. Rupert Selkirk said he phoned Sid en route. That's the very first time Sid learned she was taking possession. Do you follow? For three years, he didn't have to worry about anyone snooping around. Now he has to give a tour."

"Go on," Fleet said, though he looked less than convinced.

"Assume, for argument's sake, that Sid *did* want the painting—it's worth money and he wants to sell it. Rupert doesn't seem to know about it, and if no one knows about it, no one can report it stolen."

"You're suggesting he took it off the wall so Jo Jones would not see it upon touring the house," Fleet asked.

"I am."

"But Ms. Jones found it anyway," Fleet reminded him. MacAdams just managed to stifle a laugh.

"Well, that's Ms. Jones for you." MacAdams couldn't imagine another soul working so hard to break into the room, then hunting about under a potentially collapsing ceiling until she found all its hiding places—nor becoming completely obsessed with the object once found.

Struthers frowned and scratched his ear with the penlight. "Problem. If he knew the painting was worth something, why not sell it off ages ago?" he asked. "Why wait till the place was about to be repossessed?"

It was an infuriatingly excellent question. MacAdams sighed. "I don't know."

"You also don't know if we're looking for a painting or something else entirely," Fleet added. This, too, was the damn truth. Maybe Sid took the painting just to get back at Jo for turning up to boot him out. Maybe he planned to sell it—or maybe he torched it in revenge. To be honest, he could see him doing either.

"Let's see if they've turned up anything downstairs," he said.

The three men descended amid a chorus of creaking beams. Green met them at the bottom.

"I had the team look for evidence of drug chemicals or paraphernalia—as predicted, nothing of note. And no trace of Sid's money exchanges, either," she said.

"No receipts? Notebooks? Paper trail?" Fleet inquired.

"Not even a Post-it note. Frankly, apart from the electric bill, that was true of Sid's flat, too. If I didn't know better, I'd think he was illiterate." She rolled the nitrile gloves off. "But I *have* been thinking about this morning. Something's not right about Lotte. Like, she *should* have been hungover."

"More like Olivia?" Fleet asked.

"Kinda, yeah. And see, I thought Lotte *was* hungover when the two women came in together. But when it was just the two of us, her symptoms vanished."

"She's younger, maybe she shook it off better?"

"Look, I've had my share of benders. You might feel better, but you don't usually *smell* better, too."

MacAdams caught her meaning.

"Lotte was *fresh*, I think you said?"

"Exactly." Green furrowed her brow. "I didn't register it consciously, not until I was here in that library. Everything has a heavy, musty smell. You can't fake odor."

MacAdams had noted the lingering scent of too much hard liquor on Olivia; she was sweating it through her pores. Beside him, Fleet was rocking slowly on his heels.

"You think Olivia drinks and passes out, but Lotte only pretends to?"

Green nodded.

"I know it's a stretch, but if she's faking the booze-up, that would put a dent in her alibi for the night Sid died."

"You think she might be our murderer?" Fleet asked.

"Maybe not," MacAdams said darkly, "She could be his accomplice, and in very real danger if the murderer is still out there."

19

It had taken a few hours to get to Newcastle from Abington, and the air had grown paradoxically warmer as the evening progressed. MacAdams opened his driver's side window, feeling the moist breath of early spring. He'd parked on a narrow street, just in the shadow of a streetlamp, lights out. It didn't offer a scenic view—three bins, one overfull, and the backside of an allotment—but he had good vantage on the house shared by Lotte and Olivia. It wasn't the best part of Newcastle, but was a lot cheerier than Elsie's concrete block. He checked his watch: half past eleven. The lights had gone out downstairs in the house; now the windows above darkened. No movement outside, and no stirring within. MacAdams adjusted himself, trying to make the seat more comfortable; he didn't relish night watch, but Green needed a break… And Rachel might never forgive him otherwise. Tomorrow, he'd put Tommy on it. He was the new guy after all.

His phone rang.

"Speak of the devil," he said.

"Should I resent that?" Green asked. "Just turning in for the night and wondered how things were brewing."

"Pretty damn dull. I have begun counting stray cats." It was also, however, good brain time. "Didn't Lotte tell us Olivia sold her car?"

"Lost her license, so yeah."

"How did they arrive in Abington?"

"By train, I'm guessing."

"Don't guess." MacAdams scratched his chin. "If Lotte *was* spending ongoing time in the cottage with Sid, even recently, how'd she get there? Was it a regular thing? There might be CCTV of Sid's trek to and from—" MacAdams didn't finish the thought. Up at the house, a door was opening. "Green, I have to go."

The front door had opened and shut. The figure on the step appeared to be locking up behind her; slim, dark-haired. Even at distance he could recognize Lotte; she leaned back and cast a furtive look at the upstairs windows. They remained dark. Lotte pulled her coat a little tighter at her throat, looked both ways, and then disappeared down the street. MacAdams counted five and started the engine. By the time he'd backed out, Lotte was about two blocks ahead and moving quickly.

MacAdams didn't want to frighten her, or to give himself away—but he *did* want a closer look. Under the streetlamps, Lotte flashed back to full color: scarlet pants, second-skin fit, and chunky high heels. She couldn't be planning to go far, surely? The street cut across a back alley, and she took a sudden hard right into the lane. *Dammit*; MacAdams passed her by—but she was headed in the direction of Arthur's Hill. He made the next right, turning on his GPS as he did so; the lane would set her out on Dilston.

MacAdams pulled up at the next stop with his lights out and waited; *four, three, two*… Movement. Lotte exited the alley but clung close to the wall. He could make out the shake of her bobbed hair as she checked the street before and behind. Convinced all was clear, she moved ahead.

And she wasn't alone.

MacAdams started. From the far side of the street, a shadow moved. He couldn't make out more than general shape, but their movements were far from *casual stroll*. Hunched, tight, keeping to the blank, empty spaces between. MacAdams could see Lotte at the end of the street ahead of the figure, silhouetted against the city apartments.

Her strides lengthened. Had she seen her pursuer? No other cross streets offered themselves between there and Crossley Terrace—but the street ended in a pedestrian mall.

Fuck. MacAdams switched on his high beams and hit the gas. The engine growled, and Lotte *ran*.

He wasn't prepared for her burst of speed, but she wasn't his concern. MacAdams banked across the street toward her pursuer as if he planned to ramp up the curb; he had one full glimpse of a black neoprene jacket, dark hair, and the briefest flash of face. A man, clean-shaven, youngish. Then he was gone. MacAdams threw the car into Park and leapt out.

"Stop, police!" he shouted, giving chase. The man had the start of him, however, through the side yard of an end-of-terrace, then up and over a fence. MacAdams managed to haul himself up in time to watch him cross the next street.

"Dammit." He dropped down; he'd have to turn around, backtracking. By then, there wouldn't be much point. He returned to the car, expecting to have lost Lotte, too. Instead, he could see her hunched against the shop door of a closed salon. She held a broken shoe in one hand, tears streaking her mascara.

"Why—*why*?" she demanded, when MacAdams knelt next to her.

"We can get you someplace safe," he panted. "I know you were being followed." Lotte's large, damp eyes stared at him in disbelief.

"Followed?" she asked, lips curling in disgust. "*You* followed me! I was running from *you*!"

MacAdams sat back on his heels.

"I saw a man," he said, trying to offer her a hand. She swatted him away.

"*What* man? I saw a car chasing me—I didn't know you were a cop till you yelled." Lotte frowned, tried to get up, failed, and finally accepted MacAdams' help. "That's why I ran down that alley."

"Lotte, a man was walking along this street, right behind you. I think he meant you harm." MacAdams scanned the street behind them; in theory, he might *still* be planning harm, and they were exposed. Lotte tottered on her single heel; the look of disgust had hardened into something he might have expected from Olivia.

"God, you pigs," she spat.

"He ran when I tried to apprehend him," MacAdams tried to explain. Lotte shook her head.

"*I* ran. And he was probably just some guy. I'm glad you didn't catch him. Probably try to pin something on him, too." She shuddered slightly. "Why can't you just leave me alone? I ain't done nothin!"

"Then why are you sneaking out in the middle of the night?" MacAdams asked in exasperation. He tried to take her elbow. "Come on. You can't walk home by yourself."

"Watch me!" she snapped. But she stayed where she was, anyhow, still cradling the busted heel. MacAdams approached and guided her into the passenger seat.

"Now," he said, backing away from the curb. "I want to know what you aren't telling me. You told my sergeant that you and Olivia weren't out the night Sid died. Will your neighbors say the same thing?"

Lotte had hunched low in the seat and was pouting fiercely. "I can go where I want—when I want. It ain't a crime."

"Lying to the police is, however," MacAdams said. "Listen, Lotte. You might be in danger. Do you understand that? If there's something you know, you *need* to tell me."

They'd come within sight of the house. Lotte sat up straighter.

"Stop here," she demanded. "Stop right here. I'm getting out. And I have nothing else to tell your lot. It's *harassment*."

She got out of the car and slammed the door behind her. MacAdams watched her stork-walk to the front door and disappear inside, thinking perhaps they should have charged her for assault against Green after all. At least that would give them leverage.

"This is MacAdams," he said when he reached the station. "I'm in Newcastle. I'm going to need someone here to watch Olivia and Lotte's place."

"Think you have a runner?" asked the sergeant on the other line. MacAdams found himself scanning the darkness on impulse.

"Not quite. I think they might need protection."

Thursday

MacAdams' sartorial choices probably left much to be desired, but he could not care any less than at present. He was on his way to York—with Fleet—as promised, to pay a visit to Elsie's brother Jack. But it was seven in the fucking morning, on three hours of sleep. The previous night had resulted in more paperwork than expected, and Fleet was lucky he'd managed to shower and shave. He had *not* managed to eat anything, however, so a petrol station breakfast off the A1 would have to do.

"You don't go to York often, I gather?" Fleet asked at the checkout. Tea for him, as usual; MacAdams with his coffee and a packet of McVitie's digestives.

"Not really," he said. Fleet's expression remained expectant. MacAdams sighed. "My in-laws live there. Ex-in-laws."

Annie lived there, too, in a nice house near a pleasant pub and in walking distance of the local primary school. Her father owned a florists' shop, and she'd taken over most of the work-a-day business when her mother got ill. Not that he'd been checking up.

"I don't know where *you* live, though," MacAdams pointed out as they pulled onto the main road. "We can stop on the way."

"Not in Bootham," Fleet said. He smiled under his brush mustache, though it lacked any warmth. "There are no wealthy aunts on my side, so city center is rather above my pay grade."

It wasn't the first time expenses had ever come up in their scant conversations, and this time MacAdams agreed.

"A bit rich," he said. "Elsie's aunt is Canadian by birth, married a Yorkshire man and emigrated in the early nineties. Elsie and Jack are blood relations to him, the now-deceased uncle. He'd been living in Canada, himself, most of their lives."

Fleet had been watching the windows, and MacAdams had the distinct impression that the wheels were turning in there.

"Do you know Jack Turner?" he asked.

"By reputation," he said. MacAdams spared a look in his direction.

"And? Were you around for the murder trial?"

Fleet's thin smile returned.

"I didn't relocate to York until after his arrest five years ago. But I am familiar. I did *not* know he has a sister, however."

MacAdams frowned.

"I'm not sure *he* knew at first; Gridley had a look at their social service records. Elsie got adopted out when Jack was four years old." In fact, MacAdams would have considered this a wild chase if not for Lotte. If she knew they were related, perhaps they were better acquainted that he first thought. "Anyway, Jack bounced around the system till eighteen, then joined the military. RAF, like yourself."

Fleet visibly bristled—one of the only times MacAdams had seen a break from the usual mundane politesse.

"The military should build a sense of service, duty, *loyalty*," Fleet said forcefully. "A sense of what you owe."

"I thought *we* owed veterans," MacAdams offered. "That's the usual line, isn't it? A debt for your service?"

Fleet took the moment to drink rather magisterially from his paper teacup.

"You are quoting the Commodore, I take it?"

"You heard him say it, too, eh?" MacAdams said. The creep of bitterness had got into his voice again, and unfortunately, Fleet was very good at noticing.

"You asked me once why I liked Commodore Clapham. Now I'm curious to know why you *didn't*."

MacAdams sighed. What good was having an expressionless face if he couldn't keep his own mouth shut?

"Bloody big estate, isn't it? You think Bootham is pricey? How in hell does a retired airman become a land baron?"

"You disliked him for his money."

"No," MacAdams said, a little hotly. "I dislike it when I can't work out where money *comes* from."

"You think it's ill-gotten gain?" The question hung in the air, because MacAdams couldn't bring himself to answer. *No*. Not really. Not even though the Commodore styled himself a Lord and made sure everyone knew it, most especially his daughter, who now proselytized on his behalf. It wasn't jealousy of luxury, though; not for all the money in the world would MacAdams be that pompous.

"Do you know what I believe, MacAdams?" Fleet asked.

"I'm sure you'll tell me."

"You have a curiously antique sense of just desserts," he said quietly. "It doesn't trouble you that Ardemore House belonged, unearned, to the gentry—or that a diminutive American has inherited it by blood alone. But you disdain a man who made his own money and spent it on the same sort of estate."

MacAdams did not like this theory one bit. Mostly especially because it hit a little too near.

"So you think I'm a hypocrite?" he asked. Fleet looked out the window, then folded his hands neatly in his lap.

"I *think*," he said, "that you've missed our turnoff."

Part of Her Majesty's Prison Service, HM Full Sutton operated as a maximum security facility, which meant it housed some of the most hardened and dangerous criminals. And yet, it nestled in the bucolic landscape outside York, separated by farm fields with rows of trees meant to hide the premises.

"Over six hundred prisoners," MacAdams murmured. "And expansion plans."

"One of ten thousand proposed by the Prisons Minister," Fleet added. MacAdams knew about the proposals; plenty of complaints were lodged against it, too. The idea—that large prisons somehow meant fewer reoffenders—sounded a bit American to MacAdams. As far as he could tell, it wasn't working out so well over there.

"Seems like overkill. Do you have the file Andrews gave us?"

Fleet turned in his peculiarly military way, a ninety-degree that put him face-to-face with MacAdams.

"I left it in the car. Turner is serving life for voluntary manslaughter. Five years into a twelve-year sentence, and unlikely to be released on good behavior."

"Charming. Let's see if he can tell us anything about Elsie."

Fleet led the way, and soon the two of them waited in a long white room bisected with a beige stripe.

"Incarceration decor applies psychological principles to color choice," Fleet said, as if that were foremost on MacAdams' mind. "It's supposed to act as a calming influence."

"It leaves a lot to be desired, if that's the case."

"Because you don't feel its effects?" Fleet rapped the table softly. "Of course, you aren't the target audience."

"I bet no one asks the target audience, though." MacAdams shrugged off his coat and slumped into the nearest chair. He could use another coffee. And an actual meal. Fleet, thin, razor-sharp, and straight-arrow, seemed above such human needs. He did sit, but always as though he would rather be standing.

Jack Turner entered with a determinedly recalcitrant air. In his midfifties with a complexion pocked here and there from long-ago acne and dark hair with no signs of thinning, he managed to look younger than his years. That offered some family resemblance to Elsie and added to it were the slate gray eyes and turned up nose. Otherwise, Jack had a face like a brick, and presently looked like he'd be happy to put it through MacAdams' window. The guard walked him to his chair and tugged at the cuffs resting against his jumpsuit.

"Do you want him loose?" she asked. MacAdams nodded.

"I don't see why not."

"Don't expect a thank-you," Jack said before slumping into his seat. He wasn't looking at MacAdams, though. "Wot's this, two of you, now?"

"I am DCI MacAdams, and this is DCI Fleet," MacAdams said.

"Yeah? You work for *him*, or he work for *you*?" Jack clearly had a tendency to spit his words. It wasn't pleasant. MacAdams opened his mouth to answer, but Fleet got there before him.

"We do not work together at all," he said in a voice that probably made RAF cadets jump to attention. "I am following the detective's lead as he pursues inquiries into the death of a man in Abington. That is my only role. And your only role is to answer *his* questions. Is that understood?"

Jack sucked his teeth in silence, eyes darting and furtive.

"You—wanna ask me—about a murder?" he asked. MacAdams shook his head.

"No. I want to ask you about your sister, Elsie. We'd like to know where to find her."

Jack sat back in his chair. He seemed utterly impassive, or would to most people. MacAdams had an eye for subtlety, however, and at the moment, a ripple of emotion seemed to be fighting its way to the surface of Jack's brick wall face.

"You expect we talk regular, is that it? We don't. We ain't family like that."

"When was the last time?"

Jack shrugged.

"Holidays?" MacAdams pressed, and this time Jack let out a harsh bark of laughter.

"Shite, you think? Got herself adopted, heard she got married, probably lives someplace real cozy. But I wouldn't know, would I?"

"She did get married. To Sid Randles. Do you know him?"

"Knew his face, like," Jack said, though he kept darting glances at the now-silent Fleet. "Wot's this about?"

"Sid Randles has been murdered," MacAdams said flatly. "And so you can see why we might want to get in touch with Elsie."

It was a touch misleading, yes, but these *were* the basic facts. Jack stared a minute, a slow turn of gears. Then, he leaned forward toward MacAdams.

"I need a smoke."

MacAdams dug into his pocket for the emergency pack.

"I've nothing to light with," he confessed, handing it over. Jack just took the whole pack and tucked it into his jumpsuit pocket.

"Well. I'll be sure to think of you when I light up later," he said. "You say Sid's been murdered. Elsie in trouble or something? Wot you really wanna know?"

MacAdams took a breath. He wanted to know where Elsie was hiding. He wanted to know whether Elsie might be a victim among victims…or the perpetrator of a murder. But he felt in his gut that the answer to both began with the five thousand pounds Sid had been collecting in secret—*from* and *for* whom. It was an out-on-a-limb hunch, but he'd paid his last pack of cigarettes and might as well aim high.

"I want to know who Sid was blackmailing."

Jack froze up, a calcification of shock. MacAdams kept his eyes upon his face, looking for giveaways.

"Sid?" he asked. "I don't—don't see it. Sid couldn't—"

"You seem very sure." Fleet's words fell cold on the metal table, and MacAdams mentally throttled him for it because the interruption worked a sudden change on Jack. He looked square at Fleet and announced:

"I don't know nothing about it. But if Sid was blackmailing somebody, then he got what he deserved, that's all." Jack was looking at the guard, now; MacAdams felt the moment slipping away.

"What about Elsie, Jack?" MacAdams asked.

"What about her?"

"Might she also think Sid deserved it?" he asked. "Did she have a reason to want him dead?"

He thought this would get traction. Jack, however, had lost all focus.

"Dunno, do I?" He trailed off. "Look, is that all you want or what?"

Fleet unclasped his hands.

"You are absolutely sure there's nothing else you'd like to tell us, Mr. Turner?"

"Absolutely sure," Turner repeated slowly. "I got nothing to say, 'cause I don't know nothing. Hell, I been in here, ain't I?" He stood up and held his hands out to the guard, who stepped forward with cuffs. While they were so engaged, Fleet stood up to go, and MacAdams intended to follow. With one detective out of the room and the other's back turned, however, Jack had a fit of venomous courage.

"Trying to pin something else on me, eh?" Jack spat for real this time, right at MacAdams' feet. "Bent fuckers, all of you. Bent and dirty."

MacAdams tipped the hat he wasn't wearing:

"Cheers, Jack," he said. "Enjoy the smoke."

The ride to Fleet's place in Stamford Bridge was a quiet one. MacAdams, because he was lost in thought, Fleet, because MacAdams kept ignoring him. Blackmail hit a nerve for Jack, or seemed to shock him, maybe? Murder, by contrast, hardly interested him. Then again, he was already serving a sentence for unlawful death. MacAdams shook his head. There were connections. He just didn't see them. Once again.

"Left here, please," Fleet said.

MacAdams stopped in front of a brown-brick facade in a row of squat terraced houses.

"A duplex, is it?" MacAdams asked.

"Very spacious, however." Fleet unbuckled the belt. "I'm sorry the interview was something of a waste, but you may as well enjoy your time in York."

MacAdams did not, as a rule, enjoy York. But that was mostly the lingering sepia of personal tragedy. *Mostly.* The city center always looked a bit like a BBC historical production. The Shambles, where the buildings were so old that windows bowed and eaves pitched sideways, leaned into York's foundations at a tilt. In summer, you could scarcely walk the narrow alleyways for the crush of tourists, half of them flourishing props from the numerous *Harry Potter* knockoff shops. It just didn't appeal. At least it was a quiet Friday, the cold damp keeping most everyone indoors. MacAdams had parked up in Bootham Row and satisfied himself with a brisk walk—to the florist on Davygate.

He had a reason, he told himself: ask about the funeral flowers. But walking through the door anointed him with the unmistakable green smell of stems and cuttings, and for a moment he'd fallen backward about five years.

"James! I don't believe it." Annie stepped through with an armful of hothouse begonias. She laid them on the counter, which revealed the apron stretching over a heavily pregnant middle. "You should have called ahead—we might have met Ashok for lunch!"

She'd invited him before. And to dinners, too. And Ashok was, in fact, an entirely pleasant human being. But as usual, MacAdams felt a wave of uneasiness around such kindnesses.

"Business and not pleasure, I'm afraid," he said. Annie brushed pollen out of auburn hair.

"Not just checking up, then?"

"I never check up."

"You are a perfectly terrible liar, James MacAdams." Annie leaned upon the counter. "So, what can a humble florist do for you today?"

She was right. He was a terrible liar, at least when not specifically on the job. And he felt foolishly relieved to have the pleasantries over.

"I suppose you heard about Sid Randles' death?" he asked. A soft crease appeared between her eyebrows.

"The odd-jobs fellow, I remember him. Didn't he do some gardening for us once?"

MacAdams winced; he had—and kept calling Annie *sugar-pet*.

"That's the one," he said. She gave him a gentle smile.

"You knew him pretty well, didn't you?"

"Apparently not, as it turns out." MacAdams sighed. "Right now, I'm trying to track down Sid's first ex-wife, and she bought lilies for the funeral. A lot of them. She didn't get them in Abington, and I'm beginning to doubt her Newcastle address."

"It really *is* business? I can't decide if I'm honored or not." Annie tapped at the computer screen. "I'm sorry to say there have been a lot of orders, and lilies for funerals aren't unusual. It could take a while."

"I figured. If you sort out who bought them, can you give Jo a call?" MacAdams said.

"Jo?" Annie asked, and only then did he realize the mistake.

"Not her. Sorry. *Green.*" He'd not even been thinking about Jo, dammit. Why had *that* come out? "Call Sheila Green. I have her number if you need it?"

"I don't need it." Annie's lips curled to a lopsided smile she always wore when she had the upper hand. "So, who is this *Jo*?"

MacAdams' expressionless face did its best Easter Island.

"Just part of the case, that's all. Jo Jones owns the cottage where Sid was murdered—she found him, in fact."

"She. Hmm." Annie tapped her chin with an index finger. "You don't normally get your suspects and sergeants confused."

"Annie..." MacAdams rubbed his forehead. "It isn't like that."

Annie came around the counter. Then she reached up and straightened his mussed coat collar.

"Have you considered, James, that maybe it *ought* to be like that? With somebody? At some point?" She took a step back, as though admiring her handiwork. "It's time, you know."

"You'll give Sheila a call for me," MacAdams confirmed. Annie just smiled.

"Of course."

"And you won't ask her about my private life?"

"This time?" Annie winked at him. Then went back to arranging begonias. MacAdams took leave, noting with some dismay that his body temperature had risen and that he had very possibly been blushing.

Did he still love Annie? Sure. Who wouldn't? Did he want to still be married to her? He didn't, and sometimes wondered why not. They stayed friendly. But it tended to be MacAdams that put up the barricades and maintained the distance, so much so that he'd only seen her daughter, Daya, once, and she was nearly two, now. Maybe it was the sense that Annie wanted what was best for him...like solidity and comfort and smart decisions and a *plan*. Should be desirable qualities in a mate. But somehow it wasn't, not for MacAdams. If he had to look it squarely in the face, maybe that was why he liked Jo Jones. Unsinkable, half-cocked, wholly impractical. But unfettered, too. And very likely to get him into trouble.

That should *not* be attractive, he told himself. It was, though. It really was.

He'd managed to think-walk his way into Bootham, and now stood at the end of a stately brick terrace. The last home bore the correct numbers. Stone steps, a hedged front garden, two—maybe three stories. Judging by size, at least three bedrooms. Hannah Walker had done very well for herself, indeed. He approached and prepared to ring the bell—when the door swung open, and he was nearly knocked sideways by a woman hauling two overstuffed bin bags.

"Oh!" Her mouth hung open a moment, a perfect oval of shock in pink lip gloss. MacAdams had a shock, too, but recovered first. He didn't offer to take her burden, however. He merely displayed his credentials.

"Hello, Elsie. We've been looking for you."

20

Jo pulled into the drive behind a large Fiennes & Sons work van. She'd slept in and let them get a good head start, but it was still surprising to see the scaffold nearly put together already. Largely freestanding, it reached all the way to the mystery room window, and two burly-looking fellows were busily attaching one more level to reach the roofline.

"They didn't waste any time!" Ben was just climbing out of his Scout; he'd offered to help cart off the debris she'd bagged before. "And the fog is burning off. Should be decent weather for it."

Jo saw no sign of fog burn off. She'd come prepared with a fuzzy brown sweater under her raincoat, and it hadn't been overkill.

"I hope so." Jo pulled a couple of paper sacks from the back seat—lunch provisions—but paused at the open front door. "I'm a little worried about going in, to be honest."

"Maybe you should get them to send the uniform back up

here, like they have at the cottage?" Ben suggested. He'd got the wrong end of the idea, though.

"No, not because of *that*," she assured him. "It's their presence that bothers me. A *lot* of people were tramping around in here yesterday. And now there are big-footed roofers, too. It just…it's a lot."

"Oh." Ben balanced the sacks on top of another load of supplies while Jo opened the door. "They didn't find anything, though, did they? The police?"

"No paintings. No money hidden in the walls."

"No skeletons in closets," Ben added. Jo shook her head.

"Nope." That would at least have been interesting. The front hall smelled a lot less of rotting books and a lot more like sawdust: an improvement. The parlor table had been pressed into service as a way station for the roofers. She could see pale footprints tracking up and down the stairs in pine dust and felt the impractical urge to sweep what would just get dirty again.

"I worry I've let them get too heavy," Jo said, giving the smaller bag a tug. She could drag that one. Ben lifted the biggest and steadied it against his shoulder.

"Shame about the books," he said. Jo bit her lip. He had scarcely any idea how *much* of a shame. All those gorgeous gilt covers, the heavy paper so much sturdier than what was printed presently.

"It's tragic," she agreed. "But this place *is* tragic."

"Haunted," Ben said, but Jo shook her head.

"No, that's not right. Haunted would be full of *something.* Ghosts and memories, at least. This is—worse. Hollow." She'd been fighting off a growing sense of disappointed anger, mainly toward her mother. *Don't think ill of the dead*, she cautioned herself, but the feeling remained, like a pulled thread threatening to snag wider. "I mean, the place gets abandoned twice—first by the Ardemores, and then by mine. The way Roberta talked about it, the staff cared more than any of the inhabitants, at least after Sir Richard."

"Well, they were from here. I mean, you can't abandon it if you've no place to go." Ben had stepped out the front door; now he leaned back in. "There's a skip out here—think we could use it?"

Skip meant dumpster and, Jo realized, would save them from hauling loads off property. It also meant interrupting men at work.

"We can but ask," she muttered.

The hallway echoed with voices and banging, and Jo resisted the urge to cover her ears. Light flooded out from the narrow door; her mystery room had four full-grown men in it, throwing off all sense of proportion.

"Wow, that *is* a hole," Ben said. Jo stifled a gasp; what had been a ragged foot-wide slash over the rear-facing window was now an open rectangle through which a grown man could climb. Had climbed, in fact. Because his arm had just reached through it for a hammer.

"It's...much...bigger," she said, blinking dust. An older man, shorter than the others and grizzled about the beard offered her a calloused hand.

"Ms. Jones ? I'm Fiennes Sr. 'Tis bigger—had to cut out a lot o'rot."

"Oh." She shaded her eyes and looked up. "New beams?"

"Aye. Sistered them" Fiennes began, and Jo jumped at the word, "to this big 'un." He tapped the enormous beam that plugged into the brickwork of the chimney. *Ah. Of course.* With the addition of skylight, Jo could see the difference between wet and dry woodgrain.

She could see something else, too.

Words.

"There's writing up there," she said. A slant of letters, possibly carved. She walked just beneath it, forgetting the others crowding about her. "You see that?"

"I can probably reach it," Ben offered. They'd taken the furniture out, but he just caught hold of the beam itself and pulled himself up like a gymnast.

"Capital letters," he grunted, dropping down again. "E and I think a G."

"Initials?" Jo asked, then, more excitedly, "Code?"

Ben's reply was cut off by shouting from the roof. A moment later and a bearded face appeared in the hole above.

"The fog's lifted, Da—and there's something to see up here!"

The elder Fiennes moved the ladder from the joist to just beneath the hole. He disappeared in seconds, shimmying up like a squirrel. He was down again in a moment.

"Ms. Jones? Oi, you want to have a look, *you* do."

"I don't think—" Jo managed, but Ben was already up and through like some sort of British Olympian. He reached his hands back down, presumably to help Jo follow. Her stomach didn't just churn, it heaved.

"Would you rather come out through the window and climb the scaffold?" asked Fiennes Sr., and probably he meant to be helpful, but that was the worst idea she'd ever heard. She opted to take hold of Ben's hands, instead. One rung, two—and then a heave upward from darkness to bright light.

Ah shit. The horrible swooping feeling hit her immediately. Jo squeezed her eyes shut to stop the ground rushing up to meet her. *Conflict between vision, vestibular, and somatosensory system*, she assured herself. It didn't help much. Ben meanwhile had just let out a long, low whistle.

"Damned impressive, isn't it?" the roofer agreed, and with that kind of encouragement, Jo opened her eyes. *Look up first*, she told herself. Sky, which had started to turn blue. Then a little lower, she saw the broad sweep of North Pennine hills, and a patchwork hedge of yellow and green where fallow fields were coming up spring. And then, against her stomach's protests, she looked down.

"Wow."

Roberta had told her about Ardemore gardens. Jo had seen the plans. She had measured the length of the stone wall and done the math. Hell, she had even been *in* the garden, albeit at weed level. But nothing, not a damn thing, prepared her for such a view. Arrayed beneath her was the living embodiment of the drawing she'd found in the library: sweeping terraces, labyrinthine walls of stone, trees of every variety marking off separate plots of overgrown garden, copse, fountain—and a yew hedge and stone wall all round. She could see some color, too, just starting in the undergrowth: a gentle wave of blue. *Violets.* Jo leaned slightly further, gripping Ben's arm hard enough to leave marks.

"How?" she gasped. "I mean—that's like something from *Gardens of the National Trust*!"

"Messier, but yar," Ben agreed. "You own the meadow and those trees behind the cottage, too, don't you?"

"I think so."

"Well, see that ribbon there, running through? That's the trail you walked with Tula."

"*All that* is Richard's garden?" Jo shook her head. No wonder he impressed Roberta, with her love of horticulture. It meant something else, too, though. Jo might be house poor—but surely she was land rich? She could maybe sell some bits of it away and fix the sagging house…

"Watch it!" A loose slate suddenly rattled down the side and over the edge. It hit the drive below with a distant shattering sound, and Jo's knees went weak. *Solstice, solipsist, sssshit—*

"BackInBackInBackIn!" she squealed—and in fact Ben nearly had to carry her through the opening. Her whole body had simply seized up.

"I, um. Don't do heights well," Jo said when they had returned to the car. Ben didn't laugh at her. It was an excellent quality. He did pour her some cocoa from the thermos she'd brought. She sipped slow, till she could feel her heart settle. Then she sighed.

"I forgot to ask about the dumpster."

"S'right, I'll pop back up and ask," Ben said cheerfully. "Maybe get a photo of those letters for you."

"Oh! Yes. EG, you said?"

"Yeah, but not like that. It was E, a plus sign, G."

Jo felt a thrill run down both arms and benumb her fingertips.

"Like—like lovers? Oh gosh. You know what this means, don't you? Evelyn must be E. Oh my God."

"What's the matter?"

"She was really *here*. I mean, she must have lived here, with them." Jo felt strangely dissociated and clutched one hand against the stonework for support. Not just a painting, not just a photo, and not a figment of Jo's imagination. "Evelyn lived with her sister. Just like the ex-Sids." She was doing it again—connecting dots that might not be connected. But she didn't care. A sort of rush was coming over her synapse; it felt euphoric. Everything about the place was *sistered*, wasn't it?

"Way out here? A lot less lively than the Davies' home in Cardiff, for sure," Ben said. Jo nodded appreciatively.

"Tula said something like that. Maybe she had a lover and no one approved, so she was sent off to the countryside." She tapped her chin thoughtfully. "Let's get these bags hauled away. I want to get back to Roberta's museum."

Gwilym was, of course, already there. Jo climbed down the precarious mill stairs, still picking thistle burrs from her sweater hem. He waved a worn-looking library book in her direction (without taking his eyes off the screen).

"Guess what? *Cysts!*"

Jo blinked at him.

"As in sac-like pocket of membranous tissue?" Brain citation: *Medical history, second series, volume one.*

"Yes, ma'am. Doctor's casebook, from a practice right here in Abington. Here." He spun about and flipped the pages to *case 36*. "G. A. née D. is the patient. And I'd bet real money that refers to Gwen Ardemore, previously Davies."

"A medical record!" Jo repeated, her eyes growing wider with interest.

"Yeah. The diagnosis is hard to parse, but the symptoms suggest something major. Ovarian cysts, I think."

Jo sank into the chair and opened the careworn covers. Typeface, Garamond—or like it. Dark and light, they had a taste and a feel. She could feel her heart racing a little as the words slid through her brain—page, after page, after page. The words came together like a Rubik's Cube; a piece from the text would float out, find its mate in her memory of other works, attach, reform, change color.

"Are you actually reading it that fast?" Gwilym asked, and Jo jumped out of her skin. She'd forgotten he was there.

"Yes—erm. I know, it's a bit—"

"Amazing." Gwilym turned his chair about to face her, hands on his knees. "I could just watch you doing it! Hell, I don't know why you even need me here!"

"Partly because I can't be in two places at once." Jo frowned. That was the dream; she could get through whole libraries like that. But she thought to close the book and focus on Gwilym. "Sorry. It's good to have an out-brain, that's why I need you. Tell me your theories."

Gwilym seemed extremely pleased by this.

"Sure thing. See, I think there was baby trouble. The Ardemores weren't great breeders, right? I said it might be William and syphilis. But now I don't think so. If G. A. is Gwen Ardemore, then she must have been having fertility issues because they try all kinds of odd remedies. Even the rest cure."

"But that's for hysteria?"

"Ehm. Well, her physician seemed to think her infertility was…you know. All in her head?"

Jo recoiled.

"That's horrible."

"I know. I feel dirty saying it. But it could explain why Evelyn turned up. If Gwen has ovarian cysts and is either ill or on bed rest or both, Evelyn might have come to *help*." Gwilym swiveled back to the microfilm reader, scratching at new stubble. "This is pretty intimate business, and you wouldn't necessarily want the servants to know."

Evelyn as a nursemaid simply had not occurred to Jo. She rolled the idea around her head.

"Thing is, there are plenty of newspaper mentions of William, and several mentions of Gwen at garden parties. Nothing on Evelyn. I wonder why not?" Jo weighed this against her connected dot notions.

"Okay. What if there are two things going on at once?" she asked. "Her sister is ill, *and* she might have been sent away by her family. Perhaps she had a disreputable lover. We found some carved letters on a beam at the house."

"An Arborglyph?" Gwilym asked. "Like lovers?"

"Think so. It's E + G. It could be Evelyn plus Gwen, of course. A sisters' pact. But that seems slightly strange when one of them is married, doesn't it? G could be Gordon, or George. We just have to figure out who."

Gwilym mussed his hair and gave her a grin.

"Do I feel another extensive search coming on?"

"You hunt the books," Jo agreed. "And I'll read them as fast as I can."

21

Elsie Randles stood as if transfixed, eyes wide. She also bore the distinct look of being caught with her hand in the till.

"May I come in?" MacAdams asked. For one brief moment, he thought she might say no. Then she relented.

"I guess," she muttered and led the way. It gave MacAdams a minute to disguise his own sense of shock. Elsie was wearing a pressed suit of fine wool, double-breasted. She suddenly required refitting into his brain.

"Spring cleaning?" MacAdams asked of the bags, misshapen and jagged at the edges. She deposited them on the sofa, then sat between them.

"Donating to Oxfam." After a pause: "For my aunt. She's traveling."

MacAdams sat in the nearby armchair, though she hadn't asked him to. It wasn't just the suit and the surroundings; Elsie looked wholly *different*.

"Enjoying the view?" she asked and lit an unfiltered menthol.

"It's a very nice house," he admitted. "And I wasn't expecting to find you in it."

"Ain't a crime, is it?" Elsie blew smoke, and with that her face resettled into more familiar lines. "What do you want?"

"To begin with, I would like your statement. About Sid's death."

"Can't help you. Wasn't there."

"Where were you, then?" MacAdams asked. Elsie leaned against the sofa arm and flicked ash into a nearby ceramic dish.

"With a man."

"Can he vouch for you?"

Elsie might be sporting pastels, but the look she just gave him was lurid. She recrossed her legs, rather suggestively, and leaned forward.

"Depends on what sort of checking up you want. Knows me inside and out." She snapped back. "And no. I won't give you his name. Client privilege."

"It's important we check every alibi. To eliminate you from our inquiries."

"Eliminate me, then." She took another drag. "You think I'd come to his funeral if I murdered him?"

"Some murderers do."

"Fuck them. And fuck you. And fuck your groveling little town and *especially* fuck that drunk and her sister."

"Yes. We spoke to Olivia and Lotte already."

Elsie's eyes glittered like hard little gems.

"I'll just bet," she hissed.

"They say you never stopped seeing Sid. Is it true?"

Elsie drew her knees in and stubbed out the cigarette. She rocked gently, her face twisted away from him. When next she spoke, her voice was higher, strained.

"I last saw Sid *in a box*. And you cops, you bent motherfuckers, what have you done about it? Listened to a sob story by those greedy bitches?" She stood up and paced, hip bones and elbows at angles. "Because you hate women like me, don't you?"

MacAdams knew better than to take that bait.

"And what kind of woman is that, Ms. Randles?" he asked. She stared down at him, imprisoned in her aunt's armchair. Then she swept her gaze about the room, as if to say *not the sort of woman who lives in a place like this*. Finally, her eyes settled on the bin bags, which MacAdams strongly suspected were pilfered from Aunt Hannah and meant for the pawnshop.

"I think you'll find charity don't begin at home," she said. "And I think you better get out."

MacAdams stood to go, though he paused at the threshold.

"Ms. Randles, were you aware that someone was paying Sid almost five thousand pounds a month?" he asked.

Elsie's lips hardened around prominent teeth.

"Proof there's bigger fools in the world than me," she said. And then she shut the door in MacAdams' face.

It was late by the time MacAdams got home—alone. Fleet had decided to sleep in his own bed, run errands in his own car, and promised to return the next day, early. More than fair; he'd been in Abington a week and deserved to have a Saturday night to himself. MacAdams got as far into dinner plans as pouring a glass of Highland single malt when a knock sounded at the door.

"It's open, Green," he said.

"Hi—um, it's Jo?" She stuck her head in, comically disembodied, and held up a takeaway bag. "It's a meat pie. From Tula."

MacAdams had questions. But instead of asking them, he led the way through to the kitchen. Jo kept talking.

"Your sergeant came to the Red Lion for dinner with her girlfriend and said you would be having whisky for dinner otherwise." She paused. "She gave me your address."

MacAdams was treated to the unusual image of Tula, Sheila,

Rachel, and Jo in cahoots over his gastronomic choices. He gestured to the kitchen stool.

"Have a drink?" he asked.

"If you're not worried I'll pass out and have to be carried home, sure." Jo pinked slightly, but possibly not as much as MacAdams just had. He busied himself by fishing for ice in the freezer while Jo unpacked the takeaway. Two portions.

"Forks?" she asked.

"Second drawer to the left." MacAdams winced, trying to recall what else he'd crammed into that drawer, and handed her a whisky. Jo clinked her glass to his and took a good look around.

"It's nice," she said.

"I know it doesn't do first impressions," MacAdams admitted. "But it grows on you."

"Oh, I wasn't being polite." Jo leaned on her elbows on the counter. "The kitchen faces the front room and has a window. And it's tidy."

MacAdams unconsciously looked for untidiness, happy he hadn't left pants on the radiator or something. He settled into the other stool and opened the dish—only now realizing how hungry he was. A greedy noise escaped him that might've been a little indecent. Jo wouldn't have noticed; she'd just taken a large bite, savored it loudly, and followed it with a sip of whisky in the most uncultured way possible. MacAdams almost relaxed. Enough, at least, to ask about what she'd been up to. Jo responded by reaching into her bag.

"Reading." She lay a stack of paper on the counter. "I suspect foul play."

MacAdams paused over a bite of beef in pepper gravy.

"Again?"

Jo giggled inappropriately.

"Yes? It's ridiculous, I know. Just a story I have in my head based on tiny little clues."

MacAdams swallowed, then did his best to approximate a smile.

"That is the whole of detective work," he told her. And it wasn't far wrong. Jo considered this, shrugged, and went on.

"I'll tell you. But don't laugh." She took a breath. "I think Evelyn Davies was shy and not as traditionally attractive as her sister. Maybe in her shadow a bit, too. But she had money, so she'd have been bartered off one way or another into marriage. Her dad was something of a social climber."

About her mystery relative. MacAdams congratulated himself for catching up *in medias res* and topped off her whisky as encouragement.

"But! What if Evelyn didn't want to oblige? Maybe she took a lover her father didn't approve of—so he sent her away to the married sister. You know, keep a low profile, keep her out of the society pages, basically hide her away so the lover doesn't find and rescue her like 'Copper Beeches.'" Jo was kicking her foot as she spoke, tap-tapping the side of the chair. Now she paused, and the embarrassed look came back. "That's a Sherlock Holmes story."

"I'm aware." MacAdams picked up his whisky glass and swirled ice. "Here's another story. Two sisters married the same man. He horribly mistreated each of them. Yet neither likely wanted him dead—in fact, one seems to still love him. I can't figure out why, and that's apart from sorting out his murder."

"We each have a problem with sisters," she said.

"And foul play for your mystery is?" MacAdams asked. Jo bounced the takeaway container with her fork.

"With the help of Roberta and Gwilym, I've found a birth record for both sisters, but a death record for only Gwen—and not another mention of Evelyn ever again. People don't just vanish. Not even in 1908."

MacAdams appreciated the sentiment, even if he wasn't sure

he agreed with it. People *did* vanish. Otherwise, it wouldn't have been so hard to pin down Elsie Randles/Smythe.

"You have one advantage," MacAdams said, clearing away the dishes. "Even if your Evelyn met a bitter end, at least *her* killer isn't still at large."

"Oh. Well, yes." Jo frowned. "I suppose you've made progress, though?"

MacAdams didn't even bother to use the "can't share that with you" line.

"Not especially grand progress, no," he said, seeing her to the door. "I do have a question, though. Did you say it was Green's suggestion you drop off dinner?"

"Yes. Well, no, actually." Jo tilted her head and looked over his shoulder to the distant cabinets. "Someone called her. I didn't catch her name."

MacAdams shut the door behind her and returned to his whisky. *Annie.* Of course.

Jo walked back to the Red Lion. She was parked there, and anyway, she wanted the headspace.

She just told MacAdams that Evelyn met a bad end. Why had she done that? She didn't have a shred of evidence. It *was* an idea she'd wanted to try out, yes. And she didn't want to distract Gwilym from hunting his accounts for the photo purchase. But she could have bent Tula's ear, for God's sake. Maybe, it was just easier to talk about murder to a detective?

Jo skirted the edge of the main roadway and crossed to the opposite sidewalk. MacAdams lived on a quiet street, in a quiet town. Murders *should* be thin on the ground. But what had Sherlock Holmes said about the dangers of a country mile? Plenty of room for crime in quiet, abandoned places. Sid's murder proved that. The estate afforded everything you would need to commit and even hide a crime—then, as now. What sort of crime, though? Evelyn might have been killed by her lover; she might have died by suicide after a jilt; she might have just run off, started a new life somewhere else, like Jo's own mother. All were things an affluent family on the rise might want to hide. But then, who kept her photograph?

Jo had just reached her car when the phone buzzed in her pocket. A text, from Gwilym.

I know you hate phones but call me. It's important.

Jo dialed in resignation.

"You better have a name," she said when he picked up.

"I don't—but don't hang up! I have a *place*. Are you still meeting Roberta tomorrow?"

"She said she'd come, but I can cancel—"

"No, no! You'll want to see her." Gwilym's voice had just risen an octave, as if he was keeping in a squeal of delight. "Remember how I said I can't throw anything away? That was a genius move, in the end. I couldn't find receipts, but I found the actual box it came in! Packing slip still taped on top: *daguerreotypes, allotment 19*!"

Jo thought her head might explode before he came to the point.

"AND?!" she asked. At last, the squeal made its way out of Gwilym, who sounded like an excited Irish setter.

"Sorry—sorry—" he said upon recovery. "The photos came with a certificate of authenticity. It's signed *Wilkinson*! These came from the Abington Museum!"

MacAdams fumbled with his alarm clock, but it didn't stop the buzzing. He stared at the numbers, bleary-eyed: 1:00 a.m. He'd only been asleep since eleven—the noise was coming from his phone.

"Hello?" he asked, voice scraping and hoarse.

"It's Gridley, boss, there's been an incident in Newcastle."

"What—where?" MacAdams demanded.

"Olivia Randles reported a break-in."

"And Lotte?"

"No sign of her, sir."

MacAdams had already thrown himself out of his bed and was scrambling for loose clothing on the floor. The jolt into waking had come with adrenaline and his fingers fumbled numbly with shoes and socks.

"Tell me the details," he said, phone wedged between shoulder and ear. "I'll get there as fast as I can."

He'd broken limits getting to Arthur's Hill, but MacAdams found both Green and Gridley already there.

"I thought Andrews was on watch?" he asked at the front door.

"He was," Gridley assured him. "But Lotte went on one of her walkabouts, so he followed. Lost her near the park, still looking. The break-in happened about an hour later."

"Nothing taken," Green said, stifling a yawn. "At least we don't think so—" She indicated the state of the house generally as if to say *how could you tell.* "The perpetrator was loud, though. Apparently waking Olivia is like waking the dead."

"Knocked over a bureau while rifling through it," Gridley added.

"Looking for something," MacAdams agreed. "Where's Olivia?" Green and Gridley led the way through to the house's dingy kitchen. A constable was with her; she'd been provided with tea and a blanket but was staring like a wild animal. MacAdams sunk to a crouch just in front of her.

"Olivia, did you see who it was?"

"Where's Lotte?" she asked.

"She'll be here soon," MacAdams said, hoping it wasn't a lie. "Tell me about the break-in." Olivia brought the teacup to her lips; her hands were shaking badly.

"I went to bed early. We both did."

"You and Lotte."

"Yes, nothing unusual. I had a—a little to drink. And I was so tired." She gave up on the tea. "There was the most awful sound. I thought the roof had come in. I went out in the hall."

"What did you see? Think carefully," MacAdams encouraged. But Olivia shook her head.

"Don't know. It was dark, wasn't it? A coat. Someone in a long coat. Raincoat? Trench."

MacAdams made a mental note. Not a black neoprene zip-up. "Face?"

"Had his back at me—and anyway, I screamed and locked my door." She craned her neck about, suddenly. "Where's Lotte?"

Green signaled MacAdams and he left Gridley to continue the interview.

"I do have some news about Ms. Lotte," she said, smoothing her trousers. "The neighbor in the next terrace is elderly, bit of a shut-in. She's certain Lotte doesn't leave the house during the day—says their front door makes a racket and they won't fix it. But that means Lotte also lied about the temp agency she works day shifts for."

"So where's she getting her money?" MacAdams nodded—but a Newcastle constable interrupted before he could say more.

"Sir? Your sergeant Andrews is back. He has the girl, but she won't come inside."

MacAdams found Lotte outside near Tommy's sedan, hugging herself against the cold.

"I'm freezing," she complained.

"Come on in, we'll get you some tea," Green suggested.

"No. I'm only talking to *him*," she said, nodding at MacAdams. "And not in front of Olivia." She shivered as she spoke, and well she might. Lotte wore a short pleated skirt, and though she had a coat on, its faux fur faced outward for looks, not inward for warmth. Tommy handed MacAdams his keys.

"Let's get you out of the cold," MacAdams said to Lotte, gesturing to his car. She got in, stretching fingers to the heating vent.

"Is Olivia okay?"

"Just shaken. I take it Tommy told you about the break-in?" Lotte nodded. Her face was pinched and red, but she didn't cry this time.

"You don't know what it's like, living with her. Boozed up all the time. But she still thinks she's better than everyone." Lotte took a shaky breath. "Better than me. Did the neighbors really tell you I was sneaking out?"

With that kind of admission, MacAdams figured they didn't exactly have to.

"Why not give me the truth this time?"

Lotte half turned in her seat till she could look MacAdams in the eye. He was struck by the fact she looked younger than her years—and with an odd paternal feeling that she needed protection. Which he resisted.

"I'm gonna tell you. But you can't tell Olivia. You *heard* her call Elsie a whore—she'd kick me out on the street." Lotte sniffed and shrank into her fur collar. "I just needed some extra money, that's all. To help me get by. Sid never made money, as you know, but at least he knew how to *get* it."

"Sid?"

"That's what I'm trying to *tell you.*" Her voice took on a plaintive tone. "The cottage is where it started. Sid's idea, you know. He had some friends, and they were looking for a good time. It was easy money. It was fun, even. So, I kind of kept it up regular. Sid would check guys out first for me, to make sure they were safe."

For some reason, MacAdams was unprepared for the specific manner in which Sid turned up in this narrative.

"I'm sorry, do you mean Sid *pimped* for you?"

"No!" Lotte gasped. "No—I just—he was like a, a business partner."

MacAdams felt an icy prickle run down his spine. This was, after all, the definition of a pimp—and he imagined this might be why Ricky and the drinking club at Red Lion gave Sid such a warm send-off.

"And did he take a cut of payments?" he asked.

"No! But—I mean. They paid him, too, maybe. It was like a club. And it meant I could see Sid sometimes."

"For sex. For free," MacAdams clarified. Lotte nodded slowly.

"See. I s-saw him. On Tuesday night." The corners of her mouth drooped involuntarily. "I didn't want you to know I'd been there. It's so awful!"

Her composure broke, and MacAdams managed to find her something suitable to cry into. He was also checking off a mental list; Lotte was the woman he met on Tuesday, after failing to convince Jo about the cottage.

"Go on?" he asked.

"We were smoking in bed, after. He told me he'd miss our arrangements, but that he was cashing in, moving on." Lotte blotted her eye makeup.

"What did he mean by cashing in?"

"You think he told me? He laughed when I asked. Said to me, wouldn't I like to know." She blew her nose, then took a deep breath. "I told him I didn't care. And good riddance. Now… now he's *dead*."

MacAdams could see emotion in the slight collapse of her throat, a swallow that didn't quite make it. Guilt? Shame? Fear?

"Sid told you he was moving on—is that right?" MacAdams asked.

Lotte sniffed and nodded.

"Said the gig was up—he was getting a big score. No more sex club. No more money. So I—I been trying it out on the streets up here. Last night, you chased off my John."

MacAdams didn't need exact numbers to do the math; at the cottage, Lotte had a safe place for sex work and Sid for protection. It wasn't hard to see the decline in fortunes. "Tell me exactly what happened," he said as gently as he could manage. "You drank whisky together. Then what?"

"I don't drink whisky. Can't stand the stuff. He brought champagne." Lotte gave a mournful little laugh. "Cheap champagne. Ricky Robson drove me back to Newcastle, after."

MacAdams suddenly had a *lot* of questions for Mr. Robson. But if he corroborated, Lotte was in the clear. And of course, Ricky was back at the Red Lion for Sid's altercation with Jo.

"All right, Lotte. One more question. The thief was looking for something. What might that be?"

Lotte gave him a look both long-suffering and full of accusation.

"Well, it sure as shite ain't money."

MacAdams drove her back to the house and delivered the keys to Tommy.

"I want forensics all over this, and I want uniform guards posted," he said. Sid Randles' killer (and MacAdams felt this was a safe assumption) had broken into the cottage, Ardemore House, and now Lotte and Olivia's—but they *still* didn't know what he was looking *for.*

"My money is on *money,*" Green said. MacAdams gave a minimal shrug.

"Lotte doesn't think so. And I am starting to agree. Look at this place." He gestured to the opened drawers, papers and bric-a-brac in heaps. "He even went through the jewelry box over there on the dresser."

"What else, then?" she asked. But of course, the answer was *everything else.* A painting. A valuable. Compromising evidence. *Dirt.* No closer to finding Sid's murderer, they had a damn fine collection of motives. Sid stole from Olivia and broke her heart.

He might have stolen from Elsie, too. But what he'd done to Lotte seemed even worse—pimping her to his friends while gaslighting her into thinking it was some kind of favor. It left a stain against MacAdams' consciousness, an unexpected shadow. He'd never thought Sid Randles was a *good* man, but he hadn't ever considered him quite this *bad*. Who else had he crossed?

"What if Sid crossed Jack Turner?" he asked aloud. Green creased her brow.

"Say what? How does he come into it?"

"I don't know," MacAdams admitted. "But he's a nasty character—and Elsie is his sister, after all."

"Boss, I don't mean to be the jerk of reason," Green said with a yawn, "but Jack's been in prison. He can't have murdered Sid."

"No. He can't have. But what about blackmail? Money went into Sid's account—and then out of it, again. What if it's not Sid *doing* the blackmail, like we thought with Rupert. What if he's *being* blackmailed." MacAdams knew how mad the theory sounded; what could you threaten Sid with, after all? But blackmail certainly got a rise out of Smythe. And it was at least something to go on.

22

Saturday

Meadowsweet. And cowslip. Jo sat cross-legged on a flagstone outside the cottage, one of the salvaged garden books open across her knees. The morning had dawned bright and promised fair—and she was trying to distract herself while waiting for Roberta.

"Hallooo," came the war cry. Jo stood up and shielded her eyes from morning sun. Making her way along the footpath in knee boots (and wielding a formidable walking stick) was the woman herself.

"Passing fair," she said, appraising the cottage. "You've moved into it, have you?"

"Well, I keep trying to."

"Built in 1817 by Constance Shearwater after a fire took the existing bothy and barn." Roberta sniffed, her sharp nose turned up into the wind like a dog's. "Farm country, you see. Scottish blackface sheep. But he sold the land to the Ardemores shortly after *William* inherited the baronetcy. You know he was only second to the peerage, don't you? His father, Richard, had been declared for service during the Crimean War."

Jo was having trouble absorbing the information. She was too busy biting back on her own burning questions. Gwilym had suggested a frontal assault might not be the best way to go. *Show her the garden first.*

"Let's go," she said. If it was abrupt, Roberta didn't seem to mind. She gave the ground a thump with the end of her walking stick, presumably permission to proceed. Jo started up the hill.

"You can't really see it from the ground," she said.

"Of course not." Roberta sniffed. "That's the point of the spyglass room."

"The—what?"

"Up there." They had made it to the garden wall, and Roberta pointed to the mystery room high above. "Sir Richard had a spyglass—a small telescope—installed there so he could see the garden at its best."

Jo stopped walking.

"Wait."

"Beg your pardon?" Roberta asked, wheeling about on her. Jo held her hands up, a bit helplessly.

"I have to give my brain a chance to put that somewhere." She scrunched her eyes shut. *A spyglass room.* "That's what it's for? It has a lock but Sid never gave me a key—I broke a skeleton key trying to open it. What did he keep in there?"

"Lep-i-dop-ter-a," Roberta said, pronouncing each syllable separately, as though Jo were a bit slow on the uptake. "Butterfly specimens. And rare orchids. Pressed flowers." She removed her lenses, marionette frown still in place, but a softening around the eyes. "Are you ill?"

"I'm fine," Jo said, putting on what she hoped was a suitable face to prove it. "I think I mentioned the missing painting? That's where I found it."

"Don't know anything about that," Roberta said.

"But you saw the photograph!" Jo erupted. *Smooth.* Roberta frowned, and Jo, well. She just kept talking. "I found the same picture in the archive with Gwilym. He got the original at an auction, and he just realized *you* were the signatory—it's all cut out from the wedding photo of Gwen and William. And her painting was up there! In the house. Until it wasn't." The sudden stop was nearly as inelegant as her charge forward. Roberta drew herself up slightly.

"Are you quite finished?" she asked. Jo nodded meekly. She also handed Roberta her phone, with the photo displayed.

"That—that's her." Jo felt the flush go in and out of her cheeks, and a welcome prickle of wind through her sweater. Roberta's posture hadn't changed; rough wool tweed, walking stick, wellies. She looked like she belonged exactly where she was, against a backdrop of stone and overgrown garden.

"Landscape photos," she said at last. "Mostly amateur. I kept two of the gardens, here, taken before the worst decay. Didn't see a point in keeping the others, so, yes, I sold them at an auction. This was among them."

The prickle at Jo's back threatened to become a shiver. The sun had just darted behind a cloud.

"Where did it all come from?" she asked, and her voice sounded small.

"What do you mean? Here, of course." Roberta nodded in her usual austere manner. "Aiden Jones gave them over before he died."

Sometimes, Jo's brain and body connection just failed. Not the way they had at the Red Lion when she couldn't make herself understood; no, this was a brownout. Noise fuzzed, the world got gooey at the edges, and Jo sat right down on the damp grass.

"Goodness!" Roberta barked. Jo just held her hand up.

"Hold—hold on." *Discord, disgraphic, dysphoria.* She looked up past Roberta's careworn leather face and beyond to the bright, whole series on stages of pregnancy." Jo had to get up and do a circuit of the table; they were getting *close*, which made her almost shy of it—like flirting with the denouement of a favored novel.

"Good God, imagine her stuck *here* with the rest cure doctor." Gwilym gave an exaggerated shiver. "Like a horror novel. I confess I don't really want to give these back to Roberta."

"She *will* kill you." Jo had started reading again, her eyes flying along and stopping only when the writing couldn't be deciphered. "What would you do with all these things, anyway? Sell them?"

"Lord no. I'd hide them in my treasure room with all those glorious atlases. What else is in the box?"

Jo dug around, eagerly but carefully. *Please be a patient register and photos.* It was neither. She weighed it in her hands: a rectangle of papers, enclosed in wrapping and tied with twine.

"They look like letters," she said, and if Gwilym was excited before, he now looked positively incandescent.

"Oh my God." He twitched his fingers. "I *love* old letters—open them, open them!"

"You say that about almost everything," Jo said, getting a fingernail under the knot. "I have known you less than a week, but I've lost count of your hobbyhorses." This wasn't true; she'd been making an unintentional list; *antiques, photos, microfilm, obscura*—along with a surprising grasp of Roberta's agriculture and the desire to be an editor, too, "someday."

"Oh I know," he said, eagerly taking half of the letters. "I can never quite finish anything because I want to do *everything.* You're not so different."

"Mmm," said Jo, because she'd already started reading.

"It's true, though! You're a walking encyclopedia. And I'm a walking junk attic. We've both got all the *stuff* up there, for certain. But you've a much better search engine—"

"Gwilym? Shut up, please." *December, 1906. To Ida Hobarth, MD; from Lady G.A.* "I've just found something."

bright sky. "My uncle Aiden gave you that photograph. You're serious."

"I didn't realize it would be a shock." For once, Roberta looked discomfited. Ironic, since Jo was the one sitting on the ground. She got back to her feet and brushed off her jeans.

"I just don't know anything about anything! I don't know why they left. I don't know who Evelyn was or why her painting was upstairs. I don't know why Aiden had her photograph, or even anything about him—or about the Ardemores, either."

"Ah." Roberta packed a lot into a syllable. She wasn't even looking at Jo, but at the corners of the house, the anchoring points of Richard's gardens. "Well. Your uncle wanted to know about the Ardemores, too, I gather. Came to the archive a few times. I told him the same thing I told you."

"You told me to talk to people that are already dead," Jo said.

"I told him to speak to Sid," Roberta corrected. And there was a hint of gentleness to it. "That's when the family went wrong, you know. The Randles put everything into this place. They'd been promised something in return. A piece of the land, even. Never happened. Family went broke, rather did Sid's father in."

Jo thought about Sid on the first day, a fox surprised in his burrow. His family had been let down—by her own. His immediate dislike suddenly made a certain sense.

"I don't know a thing about this Evelyn, or that photograph," Roberta continued. "It's original—I could see that. But I suspect Aiden framed it himself." Roberta cleared her throat. "Now, still planning to show me the gardens, or are we through being pleasant?"

The words came out before Jo could stop them:

"You have never been pleasant."

Roberta blinked at her. And then laughed. It snapped a tension wire in Jo, and she felt herself settling into apology.

"I am *so* sorry—"

"You're not. You meant it," Roberta said, her eyes still in crow's-feet. Jo puffed air.

"I did. And you aren't. You scare me a little. Do you want to see the spyglass room or not?"

"Lead the way. Please."

The house's weathered front now appeared to be spying through its single unboarded eye. Jo walked through to the cavernous front hall and up the grand stair.

The roofers took weekends off, apparently, but evidence of their presence had been strewn everywhere. The hole had been tarped over again, and some of the debris swept away. Better, the window had been opened up. Jo could see the scaffolding outside, like a metal skeleton, but now the gardens were visible without recourse to the roof.

"That's it exactly," Roberta said, looking over the damp sill. She leaned her walking stick against the wall and pressed her gnarled hands together, almost as if she were planning to say a prayer. "*Look* at it. A sad ruin, now. But it *was* glorious. You—come and stand here."

Jo joined her at the windowsill; Roberta nudged her slightly left.

"Lining up your view," she said, and then handed her a folded piece of heavy paper. "Take a look."

"Oh!" Orange trees bloomed under Jo's fingertips among bee balm and lavender and shaded lime walks. *Watercolor,* she thought. Art print. The caption, tilting in scripted font, gave Richard's name, *fig 3.* "It's from a book!"

"Sir Richard's botanical. He did most of the landscape paintings," Roberta told her. "Now look there"—she pointed out past Jo's shoulder. She was looking at the same scene, precisely the same, plus a hundred years and some.

And it reminded Jo that she had her own show-and-tell.

"I told you I had a garden plan," she said. "It's downstairs." She left Roberta at the window, rocking on her heels, hands back in the pockets of her goose-down vest. *Obsession*, Gwilym would say. But everyone deserved their private joys.

"Here it is," Jo panted once she returned, waving the crisply refolded document. Roberta had moved to the other side of the room. Bent at an angle—*acute this time*, Jo thought absently—she appeared to be examining the wallpaper.

"They've changed the wallpaper," Roberta said. "I've a photograph of this room and his orchids. It should be printed in florals."

"I thought it was Victorian paper—isn't it?" Jo asked. She ran her finger along the faded print.

"Pink, is what it *is*," Roberta huffed. "Looks like a bleeding nursery. Whose painting did you say was in here? The wife? Probably wanted a girl."

"Oh no, it was Evelyn's. And anyway, Gwen and William never had any children—" Jo stopped midsentence as her brain ground gears. Then she grasped Roberta by her stick-free hand and squeezed it. "You. Are. A genius."

"Good heavens, girl." Roberta was flustered and pulled free, but Jo scarcely heard her. She was too busy digging for her phone in the too-many jacket pockets of her mackintosh. She texted fast enough to require spell correct:

Gwilym! I know why Evelyn was hiding out in the country!

Jo and Gwilym sipped tea in the mill-museum kitchen. Roberta, who had softened considerably since being called a genius, had provided them with sweet brown bread, jam, and eleven archive boxes from the city hospital.

"You think our Evelyn was pregnant?" Gwilym asked, trying to read labels without his glasses.

"I *know* it," Jo said. "I should have thought it before now."

"Okay—I'm not disagreeing!" Gwilym assured her. "And if you were hiding a pregnancy, you would definitely be camera shy—and wouldn't be turning up at garden parties."

Roberta gripped elbows across her chest.

"In 1908, Abington had the dispensary and two private doctors. Prior to the establishment of the NHS, of course." She took a seat. "One of the doctors was a woman."

"Really?" Gwilym asked. "Isn't that pretty progressive?"

"Hardly." Roberta had resumed an imperious look. "The only places you ever saw them were little towns like this. Couldn't make a living in London, could she? Ida Hobarth. She's buried in the cemetery by the park."

"Still, that seems like a good place to start, doesn't it?" Jo asked.

"The aristocracy tended to favor physicians over midwives," Gwilym suggested. "Evelyn wasn't married, so perhaps Ida would have been her first choice over a man?"

"We've a reading room," Roberta said. "But you've only got till three-thirty. It's choir night."

Jo checked her watch. It was three…and even hyperlexia wouldn't get them through all the medical detritus in an hour. Gwilym was watching her and seemed to catch the thought midair.

"Ms. Wilkinson?" he asked, "I know this is a big ask, but is there any way we might borrow these for tonight?"

He'd pushed his glasses on again, as if that would help. Roberta scowled.

"Remove them from the museum library? And take them *where*?"

"I know how precious these are to you," Gwilym said, resting one hand on the nearest box. "We'll sign any waiver or agreement you like."

We will? Jo wondered what that might entail. Maybe a trade?

"You can keep the garden plans," she said suddenly. "They're original, and you can keep them till we bring all these back."

"And we'll return everything tomorrow morning, first thing," Gwilym pursued. He gave the box a loving tap. "You don't know it, but Jo here is an editor—a research editor. And an amazing reader."

That part might not have been a lie, Jo admitted, but it was definitely pandering to the audience. Roberta gave a curt little nod.

"Understood. And you *will* sign for them. And I will have them by eight tomorrow."

"Yes, ma'am."

The upside, Jo supposed, was freedom to peruse the documents at leisure. The rest were downsides, including walk-racing back to the Red Lion for Jo's rental car, followed by hauling and packing all eleven boxes under Roberta's discerning gaze.

"There's a curry house around the corner," Gwilym said as they pulled away.

"I thought you paid board in advance at the Lion?" Jo asked.

"Yeah. I just feel a curry. You don't care for it?"

Honestly, there wasn't much in the world of food Jo didn't like. She shrugged and pulled onto the appropriate side street, which resulted in a twenty-minute wait…but also chicken tikka masala.

"If those boxes smell of curry, Roberta will murder you," Jo cautioned. "Now, where are we supposed to do this midnight research?"

"The Red Lion pub room is too loud."

"We aren't doing this in your bedroom, fella."

"I wasn't even flirting that time!" Gwilym protested. "I was thinking maybe we could do this on-site."

"You mean *at* Ardemore house?"

"Why not? Come on, please? Even Tula and Ben have been there!" He cocked his head like an expectant dog. "What if I buy beer?"

"All right, fine." Jo watched Gwilym do a celebratory fist pump. Then he folded his hands in his lap and went suddenly, almost alarmingly quiet. His face had gone a bit red, too. None of this squared with her read of the situation.

"You look like you're holding in a hiccup."

"Sorry!" Gwilym squeaked. "It's like a *date*!"

Fleet had returned, not by train but by car. MacAdams rather thought he might have done that in the first place and saved everyone the trouble—but felt a little too in his debt to say so. They convened in the incident room over coffee, and he told him about the break-in.

"And no one saw the perpetrator?" Fleet asked. MacAdams shook his head.

"Not in any useful way. Olivia saw someone—a man—in a trench. That's all we got," he said. Which described just about every bloke in Yorkshire. "I can gather a few other things, just from circumstance. He's bold, breaking into a woman's house in the middle of the night. He must surely have known the occupants would be around this time."

"You've no proof he didn't know that before, when he broke into the cottage," Fleet reminded him. It was true; Jo happened to be out of town. The killer may or may not have known that.

"Fair. But that doesn't change the profile—our suspect takes risks. And he has to be reasonably athletic. I doubt he *meant* to overturn an antique bureau, but even so, it takes some force."

"Or heft," Fleet mused over his tea.

"Doubtful. The only other thing Olivia made plain was that our perpetrator was tall and thin." What she had *actually* said was "not as heavy as you are, Detective." MacAdams wasn't exactly the Olympian standard, but he wasn't overweight. Not clinically, anyway. Thus, the perp was *thin*. He cleared his throat. "We know he's looking for something. We don't know what. And it's increasingly unlikely to be cash, as the sisters are more or less broke now."

The perp was also unlikely to *be* Lotte or Olivia. MacAdams plucked them from the whiteboard and stuck them in the further column.

"You are removing them from suspicion?" Fleet asked. "Despite knowing that Lotte and Sid were in business together?" *What a way to put it*, MacAdams thought.

"I'll agree that Lotte had something to lose without the cottage arrangement," he said. "But that wasn't Sid's fault and killing him certainly wouldn't solve it. She thought he might continue clearing customers for her, despite his claims about *cashing in*. Sid's 'wins' never lasted very long." Olivia was case in point. Her ten grand disappeared in less than six months. Sid must've used part of it to pay off creditors—and the rest to get new ones.

"I see." Fleet rocked slightly, peering over his teacup at the woman who remained front and center: Elsie Smythe. "And now we know criminality runs in the family."

"We do," MacAdams agreed. It had been rather gratifying to discover the Elsie-Jack connection ahead of Fleet. But there were still problems with the theory. "Only one problem—Elsie is certainly hard enough, I think. But she's also not a tall, thin man."

"People see what they want to see," Fleet said. "Olivia sees a trench coat. She may have seen anything."

"I saw a man, too, Fleet. At the cottage break-in. Remember?" MacAdams pressed. Fleet took a long sip in silence before casting him an appraising glance.

"You saw a gloved hand."

MacAdams was presently squeezing his own hand into an irritated fist. Mainly because Fleet was, again, correct about this.

"What I am *saying*," he said stiffly, "is that more than one person may be involved."

A two-dimensional Elsie stared back at them; the photo had to be a decade old. Unsmiling, with the same fierce eyes as her brother. Was he imagining their connection? He knew better than to surmise without facts. The Full Sutton register hadn't logged any visitors for Jack at all, much less a family member. But then, who—or what—else did she have to hide?

"I know she's involved," MacAdams said slowly. "Otherwise, she wouldn't be so damn hard to locate."

"You have been watching her aunt's house in York?"

"*Yes*, Fleet, and no, she hasn't returned to it. She hasn't been back to the Newcastle apartment, either."

Fleet's bland look had changed to something less meritorious.

"You should have brought her in for questioning while you had her," he said bluntly, "And you should get a warrant to search both her homes."

MacAdams turned back to face the board. He had *plenty* to say to that—but not within shouting distance of Cora's office, not on your life.

"I can't haul her in without evidence," he said through his teeth. "And I *do* have a warrant for her apartment. I've been there, so have Newcastle uniform. It's empty."

Of course, he wasn't really angry at Fleet. It was the truth that rankled him. He had Elsie in reach; he'd caught her off guard. It would have been the perfect moment, the perfect time to bring her in for questioning. But on what grounds? How did you corner Elsie Smythe?

There had been aspects of performance to all the ex-Randles women. Lotte played at rebel kink, but her sexual emancipation was tied up in economics—and she feared Olivia's disapproval. Olivia might be earning her stripes as a drunken cynic, but she'd also been the hardest worker, the biggest giver, and still her sister's primary support. Both also played at being grieving widows, looking for sympathy and revising their histories with Sid. Elsie, however? *She* was something else. A different level. When he closed his eyes to try and picture her, he kept fumbling, seeing instead a mishmash of her two looks: the red dragon heels and leather skirt with the soft pastel blouse under sharp business suit. He might describe Jarvis Fleet as a mask with a mustache…but Elsie? She was the whole damn costume.

He suspected her, yes. A lot. But was she murderer or accomplice—or both? By her account, she'd not seen Sid since the divorce, and her neighbor in Newcastle hadn't seen him coming and going. Her brother Jack had been evasive, too, but who else was there to ask if they couldn't produce the aunt? Elsie appeared where she didn't belong, vanished from where they expected to find her. He might as well have asked Jack about a ghost, for the way he blanched when the subject of murder and blackmail came up.

MacAdams tapped the tabletop.

"We need to do some more digging on Jack Turner. I want to see him again. By myself, this time."

"Alas," said Fleet, and this was not the response MacAdams expected.

"Meaning?"

"I meant to tell you. York received a call from Jack's legal counsel. He's cited us for harassment."

"He—what?" MacAdams had been standing. Now he threw himself into the nearest chair, which happened to be Gridley's. "I'm sorry, but that is bullshit."

"We can fight it, but it's an injunction against speaking to him further."

MacAdams rubbed his temple with a free hand. Why in hell would Jack do something like this?

"Fuck, Fleet—it's your people up there! Do something, would you?" He'd raised his voice. And he'd used a word Cora blacklisted from the office. And she had *fucking* supernatural hearing. He heard the door open and the sound of sturdy shoes.

"Is there a problem, James MacAdams?"

MacAdams faced a solid block of irritation in navy blue. He had barely slept in a week, ferreted out the semi-illegal mishmash of both Rupert Selkirk and Lotte Randles, and chased a perp on foot.

"There is *not* a problem," he said as steadily as he could with his jaw clenched shut.

"Good. You are on very thin ice. Jarvis? You said you'd like to see the War Room?"

"For old times' sake, yes." He turned to MacAdams. "I haven't been since the funeral."

"Right, you two and all that military machinery."

"Military *process*," Fleet corrected pertly. "Good day."

MacAdams nodded agreeably to the idea of losing Fleet for the afternoon. He leaned back in Gridley's chair and dialed Tommy in Newcastle.

"Anything to report?"

"All quiet here, sir. And Newcastle forensics have nothing to report—suspect wore gloves."

Yes, thought MacAdams. Black ones. To think: if he'd caught the burglar that night at Jo's cottage—

His phone buzzed in his hand. An unfamiliar number was trying to reach him. He put Andrews on hold to answer.

"Hello?"

"Areet, am gan to the toon, but that lass is back." *Geordie*—thickly accented.

"Is this Edith?" MacAdams asked, "Elsie's neighbor?"

"Aye. Just back. Saw her out in the skip."

Oh God.

"You found her *body*?" MacAdams demanded.

"Nar, nar! The bags is in. She gone off agin. And I took 'em, too, though the meter man giving us hackies."

"The bags. She put bags in the skip—and you took them out?"

"Aye, told yer. Big black uns. Wants 'em do yer?"

MacAdams assured her that yes, yes, they very much wanted them. It took him less than two minutes, but he was already at his car.

"Boss?" Andrews asked, when MacAdams managed to get him on Speaker.

"Sorry—yes. I'm picking up Green. We'll meet you in Newcastle."

Green stood in the doorway of Edith's tiny apartment, her tan raincoat hanging loose on her shoulders.

"I can't believe we are doing this," she said.

"Patience," MacAdams encouraged. The living room had a distinctly oily feeling, like too many fried up dinners had accumulated on its surfaces. Not unclean, just oddly filtered; everything seemed to have gone slightly red-brown in tint.

"Think I'm a right nebby bugga, but here y'go." Edith stepped in from the adjoining room and plopped two black sacks on the rug.

"Good work, ma'am," he said, leaning to take hold of them. Green clicked her tongue and asked, quietly: "Is this perfectly legal?"

"We have a warrant for her apartment," he said, and after all, the items must surely have started out there… "Help me get these in the boot."

"Divvent want to open 'em first?" Edith asked. "Mehbee garbage."

This made more sense than he wanted to admit. MacAdams put the first bag on the plastic doormat, hooked one finger into the plastic knots and gave a stiff pull. The lip slackened and a pair of men's shoes spilled out. MacAdams picked one up in gloved fingers; well worn, large size. He gave the bag a shake, redistributed its goods, and shone his penlight within.

"Green, what do you see?" he asked. Green peered over his shoulder at a men's shaving kit, toothbrush, and belt—among other things. She crouched next to him for a better view.

"That would be…all the things we *didn't* find in Sid's flat," she whispered huskily.

"Nor in the cottage," MacAdams reminded her. "Now, what would Ms. Elsie be doing with those?"

"Giz a deek at that," Edith said. "And she calls *me* the wazzock? Bloody bint, she war." MacAdams had only a faint idea of what she meant, though *bint* and *bitch* were sister-terms. Either way, it reminded him that here was not the place to be going over potential evidence. He nodded to Green, who donned her own gloves and began tying the bag back together.

"Was Elsie alone when she came round?" he asked the bent little woman.

"Aye."

"And how did she come? By car?"

"Oh, aye. Nicest thing I seen. Nar a sound, neither. 'Lectric."

MacAdams recalled the BMW i3, sleek and well shined on the day of the funeral. If it were just a rental, as Elsie claimed, why might she still be driving it around? And if not a rental… then she was making a sight more money than her accounts led them to believe.

"So what now?" Green asked as they loaded the bags into MacAdams' trunk.

"I need forensics to go over it, but I don't want to wait that long to bring Elsie in." He was, in fact, afraid this drop-off meant she was about to do a runner. "I want a warrant for Elsie's arrest—and a manhunt if that's what it takes to find her."

"No need," Green said, smiling broadly at a text on her phone. "Look here! York uniform just saw her. She must have gone *there* straight after dumping things here."

MacAdams took the phone from her and dialed.

"This is DCI MacAdams. Do NOT let her out of your sight."

23

Seven candles, each in a different holder and at different points of waxy disintegration, surrounded the library's low table. The electrics had shorted out again, so Gwilym and Jo peered over the well-lit middle, heads bowed, fingers tracing neat, compact handwriting. It occurred to Jo that the arrangement resembled a séance, and that this might be highly appropriate. They were raising the ghost of Ida Hobarth and her mostly anonymous clients. The carefully preserved binders included hand-drawn pictures of medicines, preparations, test tubes, and even wound-closing in colored inks.

"A hemoglobin precipitin test!" Gwilym bent closer, his glasses almost touching paper. Jo squeezed in for a closer look.

"That's blood analysis! They injected rabbits with human blood to develop the antibodies—" she said, and Gwilym made a squeeing sound.

"You *know* about the rabbits!?" He shook his head. "You're a blooming wonder."

"Well, *you* know about them, too—look at this. She did a

Dear Dr. Hobarth, it read,

> *You will forgive this second intrusion upon your time but I was too distraught to think clearly after our meeting. They told me I needed only to rest. The doctor prescribed powders, and I used every one, thinking we had hopes. You have dashed them, but I thank you for it; who knows how long I would have hoped in vain when nothing will ever help? It hurts more than you could know. I have to tell William I cannot give him an heir…*

"Shite," said Gwilym, but Jo was on her feet, flapping her hands at the wrist.

"Gwen can't have kids. Ever. Get it? *Ever.* But the room is made into a nursery, right? And the only other woman living there is her sister."

"Is that proof, then? It's not exactly a dead ringer for evidencc," Gwilym pointed out. "There's no record of a baby, no birth certificate." Jo ignored this setback and shook her head firmly. A whole picture was forming in her mind: Evelyn may have hidden the pregnancy at first, but what would happen if her father found out she was carrying the child of her lover, out of wedlock?

"You said Davies was a social climber, yes?" Jo's circles had gotten smaller; she was just turning in place, now. "If Evelyn got pregnant, he couldn't marry her off to suit him. If the father hasn't turned up to claim his child, no one will believe that it wasn't her own fault. She's damaged goods. Either she is sent—or runs—away. She goes all the way to Abington to live with people who at least don't hate her for being pregnant out of wedlock. People who want a baby, too, and can't have one."

Jo had started to get dizzy; she steadied herself against the mantel. Her heart was beating fast. Above her, the portraits looked down, as austere and poised as ever: *she* had been Evelyn's only haven—Gwen—even as Aunt Sue had been her own mother's only refuge when she was pregnant with Jo.

"It runs in the family," she said, still not looking at Gwilym but settling on a space in the middle distance.

"Do I get to hear this story?" he asked. Jo picked at her cuticle.

"It's not something we talk about," she said. But there was no *we*. Not anymore. She felt a stab of loneliness. "I didn't even tell Tula about it—though I don't know who I'm protecting." Jo sat down on the settee. "My mother left England because she was pregnant. She told me she didn't know who my father was. Except she *lied*."

It happened in the strange half-lit days after Aunt Sue's funeral. Jo was in college, then, about nineteen, and her mother had gone to pieces. She remembered the strange, hollow way she moved—as though every muscle had to be reminded of its job, as if her mum walked and breathed in pain. She leaned heavily on Jo, and Jo tried to bear up, and to anticipate her need. She'd been doing that her whole life anyway: how could Jo be more useful, more fit, and less of a weight on the tiny, fragile family to which she belonged? Now that family had been reduced to two. Jo went to the funeral homes, was there to answer questions when her mother had been too distant or too wounded to approach. The arrangements for burial, for viewing hours, even how to serve as executor of a will technically entrusted to her mum—these became Jo's employment by day, leaving her alone with her grief by night.

Did Jo miss Aunt Sue? Yes. She loved her, too, as much as she could. As much as Sue let her. Her aunt married an American serviceman at seventeen (and a half) and moved with him to the US. She dreamed of a big family, something the Ardemore/Davies never had. But her husband died in an artillery accident on base only two months later. Sue wanted kids; she got half of Jo. It just never seemed to be the right half. Jo lay awake at night trying to parse her own feelings, but mostly she nursed a horrible loneliness. And then, while searching for necessary account numbers in her mother's bureau, she found the *book*.

Held together with rubber bands, it had been tucked into the very back of her mother's bedside table. It was secret, and Jo couldn't pretend she didn't know better. But here it was, her mother's cramped handwriting in blue on faded lines: a diary. About the past. Jo felt an almost electric jolt; it tingled her fingers, and the sensation was still as vivid as ever. She held the key, maybe, to all her mother's silences. She'd hoped for talk of the old country—the old family—even Uncle Aiden. Or maybe it had just been her usual raw curiosity for the written word. Either way, what she read couldn't be taken back: *I am pregnant with his child and I don't know what to do.* His child. *His.* But there wasn't a name.

Jo had read greedily, guiltily. Her mother had been ostracized by her father. And then, by her brother, Aiden. *They don't believe me. My God, they don't believe me.* Her side of the story didn't mean anything. And she would not live like that.

"My aunt Sue was really my *mother's* aunt," Jo explained to Gwilym. "The much younger sister of my grandfather. But she was more like a sister to my mum. They both felt alone in their family." Jo hugged her knees on the sofa. "I know, because she wrote *that* down. But in all those pages, she never said my father's name. Only that it was her brother Aiden's best friend… And that he was married to someone else."

"Then what?" Gwilym asked. He'd inched forward so far on his chair that he practically hovered in thin air. Jo gave a shuddering sigh. The next part was worse. So much worse.

"Then," she said slowly, fighting the urge to chew the words back. "*Then* my mother walked into the bedroom and caught me reading."

It had all begun so innocently; Jo hadn't trespassed against any known prohibition. But she'd also been the first to speak, to apologize, to make it right—

"I didn't mean to," she said. Those weren't the right words, though. She *had* meant to; she always wanted to know and to be known, and it was always denied. Now she saw a part of the truth, and it was good, like clear water after so much dusty silence. Her mother was better and bolder in Jo's eyes. The fumbled apology did not communicate this. And her mother could spot a lie.

When Jo turned to face her, it wasn't the mother she'd always known. All the familiar lines had been smoothed out, and in their places were the alien contortions of abject horror.

"How *could* you?" her mother asked in a voice desperate and shrill. "How *dare* you?"

Jo didn't know what to say. Her words evaporated, even as they had in the front room of the Red Lion. Nothing would come. Her mother crossed the room; it seemed to take eons. Jo remembered every muscle as they expressed themselves in order, the strained white lines that pulled back from her mother's eyes, the teeth bared under thin and panicked lips.

"Give it to me. It is mine and you have no right to touch it."

But Jo wouldn't let it go. In it was the only proof of a family, albeit unnamed, beyond her mother and now-deceased aunt.

"I have a right," she'd managed to say. Quietly. Almost a whisper. "I have a right to *know.*"

Jo had a father. She might even have siblings. And maybe—just maybe—some of them were *like her.* Maybe somewhere there were blood kin who saw the world the way she did, the way she always had. Her mother closed one hand on the book. Jo did not relent. Feelings were rushing up out of all the places she carefully hid them, unruly, messy. Angry.

"How could you hide this from me?" she asked, voice shaking. A tremor had started in her legs and traveled up her torso until her arms and hands were vibrating, too. She let go of the book, and her mother hugged it to her breast as if it were a baby.

She rocked there, in place, chin folded down over something precious and strange and forbidden. Then she spoke:

"You are a hard-hearted, unfeeling girl. You have never loved me the way a daughter should."

Jo had just spoken the words out loud, in the ruined library. She heard them in her mother's voice, even so, as clear as the day they were spoken. On the other side of the table, Gwilym heaved a tremulous sigh.

"Oh, *Jo*," he said. Jo wished he hadn't said it so gently. It threatened to spring something inside her.

"We never spoke of it again," Jo said, biting her lip. *Keep your shit together.*

"Can I ask—and tell me if I shouldn't—did you ever reconcile?"

Jo curled her thumbs in crushingly tight fists. She felt the pressure of something big and ugly pressing against her ribs.

"I tried. I told her what she had said, and how it hurt me." The words were coming faster, pacing with her heartbeat. "But it didn't matter. She'd just—*forgotten it*."

Jo's body betrayed her. Sobs came, and hot tears. That day, the horror of being discovered, of being accused, of feeling small—it had been one of the most awful moments of Jo's life. But for her mother, it was just a Tuesday. Not worth remembering. And so it wasn't *real* to her. Jo may as well have been hurt by someone else, someone who didn't even exist anymore. They never spoke of it again, not when her mom became ill, not in the months of watching her decline. Her mother died without telling her the truth, the last link in a chain to some other family, somewhere else. And then the lawyers called to say she'd inherited a house in England. And Jo had come and hoped.

"So-s-sorry. I'm not sup-posed to be cry-ing," she stuttered over the hitch of a sob. Gwilym was still there, not speaking, just looking on. He looked puzzled.

"Why?" he eventually asked. "Why should you not cry?"

"I'm sup-posed to be *bouncing back*. I'm s-starting over. I'm—" Jo gestured at the things she'd tried to do already: the library, the estate, the roof… She felt pathetic. "This isn't what it's supposed to look like."

Gwilym got to his feet and joined her—not *on* the sofa, but the floor. Then he took a diver's breath.

"To whom? Who gets to decide what anything looks like?" he asked. Jo sat straighter and tried to claw back a bit of dignity.

"I'm not weak," she said, but Gwilym was shaking his head before she finished.

"No—I *know*. It's an act of revolution just to be what you are."

"And what's that?"

"Whatever you want! But not because someone else wants it. Shite, your mum said terrible things to you. And you just carry it around by yourself. My trauma's not anything like as bad—even with an overprotective mum, and a da that didn't believe ADHD was a thing."

Jo unbent herself and rubbed the salt from her cheeks. She'd never heard anyone call her life *traumatic*; it sounded alien and strange.

"I loved my mother. I miss her every day," she said, standing up slowly. "But I only ever had bits and pieces of her, I guess, and I just keep losing more family. I wanted to know more about Aiden. And—it matters, you know. That he was looking at our history. That he had the photograph." She walked to the mantel and peered up at the portraits. "Maybe he was lonely, too."

Gwilym joined her and patted her shoulder tentatively.

"We'll find Evelyn," he offered. "We still have boxes left." It didn't have the cheering effect he expected; Jo had an emotional hangover already, and her head hurt from crying.

"It'll keep," she said.

It would take a few trips to stow it all back in the car—but Jo's phone double-buzzed as soon as she stepped outside.

"Hang on," she said, steadying a box against the hood and chasing the vibration. She didn't recognize the number—but it appeared to be local to Abington. "I just can't," she said, handing it to Gwilym.

"Oh, er. Jo Jones' phone?" he said into the receiver. "Roberta! We're just—what? When? Um. Okay, I'll tell her."

"What was that all about?" Jo asked. Gwilym handed back the phone.

"I have no idea. But we're supposed to be at the museum tomorrow—and an hour earlier, too. Seven sharp."

24

Sunday

MacAdams started his morning at York Police Station. Elsie Randles had not come quietly.

"She has an impressive left hook, I'm told," Fleet said to MacAdams. MacAdams was quietly grateful that it hadn't been *his* sergeant this time. Meanwhile, Elsie had just made a rude gesture at the two-way glass and overturned the chair before resuming her anger-walk around the interrogation room.

"She says it's harassment," Green explained, joining them.

"Funny. Her brother said that, too," MacAdams mused. "Ready?"

"Nope, but that's never stopped me before." Green led the way, leaving Fleet behind. MacAdams had taken the precaution of detaining Elsie's solicitor until the very last minute, assuming that entering together would divide Elsie's attention. Caught between pleading her case to *him* and spitting daggers at *them*, she might say something useful. The tapes began rolling, and after some resistance, Elsie finally sat at the table across from them.

"Can I smoke?" she hissed. It wasn't a question, apparently, as she promptly lit up. Her white sleeves had been rolled to the elbows and the buttons of her blouse left undone dangerously low, so he could see the lace of a bra beneath. Her lips were a glaring red.

"Do you know why you're here, Ms. Smythe?" Green asked.

"Because you fucking *arrested* me for fucking *murder*." Elsie's words seared like the trail of smoke, her voice almost shaking in fury.

"On suspicion, not on conviction," MacAdams clarified. "You lied to me about your relationship to Sid Randles." He raised his hand, and an officer entered the room carrying a folded stack of clothing along with a paper bag. MacAdams unfolded the topmost article.

"Men's shirt, fifteen and a half. Slightly stained around the collar, but recently ironed. And—" He picked up the next piece. "Men's canvas trousers. Looks as though a pair of men's boxers are in here, too. A pair of dress shoes, nine and a half."

Elsie had been provided an ashtray. She did not use it, letting ash flake onto the table with each drag.

"So?" she asked.

"You put these in the bins behind your Newcastle apartment. There is a witness."

Elsie leaned forward over the table.

"So?"

MacAdams hadn't expected her to be easy. He nodded to Green, who reached into the paper sack and began depositing items on the table.

"Aftershave, used. Men's cologne, half-bottle. Men's shave kit. Extra toothbrush. Gold chain. Wristwatch, new," she said. Elsie shrugged, a defiant gesture, all shoulder.

"I have men around, don't I?"

"You have a *man*," MacAdams corrected. "Those bags came

from your aunt's home. You've been living there. And until a few weeks ago, Sid Randles was living there, too."

Elsie had eyes the color of stainless steel ball bearings, and just as cold and hard.

"Fuck. You."

It was Green's turn. She slipped a piece of paper across to the solicitor.

"Sergeant Green has shown the suspect a forensics report. Analysis proves that fibers found on the clothing and personal items match those of Sid Randles, deceased."

Thank God for York's sizable forensic lab. MacAdams waited for Elsie to make her move. But Elsie only smoked in silence.

"You said you hadn't seen Sid Randles," MacAdams pressed. "I asked you at the funeral and later, at your aunt's house."

"I told you I last seen him in a box. And I did. And the rest ain't none of your damn business."

"It is when it's a murder investigation," MacAdams assured her. "You see, we searched his flat. And we searched the estate cottage. And you know what we didn't find? Evidence of him actually *living* there. He was living with you right up till the day he died, and you didn't just lie, you covered it up by trying to dump his belongings."

Elsie leveled her eyes at MacAdams.

"Why don't you ask me where I was the night of the murder?" she said. It was smooth, and it was as icy cold as it was unexpected. "A casual friend, you might say. For casual sex. I've got his address, and I'm sure he'll remember me."

She flicked ash. MacAdams cycled through fourteen revolutions of thought. She wasn't ready to give even his name before, but she was ready to serve up addresses now? So much for client privilege; if she could cook up a believable alibi, they were sunk. He needed her to give up *something* in the interview. Some tiny crack in the armor.

"All right then." MacAdams sat back in his plastic chair. "If you didn't kill him, who did?"

"How would I know?"

"You certainly saw a lot of him." Green said it, while toying with the aftershave bottle. "Did you buy him this? His favorite kind, was it?"

Rather a bullish move. MacAdams liked and followed it.

"It's the little things we hold on to, usually. But not you. Some might say you're just unsentimental and unfeeling. But I don't think that's it." MacAdams leaned forward again, hands outstretched and neutral on the table. "You know, Olivia claims she still loved him—"

"Hah." Elsie took another drag of the cigarette, mouth twisted with derision.

"Lotte, too," MacAdams added. "They say they cared for him, despite everything. They say they cared for him more than you ever did."

Elsie puffed in silence. Green took another shot.

"Lotte was still shacking up with him. Did you know? She was proud of it. She liked to talk about it." Green waited until Elsie made eye contact before adding, *"A lot."*

There it was: the tell. Elsie's face remained almost unchanged, but the heave and hitch of her chest betrayed emotion, and the hand holding her cigarette trembled slightly. She raised her chin, a mark of pride. MacAdams aimed for that.

"See, they talk about you like you don't give a damn. But they don't know you, do they, Elsie?" MacAdams took a breath. *He* didn't know Elsie, either. And he was about to do some dot-connecting that would make even Jo Jones blush. But it was now or never.

"You stood by him, didn't you, even when he slept around, even when he got that divorce. Maybe you knew about the money he took from Olivia. Maybe you knew about the pimping he did for Lotte. Maybe you loved him through it all."

He'd been watching her the whole time, looking for a softening. He saw something else, a bit like the tightening of a spring. MacAdams felt a tug at his insides.

"You *did* know," he said, to himself as much as to Elsie. "Business partners, were you? With your aunt's house, your apartment, the cottage, and Sid's flat in Abington—that's four homes between you. Just what sort of scams might you be running, I wonder?"

The spell had broken; Elsie laughed and stubbed out the cigarette.

"You don't know a damn thing. There's no *scam*. For one, I come and go as I want at Aunt Hannah's. She never gave a shit about me all those years, so she's making good now before dying. Sid stayed because he had money, and I had time."

They'd circled back to cash, and that suited MacAdams very well.

"Oh, he had money, absolutely," he said, nodding at Green. She'd brought evidence of exactly how much and presented it for the tapes. The pages lay before Elsie and her solicitor, though she wouldn't look at them.

"Go ahead. Look at just how much," MacAdams encouraged. "Enough to keep two people comfortably."

"I don't know anything about it." She was cold again. Not a twitch. *Think*, MacAdams commanded himself. The money comes and the money goes…

"Maybe Sid had a secret worth keeping," he said, cautiously. "Maybe you knew what it was."

"Fuck you," Elsie spat.

"It's called blackmail, Elsie," MacAdams said. He'd been weighing whether to bring her brother into the matter. Now seemed the time for it. "We spoke to Jack at Full Sutton."

"So?"

"I told him Sid had been murdered. Then I asked about you. He claimed the two of you weren't in touch."

"We aren't."

MacAdams turned to Green; it was time for one last item rescued from the refuse bin—or rather, from the pocket of Sid's trousers within. Green unfolded a bit of lined notebook paper.

"Presented to the suspect, a letter from Jack Turner to Elsie Smythe."

Elsie had frozen again, though this time the expression seemed half-formed. MacAdams had seen that before, when he surprised her in York.

"When you come next time, bring 20 pack, L&B—not the cheap fags. God knows you can afford it," Green read out loud. MacAdams tapped the tabletop.

"You both lied about contact. Why would that be? Maybe he knows more than he claims; maybe he's trying to protect you. We have some options, here, Elsie," he continued. "Were you blackmailing Sid? Or was he blackmailing you? The thing is, no matter which direction it goes, I think *you* know the answers. So I'm going to ask you one more time. If you didn't kill Sid, who did?"

MacAdams waited. And the silence stretched. He'd noted before that Jack and Elsie had similar eyes, and right now Elsie's were mirroring the expression MacAdams had seen in Jack's. The one that might be fear. It would have made life a lot simpler to think Elsie was the murderer as well as the accomplice; some part of him still believed it. And yet...and yet... He nudged Green, who passed him the photograph of Sid, in situ at the murder scene.

"Elsie. Sid was murdered. I need to know why." He pushed the photo forward, in all its dreadfulness. "Because, you see, the killer wanted something. And they didn't get it. And if the culprit isn't you, I don't need to remind you that the murderer is still out there and still looking. So if you know something, now is the time."

Elsie took a fleeting glance at the photos and then scrambled for another cigarette. Her hand trembled; the solicitor ultimately had to light it *for* her. Once the tip glowed red, she blew a thin ribbon of smoke and looked over MacAdams' shoulder, directly at the distant two-way glass.

"There was a painting," she said. "It belonged to the American woman."

Jo backed the Alfa Romeo toward the museum's entry door. It only took three tries to get it right—but it beat walking the archive boxes across the wet parking lot. Jo used her hip to shut the door; the lights weren't even on in the galleries.

"This is a bit weird," she said. Gwilym hefted two boxes at once.

"I told you to call her back," he reminded her. And so he had. And she'd thought about it until well past normal people's bedtime. Jo got the door, which was thankfully not locked.

"Hello?" she asked. It echoed.

"We can bring them downstairs," Gwilym suggested, wandering toward the basement. Light filtered up; someone was already down there.

"Roberta?" Jo asked as she cleared the lintel.

"Yes, and you're four minutes late." Roberta sat at one end of the reading room table, and at the other—Rupert Selkirk and Emery Lane.

"Who are they?" Gwilym asked.

"Um?" was all Jo managed. Roberta, clearly at the gavel, motioned for them to be seated. They obeyed, boxes and all.

"I've called you here for a moment of clarification. Mr. Selkirk, the document."

Selkirk rose and handed along what appeared to be Jo's garden map. Roberta spread it before her.

"These are *not* the plans of Sir Richard Ardemore," she announced. "It has come to my attention that the gardens were, in fact, designed by Gertrude Jekyll."

Jo found herself blinking hard, as if that would clarify things. Gwilym, however, gave a high-pitched wheeze.

"Gertrude Jekyll designed at least 400 gardens in the UK!"

"Quite so," Roberta said, cutting him short. "Most have been lost to time and mismanagement. Only Upton Grey in Hampshire has been fully restored, due to the plans being located. Plans like these." Jo's brain took notes, but so far nothing had the faintest ring of familiarity. Rupert, still standing, bowed slightly to Roberta.

"May I?" he asked. "Gertrude represents a notable figure in British history, and is considered a worthy cultural icon. To discover that the Ardemore gardens were in fact designed by her makes your property of national significance."

"Wait—wait. Half this *museum* is about Richard Ardemore," Jo said, gesturing vaguely upward. "How can the gardens not be his?"

Roberta rapped her knuckles on the table with some force, as if she just needed the noise of it.

"An homage. To an *imposter*," she said sourly. "He may have *owned* the grounds, but the talent for design, the orangery, the underground heated pipes? The grand sweep of the sunken gardens, the wall, its arboretum?" She sniffed derisively. "Never *his*. Damn the man. We'll rename the entire gallery."

Jo sank a little lower in her chair.

"Am I in trouble?" she asked.

"No," said Gwilym and Rupert, and across from her, Emery fluttered.

"The one absolute truth was the sorry state of the Ardemore fortunes," he said, hands finally landing in his lap. "We would never mislead you about *that*. But if these are truly the Jekyll Gardens—well. It's a bit like buried treasure."

Surprising, but not helpful. Jo needed *someone* to explain *something*—not lay on more vague innuendos.

"What. Are. We. Talking. About," she demanded.

"Ms. Jones," Rupert said, passing her an official-looking paper, "The garden plans you so kindly gave to Roberta are signed and stamped by Ms. Jekyll. I am in the process of independently verifying the claim, but Roberta is—herself—one of the experts on such matters. As such, the Ardemore Gardens are of infinitely greater value. Because of her name, you see. And the rarity of an intact garden as yet undiscovered."

Jo stared at the document in front of her. It was a draft re-evaluation of the property. With more zeroes.

"You're joking."

"I am not joking—however, this is not yet finalized. The estate was too small to attract the attention of the National Trust *before*, but they may well be interested now. The gardens will be a crucial landmark," Rupert said. Roberta nodded, still solemn in repenting her idol.

"I never liked your *William* Ardemore," Roberta said to Jo. "But his father, it seems, was no better."

"Sorry?" Jo said, looking up. Roberta's lamp eyes blinked at her.

"Why should you be? You're trying to find a woman, aren't you? *Richard* tried to erase one."

Roberta meant it, possibly, as a compliment, but it had an unsettling effect. Along the table, Rupert, Emery, Roberta, and Gwilym continued to discuss what all this might mean—but though Jo managed to nod in the right places, she wasn't with them any longer. In her mind the pieces of Evelyn Davies rearranged in a new order.

What if, like Jo's mother, she had been pregnant against the family wishes.

But what if, instead of being cast out, she was erased in a much more final, and fatal way.

Fuck, fuck, fuck.

MacAdams banged his head (gently) against the concrete walls outside York station. No one in the bloody place still smoked, apparently, and he wasn't about to borrow one from Elsie, so he'd resorted to stale chocolate biscuits and a good shout in the alley between the gate and car park.

Elsie claimed to know nothing about the incoming (outgoing) cash over the previous three years—nothing she would admit to, anyway. What she *did* say matched Lotte's own assessment: Sid had a "big score" planned. Exact numbers weren't forthcoming, but according to Elsie, Sid was planning to trade in his "small business" for a "final payout." He had something to *sell*. If you replaced the terms with "regular blackmail" for "ultimate buy-back of evidence," then a lot began to make sense.

But that *wasn't* what Elsie told them after she began her story.

Some seven or eight years ago, an ailing Aiden Jones had come calling. He was dying, apparently, and knew he didn't have long. Elsie made a great noise about him—and the family—being lousy, cheating "rich tits" who thought they were better than everyone else...but if you waded through her rant, the basics seemed pretty clear: Jo's uncle had been searching for information about original Ardemores, and thought Sid could help, given the family connection. Sid, meanwhile, meant to make a few pounds off the deal, and went to see him at the estate. According to Elsie, that's where he saw the painting.

Aiden meant to have it restored; it was worth something. *Priceless*, he'd said. The work of a rare and gifted artist. Sid duly told him what he knew about the Ardemores—probably not much, possibly made up, MacAdams thought. But Aiden never paid him for his trouble, and threatened to call police when Sid pushed. Then, Aiden up and died, and low and behold, Sid becomes groundskeeper of the old property—by blackmailing Rupert.

So far, so good. But Sid didn't know how to sell it or to whom; that's why he went to Elsie. He went to Olivia for money, Lotte for sex, but Elsie had a brain—and he'd give her a cut. And that's where the story broke down. Elsie claimed she couldn't work out how to hock the art; plausible, perhaps. But why did Sid keep it on property? And why take it away again so suddenly when Jo Jones turned up? Elsie claimed "the American" recognized its value and agreed to give it to Sid for safekeeping, where it probably still was, and now Jo was only pretending it was stolen. No, Elsie didn't know why. When pressed, she curled her ruby lips: *maybe they were shagging.* MacAdams didn't believe this.

But Fleet did. Hadn't he *told* MacAdams that the American woman was odd? Hadn't the body been found in her cottage? Wasn't she the only new addition to the equation of Sid Randles?

But then why would Jo blame him for the theft at all? That happened *before* the murder, and—

"Boss?" Green peered round the corner. "Pint?"

"Yeah, could use one."

Green led him around the corner from York CID to a little pub. *Off the hen path*, she said, meaning quiet and slightly gritty, and probably only for locals. People who were *not* MacAdams came to York on the regular; he forgot that sometimes. Green ordered two pints of porter and two bags of crisps.

"The hotel isn't bad," she said. "Not exactly the Churchill, but it's fine."

MacAdams drank his beer and did not admit that his wedding reception had been at that fine establishment.

"Better than staying with Fleet," he said. "His place is a tiny wee hole."

Green laughed.

"Cheers to that." She opened her crisps. "You think Elsie was lying about Jo, don't you."

"Yes."

"Fleet thinks it's because you like her."

"Do you think that?" MacAdams asked and was surprised to find how much he cared about the answer. Green leaned her elbow on the bar and looked at him with her wide, clear eyes.

"Well. I can't think why Jo Jones would give a painting away, and then tell us it was stolen. And we *know* Jo got here exactly when she said—I checked. Sid's call records, his traceable ones, anyway, don't show any contacts in the US. When was she supposed to be shagging him? While on tour through the estate house?" She drank her beer to the half point, then gave the bar a rap with her knuckles. "Anyway. I hope to God Jo has more sense than that."

Sheila Green did have a way of putting MacAdams' general feelings into words. Green ordered her second and some curried chips.

"We took Jo's statement. And we searched the cottage, then we searched the estate. It's a big bloody thing, it would be hard to miss. I mean, what the actual *fuck*?"

It was a "big bloody thing." Small enough to tote around, yes. But too big to hide on your person. It had to be somewhere, and the big house in York seemed like the most obvious place. Far from incriminating Jo, Elsie had just proven she knew the painting existed.

"Sheila, I need to tell a story," MacAdams said. *A story in his head, based on little clues*, as Jo would say. "What if the painting isn't the point?"

"Um. Didn't we just decide that, given Elsie's statement, it *must* be the point?"

"Hear me out." MacAdams snatched the bottle of brown sauce and put it on the bar between them. "Okay. Elsie said Sid told her about a painting—that it was locked up, and he needed to go back for it. That squares. Sid found out Jo was on her way, locks the room the painting is in. But remember, the painting was on the floor."

"If you say so." Green shrugged. MacAdams pointed to the bottle.

"It's on the floor," he repeated. "But it *wasn't* on the floor to start with. It had been on the wall."

The chips arrived. Green hesitated over the brown sauce.

"I want to use that on my dinner—is that allowed?"

"Pay attention to the evidence." MacAdams laid the bottle on its side. "Why would it be on the floor at all? If already on the wall, locked away, why would Sid take it down?"

Green leaned on her elbow.

"He planned to move it?"

"Possible," MacAdams admitted. "But let's imagine you're Sid."

"Let's not."

"That *I'm* Sid, then. I find out Jo Jones is coming to the property. The painting is locked in a room, but I panic—I take it from the wall and shove it behind a dresser, then I lock the door. Now, *one day later*, I am going to put that painting in my van and drive off with it." MacAdams had scarcely finished speaking, but he could see the light dawning in Green's eyes.

"I see. If the painting was the point, why not remove it that very night," she said, sitting up straighter. "Instead, he really must've thought he could talk Jo into leaving him in charge, which would buy him some time. He could keep the cottage and continue hiding the painting."

"The cottage he needed in order to keep his side business going, pimping Lotte," MacAdams said. Green nodded slowly.

"Right. So, on Tuesday night, Sid is more concerned with keeping that going, than he is with the painting. But still, why not take the painting that night?"

"Assignation," MacAdams said. "Jo is moving in, and he is about to lose the cottage, so he meets up with Lotte for a last rendezvous, and returns Wednesday to take the painting?"

"So he's giving up on the pimping job. That loses him cash, but he's still got the mystery five grand—oh. *Oh.*" Green rolled her head around on her shoulders. "Shit. Sid isn't *getting* all that money—he's splitting it or paying it out. To who? Elsie? Jack?"

"We have been assuming there is one crime and it's all connected. What if there are separate crimes? Lotte called it Sid's big score; he *needed* a big score. Even if he and Lotte brought in a thousand or more a month from his pimping, that probably would only pay bills and keep gambling debts at bay. And then separately, there's the five grand going in and out of his account, which he's not pocketing or hiding. So he needs to *sell* something—for cash." MacAdams had barely finished speaking when Green slapped the bar top.

"The *letter*!" she said. "It's between Jack and Elsie, right? But it's in Sid's trouser pocket."

"And in it, Jack tells Elsie *she can afford it.* To send things to Jack." MacAdams rubbed his chin. "Maybe Sid found the letter and didn't like it. Maybe he decided to punk Elsie after all; take the money he was supposed to pay her and run instead. Maybe Elsie really didn't know about the final payout plan."

"Wait a tic," Green said, leaning on her elbow again. "If he had wanted to sell the painting for cash, why hadn't he sold it yet by the time he died?"

That was the question, wasn't it? MacAdams shook his head; it wasn't that hard to shop things on the black market. You could find a fucking tutorial on YouTube. Sid kept it. Why?

"Perhaps the painting served an additional purpose that made it worth holding on to." MacAdams stood the bottle right side up again. "This is about six ounces of glass. But it isn't much use when empty, is it?" He handed it to her, and Green removed the lid.

"You think—are you saying the painting was some sort of vessel?"

MacAdams had been feeling a slight rush—partly the excitement of bringing her along, partly the buzz of two large porters. Now he sighed.

"I do. But it's a very thin theory," he said. "I may also have taken it from a Sherlock Holmes mystery."

"Oh. I don't read those."

"It's not a perfect match anyway," MacAdams admitted. (It

was, in fact, a sort of mash-up between "Second Stain" and "Naval Treaty.") "I'm just trying to account for why the sudden interest in the painting or the estate. Sid's not the sort to have a safe-deposit box."

"You think he was hiding something inside of it?" Green offered him a chip.

"It's dumb if the painting is just some bit of decoration. But now we know Sid thought that painting was valuable, so if he didn't sell it for money right away, it had to be valuable for an additional reason." MacAdams took a breath. The next part came from his experience of the man, more than anything. "Sid also thought it was rightfully *his.* That he was owed the painting and all it was worth, probably all the more because Aiden and the Ardemore family did his family wrong, never giving them their piece of the land. And more recently, because Aiden wouldn't pay him."

"It's still pretty damn thin," Green said. "But I concede a point—the painting and something else, money, or a will or other blackmail-worthy item, for instance, may have gone missing together. And maybe Elsie killed him for either. Or both."

MacAdams took Green's proffered chip and let his eyes wander the dark wood interior. There was a woman at a booth just beyond them, checking her phone and watching the door. Waiting.

"Maybe Elsie is an accomplice, but she isn't the killer," he said. "The killer wouldn't *expect* Sid to come back. She still had all his things."

Green trailed her finger through chip-salt on the bar top. "She dumped it in a skip, remember."

"Only after we were on to her," MacAdams said. "That's an act of self-defense. And there's something more. She's afraid."

"Shite, how can you tell?"

MacAdams agreed it wasn't easy to read the woman—he's said so himself. But he also had a psalter—her brother Jack. He remembered the same trip wire jaw, the same steel pupils, the same slight catch in manner. Hard as they were, they were both scared shitless. He just didn't know why or of whom.

Green's phone rang. She wiped salty fingers against her trousers and picked up.

"Really? Perfect. No, call as soon as you hear," she said. "That was Andrews. This Aunt Hannah is in Calgary."

"Canada? All right. When is she back in England?" he asked. Green chewed her lip.

"That's the weird bit. She's been there for years."

Back at the hotel, MacAdams made a call to Fleet, but couldn't reach him. He left a message instead: MacAdams had decided to let Elsie stew overnight. It meant he would have to wear the same suit the following morning—he should have planned better. Of course, Elsie would be sleeping in her clothes again, too. That might thaw her a bit.

The room had a minibar, but for once what MacAdams really wanted was a strong black coffee.

Elsie and Jack. Sid and Elsie. Jack, Elsie, and the absent aunt, Hannah Walker. The word *blackmail* got a rise out of both Elsie and Jack—but why? What on earth did *he* have to do with it? MacAdams dug about in his bag for Jack's felony file. Fleet had tried turning it in after their last interview, but MacAdams checked it out again. He wanted it with him in case they could work around the injunction against a second interview. Now he settled into a highly uncomfortable half-moon chair and thumbed the contents. The history was succinct: dishonorable discharge from the military; end of his career as a pilot; a smattering of petty thefts. He was looking for the manslaughter indictment when his phone vibrated.

It was a text from Annie.

She was in the lobby.

"Hi! I called your office and they said you'd be here." Annie waved one hand as he met her downstairs. The other was wrapped around the tiny fingers of a small girl with large, dark eyes. "You remember Daya?"

He hadn't seen Daya since she was practically a newborn, but he nodded.

"Do you want a coffee?" he asked, looking behind him in hopes of finding a kiosk or coffee bar.

"No thanks. My parents are coming for dinner. Ashok just went to pick them up." She twisted blond hair into a knot and smiled. "I *did* try to invite you."

"Work," MacAdams said hoarsely.

"I know. That's actually why I came. Your hotel is on the way. Can we have a sit-down? It's not exactly top secret, but I don't want it to get round that I've been peeping into customer records."

MacAdams felt a fool for not suggesting it already. He ushered Annie and Daya, who kept peeping at him from her mother's coat sleeves, to a group of chairs in the corner.

"I shouldn't have asked. I'm sure it has nothing to do with Sid Randles' funeral," he said.

"Oh, but it did!" Annie pulled a folded piece of paper from her coat pocket. "The card had a personal note attached: *For Sid.* See? I also looked up the credit card details."

"Makes sense," MacAdams said. "We know Elsie had been living here at least part time."

"Elsie? I don't recognize that name. The woman who bought them was a bank teller from town. She'd been in before—I checked with the clerk. Anyway, I brought the receipt in case you needed it."

She handed it over, along with the crumpled funerary message, then got unsteadily to her feet.

"Careful," MacAdams said, trying to offer his hand. She smiled at him…a touch indulgently, he thought.

"It's fine. Baby will be soon, though—won't it, Daya? You'll have a little playmate." Daya hid at the mention of her name, and Annie gave MacAdams a smile. "I hope this is helpful to whatever you're up to."

"Me, too," MacAdams agreed. "Thank you for doing it."

Annie was already on her way out, but she turned to wave. "Give my best to Jo, by the way," she said. MacAdams waited until they'd turned the corner outside before doing what he'd been itching to do from the first—and unfolded the receipt. He'd expected half a dozen names in the last thirty-eight seconds.

But none of them had been *Hannah Walker.*

25

Monday

Morning light caught the spire of York Minster, bright and clear against ribbon-pink sky and mirrored in puddles of rain. No wind: the air lay still as a held breath. There were storms coming, they said, from the north. From *home*, MacAdams thought. And well they might, because his mood had blackened with every tick of the clock. Elsie had played a dealer's hand.

"Got it." Green stepped out of the bank, a plastic sleeve clutched in her hand. MacAdams slipped the identification card out. A bright photo, soft blond hair, pastel suitcoat. Elsie Randles—but of course, *not* Elsie Randles. The badge read Hannah Walker.

Andrews had spent the night on the phone to Calgary which, aided by time zone, had managed to finally track down the real Ms. Walker. Elsie and Jack's aunt had returned to Canada after the death of her partner and had been living in a retirement community for the last seven years.

She didn't own a home in York. And she sure as hell didn't work as a bank teller. Elsie had been living two different lives.

"I can't believe it," Green was saying as they made their way back to York station. "I just *can't.* Branch manager said she was the model employee. Smart. Efficient. Good manners. But I *met* her, and I'd have sworn she was a cheap slapper with a side of street tough."

"What she is," said MacAdams through his teeth, "is a damn genius." It wasn't merely that she played a part; Elsie did have sex clients (one of whom made for a useful alibi). Elsie *also* worked in a nice office at Lloyds, originally as a teller, and then later as a loan officer. He'd seen the mask slip when he surprised her in York. She had to decide which person to be on the spot, and the incongruity stayed with him…he just hadn't known what it meant.

"But why?" Green asked. "I mean, why bother being both—why have the shitty Newcastle apartment and the shitty johns? Why not just steal your aunt's identity and get on with it?"

"Because a tidy row house in Bootham requires more cash that she could turn either way," MacAdams said, crossing the street against traffic. "About five thousand a month would help, though."

"You're saying she treated blackmail like her third job?"

"More likely she got the job at Lloyds to cover the blackmail." MacAdams hadn't given her enough credit by far. Elsie *planned ahead.* Acting the model employee (and possibly shagging around) meant she had climbed quickly—and learned fast. A bank could be a great place to hide and launder money; she may have made false accounts. "Gridley and Andrews are both working full time on the accounts and the bank managers are on alert. I want a better look at her early years. She's definitely had a better education than she lets on."

Green rolled her neck.

"So—let me just get this straight in my own damn head. She is the one on the receiving end of Sid's money. And she launders it. But it doesn't go back to Sid?"

"Not most of it, I think."

"What, she gives him a cash allowance? This is just getting weirder." Green stepped ahead and opened the station's front door.

"Sid is terrible with money. Elsie wants to live comfortably. She pays her rent in cash, and probably paid his creditors for him."

"So we know where the money went," Green said as they wound their way toward the interrogation rooms. "But we still don't know where it came from."

"We don't. But Elsie does. She must."

MacAdams set his coffee on the table and peered through the two-way glass. Elsie looked a little worse for wear, having spent the night in a cell. She also, however, looked highly composed. What did Elsie want in life? For that matter, what did Lotte and Olivia want. Each of the sisters, in different ways, had traded security for holding on to Sid. Elsie certainly took risks, but for wholly other reasons. Elsie was after security *itself.* The house, the identities, the jobs were just eggs in different baskets. Elsie was a *survivor.*

"Green, I want you to do the interview."

"Why me?" Green asked. "What about Fleet?"

For one thing, Fleet had yet to appear—or to answer any of MacAdams' calls. But that wasn't the only reason.

"Frankly?" MacAdams said, leaning against the windowsill. "Because she already knows her way around me. And because I think you'll be far more proficient at bringing out the best of Ms. Hannah Walker."

MacAdams watched through the glass as Green, sharp as usual in her blue wool suit, took the seat opposite Elsie.

"I think you know why we're here today," Green said, pushing the bank badge across the table. "Do you want to tell me about being Hannah?"

It was an interesting segue. And Elsie seemed to be considering.

"What do you want to know?"

"Well. I have an honest question. Why two identities? You have a job and impressive credentials. And a house. You must have enjoyed being Hannah. Surely."

Elsie's fingers curled around the ID badge. The steel-bearing eyes were just as cold and edgy as before, though the voice she now used was far smoother.

"Do you enjoy being Sheila Green?" she asked, the faint lines at her mouth appearing in half-smile.

"I do."

"Then you realize it's a stupid question." Elsie tossed the badge back at her. Green kept her composure better than MacAdams expected, and merely folded the ID into her notebook.

"Are you suggesting that you think of Hannah Walker as your own identity?" she asked.

"It is my identity."

"And not Elsie Smythe?"

"That's mine, too."

"You can't have both," Green insisted. Elsie laughed, and that was the same in either role she played, harsh and hard.

"Call one my stage name."

Green leaned across the table, her chin thrust out and sharp.

"Let's call it an alias. That's what it is, isn't it? Because you're the smart one." Green's eyes flickered to the window, though MacAdams wouldn't be able to give her a sign regardless. "You know we'll sort it out in the end. That's why you gave up the rouse. We'll pick through your accounts, all your little transactions. We'll discover that Sid transferred the five thousand pounds to you. So why not tell us where Sid was getting that money in the first place? Who did you have on the hook?"

MacAdams had a pretty good idea what Elsie would do if *he* said that. But right now, it was two fierce women facing each other over a sterile metal table. And he wasn't really sure what to expect. Ultimately, Elsie eased up first.

"You're trying to pin the blackmail on me," she said slowly. "I won't let you."

"I didn't say blackmail," Green said. "I said money laundering. Smart people don't blackmail. They just know how to hide it when someone else does."

Elsie lifted her left hand, as though she held an imaginary cigarette—probably muscle memory. Her eyes fluttered slightly to the glass, where she must know MacAdams waited.

"Perhaps I discreetly managed some money. Cleaned it, let's say. How should I know where Sid got it? It was all his idea, anyway. We had nothing to do with it."

She had played the part perfectly, her face, now without makeup, pleading in a way that would have moved MacAdams had he not seen her other performances first. But this was Green's show. And she was asking the questions.

"Elsie? What do you mean *we*?"

Behind the two-way glass, MacAdams was already rifling through the case notes. He heard Green enter behind him—felt it, almost, a rush of energy.

"Jack Turner. It has to be," she said.

"Ahead of you," MacAdams agreed. Elsie hadn't given Green a name—she'd given total silence and refused to speak more, but that of itself was an admission. So far, the only people they hadn't thrown under a bus were each other. "Dammit, where's the manslaughter file?"

Green ducked under the table and looked beneath her own case notes.

"It was right here the day before yesterday. Fleet read it to me." MacAdams shook his head. "Doesn't matter. This is York station—they'll have it. And just where the hell is Fleet, by the way?"

York CID offered considerably more space than Abington,

and some half dozen spare sergeants and unattached detective constables. MacAdams seized upon a likely subject, still nursing a raspberry bun and coffee for breakfast.

"We're looking for everything you have on this incident," he said, passing him the file folder.

"Oh." The DC dusted powdered sugar from his tie and sat up straighter. "This have to do with the Sid Randles case?"

"Yes. What I want, though, is everything on Elsie's brother Jack Turner. I know he had a conviction and I'm missing half the case file. And get Fleet on the phone, would you?" MacAdams took another sweep of the room, to make sure he wasn't tea-drinking in a corner. "I want that injunction against interviewing Turner lifted."

"Yes sir. I'll start pulling the files. The Turner case was five years ago, I think."

The DC went off to retrieve things from the nearest printer. Green took the liberty of scrolling through the file on his desktop.

"Did you say you *read* the file?" she asked.

"Not beyond the basics; Fleet was with me in the interrogation."

"Oh SHITE. Boss—look here." Green pointed to a clipped photo of Douglas Haw, Jack's arson and manslaughter victim. "Douglas had turned police informant!"

MacAdams stared over her shoulder.

"Informing on Jack Turner—"

"On the whole damn outfit, looks like. No wonder the Met police were all over this—they thought Douglas would help them bring down the ringleaders." Green stepped back to let the DC back at his desk.

"Here you are, all the missing pieces," he said, handing it over. "Douglas Haw, Jr. had been caught jacking a car in Hexham. He agreed to act as informer for a lighter sentence."

"And he got torched for it, but it went down as manslaughter?

How?" MacAdams demanded, "And *where* is Detective Fleet for God's sake, we need him on this."

"Sorry sir, he's out for the day."

MacAdams growled under his breath, shuffling the papers off to Green so he could dial Fleet's mobile. It rang without going to voice mail. "Oh hell with him. Who among your lot can get us an interview with Jack Turner over in Full Sutton?"

"Boss!" Green's eyes were switchbacking across the pages. "Oh damn." She tugged him away from the row of desks (and listening ears).

"*Look* at this. Undercover operation, surveillance, people watching Jack's house. I haven't finished, but this looks like a big fucking deal. No way Fleet didn't know about this."

MacAdams picked up his phone to dial Andrews.

"Tell me something, Tommy. When I asked you to look up history of Jarvis Fleet before his arrival, did you keep a file?"

"I always keep a file, boss."

"Good. Tell me *exactly* the timeline of his semiretirement to York."

"Sure thing." The ghost of typing echoed in MacAdams' ear, and he held up a finger to encourage Green's patience. "Five years ago, last August 13."

That was a full three months *after* Turner had been tried and convicted. MacAdams tapped the phone against his cheek.

"Okay, okay, fine. Wait—while still with London Met, did he by chance work in York on an undercover case?" MacAdams asked. But he needn't have. Green's eyes had gone wide, and she held up a page from the new-printed file on the Jack Turner case. Above the indent of her fingernail, in a list of leading officers, one name stood out perfectly clear: *Jarvis Fleet, Principal Investigator.*

Jo hummed to herself.

The lights were still out at Ardemore House, but she'd made

a little nest in the library. She'd relit the candles and brought in a few more but was presently curled under a blanket and reading by flashlight.

Gertrude Jekyll was, it turned out, a *prolific* writer. Thousands of articles, at least forty books, notebooks, and drawings—most of which were held by the Godalming Museum (now the envy of Roberta Wilkinson). Jo had two of her flower books open in her lap; it was probably where Ardemore got his "language of flowers" turn: lilies for purity, lavender for distrust, baby's breath for everlasting love. She could memorize later; for now, she had a printout of Jekyll's online biography; *Gertrude's brother was a friend of Robert Louis Stevenson; who borrowed the family name for his famous Jekyll & Hyde story.*

Jo leaned back to stare at the (still ruined) ceiling. Gertrude had been a scientist, of a sort, herself—"allowed to flourish" in "manly" disciplines by an indulgent and understanding father. Jekyll, and not *Jane Eyre* after all.

Jo pushed the blanket aside and stood up. It was nearly noon, but outside the sky remained dark and forbidding. Tula had warned her of a storm coming; Jo tried to get signal enough to check the weather, but no dice. She replaced a guttering candle for a bit more light, and then brought out the glass tumblers from the China cabinet. They sat next to a decanter, big and thick and square—but too heavy to be bothered with. Whisky from the bottle was good enough. She lined them up on the mantel, beneath the portraits of William and Gwen, and poured a little whisky in each of four glasses. It was a family meeting, after all.

Jo stood before the fireplace and sipped her whisky.

"I don't know what happened to Evelyn's painting," she said out loud. Her voice echoed oddly in the room. "But I think I know what happened to Evelyn."

Predictably, the paintings said nothing. Jo's gaze followed the severe lines of William's aristocratic forehead, right down to his blue cravat, where the varnish had cracked. Gwen was more pleasant to look at, if slightly more hollow, too. Less fully there.

Sister wives; that had been the problem with Sid Randles, too. But this? Jo turned her attention to Gwen's portrait.

"Was it your idea?" she asked. Did Gwen offer shelter, the way Jo's own aunt had done? But what would William think? New to the aristocracy, the Ardemores had certainly taken to it—even to the point of having a garden fashioned by the famous Jekyll, for which Richard then took credit. Would he be content to let a "ruined" woman live in the house? She could imagine Gwen insisting, promising to help raise the child. Just as Sue had helped raise Jo.

Except there was no baby. And no Evelyn, either. The Ardemores left town and didn't come back. Jo swirled her whisky, making "legs" of amber liquid in the glass. Jo's uncle Aiden and her grandfather *pretended* her mother was as good as dead when she left England.

What if Evelyn, however; died in fact? During childbirth, maybe, tragically, because she was afraid to call a midwife and out her own secret. Gwen, heartbroken twice over.

Sid Randles had been right about at least one thing. People *don't* just up sticks and move, never to return. Not unless something bad has happened.

Sid, the sly fox. Jo lifted her glass in a silent toast. Something bad happened to him, certainly. To his whole family, from the sound of it. Jo shifted her gaze to William once more. She'd begun to see Roberta's side of things. Promises broken, families left in hock. She hadn't liked Sid, but whatever he'd got himself into—and it was probably a lot—he hadn't deserved to end up facedown on her rug.

Of course, murder in your home was also "something bad." But Jo didn't feel like packing up and leaving, and it wasn't just that New York and Chicago didn't have anything for her. She'd only come to terms with it two nights ago, sobbing right here, in the library—and only because Gwilym said it first. Jo might not be very good at peopleing, but she was sure as shit tired of being alone. She'd come all the way to Abington to find—something. Someone. Evelyn Davies. Her own father. Herself.

Jo didn't see the lightning, but the thunder clap echoed like the boom of too-near fireworks. She covered her ears, grimacing at the reverberation as fat raindrops began slapping against the windows. Outside, the gravel lane changed from white to dark gray. The wind was picking up, too; if she didn't leave now, she might be stuck there a long while—

Three sharp bangs sounded from the hall. Jo knew it was the door knocker, but it scared her anyway. Maybe Tula had come in the truck to rescue her? She slid the bolt and pulled the heavy door open to find a very wet mackintosh, broad brimmed hat, and a detective's badge held at arm's length.

"Detective Fleet?" she asked. He smiled under his brush mustache.

"Hello, Ms. Jones, may I come in?"

"What are we looking for?" Green asked. She was standing guard as MacAdams rifled through papers on Fleet's desk. The firearms and forensics division shared the lower floor with secure storage for search and seizure, which had worked very much to their benefit. Fleet had only a single office mate, who was presently not...present.

"He lied. He told me he didn't know Turner, that he hadn't been part of the case." MacAdams accidentally overturned a framed photo of Fleet in full RAF uniform. Is that why Fleet had prickled when MacAdams said Turner was also a veteran? He picked it up and shook his head. "It doesn't make any *sense*, Sheila. Why would he lie?"

"Embarrassment?" Green asked. "He essentially testified *on Jack Turner's behalf.*"

MacAdams furrowed his brow further (if possible). According

to the case details, Douglas helped the police against an organized syndicate operating out of London. He fingered Turner as the point of contact—not a big player *yet*, but a lot more committed and climbing the syndicate ladder. Follow Turner, find bigger fish to fry. Unfortunately for Douglas, Jack Turner got the wind up. He knew exactly what he was doing, too. Facing a murder charge, he *should* have been sent away for the max sentence *or* singing like a canary for a plea bargain. Neither happened. Instead, he got a reduced charge, a reduced sentence…

"It doesn't make sense," Green continued, coming fully into the office. "Fleet ends up being a witness for the guy he was supposed to catch, right? Says he saw Jack try and save Douglas, that it had meant to be a scare, not a murder. Bang, reduced to manslaughter. It's the worst kind of shame because on one hand, *not* to witness would make him a crooked cop. But standing up for Smythe lost him his chance at a win for Met police, and I can bet they forced him into retirement because of it."

"Okay, I hear you." MacAdams replaced the military photo on the desk. Fleet seemed to have been retired out early more than once… "But answer me this—why *here*? He's got no family here, Green. In fact, the only connection he has to the place is one fucked up case and Jack Turner, himself down the road in HMS Full Sutton Prison. There *has* to be a reason. The man had a flat in London somewhere, he must have. Would you trade that for a rented '70s row house in Stamford Bridge?"

"He lives in a rental?"

Green's question threw him off. But yes, Fleet had said as much—*the rent was cheap for the size.* A sudden, numbing prickle ran through MacAdams, collarbone to clavicle.

"Oh my God. He's *broke*."

"A single white man retired from both the service and the Metropolitan Police? He can't be," Green said. And then, it hit her, too. "Ah shit. He's broke—because someone's been taking his money?"

"Pardon me? Can I, eh, help you two? This *is* a restricted area."

MacAdams saw the man some three seconds before he spoke—and had already reached for his identification. Fleet's office mate. He hoped his own officiousness would cover Green's nervous leap to one side when she saw him a moment later.

"DCI MacAdams and this is DS Green, Abington CID. We've been working with Jarvis Fleet on the Sid Randles murder."

"Ah yes! The German derringer!" The man rocked slightly on his feet, clearly pleased by the remembrance of such a gun.

"We were pursuing inquiries into Elsie Randles," MacAdams went on. "DCI Jarvis Fleet led the case against her brother, didn't he? Jack Turner?"

"Something like that, the great bloody ponce." The man reached a hand forward. "I'm Franklin, by the way."

MacAdams warmed to Franklin with alacrity.

"Still with the Met back then, wasn't he?" he asked, shaking his hand. "Still behaves as though he might be, yet."

MacAdams couldn't watch both Green's expression and Franklin's at once, but he hoped she had cottoned on to his strategy. Meanwhile, Franklin's well-worn face creased into derisive mirth.

"Aye, I don't doubt that."

MacAdams surveyed Fleet's desk again.

"And of course, the military bearing," he said, pointing to the photo. "You know he left the RAF for the police?"

"God. Don't I." Franklin sat at the desk opposite and made a *see?* gesture with both hands. "I'm a captive audience. Have been since they moved him down here, a supposedly temporary arrangement."

A grudge-bearing office mate was just what they needed. But MacAdams didn't want to make a wrong step. In his mind, a cursed rolodex was flipping back and forth: Sid, Elsie—Elsie,

Jack—Jack, Fleet. Connections. Where were the bloody connections?

"Jack Turner was in the service, too," he mused, and could see Green suddenly fumbling through Jack's file out of the corner of his eye. "Did Fleet know him by chance? I mean before all of—this."

Franklin shook his head.

"Can't say. I'll tell you what, though. The case was a bloody cock-up. They should never let military witness for military."

Well. There was one connection made for him…

"You don't think Fleet should have testified because of the bias?" MacAdams asked.

"I'm not saying he should have kept mum—don't get me wrong. We've enough bother from barristers claiming falsified evidence—and the papers are only happy to repeat it."

"Bent cops." The words came out of MacAdams own mouth, but in his head, it had been Elsie and Jack in stereo. "You're saying if he *hadn't* testified, the force would have been accused of hiding evidence?"

Franklin had been halfway to a sip of cold coffee. Now he paused.

"Hard to say, I suppose. It would just be Turner's word against a Scotland Yard DCI." He shrugged. "Pointless, anyhow. Turner got fifteen years when the average life sentence is what, twenty-five at most? That's the worst of it. Fleet loses a chance to bring down organized crime, and the only gain is a man like Jack serving some years fewer. Travesty. He had to have had a bias."

MacAdams had finally turned his eye on Green. He could tell by the pursed line of her mouth that the contents were under pressure.

"Served under Clapham," she said quietly.

Which meant, of course, *also* under Jarvis Fleet. MacAdams' scalp prickled. Would *that* be enough to induce a rule-minded, stiff-backed man like Fleet to shield a potential murderer? Unlikely as hell.

"Blackmail," MacAdams said, clearing his throat. "We think Sid had extorted money from his killer—five thousand pounds to be exact—to then wire back to Elsie."

"And you think Jack Turner might have been Sid's target?" Franklin asked, mercifully getting the wrong end of the stick. "He'd have a hard time shooting him from his prison cell in Full Sutton, I think. Especially with a little tiny firearm. Have you seen it?"

"We haven't located the murder weapon," Green reminded him, but Franklin just shook his head.

"I mean ours." He was already standing. "It's worth seeing. So rare you would have to order ammunition from a specialty dealer in Germany or make your own."

MacAdams and Green followed Franklin down the hall; search and seizure was double access, keycard and pin. He left them at the steel door to fetch the lanyard.

"This looks very, very bad," Green whispered.

MacAdams agreed but waved his hand for silence as Franklin rounded the corner. The two of them stepped dutifully away while he punched in the codes, and soon they entered a large storeroom of movable shelves.

"Archives are over there. Search and seizure this way." He made a left and they proceeded down a virtual weapons gallery, from shivs and switchblades to firearms and one pair of what MacAdams assumed to be nunchucks. At the end of one steel case, Franklin retrieved a cardboard box.

"Thing of beauty," he said, unwrapping the derringer.

"James Bond," MacAdams said, as he had the first time he'd seen the photograph.

"Funny you say that." Franklin handed the weapon to MacAdams. "Spy movies. Always supposed to be hiding in plain sight, but they never are! Driving an Aston Martin, you're not exactly blending in."

"So the derringer is an Aston Martin," Green asked. MacAdams shook his head.

"No. It's—it's—" He felt the cool weight in his palm. Small. Tidy. Easily hidden in a pocket, up a sleeve. An Aston Martin was pretentious, loud, statement making. The gun was not any of those things. Rare, yes. And possibly easy to identify, too, if you knew what you were looking for. But that wasn't the point slowly taking shape in MacAdams' head. "*Why* would anyone use a gun like this?"

"Stealth, I assume," Franklin offered. "Small enough to hide. In a crowd, who would know where the shot had come from?"

But that wasn't at all what MacAdams meant. He closed his fingers around the handle, then placed the weapon back on the shelf—a shelf right there in York station, scarcely ten yards from Fleet's office. A murderer might choose a specific gun for all sorts of reasons. But a man in a hurry and under pressure would choose for only one: practical accessibility. A man is blackmailed; he doesn't know by whom; he doesn't want to take chances…

"Franklin, this gun goes to forensics. Now."

"I beg your pardon?"

MacAdams felt the sickening churn of his insides as several ideas locked into place at once.

"We didn't find the murder weapon," he said, his throat dry and constricted. *"Because we had it all along."*

26

Detective Fleet sat in the wingback armchair of the newly conversational sitting area. It was the seat nearest the hearth, just beneath the formidable painting of Lord William. Brown tweed suit, one leg crossed ankle to knee and otherwise extraordinarily stiff and proper, he might have been a painting, himself.

"You've had guests?" he asked.

"Sorry?"

"Four glasses." He pointed them out with a long forefinger—and Jo could feel the heat of a blush sliding up the back of her neck.

"I was, erm, toasting my ancestors." Jo lifted one from its place on the mantel. Was it rude not to offer? Or was he on duty? "Would you like one?"

He smiled the way waiters did at posh restaurants. Like he didn't mean it.

"I'd like you to tell me about the paintings," he said.

Jo had been left without an answer on the whisky question. She decided to set it on the side table nearest, as a neutral zone.

The Barbizon school of landscape painters and portraitist Augustus John jumped to her frontal lobe—but she felt reticent about sharing, suddenly. It was his bearing, maybe: gray hair and gray tweeds, toothless smile and fingers splayed on the chair arms. She'd associated Sid with Reynard the Fox, almost from first meeting. Perhaps because of it, Fleet now reminded her of Isengrim the Iron Wolf.

"What do you want to know?" she asked. His posture didn't change.

"Are you still looking for your lost portrait?"

"No. Well, yes—sort of." Jo cleared her throat and endeavored to think in a straight line. "I ended up being more interested in Evelyn as a *person*. She's a long-lost relative of mine. I think she died in childbirth. It's hard to tell from the records because unmarried women sometimes hid their pregnancies or were afraid to call a doctor..." Jo trailed off. She couldn't tell if Fleet had even been listening. He'd picked up the tumbler and nosed the glass.

"Talisker, isn't it? That's MacAdams' favored brand. I used to be very fond." The way he held the crystal seemed extraordinarily precise, even priestly. "Your lost painting was on the wall upstairs. I examined it with the forensic unit."

"Yes. But I found it on the floor. Maybe it fell."

"From grace?" Fleet asked.

"Um?" Jo's head was buzzing, though not from whisky. Some idea was forming just out of her reach; she felt hypervigilant and slightly unfocused. Meanwhile, Fleet smoothed each pant leg as though scattering imaginary crumbs and then got to his feet—still carrying the whisky glass.

"Everyone has a breaking point. Some fall further than others." A wind had picked up outside and it found its way through the house's cracks to flutter the candle flames. Fleet held the tumbler under his mustache, as though breathing it. A faint twitch appeared at the corner of his mouth—and without warning, he drained the glass in a single shot. Fleet then slid one finger along the mantel finial, and tapped at the whisky glass meant for William.

"I celebrated my twelfth year of sobriety last August," he said, picking it up. "It's a shame." Fleet drained the whisky glass, again in a single swallow. At odds with his every other motion and manner, it was somehow frightening. Jo pulled her knees to her chest, as if this would help anchor her somehow.

"What is it that you—want?" she asked.

Fleet turned back to the mantel, where he deposited the empty glass and picked up the last one—the one that should have been Evelyn's.

"I should say *the truth*," he said. "But people lie. For all kinds of reasons. You say you didn't know Sid Randles. And yet, he came to see you once here, twice at the Red Lion. I've thought about this a great deal."

F-f-f-f—Jo was already gripping at her thumbs, but her usual retinue of repeatable words failed her.

"He—he came the second time to—to shout at me."

"This is certainly what we've been made to think. Sid telling the room that he hadn't stolen anything—and you, half fainting from fright. And yet you've shown such remarkable composure ever since."

"You don't believe me," Jo said, feeling the sudden need to explain herself. "Why would I pretend?" She could almost hear her own pulse in her ears, but Fleet went on.

"I said before, sometimes we lie for good reasons." Fleet drank the third glass and refilled it from the bottle. "Perhaps Sid came to you that first night with a proposition. You, new to the town, would be the perfect accomplice. Maybe he played upon your sympathies—your family owed him—you guiltily oblige."

"Oblige to *what*?" Jo felt like her scalp was shrink-wrapping to her skull, and she jumped at the next peal of thunder.

"Too strong?" Fleet made another of his quarter turns. "I am willing to believe he beguiled you. I'd believe that he forced you—threatened you. Maybe you didn't understand the value of what he'd entrusted to your care."

"But the painting was mine to start with!"

"Oh. The painting." Fleet made a *tsk* sound, and then wagged a finger at her slowly. Jo had too many words trying to get out of her mouth—and so said none of them.

"You see, Ms. Jones, a detective must work backward from the fact. Mr. Randles was so keen to have this out-of-the-way hideout that he blackmailed your lawyer for it. Does that surprise you?"

It really fucking *did*, but Jo still hadn't managed to unlock her jaw.

"Not just the cottage, for his little business. But *this* place. This sad, lonely, empty house." He swept one hand around the room's dim, ragged corners. "So excellent for hiding in. And now Elsie Smythe—Elsie *Randles*—has told us *you* had the painting all along."

"But I DON'T!" Jo said, finally. She'd jumped up from her chair, every muscle twitching. "I don't—I *don't*!"

"Now, now, Miss Jones." Fleet made a sudden, erratic gesture. It halted and silenced her, because if his stiff command had been intimidating, the *loss* of it was *terrifying*. "Now, now," he repeated. "I am very generous, you see."

Fleet now made a circuit of the room—one that included Jo as its center. His gait had changed, and his tongue had loosened.

"I'm not arresting you. I *could*. Blackmail is a prison offence."

"*What* blackmail?" Jo asked. Fleet grasped at his collar with his free hand, pulling the tie loose. His lip curled up when he spoke, a tic of some sort, a snarl.

"You *must* have known what you had after Sid was—Well. *After*. But I'll believe you didn't. No one ever need know. Only you *will* give it to me!"

Jo recoiled against the mantelpiece and thought of storybook foxes. Reynard always got away. Until he didn't. A tremor vibrated in her muscles and ran stairs down her spine, with all the bells ringing.

"Sid," she said thickly. "Sid had something you wanted? He was blackmailing *you*? And you—you—" *Oh God. Oh fuck.*

Fleet drank the last glass of whisky, a tall one, and Jo felt as though a final door had just been shut somewhere.

"Now what makes you say such things?" he asked, his voice a whispered hiss. He leaned over her where she clung to the mantel—long and gaunt, a twist of mouth under the mustache. A mash of conflicting stories were screaming across Jo's synapse: Reynard and Iron Wolf, Jekyll and Hyde, Sherlock and Watson. Nothing had prepared for the real denouement—but here it was, anyway: Fleet murdered Sid Randles.

And now, Fleet knew that she knew.

"I *gave* you opportunity," he said, bathing her in whisky breath. "You could have said you didn't know—you could have produced the missing painting—or the documents within. I would have made it all go away. Why can't you just *do as I say*!"

Jo swallowed a bubble of panic and began inching backward along the mantel and its big blue vase. Blood pulsed into her ears—*keep it together.* Her fingers had reached the beveled edge. She felt the cold ceramic and took a breath.

"I don't w-want to be murdered."

"Do you think I meant to? I've never *meant* to," Fleet said. His animal breathing labored at the edge of speech, and under it lurked something raw and mean and desperate. "Killing. It's ugly. Messy. Wars are messy—but we can always make the bad things go away."

"What bad things?" Jo chirped.

"*Any* bad thing. People make mistakes. They do little things—and bigger ones to cover the little things. Soldiers, civilians. Just give it to me, and this will all go away."

Jo panted, her mind racing. She didn't know what he wanted.

She just needed to get out. *Distract him*, she told herself. *Make him look away. Buy time. Lie.*

"I—I hid what you want. In this room," she lied. "On the bookcase."

Fleet spun about to face the ruined, gutted (empty) shelves. He wouldn't find anything there. But it wouldn't matter now; Jo felt the reassuring weight of the pepper spray canister in her palm. She extended her arm, finger on the aerosol depressor, and waited for him to turn around—

"Jesus," Green breathed as MacAdams narrowly avoided clipping the car in front of them, its brake lights bleary in driving rain.

"Sorry." It had been helter-skelter since they raised alarms at York station; Green had been on some dozen phone calls already and the traffic had snarled under thunderheads. They didn't have all the answers. But they had some.

Confirmed—Fleet had gone back to Abington early that morning, without telling MacAdams.

Confirmed—he had not checked in at Abington CID. Andrews had been trying to reach Jo Jones, but no luck.

"Did you tell them to send a squad to the estate?" MacAdams asked. Again.

"Yes. Twice. But they are being thrashed by this storm, too. Power is out everywhere, trees down." Green cringed as MacAdams took another swerve round slow traffic. "We don't *know* anything is wrong, boss. Remember, we don't *know*."

"I fucking know," MacAdams growled. Elsie had played them, but she'd played Fleet, too. That was why she kept looking through the two-way glass as she spoke; she knew Fleet was bound to be there—and she wanted him to blame *Jo*, not her and Jack. "Fucking move, you slow fucking bastards!" MacAdams changed lanes again, and this time Green clung to the overhead handle.

"All right, I can believe Elsie is a guilty party easy," she agreed. "And we know Jack had something on Fleet, who helped him get the more lenient sentence."

Confirmed. Though not the sole witness to the murder (a team had been trailing Jack, after all), Fleet was first on the scene. He claimed Jack didn't know the victim was inside the car, and in fact tried to save him. Manslaughter, not murder, on Fleet's word alone.

"What I don't get, though, is how Sid becomes involved at all," Green continued. "He wasn't in service with them, and doesn't appear to have known Fleet before the blackmail started."

"Sid was married to Elsie," MacAdams said simply.

"But why would she involve him? He'd be a liability."

"Remember the dead roses, dead birds sent to Olivia? Elsie gets revenge, and Sid had wronged her." MacAdams had been falsely assuming *she* was a victim of Sid's extortion. Elsie, for her part, probably knew MacAdams was bound to see her as victim instead of the mastermind of a convoluted blackmail and money laundering plot. "I'm sure Jack used something against Fleet to get off his murder charge, but he's not the brains behind this, and neither was Sid."

Green cringed at the gap between lorry and tour bus that MacAdams had just squeezed through.

"Then why would Fleet not go after Elsie—or Jack—in the first place?" she asked. "Why murder Sid with an antique derringer in an empty cottage? Is doesn't make sense."

And of course, she was right. MacAdams was still missing something—something that predated Jack's arson conviction. Though for the moment, he didn't give a damn what it was. He replayed Elsie's words from the interrogation.

It was all his idea, anyway. We had nothing to do with it.

"Call the station again, and this time stay on the line till *someone* confirms they're at Ardemore House," he demanded.

It wasn't like the movies. A detonation of searing spray exploded into Fleet's eyes, nose, and mouth—but the overspray burned Jo's fingers and turned the air bitter in her own lungs. Fleet made a retching, coughing shriek and collided with the mantel. Jo leapt backward, only to collide with the overturned coffee table. He was cursing her, a foamy guttural over the sound of shattering glass as his windmilling arms sent vases and candles crashing to the floor.

Fuck, fuck, fuck played on repeat in Jo's brain as she slid sideways into the hallway. Her own eyes were bleary, her thoughts scattered. And Fleet was far from off his feet.

"Give it to me!" he demanded. Jo darted to the front door, but despite purpling face and streaming eyes, Fleet was taller, faster, and stronger. He lunged and Jo squealed in recoil, putting the hall table between them.

"I don't even know what *it* is!" she shouted. Fleet was foaming but focused, the startling blue of his iris floating in a sea of red.

"*Clapham's letter*, you fucking bitch," he wheezed. Spittle formed in the corners of Fleet's mouth as he spoke, his fingers clutching the table edge white-knuckled. *"Give me the letter!"*

Jo didn't know who Clapham was. She didn't care, either; one foot braced against the wainscoting and she shoved the table hard at Fleet's midsection. It bought a little time; Jo bolted through the dining room and on to the back pantry. No door—no lock. Jo sized up the enormous China cabinet and shoved with all her might. It shuddered and tipped, dust-coated crystal smashing on the floor below—but it hadn't blocked the door, and Fleet was already there. His arm shot forward, gripping her shoulder.

"I've no more money—do you hear me? It ends NOW!" She was pinned, half squatting between the wall and the hutch, fingers scrabbling behind her for a missile of some sort.

"I don't want your money!" she shouted, groping wildly.

Fleet responded by yanking her to her feet—but Jo's fingers had located the smooth neck of the decanter, still intact. She swung it by way of reflexive action, the heft carrying it on her arm like a pendulum. It connected with a sickening sound. A spurt of blood followed the crunch, and after that, Fleet's desperate howl of pain.

Oh God, oh God—Jo tore herself away, reseeing the blueprint in her head. *Through the kitchen! Wrap around the back, past the cellar, to the front hall.* The house was a circuit; if she could beat him, she could get to the front door…

But something was very wrong.

Light pooled on the hallway floor, shining and intense. She saw red and yellow, heard a sizzling that wasn't rain on roof tiles. The upturned candles had caught the curtains, and a river of hot wax spilled fire across the carpet. From their prone position on the floor, William and Gwen stared back, faces alive and glistening as heat sweated the varnish. The library—*her* library—was *on fire.*

For a moment, nothing else mattered. Jo grasped the drop cloth that once covered furniture and attempted to smother flames, but the heat billowed it back. She tried again, and again, but too little, too late. The empty bookcase spouted fire at the ceiling, and the air was growing wavy and warped in the heat. It was Jane Eyre all over again, *"the building one mass of flame."* Everything was going to burn, and Jo staggered backward from the heat.

"Going somewhere, Ms. Jones?" came the guttural growl as long-boned fingers closed on Jo's throat. She gulped and gagged and kicked the floor. Fleet responded by hauling her up to his ruined face. His nose crumpled to one side and blood fouled his mustache and ran into his spittle-flecked mouth.

"We have to get out! It's on fire!" Jo choked.

"Is it here?" he demanded. His fingers clutched the base of her neck as he jerked her along. Jo twisted against his grip, but size *did* matter; she was a rag doll in his grip. They were in the dining room again, the foxhunt winking above the table in reflected orange light.

"Clapham said just the three of us would ever know. But three can't keep a secret, can they?" He spat clotted blood. "Is it here? If so, it can burn."

If she agreed, she'd never make it out of the fire. She knew it, could see the whole plan in a flash: his word against a dead woman's… He might even say he tried to save her.

"It's not here," she shouted over the roar of thunder and fire. "Let me go and—and I'll show you—"

"WHERE?" he roared. The fire roared, too. They were running out of time.

"You can't want me dead—you're a policeman!" she cried. After it came a crackling, bone-sucking sound: Fleet laughing through his broken nose.

"That's just what Sid said," he coughed. He dragged her toward the flames, using her as a heat shield. Jo's mind spun; was he going to roast her until she gave in? Cook her to death. *Get. Out. Now.* Jo had been scrabbling against every surface, trying to free herself from his grip around her neck—but that wasn't the way. Endless courses of self-defense, but she could only remember one thing: *deadweight.* Jo dropped suddenly to the floor like a stone.

It hurt more than she expected. Fleet tipped forward and her shoulders connected hard with the floor amid his cursing and coughing. The air was better close to the ground, though, and she took grateful breaths. Fleet gagged above her, and then let her go. She was on her hands and knees in a moment, scrabbling forward in a world gone black and red. A heavy dark cloud rolled above, smothering the edges of doors and windows. *Solicitor, solstice, Sanskrit, seconds.* She'd made it to the hall, but couldn't see the front door. There *was* no door. Just a ball of fire and searing heat—and a wail that was, or should have been, human. Fleet, his coat in flames, arms waving like fiery pinwheels. *Look away,* she told herself, look away and get yourself out—except the only way out was *up.*

Jo darted for the stairs in a crouch, holding her breath. Up one. Up two, three, four. Heat radiated from the floor and all the timbers crackled. Her eyes stung with tears, but she'd come to the place beyond feeling, where only the answer mattered. Lightning flashed through the hall and the house wailed, snapping and moaning.

One way out.

Through Evelyn's room.

Smoke plumed up from below and gathered at the roofline. Jo pulled her shirt up over her nose and mouth as she approached the little door. It danced in front of her, wavy with heat. She grasped the doorknob, and it sizzled in her grip. *Dammit!* The library inferno below had made the room an oven.

In her mind, she could still see Fleet, bony, red-eyed, and blood-mouthed, filling the space like death itself. *He* was dead. She was going to be if she didn't hurry. Jo grasped the handle again, ignoring the sear of flesh, and thrust herself into Evelyn's room.

It had come alive. Distorted by refraction, the wallpaper writhed, and the ceiling beams bent. Flames licked from the floorboards and danced firefly embers against walls of sepia-pink. At the far end, she could see the open window, its purple night bisected with fractures of lighting. It might be a thousand miles away.

You will do this, though.

Jo clutched fingers to fists and ran for the black window. The floor burned, her face burned, her lungs burned. Then, she had one leg out the window, one foot dangling in empty air…

She jumped, falling onto the scaffold platform outside.

"Oh. My. God."

The ground heaved below, and a bleary streak of colored lights lined the drive. Men were shouting at her, maneuvering ladders and trucks. But *so* far down; she couldn't climb—she couldn't move. Jo wrapped numb fingers around icy steel, closed her eyes, and waited for the end.

The first murder case of which MacAdams had any part took place in Glasgow. They discovered the body of a college girl in an alley not far from Kelvingrove. Still a constable, he'd been first to find her, and he remembered the scene as if painted: her body propped against the stone wall, autumn leaves caught in her dark hair. A bicycle had been locked nearby, unrelated, but somehow part of his memory as though a key piece of it. Most young police officers could share an experience like it, a threshold moment, where you knew you were leaving one kind of lived experience for another and wouldn't go back.

This was one.

Ardemore House rose from the hilltop as a skeleton, black-rib chimney towers and a collapsed rubble of timber and slate. MacAdams stopped the car, left it running, and ran into the knot of firefighters shouting Jo's name. He didn't remember Green following him. He didn't remember his own uniformed officers, plus a rain-soaked Gridley, trying to keep him from stumbling into quarters of the still smoldering structure. It was all just raw and numb at once, the ice of dread and the gut-realization that *one of their own* had done this—that MacAdams had spent days and nights with the man, the murderer, and had never suspected—that this same man had killed Jo Jones.

Except, thank God, he *hadn't.*

"James, for God's sake! She's in the emergency van!" Green finally managed to say. And so she was, smoke-smeared and wrapped in an NHS-issue blanket. The relief he felt manifested as both a desire to yell at Jo and the desire to embrace her, neither of which were appropriate to the situation. So he stood there, mute and largely useless.

"I climbed out on the—the thing." She sniffed and pointed to a twisted wreck of scaffold, from which (Gridley explained) she'd been rescued by the fire brigade.

"I'm glad." And because he couldn't think of anything else to do, he climbed into the van and sat next to a wet and bleary-eyed Jo. "How—how did you manage it?"

"Jane Eyre," Jo said. "They ask Jane what she should do to

avoid the fire pits of hell. She tells them she must *keep in good health and not die.*" She looked at her hand, which had been bandaged against the burn. "I decided to not die."

MacAdams felt an odd hitch in his throat; the incongruity of Jo Jones wasn't easy to overcome. In fact, the whole woman wasn't easily overcome.

"The other detective is dead," she said after a long silence. "It wasn't nice."

"No. But *he* was not nice," MacAdams said. It would be quite a while before they could dig him out. Bits of him, anyway.

"He said Sid was blackmailing him." Jo said the words as if she were trying them out for the first time. "With a letter. He thought I had it."

"A letter. Not the painting?" MacAdams asked. They were searching the house in York as they spoke and would soon be overturning the hideaways of all her various aliases.

"He seemed to think it was *in* the painting?" Jo said. "Not in a clever way."

MacAdams had to sit with that a minute; she meant, he gathered, not a puzzle. "As in stuck to the back of it, or inside it?"

"Mhmmph." Jo sniffed and rubbed her nose. "I think? Clapham's letter, is what he said."

MacAdams heard the name with a jolt. *Commodore Alexander Clapham*, superior officer to Jack and Jarvis. MacAdams felt the click and lock of two separate ideas… Fleet had come to help Cora sort through "papers" at Clapham's funeral. And he had still been poking through them, hadn't he…?

"Boss?" Green had appeared with tea for Jo, and a mobile phone for MacAdams. "Back in Newcastle. You aren't going to believe this."

"Try me," he said.

"They found the painting. And that's not all."

27

MacAdams wasn't sure who he'd underestimated the most in this case. Elsie would be going to prison for blackmail, yes. But she never did have the painting. That would be found in Olivia's house, willingly hidden by the woman Sid trusted more than the rest.

At least MacAdams' gut response to Alexander Clapham had been redeemed—and as with almost every case, everywhere, it came down to following the money. Even so, he never would have guessed its path or its origin, in Afghanistan, in 2001. Back then, Clapham was a Wing Commander with a wife, a young Cora, and an unexpected newborn son. Times were tight; his wife's bad health meant the need for extra caregivers. Everything had begun innocently enough; air force parts, comms units, even electrical supplies were scarce between shipments, so you stole from Peter to pay Paul and edited the books. Supply and demand were fickle, however, and some machine parts began to accumulate needlessly, or went obsolete as new models appeared. The same was true of ground transport units, and even of airplane parts. If a few items found their way into the hands of locals for an extra quid, it hurt no one—and it helped out at home. Local demand grew; parts went for higher dollars; higher dollars led to *arrangements.* Clapham got promoted first to Group Commander, then Air Commodore, and being the generous sort, his top officers got "extras." Perks of the job, and no one asked, and no one told. Clapham retired in 2010, to lead a more retired life at the well-heeled estate he'd purchased outside Abington. And there, it might have ended.

But it didn't. "People make mistakes. They do little things—and bigger ones to cover the little things," Fleet had said, as Jo recounted. The network of goods then expanded; Clapham styled himself a businessman, an entrepreneur. He just needed someone to take over on his behalf—and so came Jarvis Fleet. Having a posh education and reasonably good breeding, Fleet took over the black market trade in air force parts and navigated the escalating demands even better than his predecessor. He was also far more ruthless; rule-bound, tidy, but ruthless. In two years, over five million pounds in military equipment from machine guns to medicine had been sold to buyers in Russia, China, Mexico, Hong Kong, Kazakhstan, and Ukraine. He didn't have to get his hands dirty; Fleet targeted soldiers with priors—men with money problems or drug problems. Men like Jack Turner.

Turner was violent but cash motivated. He was also in trouble; despite being a decent pilot, he'd been grounded for infraction and very nearly discharged. Fleet found him capable not only of theft, but of convincing others to follow suit—and of threatening them when necessary. A match made in heaven; Fleet's rule-bound persona put him above suspicion; Turner's slow wits and underclass status almost put him below it. They made money fast. They sold to friendlies and enemies alike. And…they *drank.*

Jack wore his brutality like a badge—Fleet, it seemed, had as much ruthlessness, just tucked up beneath extraordinary discipline and a sharp mind for detail. (It was little wonder to MacAdams that he did so well as a Scotland Yard Detective.) The trouble, of course, was keeping that cruelty in check. Beneath the stiffness, the oddly neutral tone, even the way he turned every corner sharp as a knifepoint, Fleet had a weakness: liquid. He was a nasty drunk with a short fuse, made mistakes, and a senseless fight broke out with Jack one night in Mazar-e-Sharif. No inquiry from MacAdams would ever discover who started it, or even who dealt the final, fatal blow, but a civilian paid the price. It should have been a court martial for both Jack and Fleet. And that's where Clapham returned to the story.

He was a civilian himself, now, practically landed gentry (and still taking a lion's share of black market business). Social affairs with elites from as far away as London, a widower known for charity balls and proud of two military kids. It was time to end their dealings. The soldiers were exonerated (quietly) and the entire operation came to a swift halt. Fleet went sober and ended up in police work, helped by his rank, his work ethic, and Clapham's connections. They settled a sum on Turner, too, but knew better than to trust him. If *two* can't keep a secret, *three* was going to be a problem. Clapham needed a threat that would stick; that's why he created the document in the first place.

MacAdams didn't know *all* the details; they were still in the process of looking for Fleet's remains, much less discovering all his motives. It might be conjecture, but MacAdams could recognize the sheer bloody-minded tidiness. The "Clapham file" as they were calling the eight-page document of incriminating details behind their operation, had Fleet written all over it. Every drop shipment, every fudged number, even the case in Mazar-e-Sharif had been meticulously recorded. Fleet had amassed a file for the Air Commodore that would put all three of them (and not a few others in service) behind bars—but which also carried the following stinger: Fleet and Turner, in their wide-ranging clientele, weren't just stealing and dealing. They sold parts to the enemy; they were guilty of treason against the United Kingdom.

MacAdams could imagine that fateful meeting; perhaps it

took place at Clapham's War Room—three men hovering over the details of their crimes, and then signing their names. If one of them squealed, they would all go down together. But Clapham, older, with more friends, money, and clout, would still come out on top. Just desserts, indeed.

We, the undersigned, agree that a copy of these records will be our check and our balance.

We, the undersigned agree never to speak of these matters again, in exchange for a clean record.

The words hung over Fleet like a cloud; no wonder he so obligingly went through Clapham's papers when he died. The more MacAdams thought about it, the more he wondered just how much Cora knew (or suspected) about her dad's precipitous rise. But Fleet had come up empty. Probably, the dying man had already destroyed his copy.

Then there was Jack.

He turned his military "training" into a lucrative criminal career. It was hard to know how long he'd run stolen cars before involving Douglas Haw, or when their operation joined with the larger ring out of London. Discovering the betrayal of his mate, Turner decided to kill Douglas and send a message all in one—and didn't know the Met were already onto him. But lo and behold! Who is it that catches him? His good friend Jarvis Fleet. *Get me in the clear.* Troublemaker Turner, with no family, kills local man Douglas, of good family, for informing on their sting? A not-guilty plea would have taken a miracle of the sort only Clapham could manage—and he was dead. So, thanks to Fleet, manslaughter was the best they could do. All things considered, the case did do one thing: it reunited Elsie and Jack. The trial went on for months; the papers and BBC carried the story. When she came to the sentencing, it was the first they had seen of each other in twenty years. It was going to be twenty *more* before Jack breathed free air—and he blamed Fleet for it.

Time for revenge.

Confessing to the authorities might get Jack in far more trouble than the now-Scotland-Yard detective. So instead, he tells his sister. Jack never received visitors, but he *did* get letters—and phone calls, too. From an ambitious Elsie "Hannah Walker." It took her a few years to be properly placed to launder money, then the blackmail started.

Elsie claimed it was all Jack's idea. MacAdams knew this was nonsense; no doubt they hatched the plot together. She'd make bank out of Fleet—five thousand pounds a month, to be precise—and save up money for herself and for Jack on his release.

But she had an even better plan. She'd get Sid to be her patsy, carry all the risk. She would keep the Clapham blackmail letters "somewhere safe" and hang it over Fleet's head. Sid would do pickup and collect cash from various drop-off spots all over the north of England. Put that money in an account (to which she had access), and off it went to be laundered. In return, Elsie paid his debts, or some of them. Maybe Elsie even allowed the creditors to keep up the pressure, just enough for a short leash on Sid…all the while creating a paper trail that would lead straight to him in the end.

The only thing she hadn't planned on was Jo Jones turning up—and a cornered Sid rifling her desk to discover the note between Elsie and her brother. Elsie had probably been lying to Sid that she was double-crossing her brother, had stolen the letter from Jack so she and Sid could live comfortably—and then Sid discovered her correspondence with Jack, and where her loyalties really lay. No doubt Sid decided to take matters into his own hands, hide the file with his other treasure back at the estate, and—

"Boss?" Green asked. "Are you with us?"

"Sorry, still thinking about the case." MacAdams had agreed to pay the first round of celebratory beers at the Red Lion—Ben had just arrived with chips.

"I thought thinking wasn't allowed after hours," Rachel said, poking at Green's shoulder.

"Oh yeah, we *never* take work outside the office, do we?" Green laughed. Beside her, Andrews swallowed a mouthful of beer.

"I might never stop thinking about this one," he said. "For one, I *still* don't get why Sid was murdered. Fleet didn't get what he wanted."

"He was willing to kill Jo, despite not getting what he wanted," MacAdams said, ordering another beer.

"The man had *rage*," Green added. "Sid made the big mistake. You don't go meeting the guy you're blackmailing in a quiet, out of the way place."

"Right, but the man was a cop. I mean, you'd have thought you were safe, right?" Andrews asked.

"Safe enough to do some bragging, I expect," MacAdams said. "He was smart enough not to name them, but Fleet knew he had an accomplice."

"And that it was a woman," Gridley added. "Or else why break in on Jo and Olivia and Lotte?" MacAdams nodded.

"He'd have enjoyed that, I imagine. Telling the detective he'd been bested by Sid and one—or more—of his women." In fact, almost everything came down to Sid's psychology in the end. He felt the estate and everything inside it—the *painting* included—was owed him, not just because it was no doubt valuable, but because it had been valuable to the people who did him wrong. Like the Ardemores, or Aiden, or Jo—or Elsie, for that matter. Sid planned to sell the Clapham file to Fleet, to get back at Elsie and make a buck all at once. Puts the thing inside the painting, hides both together at Ardemore. Jo hadn't been far off; the estate was a fox cache. When that became endangered, he needed to move his treasures to the next place—or rather, person—he considered absolutely safe.

"From Sid's perspective, Olivia is the only one who made sense. She never crossed him, never used him, seemed to genuinely love him. Was always there to bail him out," MacAdams said.

Fleet hadn't been looking for a painting, then, but a letter. All the same, it *had* been hidden—and damn well. She'd strapped it to the underside of her mattress. Olivia came clean to Lotte after the break-in that she was keeping the painting for Sid, and they turned it over to Newcastle uniform before a search warrant could even be issued or they might *still* be looking.

"I guess points to Sid for not ratting her out to Fleet," Gridley said.

"I'm not sure he had time to," Green admitted, stirring her drink. "What did Jo call him? Contents under pressure? All that tight-assed exterior just holding down a reckless murderer, I guess."

"He was a proud and selfish bastard," MacAdams said. "When he knew Sid didn't have the document, and that a woman did, he shot him. Fleet couldn't imagine himself beaten, not by Jack, not by Sid—not by a woman."

"But he *was*," Rachel said, raising a glass.

"I'll drink to Jo Jones," Green agreed. "God. Some men will do anything not to be shamed."

"Right," Gridley said. "I mean shit, Commodore Clapham? I sure wouldn't want to be Ma'am Cora right now."

Cora, to her credit, had already begun the process of recusing herself from the case.

"We see what we expect to see sometimes," MacAdams said—but the sentiment was cut short by the intrusive ring of his mobile. It was Struthers.

"Happy days, Detective," he said. "I have good news. And I have strange news."

MacAdams cupped the receiver.

"Carry on."

"Well. The good news is we found the bodies."

"The—bodies? Plural?" MacAdams asked. He could hear Struthers sucking his teeth through the line.

"Yes. That's the strange news."

28

MacAdams stood against the wall of Struthers' sterile, blue-hued room. It's normal odor of chemicals and antiseptic now carried an undertone of smoke and char, and he wasn't looking forward to the reveal.

"We can get this out of the way first," Struthers said, gesturing to the far slab.

"I should brace myself, I take it," MacAdams said, but Eric shook his head.

"Trust me, it could have been *much* worse. He is burned, yes, mostly his arms and back—but the floor collapsed. In fact, the whole house more or less ended up in the cellar. The debris mostly preserved the remains."

Struthers pulled the sheet back, and MacAdams swallowed hard. *Preserved* was definitely not the right word. The clothes had been burned into the skin, and both hands were blistered beyond recognition. The face, however, remained intact.

"Recognizable," he said. Even the singed smear on the upper lip that had once been his brush mustache.

"That's Fleet, then," Struthers said, mercifully covering him up again. "Both legs broken, one compound. Nose broken. I'm guessing from the angle that a vertebrae shattered on the way down. I won't know till I've done a full autopsy, but I suspect he was already dead from smoke inhalation."

MacAdams had walked to the far wall again to give his insides a chance to resettle. He'd noted the other slab. It had been covered but didn't look much like a body.

"Ah. My surprises," Struthers murmured. He gently picked up the sheet. "I think it's fair to say these aren't recent."

Bones. They were cracked, some of them discolored by what must have been fabric; clothing or a shroud. Arranged in human shape, the skull grinned back at them.

"At first, the boys thought they'd found Detective Fleet—but the fire wouldn't have rendered a fresh body so utterly clean. And then, of course, you have the pelvis."

"The pelvis," MacAdams repeated, staring at its discolored sockets.

"It's a woman," Struthers explained. "And that's not all. See these smooth craters on the posterior surface of the pubic bone? I'd say the woman was—or recently had been—pregnant."

"You found a baby?" MacAdams said.

"No. Just the woman. Not much to go on for identification. Based on the decay, I'd say at least a hundred years in the ground."

MacAdams weighed his phone in the palm of his hand.

"I'm pretty sure I know who it is," he said, dialing the number.

MacAdams awaited Jo's breathless arrival in the parking lot, for fear she'd otherwise barge directly into the morgue. There would be tests to run, and forensics would need to date the bones—possibly try for a DNA match with Jo. But after everything that had happened, she had a right to know.

"Where?" Jo said, opening the driver's door almost before coming to a complete stop.

"In the cellar."

"No, *where* is she? I want to see her." Jo's face was flushed and earnest—wide eyes glassy and utterly serious.

"Jo, right now it's an investigation. We'll need proof. Then, we can work on how to return them for proper burial." MacAdams delivered this knowing it would make absolutely no impact on Jo. She was gripping one thumb (the other still bandaged in gauze) and casting about her, as if looking for a handle—or a refutation.

"Identification," she said finally. "People can do that, right? I've seen it on shows."

"Jo," he started—

"Let me do it! *I'm next of kin.* I'm all the family Evelyn's got." She rocked slightly on her heels as she spoke. The words were not, by themselves, enough to move him. But MacAdams also heard what she wasn't saying. *Evelyn* was the only family *Jo* had left.

"Let me talk to Struthers," he said.

Why was nothing like the movies? Jo waited in a warm, butter-yellow room next to an old-style coffee machine. The office was empty and quiet, save for the humming of the lights. She was about to see Evelyn. Her skeleton, MacAdams warned. She would be, of course. It depended on temperature, humidity, insects—submergence in a substrate like water, and whether any embalming had been practiced. Evelyn had been a skeleton a long time, she guessed. The thought set her foot to bouncing impatiently on the tile, and she was glad when she heard MacAdams coming down the hall.

"Ready?" he asked. She wasn't.

"Yes."

"It's belowstairs," MacAdams said. He also said something about the elevator, and the weather. She was glad to have him talking. Even if she couldn't listen. They stopped at last next to a heavy door.

"He wasn't prepared for a viewing. We'll have to go inside," MacAdams explained. Jo nodded wordlessly, and then they were through the doors.

Jo had stood a long time over the body of her mother before she made the final call. It had been a surreal moment; the body was only a vessel—the life gone, Jo touched it as she might touch wood. But here, faced with the desiccated skeleton of a woman with teeth prominent, jaw receding, and a forehead of wide, white bone, the impression had reversed.

Evelyn *lived*. She was real, and present. A deep, strange sound escaped Jo's constricted throat: she had found her. She had been found.

"How did she die?" she asked, barely above a whisper.

"We aren't yet sure," said the man in scrubs. "She had been recently pregnant. So recently, that she might have died during birth."

Jo's mouth tugged down in frown.

She could imagine Evelyn going into contractions without a doctor—without help—

With a dark kick in her stomach, Jo's mind to flashed to Gwen. And William. Perhaps they never even called a midwife or doctor, for fear of letting the secret be known and disgracing their family.

But where was the *baby*?

"You found her in the—the cellar? Alone?"

"Buried," MacAdams explained. "Through the dirt floor in the far corner. Not left to lie."

"I suspect a burial shroud, as well," the coroner said. Jo tried fitting the details into her brain. It took some effort. It took some care, at least. Yet—

"They buried her in their house," she said, finally. "That's why they left."

The Ardemores had turned their home into Evelyn's tomb.

29

April came in unseasonably warm—and very seasonably wet. The office was quiet, the hum of usual county CID activities. MacAdams checked his watch, tugged on the mackintosh and reached for his umbrella.

"An early day, Detective?"

MacAdams managed to stifle his surprise; Cora Clapham's step had grown unusually quiet in the weeks since the case—from which she had to recuse herself.

"Ma'am?"

"I won't keep you. May I walk you to your car?" She kept her hands laced carefully over stiff suit lapels. Black, no cardigan. She looked like she might be in mourning. MacAdams held the door for her and followed her out, but though she'd come with the pretense of talking, she said nothing until they were both outside in a hazy drizzle.

"You're going to be recognized for your work on the Randles case," she said, finally. "As you should be." MacAdams unlocked his car.

"You didn't come out in this weather to tell me that. Do you want to get in? It's pissing rain." He'd half expected a smart reproach. But Cora only gave him a wry smile and settled into the passenger seat.

"I don't know exactly what will come of the investigation into Fleet—and my father," she said. "But your surmise was correct. I asked Fleet to sort his papers because I *suspected* him."

"And if he'd found something?"

"I was saved the trouble of moral dilemma, James. You know that already." It was true; Fleet had looked, certainly, but hadn't *found*. Cora sighed. "Imagine my relief—*the irony* of my relief. My father lied to me. And I let him lie."

MacAdams had to respect her owning it. She didn't say so, but MacAdams understood implicitly that this had been hard. He was, no doubt, her first trial.

"What now, Cora?" he asked.

"I must decide whether I'm weathering this storm as Chief—or not. And incidentally, I *did* come to tell you about your upcoming honorary. It's not the King's Police medal, mind. But it will be good for your career. If you want it to be." She'd delivered all this in the same gravel-studded tones she used to give assignments, while simultaneously opening the car door. No rejoinder was apparently invited.

"I'm not applying to be Chief," MacAdams said anyway. Cora nodded, lips pursed, but didn't answer. She shut the car door against fattening raindrops.

"Enjoy your afternoon," she said. MacAdams sat back in his seat; *that* was a fucking thing to do to a man late Friday afternoon, and she knew it. But he turned the key and put the car in gear; no time to think about it, now. He had an appointment to keep.

Jo rocked on her heels and tapped repetitively on the window glass. This did not make time move any faster, but it helped focus her thoughts.

It had been over a month since the fire, which felt like yesterday and a year ago all at once. In the weeks that followed, Jo had turned over the house's remains and all of *Jekyll* gardens to the National Trust conservancy. Rupert was handling the transfer—it meant the elimination of Jo's back taxes, and enough money to turn the cottage's attic level into an actual holiday let. Of course, it would be months before either would be finished (or started, for that matter. Things seemed to move very slowly in Britain). She'd picked up an editing gig with a previous client to keep herself in butter—and borrowed against the future nest egg for the necessities. Like a new plaque for Grove Cottage, which she'd renamed *Netherleigh*—and a proper restoration of Evelyn's painting. And *that* was what landed her here, at York Fine Arts, waiting for James MacAdams to turn up.

It had been a simple phone call. A message, rather, since Jo hadn't answered. *There's something we think you should see. Could you come down to York?* A reasonable person would have called back to find out what, exactly. Jo turned up in MacAdams' office instead and asked him to come as her second pair of eyes. To his credit, he didn't even ask why—fortuitous, since she'd have to manufacture a reason for the feeling in her guts.

"Still nothing conclusive on the remains," MacAdams was saying as they took their seats in a cramped office that smelled faintly of paint thinner. "Age about twenty-five, general health good. No signs of disease."

"Doesn't that mean *not* a natural death, then?" Jo asked.

"As in death by childbirth? Or as in murder?" MacAdams asked—just in time for the art conservator to hear it. A woman in her early thirties, very tall, very thin, and looking suddenly extra interested.

"Ms. Jones?"

"Yes! Call me Jo. And this is Detective Chief Inspector James MacAdams. He solves murders."

"But not regularly," MacAdams added, shaking the woman's hand. She affected a laugh.

"I'm Dr. Emily Strong. Good of you both to come—though I'm not sure it's a police matter. Can you step into the studio?"

They had located the source of the odor. Jo breathed as shallow as she dared; between the fumes, the crush of extra canvas stands, and misshapen heaps of drop cloths, the place wasn't just sensory overload; it was a fire hazard. And she'd had enough of those for a lifetime.

"When you told me this might be an Augustus John, I confess, I was *very* skeptical. But there are signs—" She lifted the drop cloth, and Jo gave an unexpected chirrup.

Evelyn, but as she'd never seen her. Her dress looked as though it might feel real to touch; all varnish cracks, lines, and grit banished. Around her, once faint flowers popped like brilliant stars: violets.

But Jo couldn't miss the eyes.

"They're so *real*!" Jo said, her voice suddenly thick. Deep brown wells, strange and sad, exactly as in the photograph but rendered in color. They seemed brighter, somehow, than the rest of the painting.

"That's just what I want to tell you about," Emily said. "I want you—both—to take a step back. Further yet, there! Now look again, slightly at angle."

Jo and MacAdams had rather awkwardly bumbled backward together, standing as though on a viewing deck, about a dozen steps away.

"What am I looking for?" he asked—but Jo had already spotted it.

Or rather, she'd noticed on the very first day, in the little room above the library. It had been there, in her memories, even in her dreams about it. Something tugging at the edges but not quite fully realized. A sudden hot tremor ran up her spine, and she found herself fumbling with her phone.

"Look at the eyes in the photograph," Jo said, showing him the photo. "Hold it up and really *look*."

"Perfect. They're exactly the same," he said. Jo bounced on her toes.

"Exactly!" she said. "But she's sitting at the opposite angle in the painting!"

"Well done!" Emily said, waving them back to their chairs. "And do you know why? This painting has been restored *before*. Recently, I'd say in the last ten years. Two things alerted me—first, the angle. But second, the varnish over the eyes and upper bridge of the nose was of a different kind and quality from the varnish on the rest of the painting. We decided to do some forensics."

Jo saw MacAdams perk up.

"As you would for fraud?" he asked.

"Something like that," Emily agreed. "Usually we can tell by style, or under magnification. But looking at damage required a bit of ultraviolet and infrared." Jo managed to keep herself from adding *because paint layers fluoresce to different colors* in favor of more important questions:

"Damage? Where? What kind?"

Emily traced a long rectangle across the canvas.

"Something corrosive was thrown onto the original. The canvas remained intact, but the original eyes and a bit of the nose had been destroyed."

Jo had ceased to breathe.

"And yet, you say it was restored," she heard MacAdams say. "By whom? And what does that have to do with Augustus John?" Jo bounced her foot in excitement. *That's* why she invited him; one of them needed to ask relevant questions.

"Ah. Let me start with your last question. Ms. Jones, I think it's very possible, even likely, that the painting *may* have been an original work by Augustus John. We would need an expert on his catalog to see it, and additional analysis." Emily had resumed her seat and a more businesslike manner. "The damage will decrease the value, of course. But the restoration itself is excellent. A professional, certainly. There are a few artists that could probably have done the work. It's just a matter of research to find out which, and who employed them."

"I think I know," Jo said, feeling the internal shiver again. She turned to MacAdams. "I told you about the little framed photo? It had been with my uncle's things, sent on to the museum and then auctioned."

Jo turned back to the painting, to the eyes that seemed too bright, too real, and not quite the right angle.

"Whoever he hired must have used it as a model."

"Sensible," MacAdams agreed. "But how was it damaged in the first place? The eyes—that seems intentional. Especially as it's valuable."

Emily was replying, but Jo's attention had shifted internally. Three paintings, but only Evelyn's by a master. Her haunting, faraway eyes destroyed; it felt like the erasure of identity. An unnamed painting, all but forgotten. Like Evelyn herself, buried beneath the house.

MacAdams agreed to be part of Evelyn's homecoming. For one, Jo needed help getting her in and out of the car; she certainly wouldn't be able to hang it herself. It took some doing, even with both of them, but Evelyn at last presided over the sitting room. MacAdams, who had divested himself of both jacket and tie by this point, stuck hands into rumpled pockets.

"I feel like I owe you an apology," he said.

"You have apologized an awful lot, already," Jo reminded him. He'd done almost nothing else in the scant few times she'd seen him since the estate fire.

"This is a new one," he insisted. "I'm sorry I didn't take the theft of this painting seriously. I should have listened to you."

"Okay, that's your best one yet."

"Thank you. It was painful." MacAdams picked up his coat from the rocking chair. "How goes the new garden?"

"Noisy," Jo said, opening the front door to the distant cacophony of machinery. "Until they get the house completely cleared away, I can almost pretend I'm in Brooklyn again."

MacAdams didn't answer; he was looking up the lane that led to Ardemore. A man was coming down it, and quickly.

"Ma'am?" He looked uncertainly at Jo, then with some relief at MacAdams. "Glad *you're* here, sir. It might need police. We—we found something buried."

A buzzing had started in Jo's ears, a fuzzy numb feeling that tingled in her fingertips. *Something. Buried.*

"It might not mean that," Macadams was saying at her shoulder. It was hard to know what impressed her more, that he knew what she was thinking, or that he'd caught up with her mad-dash run toward the garden wall.

The ground wept puddles in loamy soil. Just past the gash where the house used to be, a knot of workmen waved them over. Jo wandered among yellow slickers and heavy boots.

"We weren't sure if we should move it," said the foreman. "Seeing how there was the murder here, and everything. But it's just a little box, after all, buried under the jump-ups."

"Oh God," Jo panted. Two men were walking up, now, carrying a clay-covered box. They rested in on the ground between them.

"Jo—" MacAdams cautioned from behind, but she'd already dropped to the muddy ground beside it. The lid was caked shut, but the latches had long fallen away. She lifted it against a crumbling hinge.

She expected to see bones. A tiny, curled infant skeleton. There wasn't one. Jo rested her hand, instead, upon soft cloth.

"Baby clothes," she whispered. A tiny embroidered infant's dress. The clay sealed them in, but rot had eaten the fabric like lace. *She dreamt of a child, too feeble to walk, who cried in her arms.* "It's a hope chest."

"A what?" MacAdams was kneeling next to her, now, both of them bent over the contents.

"My aunt had one. Unmarried women used to store things inside for marriage—kids. The future." Jo lifted away a quilted blanket to find delicately embroidered silk. "Look, *E + G*. Just like on the rafters. And—oh my God. Letters."

Two bundles of aged and yellowing papers. They were fragile, too fragile to open without damaging, but the first lines still visible:

Dearest Evelyn,
I assure you that I have never meant to hurt Gwen. I know you never meant it, either. But I did not know love until you came…
I'll come to you on Thursday. You know where.

Love letters. Not between Evelyn and an unknown admirer. Not between Gwen and William. These were the intimate confessions of a tryst between Evelyn—and her brother-in-law. Between Evelyn and *William*. *E + G*; not Gwen, not another lover, but…

William. *Gwilym*. It was Welsh. And neither she—nor her own Welsh Gwilym—had spotted it.

Jo untied the bundle, eager for more, only to watch a single pressed violet drift from between the pages. It landed on the wet ground, absorbing water and changing to a deep purple.

"Where did you say you found this box?" she asked. The foreman pointed.

"Under the jump-ups, ma'am—little blue flowers?"

MacAdams, already standing, had been offering Jo a hand for a good minute. Now she took it and got to her feet.

"Violets," she said. "They stand for *delicate*, especially for delicate love." Jo closed her eyes, reeling back her rolodex of words and their associations. *Leigh*, English given name meaning *delicate*.

"The painting told us the whole time," she said. "*Netherleigh*.

It means beneath the violets. William wanted to leave something of their affair, for someone to find it. About how much she *meant*."

"Well," said MacAdams, not to Jo but to the fire she'd started in the grate to knock off the night's chill.

"Yes," Jo agreed. Then they lapsed once again into silence. They'd been doing that for an hour; testing single words and phrases—and whisky—while staring at Jo's hearth.

"I am not sure how to feel," Jo said, finally. The investigation into Evelyn's remains had been *inconclusive*. They would be, though, after so long. No bones had been broken before death, no violent end. Jo squeezed her eyes shut, trying to imagine the Gwen Davies who wrote so feelingly to her doctor about childlessness as a cold-blooded killer. She couldn't quite do it. Partly, because Gwen and Evelyn now wore the faces of her aunt and mother.

Then again, Jo's mother had kept secrets, too.

"She may still have died in childbirth, as you originally thought," MacAdams suggested.

"I suppose," Jo said. "But then, why try to destroy her painting. Why bury her *under* the *house*. And that's not the biggest mystery, anyway."

"You need more of them?" MacAdams asked.

"It's about the *baby*," Jo reminded him. "They should be buried together, you know? Only we don't know where to find it, and not knowing makes me crazy. It's haunting."

MacAdams wasn't looking at Jo. But he *was* ruminating.

"I think Fleet was haunted," he said. "I think Elsie *should* be. And you don't know her, but Cora Clapham is going to be haunted, too, for the rest of her life."

There was a lot going on here, Jo realized.

"What about you?" she asked. "Are you haunted."

"Yes. I'm divorced."

Jo spat whisky, but MacAdams self-deprecated.

"I didn't mean it like that! Annie is precious to me. But that's the point, I suppose. You don't get ghosts from a past you don't care about."

Jo lifted her glass to the oval face and its hooded eyes.

"I can live with that," she said. "To Evelyn."

MacAdams raised his glass, too, but not to the painting.

"To Jo Jones," he said. "It's not everyone who finds what they're looking for." Jo wondered if she was ever going to manage a drink with this man without blushing. Possibly, he hadn't noticed. Following the formal libations, he went for his coat and hat.

"Do you think you'll stay in Abington?" he asked.

"How could I leave, now? They aren't even finished with the garden!"

"Ah yes, of course," he agreed. "Do you think you'll stay out of trouble?"

"That I can't promise."

MacAdams stood in the doorway, squeezing his hat brim in both hands. It would be an uncomfortable silence, except he wasn't looking at her. He was looking at Evelyn, in state on the chimneypiece.

"Yes, well," he said. "Good night."

Jo shut the door behind him and settled by the fire. Then she typed *Aiden Jones* in her search bar. What had he known about Evelyn? For how long? Someone, somewhere, knew something. And they'd be no match for Jo Jones.

"We'll get there, Evelyn," she said, scrolling through ten thousand Google hits, "It's just gonna take a while."

★★★★★